Praise for the Rhona MacLeod series

'Forensic scientist Rhona MacLeod has become one of the most satisfying characters in modern crime fiction – honourable, inquisitive and yet plagued by doubts and, sometimes, fears . . . As ever, the landscape is stunningly evoked and MacLeod's decency and humanity shine through on every page' *Daily Mail*

'Lin Anderson is one of Scotland's national treasures . . . her writing is unique, bringing warmth and depth to even the seediest parts of Glasgow. Rhona MacLeod is a complex and compelling heroine who just gets better with every outing' Stuart MacBride

'Vivid and atmospheric . . . enthralling' *The Guardian*

'The bleak landscape is beautifully described, giving this popular series a new lease of life' *The Sunday Times*

'Greenock-born Anderson's work is sharper than a pathologist's scalpel. One of the best Scottish crime series since Rebus' *Daily Record*

'Inventive, compelling, genuinely scary and beautifully written, as always' Denzil Meyrick

'Hugely imaginative and exciting' James Grieve
(emeritus professor of forensic pathology)

Whispers of the Dead

Lin Anderson is a Scottish author and screenwriter known for her bestselling crime series featuring forensic scientist Dr Rhona MacLeod. Four of her novels have been longlisted for the Scottish Crime Book of the Year and she was shortlisted for the Crime Writers' Association Dagger in the Library Award in 2022. Lin is the co-founder of the international crime-writing festival Bloody Scotland, which takes place annually in Stirling.

The Rhona MacLeod books in order

Driftnet
Rhona investigates a murder victim who may be the son she gave up for adoption seventeen years ago . . .

Torch
Rhona joins the hunt for a terrifying arsonist on the streets of Edinburgh.

Deadly Code
A horrifying discovery is made off the coast of Scotland's Isle of Skye.

Dark Flight
When a boy goes missing, Rhona is called in to examine a chilling series of clues left behind.

Easy Kill
A sadistic killer is targeting a string of young women in Glasgow.

Final Cut
Rhona is called in when a badly burned body is found wearing a soldier's dog tags.

The Reborn
A pregnant woman is found dead – and the killer is watching and waiting to strike again . . .

Picture Her Dead
A sinister murderer is hiding the bodies of his victims in Glasgow's derelict cinemas.

Paths of the Dead
When a body is found inside a Neolithic stone circle, Rhona is called in to investigate.

The Special Dead
Rhona and DS Michael McNab look into the ancient practice of Wicca following a ritualistic killing.

None but the Dead
Rhona heads to the remote island of Sanday when human remains are discovered beneath an old school.

Follow the Dead
A killer stalks the Cairngorms in the Scottish Highlands after a mysterious plane crashes on a nearby loch.

Sins of the Dead
Rhona is being targeted by a terrifying killer whose methods echo the ancient religious practice of sin-eating.

Time for the Dead
Rhona investigates a series of brutal deaths on Scotland's Isle of Skye.

The Innocent Dead
A decades-old cold case is reopened when a body is discovered in a peat bog south of Glasgow.

The Killing Tide
When three bodies are found on a wrecked ship in the Orkney islands, Rhona is brought in to investigate.

The Wild Coast
A killer is preying on campers along Scotland's remote west shoreline.

Whispers of the Dead
When a movie star goes missing while filming their latest blockbuster in Glasgow, Rhona and the team must investigate.

By Lin Anderson

Driftnet
Torch
Deadly Code
Dark Flight
Easy Kill
Final Cut
The Reborn
Picture Her Dead
Paths of the Dead
The Special Dead
None but the Dead
Follow the Dead
Sins of the Dead
Time for the Dead
The Innocent Dead
The Killing Tide
The Wild Coast
Whispers of the Dead

STANDALONE NOVEL
The Party House

NOVELLA
Blood Red Roses

Whispers of the Dead

Will reveal the truth . . .

LIN ANDERSON

PAN BOOKS

First published 2024 by Macmillan

This paperback edition first published 2025 by Pan Books
an imprint of Pan Macmillan
The Smithson, 6 Briset Street, London EC1M 5NR
EU representative: Macmillan Publishers Ireland Ltd, 1st Floor,
The Liffey Trust Centre, 117–126 Sheriff Street Upper,
Dublin 1, D01 YC43
Associated companies throughout the world
www.panmacmillan.com

ISBN 978-1-0350-2922-8

Copyright © Lin Anderson 2024

The right of Lin Anderson to be identified as the
author of this work has been asserted by her in accordance
with the Copyright, Designs and Patents Act 1988.

All rights reserved. No part of this publication may be reproduced,
stored in a retrieval system, or transmitted, in any form, or by any means
(electronic, mechanical, photocopying, recording or otherwise)
without the prior written permission of the publisher.

Pan Macmillan does not have any control over, or any responsibility for,
any author or third-party websites referred to in or on this book.

3 5 7 9 8 6 4 2

A CIP catalogue record for this book is available from the British Library.

Typeset in Meridien by Palimpsest Book Production Ltd, Falkirk, Stirlingshire
Printed and bound by CPI Group (UK) Ltd, Croydon, CR0 4YY

This book is sold subject to the condition that it shall not, by way of
trade or otherwise, be lent, hired out, or otherwise circulated without
the publisher's prior consent in any form of binding or cover other than
that in which it is published and without a similar condition including
this condition being imposed on the subsequent purchaser.

Visit **www.panmacmillan.com** to read more about all our books
and to buy them. You will also find features, author interviews and
news of any author events, and you can sign up for e-newsletters
so that you're always first to hear about our new releases.

Whispers of the Dead

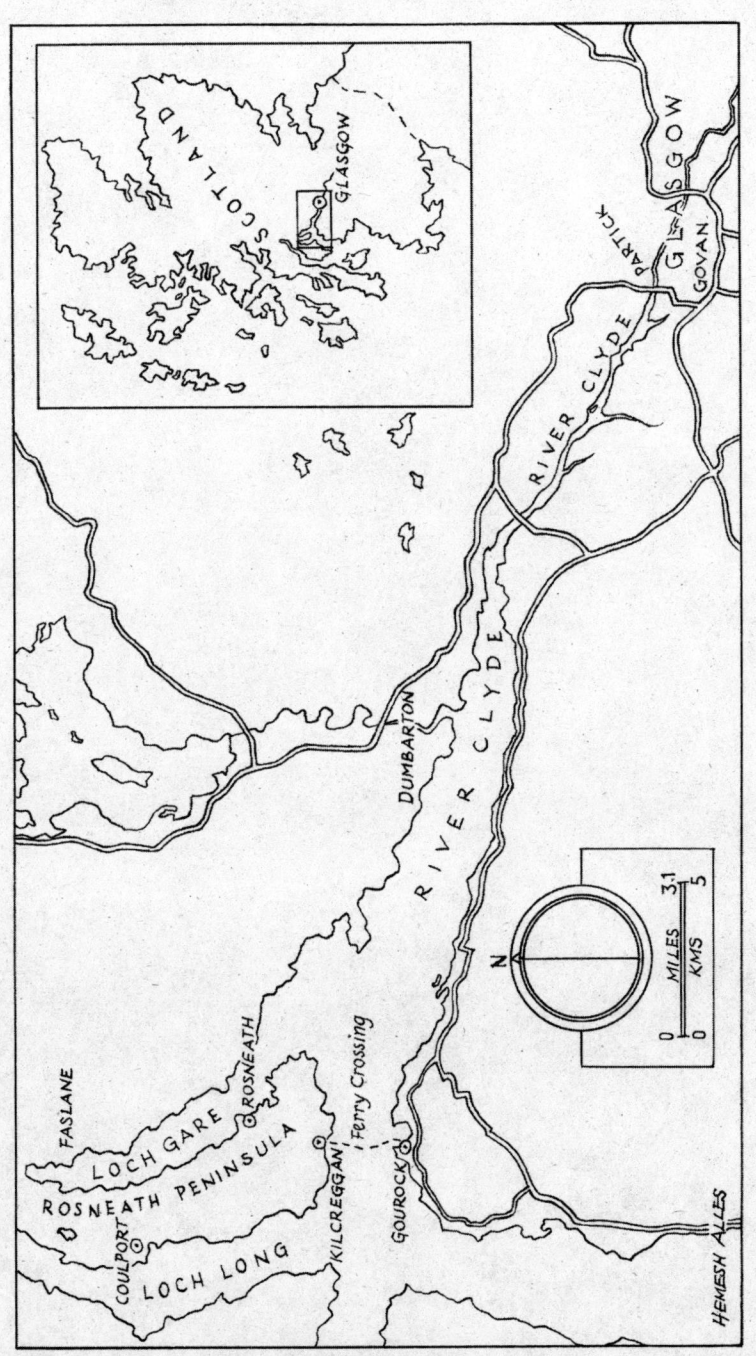

Unable to sleep, she rose from the bed and went to the window.

It's snowing, *she thought, surprised,* and it has been for a while.

Funny how a veil of white made everything seem beautiful. Even from here.

She shivered a little and thought of climbing back into the warm bed . . . soon to be for the last time.

It was at that moment the figure of a girl, dressed in a kilt and blue velvet jacket, arrived to tramp across the snow in front of the main gate. As though sensing someone watching, the girl stopped and turned to look over at her.

Marnie stood transfixed, then shut her eyes, her heart hammering.

She's not real. It's a waking nightmare. When I look again, she won't be there.

And she was right. When Marnie forced her eyes open, the figure had gone, or more likely, it had never been there in the first place.

Except . . . there were footprints in the snow to prove otherwise.

Marnie dropped to her knees. What if it was a sign that her daughter, Tizzy, was alive and waiting for her outside these prison walls?

1

He sensed the dark rather than saw it, his eyes barely able to open a crack. As for his mouth, it too had been stitched together with tight thread, which dug into the puffed-up lips.

That only left his ears, which were still resounding with the high screeching noise fed into them via the headphones, now, thank God, no longer in place.

He thought the room was empty, but as the ringing in his ears abated, he imagined he caught the whisper of laboured breathing.

Then again, it might be his own.

The sudden blast of cold air against his naked body, that he was certain of. A window had been opened or a door to the outside. He thought he felt the soft touch of wet snow on his lips and welcomed it hungrily.

The crash of glass when it came told him two things for sure: his hearing had returned; and there was definitely someone in the room with him. As the rush of cold air became stronger, it caught at his blood-matted hair and snowflakes swirled against his battered face.

Then he was moving, the chair he sat upon screeching

across the floor, pushed solidly from behind. Instinct told him to try to stop it and he forced his feet hard to the floor, but the pressure on the chair's movement could not be stopped.

He knew now where it was going, because he felt the approaching emptiness before him.

He would have screamed if he had been able to open his mouth, but it would have done him little good.

As he met the open air, his feet snagged on a jagged ridge of broken glass and he felt the warm escape of blood. Then he was tipping forward. There was a brief moment while he pivoted there on the cusp between life and death, before gravity came into play and he dropped like a stone into the swirling snow.

2

The snow was getting thicker now. Ally raised his face and opened his mouth, relishing the touch of the snowflakes on his tongue.

Dreep, standing beside him, finally abandoned his attempts to ping stones off the supermarket trolley parked in the middle of the boating pond.

'Fuck it. I cannae see it any more.'

'You didn't hit it when you could,' Ally told him with a grin.

Dreep was shivering, his narrow shoulders quaking now that he'd stopped throwing stones.

'I vote we get inside,' Ally suggested. 'Unless you want to head for home?'

'No way!' Dreep told him, jumping up and down in an attempt to keep warm.

Ally turned towards Kevin, who was putting the finishing touches to a slogan on the side of the nearby pavilion. 'You coming, Kev?'

Not waiting for an answer, he and Dreep made for the high railings that surrounded the old farmhouse at the edge of the park.

Glasgow city council had done their best to keep them out of the derelict listed building, bricking up the doors and sealing the windows with metal sheets, but they hadn't made it foolproof to Dreep, who, climbing up, over and through all obstacles in his way, had first gained them access to the upper room on the pavilion side.

Now, shimmying up the blackened and burnt trees next to the spiked metal fence, showing exactly how it should be done, Dreep was first to plop into the deepening snow cover on the other side.

Ally caught the list of expletives resulting from that. At least, that's what he thought the swearing was about.

It turned out he was wrong.

Dreep's frantic cursing continued in his half-smothered, high-pitched voice, sending a warning bell jangling in Ally's brain as he followed his friend.

Had another gang found their way in and booby-trapped the place?

'What's wrong?' he called, keen to avoid anything bad between him and the shadow of Dreep ahead.

Dreep's sudden silence freaked him even more than the litany of curses that had preceded it. As he moved cautiously forward, he heard the sound of Kev landing behind him. The usually silent Kev asked him what the fuck was going on.

'Something's freaked Dreep. I don't know what.'

Emerging from the intervening tangle of bushes, Ally was presented with Dreep's back.

'What the f—' The unfinished expletive died in Ally's throat as Dreep stood aside to let him look.

The naked shape of what might be a human was on its back, knees in the air. Ally's eyes were drawn to the blood-soaked feet, the rigid hands tied to the arms of what looked like a metal chair. The head, flung back, seemed to be looking up into the falling snow, much as he had done himself back at the pond.

Dreep was pointing at the face, his own ghost-like. 'Somebody sewed his eyes shut, and his mouth.'

As they contemplated the added horror of this, Kev said, 'Is he alive?'

'Of course he isn't,' Dreep said, open-mouthed.

'Did you check?' Ally asked, rousing from his own stupor.

'How the fuck do I do that?' Dreep squeaked.

Ally forced himself forward and reached for the neck, the way they'd done in First Aid in school. He tried to find a pulse like they'd been taught, but his shaking fingers were refusing to stay in position.

The sudden sound of a police siren heading along the nearby road ended his attempt.

Dreep took off first, his skinny legs like a deer springing through the undergrowth. He was up and over the green metal fence before Ally had taken a breath.

Even Kev got there before him and was over, almost as fast as Dreep.

By the time he'd made it out, the two of them were well on their way in their sprint across the snowy grass towards the park exit.

As he belted along behind them, Ally realized all three sets of footprints were clear evidence as to where they'd just come from. Worse than that was the memory of the faint pulse he'd felt beneath his fingers before he'd upped and run away.

The naked ginger-haired guy had been alive . . . just. But someone definitely didn't want him to be.

He thought of Kev repainting their tag on the pavilion wall. He thought of the stuff they'd planked in the old farmhouse. Jeez, whoever tortured him must know someone had been using the place as a hideout.

His mind racing as fast as his feet, he thought of his fingers on the naked guy's neck. Had he left his prints on him?

As he belted round the corner at the Vital Spark pub, he thumped into a smoker huddled against the wall. Gasping out an apology, he attempted to walk on, only to be wrenched back by the hood of his jacket.

'What's the big hurry, son? Polis after you?' a gravelly voice demanded.

Ally took a breath. 'Naw. Frozen, that's all.'

The hood suddenly released, Ally staggered off and, picking up speed again, headed for the agreed meeting point if they ever got split up.

The pedestrian tunnel that ran under the Clyde from Govan to Partick was only yards from their own street. Racing through it on their bikes was a favourite pastime. Ally wished they'd spent the last hour down here rather than in the park.

On approach, it looked as though Kev and Dreep had already bailed, and he'd almost decided to do the same, when he heard Dreep call out to him.

Small for his age, Dreep seemed to have shrunk even more in the cold light of the tunnel.

Ally heard himself say, 'It's okay, Dreep, no one saw us.'

'I dropped my phone.' Dreep's voice came out in a squeak.

'I was running behind you. I would have seen it on the snow,' Ally said, willing that to be true.

'I took a photo of . . . him,' he chittered. 'When I heard the polis car, I ran and must have dropped my phone.'

There was a sudden screech of brakes as a fast-moving bike spotted them clogging the passageway. As they dived to one side, the cyclist let rip with exactly what he thought, before whizzing on past.

Ally, still trying to process what he'd just heard from Dreep, said, 'You took a photograph of that man, then dropped your phone?'

Dreep nodded, his eyes huge with horror.

At this, Ally felt a peal of panicked laughter rise in his throat only to erupt like a volcano, and he had to lean against the tunnel wall to stop himself from falling over.

'And I was worried about leaving my fingerprints on his neck!' he gasped as he began to regain his wits.

'We're fucked,' Kev offered solemnly.

'We sure are,' Ally agreed.

3

The previous evening, Rhona had watched from the bay window of her flat as the big flakes of snow had dressed the surrounding Kelvingrove Park in a robe of glistening white.

Expecting it to be gone by morning, she'd been surprised to discover that a drop in temperature had turned the snow, on the grass at least, into a layer of frosted icing. The roads, however, didn't share the sparkle, and any remaining snow there had been beaten to a slush by this morning's rush hour, through which she had just driven.

Now entering the gates of the new custodial community unit for women, known as the Lilias Centre, Rhona was pleased to note that the cluster of attractive buildings before her bore no resemblance to the old Cornton Vale. She had visited the former women's prison in Stirling on several occasions, usually to talk about her role as a forensic scientist or to encourage inmates to take the free online introductory course offered by Glasgow University.

This morning she was here at the Lilias Centre to congratulate the inmates who'd successfully completed the course and also to meet with the members of the Fine Cell Work group, who'd been learning needlework during their incarceration. Magnus, interested in the rehabilitation of female prisoners, had been conducting a study on the positive aspects of the sewing class on the group.

Drawing into the car park, Rhona checked to see if Magnus's car might already be there, and found that it was. Professor Magnus Pirie was a man who operated in a timely fashion, unlike herself. Then again, he knew exactly when he would be called upon to give a lecture to his criminology students at Strathclyde University. She, on the other hand, never knew when the next call to a possible murder scene might occur.

Luckily, that hadn't happened this morning.

Locking her vehicle, she double-checked she had brought the personally signed certificates of completion for the forensic course participants, then made her way to reception, where she found the tall blond figure of the Orcadian professor chatting to the officer on the desk.

'Dr MacLeod, you made it,' Magnus said with a smile.

'I did.' She approached the desk and signed in. 'Are you coming to my forensic group first?' she asked.

'It seems the two groups overlap apart from one participant, Marnie Aitken, the star of the stitching class.'

'She didn't take the forensic course?'

He indicated not. 'She's coming along anyway. I understand there are to be awards?'

'I had certificates made. It's not much but . . .'

'They'll love that,' Magnus assured her. 'I hope you signed them?'

'I did.'

'Good. They may ask you to dedicate them too. For their kids.'

'That's a thing?' Rhona said.

He nodded. 'As an encouragement, I think.'

'Or to warn them how easy it is to get caught nowadays,' Rhona suggested.

At that point a young woman arrived and introduced herself as Dr Sara Masters, forensic psychiatrist at the centre.

'Dr MacLeod?' she said with a smile. 'Professor Pirie and I have already met.'

Rhona decided that the super-friendly smile Sara now bestowed on Magnus suggested the two of them may have already met outside the confines of the correction unit. Something she would need to question Magnus about later.

The area they were now walking through had been painted in soft pastel shades of green, blue and pink.

'This place is certainly an improvement on the old Cornton Vale,' Rhona said.

'And not just in looks,' Sara told her. 'There are only twenty-four women here and we use a gender-specific and trauma-informed approach to manage and support them. Plus hopefully better prepare them for their reintegration back into their communities.'

'You've been coming here since it opened,' Rhona said to Magnus. 'Is it managing to do that, do you think?'

'It's early days but it's a definite improvement on what was available before. The woman I mentioned as the star of the Fine Cell Work group?' Magnus said. 'She's being released tomorrow after serving a long sentence. Being here has definitely helped her prepare for the outside world again.'

Sara nodded her agreement. 'Marnie was incredibly withdrawn when she arrived. It took quite a while before she could be persuaded to join even the Fine Cell Work group. Then she turned out to be an excellent student.'

The door to the room stood open, the seven women seated round in comfortable chairs. One wall was lined with computer desks. The other held a display of some of the work of the Fine Cell Work group, framed embroideries and a selection of soft toys, one of which sat centre stage. It was a doll, dressed as a female Highland dancer. Even from where she stood, Rhona could see how beautiful it was.

That, she guessed, must be the work of the star of the class.

Fifteen minutes later, Rhona had happily dedicated the certificates to the various offspring of the women. After which she was questioned about her job and how she could possibly work on dead bodies, especially ones that had been buried.

It was a question she'd been asked numerous times, but she always made sure to answer it carefully and with respect.

'I never think of them as bodies but as people, each one of them unique. I try to learn as much as I can from them, so that I might understand how they died and whether someone else was involved in their death. The loved ones of the victims have the right to know these things.'

She halted there as she saw a hand raised. The small, brown-haired woman, Rhona guessed to be in her late twenties, had been the only one not to receive a signed certificate, so must be Marnie Aitken.

'Yes, Marnie?' Rhona asked cautiously.

The voice that answered was soft, yet determined. 'What if the police don't find a body to examine?'

It was obvious from the faces of the other women that they knew why Marnie had asked that particular question.

When Rhona checked with Magnus, he indicated with a nod that Rhona should respond.

'Then other forensic evidence must be brought to bear, sufficient to establish the likelihood that the missing person is dead and likely murdered.'

'But what if they're not dead?' Marnie said. 'What if they turn up alive later? That's happened, hasn't it?'

Rhona couldn't lie. 'It has on occasion,' she admitted.

Marnie nodded as though reassuring herself of such a possibility.

As calm descended once again, Magnus switched their attention to the endeavours of the Fine Cell Work team.

'Let's show Dr MacLeod what you've been working on.' He indicated that they should all approach the display.

'You too, Marnie?' he said, when she remained in her seat.

Marnie didn't respond to his invitation but rose and left the room. Magnus didn't remark on this but instead encouraged the others to tell Dr MacLeod about their own work and how it had helped them deal with their time inside.

As the women eventually began to drift off to their own rooms, Magnus asked Rhona if she had time for a coffee before she went back to work. 'There's a staffroom we can use.'

'Is it about Marnie?' she said.

'It is,' he told her.

Seated now with a mug of coffee, Rhona listened as Magnus gave her some background to the question Marnie had asked.

'I was aware you weren't involved with her case, because you didn't recognize the name and it was six years ago. A four-year-old girl went missing during the Highland games on the Rosneath Peninsula. She was never found. Her name was Tizzy Aitken.'

'Marnie's daughter?' Rhona said, surprised. 'So that's the reason for the Highland doll?'

Magnus nodded. 'Tizzy was due to take part in the dance competition when she disappeared. Her body was never found, but both forensic and other evidence pointed to Marnie being involved in her disappearance and likely death.'

'But what if they're not dead?' Rhona repeated Marnie's words. 'You think she believes her child is still alive?'

'I think it may be easier for her to believe that than the truth.'

'What forensic evidence did they have to convict her?' Rhona asked, intrigued.

'I don't know the details, but I believe Marnie was psychologically assessed by social services earlier and was found to be a fit mother.'

'When is she due to be released?'

'Tomorrow.'

Rhona read his expression. 'You're worried about that?' When he indicated he was, she said, 'Will you be keeping in touch with her?'

'She's one of the women I've been studying for a report on women who kill, so yes, I hope so.'

The ring of Rhona's mobile halted their conversation. 'I have to take this,' Rhona said. Answering, she found Chrissy on the line.

'We're wanted at the old farmhouse in Elder Park. The body of a man. I'll meet you there.' And she rang off.

'Work I assume?' Magnus asked.

When Rhona indicated it was and she had to leave, he suggested they might meet again soon to chat further regarding Marnie.

Rhona agreed; then, with a smile, she suggested that they might also discuss Sara Masters, at which Magnus looked moderately embarrassed.

'You should have become a psychologist, Dr MacLeod,' he offered.

'I'll leave that up to you,' Rhona told him. 'And Dr Masters.'

4

Heading for the Clyde Tunnel, Rhona recalled the story of two male students from one of her classes who'd told a tale of walking through the pedestrian tunnel from Partick to Govan, only to find when they emerged that they were back in Partick. 'Can forensics solve that conundrum, Dr MacLeod?'

Rhona had assumed strong drink had played a part in the story, but still hoped one day she might surface to find herself back where she started.

Today is not that day, she thought as she emerged on to Govan Road and the expanse of Elder Park, dressed decorously in white.

The Fairfield Farmhouse, Govan's oldest surviving building and its only remaining link to its pastoral past, she knew as a listed building, now in very poor condition. It stood on the western side of Elder Park, near the boating pond and pavilion. The side closest to Govan Road had served as a community garden for a time but was now shut down.

If she hadn't been aware of the location already, the obvious line of police vehicles told the story. That and the curious locals hanging about the pond and pavilion in the hope of seeing what was going on beyond the incident tape.

Spotting the forensic van, Rhona parked alongside, aware that Chrissy must already be on site.

Kitted up, she made for the gate to the grounds of the nineteenth-century farmhouse, now unpadlocked and lying open, with a scene-of-crime officer in place. Greeting Rhona, he waved her through, informing her that Chrissy was there and the tent already set up.

Once inside the perimeter, Rhona stood for a moment, taking note of her surroundings. There was a clump of trees close to the perimeter fence, their trunks burnt black from someone's earlier attempt at a fire. Between the trees and the old stone building was a thick tangle of vegetation under which the snow still lay. Close to the farmhouse itself was a blue forensic tent.

As though sensing her arrival, a white hooded and masked head popped out to order her inside.

'Come see this. It's a humdinger.'

Her forensic assistant, Chrissy McInsh, wasn't known for mincing her words. Although always respectful of the dead, she wasn't afraid to comment on the crime scene.

Rhona had already decided the setting itself to be intriguing, but now inside the tent in the full glow of the arc lights, she had to agree with Chrissy's summation of what lay before her.

The naked male body, wrists and ankles tied to the arms and legs of an upturned metal chair, would have been staring skywards had his eyes not been sewn shut with big black stitches, along with his mouth.

It was a horrifying image that was already conjuring

up in Rhona's brain what had been done to him before his death.

'A gangland killing?' Chrissy suggested.

'If it is, we haven't seen one like it before,' Rhona said, circling the body, noting the mass of contusions, the bloodied feet, the stitching round the eyes and mouth. 'Whoever did this to him, it's unlikely to have happened out here in the open.'

'My thoughts too,' Chrissy said.

Rhona stepped outside again.

The lower windows of the old farmhouse, she'd noted earlier, were barricaded with metal shutters. Of the two windows on the upper floor, only one was boarded up, the other open to the elements, just a jagged rim of broken glass left.

'Looks like he may have come from up there.' Rhona pointed.

As they surveyed the scene, a tall and familiar figure, despite the suit and mask, arrived to join them.

'You took your time,' Chrissy informed him.

'And good morning to you too, Ms McInsh.' DS Michael McNab's green eyes reflected the smile behind the mask. 'Dr MacLeod.' He gave a small bow in Rhona's direction.

'You've viewed the body?' Chrissy said.

'Not yet. Although I understand it's interesting?'

'Come see for yourself,' Chrissy said, leading the way.

The expletives were for the most part swallowed by the mask, but Rhona heard enough to gauge McNab's disquiet at what he saw. She also suspected the image of an auburn-haired tortured man tied to a chair brought back uncomfortable memories the detective would rather forget.

'Recognize the handiwork?' Rhona asked quietly.

'If you mean what the Russian gang did to me . . . no,' he said. 'Solonik's party piece was to press both your eyes into your head. Or alternatively to scoop them out and throw them away. As to stitching them shut . . .' He tailed off.

'Any idea who reported it?' Rhona said.

'A nearby nursery use this end of the park as an outdoor play area. One of the kids spotted something through the fence and told the teacher. She called it in at ten a.m.,' McNab said.

'Plenty of gang slogans about,' Chrissy offered. 'Maybe a feud over territory?'

'As to who owns Elder Park?' McNab joked. 'Don't think so. The victim is too fit and nicely tanned for any of the teenage gangs that hang about here. Seriously, though, this looks like a professional job.'

'And a personal one,' Rhona said. 'The stitching up of the mouth and eyes would suggest a warning of some sort.'

McNab nodded. 'But if it's a Glasgow crime lord punishment, it's new to me.'

'I think he was probably pushed from that upper window,' Rhona told him. 'His feet are badly cut and there are glass fragments in the wounds. We'll need to examine that room and the surrounding area once we've prepared him for removal to the mortuary.'

'Okay, we'll check for a safe way to get you up there,' McNab said. 'So how do you plan to deal with our victim?'

'We won't process him here for fear of contamination or loss of evidence. We'll wrap him and the chair in plastic sheeting, ends twisted over to make a big Christmas cracker, which we'll hold together with print-lifting tape. Also, we'll need a transit-type van to transfer him to the mortuary,' she finished.

'Right.' McNab looked relieved that she had it all figured out. 'I'll organize the van.'

'Once he's on his way, Chrissy and I will comb the surrounding area in case any other projectile landed with him,' Rhona added. 'After which we'll tackle the upstairs room.'

'On that now,' McNab said.

It all sounded straightforward, even easy, but Chrissy's expression confirmed it was anything but.

'Christmas cracker, very seasonal,' she said, with one of those looks only Chrissy could produce. 'Better get to work, then.'

It took more than two hours before they could bid the victim goodbye and move on to combing the surrounding area.

Early afternoon now, the midwinter sun was already in retreat and the temperature dropping even further. Looking up at the dimming sky, the rumble of the traffic on Govan Road as backdrop, Rhona acknowledged how lucky they'd been that the weather had stayed dry with no more snow and, thankfully, no rain.

Their search of the wider locus had produced nothing of real interest, apart from fragments of glass that might or might not have come from the shattered window. Discarded Buckfast bottles and beer cans they'd found a-plenty, plus empty spray-paint cans, the favourite colours being red, yellow and black.

It was on their final circle that the eagle-eyed Chrissy spotted something caught in the roots of one of the trio of burnt trees close to the fence.

Extracting it from beneath the now-melting snow, she flourished it at Rhona.

'A mobile?' Rhona said in a mix of surprise and delight.

'Could have been there a while,' Chrissy said, turning it over in her gloved hands.

'Or it landed here along with the body,' Rhona said.

Using a Faraday bag, Chrissy secured it with the deference given to precious finds. 'So now for the upstairs room.'

'Something to eat first?' Rhona said, aware of how hungry Chrissy would be by now.

Chrissy's eyes brightened. 'I brought along the breakfast rolls that neither of us got to eat. They won't be hot, though?'

'Who cares?' Rhona said, conscious now of her own stomach's rumblings.

Forty minutes later, replete and kitted up again, they were making their way up the narrow staircase in the old farmhouse.

As Rhona had surmised, the upper floor consisted of two small attic rooms, the one to the right showing signs of having been in use recently.

Now brightly lit, although seriously cold, the position of the chair and its tortured occupant was clearly marked by bloodstains and bodily fluids on the wooden floor. Obvious too was the chair's scraped path across the wooden floor towards the window.

'Could he have thrown himself out?' Chrissy ventured. 'Trying to escape.'

'More likely he was pushed.' Rhona indicated the footprints that followed the bloodied route to the window.

'Why not just leave him in here to die of cold?' Chrissy shivered, despite her layers of clothing and the forensic suit. 'He might never have been found.'

'Except it looks like someone's been using this place,' Rhona said, now over at the far wall where various items of clothing were heaped together with empty takeaway boxes and more Buckfast bottles.

'No drugs paraphernalia, though,' Chrissy commented. 'So not a drugs den.'

'Right,' Rhona said. 'We'll photograph and video record as before, then we'll bag everything in here and take it back to the lab. Then we'll work the area where the chair was and its route to the window. Whoever was in this room will have left their mark somewhere.'

5

From where he stood in the dimness of the park, Ally could see the blazing lights in the garden and also on the upper floor of the old farmhouse.

He'd hoped that when the body wrapped in plastic was taken away, the two women would go with it, but they hadn't. Instead, they'd gone back inside the fence and started combing the ground.

Last night, he'd told Kev and Dreep that since tomorrow was half-day Friday he would take the morning off and try to find the mobile. He would, of course, not inform his mum of this fact.

Arriving bright and early, Ally had quickly realized he could only look around outside the fence because of the folk walking through the park. He'd never imagined it would be so busy at that time of the morning.

When the nursery group had arrived at their play area near to the fence, he could have cried, especially when one of them spotted something and shouted to his teacher.

Ally had stood transfixed as the teacher approached the fence and peered into the garden. It was obvious she'd seen the body because she immediately shooed the kids away, then made a phone call.

The next thing Ally heard was the siren. That's when he knew for definite it was all over, because the phone was in there somewhere and they would no doubt find it with the body.

Now late afternoon, and fast getting dark, the police and forensic team were still here. What were they doing up in that room?

Bagging all your stuff, a wee voice told him. He tried to recall what they'd left up there. Fast-food cartons, empty bottles, even clothes. Jeez, everything would have their prints and DNA on it.

There's no way they could know whose stuff it is, he tried to persuade himself. *Unless they find the phone.*

Thank goodness he'd persuaded Kev and Dreep not to come to the park with him. Dreep especially would have totally freaked out by now. It had turned out that the mobile was a cast-off from his older brother, Darren. According to Dreep, there was stuff on there that could lead the police to Darren, who already had form for possession. Plus he was in a real gang.

To stop himself imagining Dreep's face when he told him about all of this, Ally took off for another run round the park. So as not to look like a permanent feature at the crime scene, he'd taken to running to the library in the far corner of the park and back again. He dearly wanted to go into the library to get warm, but he'd already done that once. They knew him in there, and would wonder if he kept coming back.

His most recent jog complete, he now made for the old stone portico, all that remained of the fancy mansion house that had once stood in the park. As he watched from there, he saw the two suited women emerge from the garden to load three big black bags into the back of the forensic van.

They were chatting to one another and he could hear them laughing. As they rid themselves of their forensic suits, he saw that the one doing most of the talking had pink hair.

As though conscious of his gaze, she suddenly glanced his way and he had to duck behind the portico, but not fast enough apparently.

'Hey,' she shouted cheerily. 'Can you tell us where the nearest chippy is?'

At that moment one of the two remaining uniform officers appeared and Ally realized if he didn't respond it might look suspicious, so he emerged from behind the stone arch.

'Over here,' the pink-haired girl ordered with a smile. 'We don't bite.'

His heart hammering, Ally did as commanded.

Giving him a quick up-and-down look, she said, 'I take it you're from around here?'

Ally nodded and waved vaguely in the Linthouse direction.

'Well, I'm Chrissy and this is Rhona.' She waited as though expecting a reply.

'Ally,' he muttered.

'Right, Ally, me and my boss here are ravenous. So where do we go for a good Govan fish supper?'

There was no way he was going to direct her towards the local chippy, so close to their meeting place at the tunnel, so he pointed in the other direction. 'Leo's Fish and Chips, further along Govan Road.'

'Nothing on your side of the park, then?' She was eyeing him quizzically as if she already knew the answer.

'Aye, but Leo's is better,' he said with a manic grin.

The other woman was watching their exchange with interest. Now she spoke.

'Is this where you normally hang out?' She gestured towards the pond and pavilion and eventually the old farmhouse.

He knew he could hardly say no, so muttered, 'Sometimes.'

'So which gang slogan's yours?' The one called Chrissy pointed towards the pavilion.

'None of them,' he lied.

She laughed as though she didn't believe him. 'But you come here to eat Leo's fish suppers?'

Ally suddenly understood what she was getting at. The bags they'd brought out were likely full of stuff from the upstairs room. Their stuff. And that would include carry-out cartons from Leo's.

He swore internally; then, with a quick glance at his non-existent watch, said, 'I'll have to go, sorry.'

He imagined he could feel their eyes on his back as he jogged towards the west gate.

The one called Chrissy had read him like a book, he realized. He would have to stay away from the park. All three of them would have to stay away from the park.

But if they'd found the phone, a small voice said, the police would come looking for them soon enough.

And the first person they'd come for was Dreep.

Or, even worse, his brother.

6

Now that the body had gone and Rhona and Chrissy were about finished upstairs in the farmhouse, he could leave. McNab found himself strangely reluctant to do so. The image of the dead man had imprinted itself on his brain and was stirring up old memories. Ones he'd tried hard to bury.

The victim hadn't really looked like him, but the auburn hair and the evidence of torture had been enough to make him recall how it had felt to be strapped to a chair, and had conjured up the huge mountain of a man that was Solonik staring down at him, his expression blank as he contemplated what he might do next.

McNab still bore the scars of that encounter, although the most prominent of all, the bullet to his back, he'd had covered by a skull tattoo, inked by Ellie.

The Ellie he'd eventually driven away because he always put the job first.

The buzz of his phone thankfully interrupted that depressing train of thought. Glancing at the screen, he registered that it was his partner in crime.

'DS Clark, what can I do you for?' he said, trying to sound upbeat.

'How goes it in Elder Park?' she asked.

'Weird and nasty,' he admitted. 'A naked guy, strapped to a chair, his eyes and mouth sewn shut. Looks like he may have been launched from the upper floor of the old farmhouse.'

'Jeez,' Janice grued. 'Gang related?'

'Never seen retaliation like this before and we've seen plenty,' McNab said honestly. 'Rhona's wrapped him and the chair and sent it off to the mortuary. She and Chrissy are working the farmhouse now.'

'So you're finished there?'

'For the moment,' McNab said, hearing something in his partner's voice that suggested there was another reason for her call. 'What is it?' he demanded.

'Your Harley's been stolen.'

'My Harley's been stolen,' he repeated, thinking his partner was taking the piss. 'From outside the police station? Aye right,' he added disbelievingly.

'It has.' Janice's tone didn't suggest she was having him on.

McNab, realizing she was definitely in earnest and his much-loved motorbike had been taken, swore under his breath. 'I assume this was caught on CCTV?'

'The duty sergeant saw it happen. Whoever took it was dressed in black leathers and a helmet. He said he thought it might be female. Have you pissed off any women recently?' she asked, with more than a hint of irony in her voice.

McNab, ever more perplexed, chose not to answer that question. 'Okay, I'm coming in.'

'No you're not,' Janice said. 'You're to meet me at the Hidden Lane instead. Soon as.'

He'd heard of the Hidden Lane but had never attempted

to find it. Apparently it was trendy and lay somewhere off upper Sauchiehall Street near Kelvingrove Park and Rhona's flat.

'Why on earth are we meeting there?' he demanded.

'An American film crew in the vicinity reported one of their actors missing.'

McNab made a sound that indicated how underwhelmed he was by that. 'And there's no one else available to go and play nursemaid to the bloody Yanks?'

Ignoring the question, Janice told him she would see him there in twenty minutes. 'We can have chai tea and scones in the Hidden Tearoom after we do the interview,' she said sweetly.

Pretending not to hear that, McNab rang off.

Today could not get any weirder, he decided. The see-and-speak-no-evil naked man in the chair, whose injuries had freaked him out. Followed by some woman stealing his Harley from outside the police station.

He thought of Mary Grant, wife of his once-mate Davey Stevenson, who'd given him the bike as a gift after Davey had been sent to prison. The gift had been Mary's way to keep them in touch, something he hadn't kept his promise on. Might she have reclaimed it because of that?

Or maybe Ellie, a keen Harley rider herself? Might she have kidnapped his bike? If so, why? She'd been the one to end their relationship. Although he'd been the one to ruin it. Another thought he didn't like to dwell on.

Preparing to draw away in the car, he noted that Rhona and Chrissy had emerged, and were now talking to a boy of about twelve or thirteen who looked as though he might have been hanging about the crime scene.

Something about the exchange made McNab wait, engine

ticking over, while Chrissy gave her full attention to the lad. Chrissy's interrogation techniques were legendary. If she was questioning the boy, she had reason to.

Whatever was being said, it came to an abrupt halt when the boy suddenly took off in a sprint towards the park exit on the Linthouse side.

'What the hell?' McNab muttered as he shifted into gear and took off in pursuit. A runner was always worth a follow and the lad might just know something if he spent his time hanging about the park.

Exiting the big gates with traffic lights ahead, McNab caught the tail end of the boy heading west on Govan Road past the Vital Spark pub.

If he continued into the housing scheme on the other side of the expressway, McNab decided he would follow. Maybe find out where the boy lived. Then if Chrissy indicated he might be a witness of some sort they would know where to locate him.

His hope of doing so was short-lived as the running boy instead turned down the ramp that led into the pedestrian entrance to the Clyde Tunnel.

McNab drew to a halt. Had the boy realized he was being followed and taken himself down there to get out of sight? Or was he planning a walk through the tunnel to Partick? Whatever the reason, McNab decided he wasn't about to park then follow him on foot to find out. He had a meeting in the Hidden Lane to go to. And his partner didn't like to be kept waiting.

When McNab finally located the entrance to the Hidden Lane, he realized how hidden it was. Not dissimilar to Ashton Lane where their after-work hang-out of the jazz club lay, this place had a different feel to it. Whereas Ashton was mainly dedicated to pubs, this cul-de-sac felt more sedate. Hence maybe why the tearoom DS Clark had mentioned was situated here.

Having parked the car outside on the main street, he walked in, noting the long flat stones edging the rough cobbles, there no doubt for the cartwheels in past times.

Folk from outside thought of Glasgow as an industrial city, which it was and had been, but it was also home to over ninety parks and miles of lanes behind the more gracious tenements, once used for access or stables, which now bloomed in spring and summertime like country lanes. One such lane was visible beyond the hotchpotch of low buildings painted in blues and yellows.

He halted for a moment, registering a camper-van parked to the right alongside various items of equipment, suggesting this was where the camera crew were set up, a line of tape separating it from the rest of the lane.

Two guys stood this side of the tape, chatting to his partner in what appeared to be a friendly exchange. Reading their body language, McNab smiled to himself. *Coming on to Janice is a waste of time, lads. She's happily married, and to a woman.*

Janice turned and, by the look she gave him on approach, he knew she was well aware of the situation and was in fact being entertained by it.

'Jerry Borstein, Ragnar Ryan, my partner Detective Sergeant Michael McNab.'

Jerry, McNab thought, looked to be in his mid-twenties. He was tall, blond, tanned, with hair shaved at the sides, and a serious beard, a definite shoo-in for some Viking movie. Ragnar, the one whose first name actually sounded Viking, was around the same age, but the opposite in appearance, being short and slimly built with a mass of dark curly hair.

When both fell to scrutinizing him as though sizing up how he might look on camera, McNab found himself inadvertently straightening up, which resulted in Janice throwing him one of her looks.

'A Scottish redhead,' Jerry nodded. 'Haven't seen many of those since we arrived.'

At this point Janice coughed to smother a laugh, and McNab decided enough was enough.

'Right, what's the problem here, sir?' he said firmly.

'We're missing one of our actors.' Jerry indicated the camper-van as though it somehow played a part in the story.

'Your actor was staying there?' McNab said.

'No. We're all in a hotel nearby. The camper-van's used between takes.'

'Your actor's name?'

'Jason Endeavour.'

'Jason Endeavour,' McNab repeated, feeling himself sliding into the 'Aye right' realm again. 'And what does Jason look like, sir?'

'Six feet tall, hair your colour, works out, tanned, twenty-seven. He's on the up,' Jerry added as if for emphasis. 'Two million followers on TikTok.'

McNab chose to ignore the TikTok reference and asked when they had last seen their actor.

'As I already told your colleague, it was yesterday afternoon. We stopped shooting when the snow came on. Being from California, we think the snow is great,' Ragnar said with a smile. 'Me and Jerry went to the big park nearby, Kelvingrove, to take some snow shots there.'

'And what did Jason do?'

Ragnar shrugged. 'Went into the van. Said he wanted a nap. Hasn't got over the time zone change yet. Anyway, he wasn't here when we got back and he never came back to the hotel last night. He wasn't answering his phone and we were scheduled to shoot again today. When he didn't turn up for that we began to get worried.'

'Could he just be out on the randan?' McNab said.

When they both assumed a puzzled expression, Janice translated. 'Could Mr Endeavour just be out on the town? Getting to know Glasgow?'

'Oh, he knows Glasgow already,' Ragnar told them. 'He comes from here. Studied at the Conservatoire. Came to LA six years ago.'

'I take it Endeavour's not his real name, then?' McNab said, keen to clear that up.

'Stage name,' Jerry confirmed.

'So what is his real name?'

'Lewis McLean.'

McNab ran the name through his memory banks. Had he ever encountered a Lewis McLean back in the day? In any capacity? The search came up blank. He looked to Janice. A small shake of the head confirmed she was also a no. But they could easily check up. Find out if the missing actor had ever been on their radar during his youth or student days in Glasgow.

'I'd give it another twenty-four hours,' McNab said. 'A Weegie back in his home city is liable to be celebrating that fact, especially if he's become famous in the interim. I suspect he's met up with some old pals. You could of course post his picture on social media. Try to locate him that way,' he added.

The two men looked at one another in concern. The idea

of alerting their actor's fans to his disappearance obviously didn't appeal.

'It's what Police Scotland would do,' Janice explained. 'We'd put a photo of him up on social media with where he was last seen and a description and number to call if you've seen him.'

'Do you have a photograph we might use?' McNab persisted, keen to be done with the encounter and thinking even a pot of tea and a scone in the nearby Hidden Teashop would be better than standing here with these two plonkers.

At a nod from Jerry, Ragnar flicked through his phone, then handed it to Janice. 'That's Jason.'

Janice took a look then passed the mobile to McNab.

As McNab studied the photo, a troubling thought entered his head. One he decided not to voice.

'Are you happy for us to put this up?' he said. 'Or would you prefer to wait a little longer for Jason to reappear?'

Checking with Jerry, Ragnar said, 'We'll give him until tomorrow.'

McNab nodded. 'Can you send me a copy of this? If he hasn't turned up by, say, tomorrow lunchtime, we'll post it up with a request for information on his whereabouts.'

The exchange done, they said their goodbyes, the two Americans immediately heading for the trailer, talking in a worried fashion.

'What do you think?' Janice said when they'd both disappeared inside.

'I think we should leave this place,' McNab said firmly.

'So no tea and scones, then?' Janice said with an enquiring look.

'Something stronger is required,' McNab told her firmly as they regained the main street.

'Why?' Janice said. 'Because of your Harley being stolen?'

McNab shook his head. 'Because, going by that photograph, I think there's a small but possible chance Jason Endeavour might just be the dead bloke we found in Elder Park.'

7

Ally had spotted the police car leave the park immediately after him. He had no idea if he was being followed, he just ran as though he was.

Crossing the dual carriageway, he headed down the slope into the pedestrian tunnel and waited, his heart pounding.

He should never have shown himself. He should never have spoken to those women. The one with the pink hair knew what she was doing. All friendly and it's only about a local chippy. *Aye right.*

When he was satisfied the driver following him out of the park hadn't ditched his vehicle and was following him on foot, he let out the breath he'd been holding. It didn't matter that they weren't coming for him now, because they would be in the future. They must have found the phone. Isn't that what forensic folk did? Examine the dead body and search the surrounding area for clues?

They wouldn't have missed a mobile lying near the body. *No chance of that.*

He banged his head against the tunnel wall, swearing at his stupidity for getting spotted. Knowing it didn't matter anyway because the lost mobile made sure the police would come calling and soon.

Waiting a few more minutes during which two bikes shot past, he then sent Kev a text to meet him here with Dreep. Now he had to work out a way of telling Dreep that he didn't get the phone and telling them both that their den at the farmhouse had been examined and bags of their stuff removed by two white-suited women.

Who managed to corner you and get you to mention Leo's chippy. The one called Chrissy latched on to that right away.

Kev's reply 'On our way' arrived minutes later. Kev and Dreep lived on the same street, but Ally suspected they'd likely spent the day at Kev's waiting for him to summon them.

As he walked up and down to keep warm, a text came in from his mum, ordering him home for his tea. He answered saying he'd be there in ten minutes. Her response when it came was 'NOW' in capital letters.

Defeated, he decided to walk towards home and meet Kev and Dreep on the way. He wouldn't say much. Just that he didn't find the phone. Maybe suggest it could have been spotted inside the fence by an early passer-by going to work. Which could be true, he assured himself. Hopefully it had been someone who would keep it for themselves.

Not when they saw the pic of a dead naked bloke strapped to a chair, they wouldn't.

Emerging from the tunnel, he headed up the path towards the road, aware that he didn't have long before his mother would be on the phone again. Seconds later, he spotted Kev and Dreep running towards him like they'd just escaped a burning building. Whatever had happened, it wasn't good.

When they reached him and saw his expression, both their faces assumed a look of further terror.

'The police found the phone?' Dreep wailed.

'I don't know,' Ally said honestly. 'All I know is I never found it. Plus they've searched our room and taken away all our stuff.'

He expected them to be really freaked by that last bit of news, but it seemed they had something worse in store for him.

'Darren wants his phone back,' Kev said. 'And Dreep told him he loaned it to you.'

'What!' Ally said in horror.

'It was all I could think of,' Dreep said. 'Sorry, mate.'

'Don't *sorry mate* me,' Ally warned him. 'I just hung about that park all day for you and you rat me out to your big brother?' He stopped there, seeing Dreep shrink into himself at his fury.

As his own mobile buzzed another message, he said, 'That'll be Mum about my tea. I have to go.' He took off at a sprint before Dreep and Kev had time to respond, glad to get away from them and give himself time to think. In truth, he was more afraid of Darren than of his mum and at least at home he was safe from Dreep's big brother.

Reaching the gate, he composed himself before slipping his key in the lock. He'd decided the story of his day on the way back, aware he should stick to the truth as closely as possible.

His mum wasn't a detective, but she could be. She was like the pink-haired lassie, who could wrestle stuff out of you and scent a lie almost before it came out of your mouth.

'I'm home, Mum,' he shouted in advance of reaching the kitchen.

Entering, he found his mum at the table, opposite the figure of a man who had his back to the door. As his breathing stopped in fear at who it might be, his mum looked up at him and smiled.

'Brian's big brother's here to see you.' She always used Dreep's real name. 'Something about Brian's mobile?' she said, not looking worried at all.

At this point, the dark-haired head of Darren McGowan turned towards him with a smile that would have cut glass.

'Dreep said he lent you my old phone,' he said. 'I need it back, I'm afraid.'

He definitely wasn't afraid, but he'd made sure by those eyes that Ally definitely was.

Words failed to materialize in Ally's mouth although he heard them form in his head. Eventually his mum ended the silence.

'Well, Alistair. Do you have the phone?'

He shook his head and the lie tumbled out. 'I'm dead sorry, Darren. It must have dropped out of my pocket last night in the park. I've been searching for it all day.'

Darren's eyes were now shooting bullets at him. Ally could almost feel the pain as they met his chest.

'I'll try again tomorrow,' he promised. 'There were bits of the park near the boating pond I couldn't get to because of the police cordon.' Why he said that, he had no idea, but was glad he had as Darren's threatening look now moved to one of concern.

'Why are the police in the park?' his mum came in.

'I think they found a body,' he found himself saying, 'near the old farmhouse.'

His mother looked shocked. 'I hadn't heard anything about that.'

'It'll maybe be on the news tonight,' Ally offered.

Scraping the chair back, Darren got to his feet. Ally made

a move towards his mum, in case Darren propelled him out the door with him.

'Right, Mrs Feeney. I'll be off,' Darren said, before nodding to Ally. 'Want to see me out?'

Ally didn't want to, but he hadn't much choice as his mum gestured at him to do as he was asked.

Out of sight of the kitchen, Darren opened the front door and, grabbing Ally's arm, shoved him out first.

'Right, you wee shite.' He poked Ally sharply in the ribs. 'Where the fuck is my phone?'

'I told you. I dropped it somewhere in the park. I'm sorry, Darren.'

Darren eyed him for a moment, before he hissed, 'If the polis find it and come looking for me, you're a dead man. Do . . . you . . . understand?' He stabbed at Ally's chest again, then stood back and stared pointedly at him.

'Just like that naked dead guy they found.'

8

The snow cover was fast disappearing as they left the park, only grey slush left on the tarred exit road and churned mud on the surrounding grass.

Chrissy led the way in the forensic van, Rhona tailing her. They would have to safely store all the material they'd recovered at the lab before finishing for the day. As for the body, that would be the responsibility of the mortuary staff until tomorrow when it would become the centrepiece of the secondary crime scene examination.

As they entered the Clyde Tunnel on their way back to the university, Rhona thought about the young lad hanging around the crime scene. Nothing odd in that per se. There had been a constantly shifting group of folk, wondering what was going on in the grounds of the old farmhouse. Most realized quite swiftly that there was nothing to see, other than a glimpse of the blue tent and a constant stream of police and forensic teams moving in and out of the site.

Because of fears of contamination, plus the ground and weather conditions, she and Chrissy had been the only ones to work in close proximity to the victim. When the body and accompanying chair had been brought out in its plastic wrapping, Rhona realized that the boy they'd spoken to had been watching the proceedings, again from the stone arch a little way off.

When he'd suddenly sprinted away, Chrissy had confirmed she too had spotted him there earlier.

'I suspect he's maybe been using the upper room as a den,' she'd said as they'd watched his retreating back. 'A place to drink Buckfast and eat Leo's chips.'

'So he may be a witness to what went down in there,' Rhona had said.

'Exactly. Well, we know he's from Linthouse and his name's Ally. Plus I took a photo of him,' Chrissy had told her with a smile.

Rhona had wanted to ask how, and when, but didn't have to.

'When we stopped to eat our rolls.'

It was dark when they'd reached the lab. Even darker when they'd finished recording and storing the material they'd brought back with them from the locus.

Having briefly discussed whether they should adjourn to the jazz club for a drink before heading home, they'd established that neither of them had much enthusiasm for that.

'Home, shower and food,' had been Chrissy's preferred option, and Rhona had agreed.

As she slipped her key in the lock, she heard a mewing from behind the door. It seemed Tom had sussed out her arrival and was keen to make his presence known. Either that or he'd caught the scent of the fish supper she'd bought on her way home.

Heading for the kitchen, she turned on the heating, then poured a glass of white wine from the fridge and settled at the table with her meal. Tom's attempts to persuade her into sharing eventually saw a small piece of haddock on a saucer placed in front of him.

'I'm eating the rest,' Rhona informed him. 'You've plenty of food in your bowl.'

She was finished and licking her fingers when her mobile rang. Quickly wiping her hands, she answered.

'McNab,' she said, surprised. 'Not off duty yet?'

He didn't respond to her question but instead said, 'I'm about to send you a photograph. Take a good look at it then tell me what you think.'

Intrigued, she said okay, and waited for it to arrive, wondering what this was all about. Seconds later, the attachment was with her. Rhona opened it.

The photo was of a male, possibly in his twenties. He had posed for the camera, standing side on. He was tanned and muscled with dark auburn hair that hung over his eyes. His smile was very white, wide and attractive. McNab had included a name, Jason Endeavour, and details of his height, eye colour, etc.

'Who is this?' Rhona asked.

'An actor who disappeared yesterday around lunchtime from a film set not far from your place in the Hidden Lane. Jason Endeavour's his stage name. His real name is Lewis McLean and he's from Glasgow originally. Been living in Los Angeles for the past six years.'

'Hence the tan,' Rhona said, taking a closer look. 'I'm assuming you're wondering if this could be our park victim?'

'I know his face was sewn up, but what do you think? Is it a possibility, going by the photo and description?'

'The approximate height of the victim, his build, age, the tan and hair colour are a possible match,' she told him.

'Right.' McNab's tone suggested it was the answer he'd anticipated.

'We'll be extracting him from the chair tomorrow. You could come along?'

'What time?' he asked, not sounding enthusiastic.

'First thing,' she told him.

There was a grunt in reply, which, Rhona decided, could mean anything. 'Send Janice if you're squeamish,' she said, aware that PMs were not McNab's favoured events. 'Oh, and I thought you might like to know, we found a mobile not far from the body,' she added, knowing that would bring a smile to his face.

'Excellent. I take it it's gone to IT?'

She assured him that it had. 'We spoke to a youngster who'd hung around all day at the crime scene. We wondered if it might be his mobile and he'd come looking for it. It was lodged in the roots of the trio of burnt trees close to the fence.'

'I spotted Chrissy giving him the third degree just before I left,' McNab told her. 'I followed him when he ran off, but he disappeared into the pedestrian tunnel. Did she get anything from him?'

'His name's Ally and when she asked if he was local, he waved towards Linthouse. Chrissy asked him to recommend a good chippy. He told us Leo's near Govan Cross. Then, maybe realizing Chrissy was fishing, got spooked and ran off. The room upstairs—'

'Had discarded Leo cartons in it,' McNab finished for her. 'So we need to talk to that young man.'

'Chrissy took his photo surreptitiously. I'll get her to send it to you.'

When silence fell between them, Rhona wondered if there

was something more McNab wanted to talk about but was loathe to do so. When nothing was forthcoming, she eventually said, 'Right, see you tomorrow,' and rang off.

Showered and settled now on the sofa in the sitting room, with the gas fire on and Tom nestled beside her, she pulled up the images she'd taken at the locus. Under normal circumstances she would have spent up to twelve hours with the body and written up her notes in the tent, but the circumstances today hadn't allowed for that. The photos and video would have to be sufficient to formulate her thoughts.

Viewing the set of photos she'd taken, she was struck again by the bizarre nature of the attack. The most common method of dispensing with an enemy in Glasgow was by stabbing. In this instance, the victim had been stripped and systematically tortured before being hurled through the window from the upper storey of the farmhouse, where he would definitely be discovered. Which suggested the perpetrator wanted the oxygen of publicity.

A revenge killing perhaps. Or retribution for something the victim had seen, said or done.

The significance of the stitched eyes and mouth was what struck her most strongly. She was reminded of the three wise monkeys, their hands over their ears, eyes and mouth symbolizing the belief that if we do not hear, see or speak evil, we ourselves shall be spared from evil.

In this case, the ears hadn't been stitched shut, but they had been bleeding, which suggested some sort of trauma had occurred. Torturing the victim via earphones with a very loud and continuous noise might be the cause. Or being continuously pummelled about the head.

Tomorrow, the mortuary would become the secondary

crime scene. She and Chrissy would do the original work with the body in the chair, swabbing and taking trace evidence lifts. Exactly when the body would be removed from the chair would be decided together with the pathologists involved. Every move would be recorded. Every attempt to preserve evidence taken. After which the chair would come to them at the lab along with the taping and wrappings from the body.

Bringing up the photograph of Jason Endeavour, she set it alongside the image of the victim. Might the missing actor be their victim? It was a possibility but only that. Rhona hoped McNab's fears were unfounded and Lewis or his alter ego Jason would turn up after rediscovering his home city.

Glancing at her watch, Rhona registered how late it was. She saved her notes, closed her laptop and, carefully moving Tom's supine body clear of hers, headed for bed.

9

The room was much the same size as before. A single bed, a table, a chair, a window with a different view. The social worker who had brought her here had seemed sorry about it.

'It's clean and safe,' she'd said in an apologetic voice. 'Until we find you a place of your own.'

I have a place of my own, Marnie thought. *But can I go back there?*

Standing by the window, she registered that the snow was no more. She tried to recall the image from before. The beauty of the large white flakes drifting down in the golden circle of light from the lamp post. The figure of the girl stomping through the snow to suddenly stop and stare over at her.

She'd imagined it could be Tizzy, but Tizzy was dead. She had killed her. Or so they all said. The police, the lawyer, even her social worker back then, and, of course, the jury. They had all decided that she, Marnie Aitken, had neglected her child, Elizabeth Mhairi Aitken, even unto death. *If I hadn't left her that day . . .*

But they never found her body. So how could they know Tizzy was dead?

If there's enough evidence, the forensic woman had said, then it's possible.

Dr MacLeod had looked sorry about having to tell her that. She probably knew why she'd been asked the question. Everyone in the room knew the reason. Professor Pirie, the tall blond psychologist with the lilting voice. Dr Sara, who'd tried to help her prepare for where she was now.

Released from prison. Free.

The social worker had supplied her with a mobile. On it were three numbers. One for the social work department. Plus Professor Pirie and Dr Sara.

'Call me at any time,' her social worker had told her.

Marnie remembered her expression as she'd said it and thought she would never willingly call her, although she would have to endure her visits. Her release from prison required her to stay here in the hostel and be in regular contact with her social worker.

She'd also agreed to continue to see Dr Sara once a week and to talk with Professor Pirie, or Magnus as he preferred that she call him.

She liked her time with him. When he talked of his house on the edge of Scapa Flow on Orkney, it reminded her of her own home. Of the cottage and the nearby sea. Of Tizzy's delight when paddling among the rock pools.

When another figure stalked those memories, she'd blotted him out. Inside the prison, he couldn't reach her, but now that she was out . . .

You know what you did. And so does he.

She turned from the window and sat on the bed, her unopened bag beside her. Unzipping it, she stared down at the last item she'd packed and the first she would unpack.

With it was the small kit she'd been given when she'd joined the sewing class.

She placed both the doll and the box side by side on the bed.

The thought she'd been nursing rose up again to confront her.

The way the woman, Dr MacLeod, had spoken suggested she was interested in her story. Interested enough to think about it further? Or was she just being polite?

As Marnie considered this, the mobile rang, an unknown caller image on the screen.

The social worker's name was Jean and since it was she who'd set up the mobile, it definitely wasn't her. Neither was it the professor or Dr Sara.

Marnie listened to it ring three times, then pressed the Dismiss button, telling herself it was a spam call.

Mind now made up, she opened her sewing kit and began to work on the doll that had won her so much praise when it was the centrepiece of the Cell Work Group display.

10

The desk sergeant observed McNab with a jaundiced eye.

'I told you, I only got a glimpse of the thief. Black leathers. Got on the bike. Started it up. Then away. I thought it must be legit. Maybe one of your lady friends you'd loaned it to?' he added with more than a hint of sarcasm.

'My lady friends?' McNab repeated, only wishing he actually had some. Or even one.

'They had a key,' Officer Beath said. 'And, as I said, they didn't act suspicious. Have you checked the CCTV footage?'

McNab had and got nothing from it, apart from the thought that the cool thief looked female and very much at ease when removing his bike.

Catching the desk sergeant's look, he saw no sympathy there. In fact, he almost looked pleased by his predicament. What followed confirmed he was right.

'Never mind, Detective Sergeant McNab. I hear you have an excellent clear-up rate. I have every faith you'll root out the culprit.'

The manner in which this was said convinced McNab that Officer Beath, like many other innocent officers, was still smarting from the recent investigation into rogue cops in the force, for which he could be held responsible. And obviously was, judging by Beath's barely concealed anger.

Managing to stop himself from rising to the bait with a suitable retort, McNab directed his steps towards the coffee machine. Choosing a double espresso, he replayed the grainy image from the CCTV once again in his head.

The thief had a key. Mary could have kept one when she gifted him the bike. What about Ellie? She may well have had one made while they were together. Mary definitely wasn't a fan of riding motorbikes. Ellie was and had one of her own. Plus she worked in a Harley Davidson store. But he couldn't be sure the figure in the leathers on CCTV was her.

Maybe she'd got a mate to take it for her? She rode with three female pals, Izzy, Mo and Gemma, all of them capable of playing such a trick on him. Pretty fearless too, he thought, remembering the role all four women had played in a previous case.

Then again, maybe it wasn't personal at all. Maybe there was a Harley thief about and stealing one from outside a police station was just too sweet an opportunity to miss. Especially if the owner was a cop and one you knew and disliked.

McNab quelled that train of thought. If he was to go through the list of everyone who held a grudge against him for whatever reason, he'd be here all day.

Choosing a latte for Janice, he headed for his desk, thinking about the post-mortem on the farmhouse victim. He didn't like post-mortems in general, but this one wasn't just a PM, it was a secondary crime scene examination of the naked and bound victim and he should be there.

The sudden momentary flashback to his own similar

incarceration stopped him in his tracks for a second, causing the hand holding the espresso to shake a little.

Swearing to himself, McNab drank it swiftly down. Dispensing with the cup on the way, he composed himself before appearing at his desk and placing the latte next to Janice.

'Any news on your bike?' she said with a thank-you nod.

'None. Any news on our missing actor, Jason Endeavour?' He pronounced the name with what he thought was a half-decent American twang.

By the look Janice threw him, she didn't agree. 'A few images when he was a drama student. Take a look.' She turned her screen towards him.

McNab studied the collage of photographs, thinking that Lewis McLean had definitely improved in the intervening years. Bronzer and more muscular now, the face and body from before had had more of a brooding, gaunt look.

'The States have done him a power of good,' McNab offered. 'I take it he doesn't have a record?'

'Not here anyway,' Janice said. 'Shouldn't you be heading for the PM on our Jason lookalike?'

McNab tried not to groan at the prospect. 'You'll message me if Jason turns up unharmed? Then we can cross him off the victim list.'

'Will do,' Janice promised, turning her attention back to her screen.

The snow having mostly melted, the city had taken on a grey washed-out look to match the piles of hardened slush that lingered in the gutters. McNab wasn't a fan of snow, but even he had to admit that his home city looked beautiful when wearing her white frosted cloak.

The city mortuary, in its new home in the Queen Elizabeth University Hospital, lay on the south side of the river. McNab decided to take the route through the Clyde Tunnel. He knew he was unlikely to see the boy runaway en route, but he was toying with the idea of taking a turn round the nearby housing estate after the PM, maybe show the photo Chrissy had sent him to the local residents. See if someone could identify this Ally who had taken fright and run off yesterday.

He was aware it would have been better if Janice had been with him. Folk were more likely to talk to a female officer, but if he failed to have the boy identified, then his partner could give it a try next time round.

Emerging from the tunnel, he soon saw the looming monstrosity of the hospital complex, known locally as the Death Star, and felt the familiar distaste at having to be back here again.

Dead bodies go with the territory, he reminded himself as he parked the vehicle and made his way to the mortuary. And at least he wasn't a forensic pathologist who had to do post-mortems for a living. All that was required of him was to stay long enough in that room to find out whether he might be the missing Jason, and hopefully how exactly he had died.

Although he was also likely to discover what had been done to the victim before he was catapulted from the room. That was the bit he wasn't keen to hear about.

Entering the mortuary, he registered that it was always the smell in here that got to him. Even in the suit and mask, he could feel it invade every pore in his body. He'd been at countless loci, each seemingly more horrible than the preceding one. Sometimes the death scene was in the open air where the victim's eyes had already been feasted on by crows. Sometimes inside houses where folk had lain dead for weeks or more. All the bodies had been in various degrees of decomposition, the smell of which he knew only too well.

But the smell in the autopsy room was indescribable. It lingered on his clothes and hair long after he left. Even his stubble released it hours later if he rubbed his face.

He knew that staff cleaned all surfaces religiously with strong disinfectant. Maybe that was the root of the problem. For him anyway. That hideous mix of decomposition and disinfectant.

Robed now, McNab took a deep breath, fastened his mask in place and stepped into the room.

11

The body, still enthroned, looked different in the mortuary, although Rhona felt the same affinity with the victim as she had during their time spent together in the tent in the frozen grounds of the old farmhouse.

She'd observed the studied reaction of those present as she and Chrissy had carefully unwrapped the plastic parcel they'd brought from the locus. Listened while everyone involved in the study and recovery of evidence from the body and chair discussed the least obtrusive and most comprehensive way to preserve that evidence.

The order decided, they'd worked individually or in tandem, depending on the task, the photographer capturing every decision and move that followed.

Now that the swabbing and trace evidence lifts had been completed, and the bindings finally cut and carefully stored for transfer to the lab via Chrissy, the victim could be removed from his chair. This was the moment they had all been waiting for. The moment when the twisted, confined body might be released and laid out on the metal table.

Although always human, now he seemed even more so. It caused Rhona to remember how it was when she and

Chrissy would be called upon to unearth human bones, ticking each one off on a chart as it was recovered. Laying them out in the lab to form the skeleton and make them whole again.

Now this victim seemed whole again. She could properly consider the length and breadth of him. She could imagine him when he'd been upright, warm and very much alive.

Even as she thought this, Dr Sissons pulled the overhead mike towards him and began to record what he could observe. The evidence of beatings and burns to the upper torso were described in minute detail. As was the attack on the genitals and finally the sewing up of the eyes and mouth.

Watching McNab's eyes above the mask, Rhona tried to imagine what he must be feeling as he listened to the catalogue of abuse experienced by the victim. Some of which he himself had endured at the hands of Solonik, his torturer.

At one point he caught her eye and gave her a little nod, which she read as 'I'm okay'.

As Dr Sissons prepared to remove the thread from the eyelids and mouth, he asked McNab if they had any idea who the victim might be.

McNab hesitated but only briefly before explaining that a man with a similar description had been reported missing from a film set in central Glasgow around the time the body was found.

'And that man is?'

'An actor called Jason Endeavour,' McNab said.

'Jason Endeavour.' Sissons repeated the name in his signature droll manner. 'American I presume?'

'A TikTok star and actor whose real name is Lewis McLean,' McNab told him. 'He moved to the States six years ago from Glasgow. Ended up in LA.'

'And the body measurements we took from our victim are similar to the missing actor?' Sissons said, interested now.

'Yes. Plus the tan, hair colour, muscles and age range,' McNab confirmed. 'I have a photograph of the missing Jason. And there's a likeness but—'

'With the eyes and mouth sewn shut it's difficult to decide how strong that likeness is,' Sissons finished for him. 'Well, we're about to free those, although I believe it unlikely that will be enough for a facial ID. Dr MacLeod will have samples of the victim's fingerprints and DNA, which will provide a more reliable comparison with your missing actor.'

He halted then to concentrate on carefully snipping and gently pulling out the criss-cross thread on the eyes to hand it to Rhona for an evidence bag. After which the mouth too was set free.

Just as anticipated, it made little difference to the puffed-up mottled face.

'Right,' Dr Sissons was saying. 'I believe we've learned what we can from the body as it is. Time to take a look inside.'

Those were the words McNab had been waiting for. With a glance across the table at Rhona, and a 'thank you' to Dr Sissons, he made his escape before the noise of the drill or the saw began.

Indicating to Sissons she would be back, Rhona followed McNab into the changing room, where she found him, mask discarded, bent over the sink, his open mouth under the gushing tap.

She waited, well aware of how much he needed to get rid of that taste and perhaps too the replay of the torture scene.

Eventually registering her presence, he stood up and, spitting out the remaining water, turned towards her. She was perturbed by how pale and drawn his face had become. Without speaking, he unzipped the forensic suit, stepped out of it and threw it in the nearby bin.

'A shower would help,' she suggested.

'Not if I put the same clothes back on.' He made a face. 'I'll survive until I knock off tonight. But thank you, Dr MacLeod, for your concern.' He stood for a moment, collecting himself, before saying, 'The clothes you took from that room. Could any of them have belonged to the victim?'

'We didn't examine them in situ for fear of losing evidence from them,' Rhona told him. 'They're all at the lab now. We'll check through for anything that may have been worn by him.'

'What about shoes?' McNab asked.

'None recovered inside the farmhouse or grounds, although we did find footprints, which the SOCO team lifted.'

He accepted this with a nod. 'I plan to go and check the estate near the pedestrian exit to the tunnel. See if anyone recognizes your runaway Ally from Chrissy's photograph. After which I'll check in with IT about the phone you found.'

'Chrissy spotted it lodged in the roots of the burnt trees that border the fence. I think that's maybe where Ally and his pals have been climbing in.'

'So you think it's his phone?' McNab said. When Rhona indicated she did, he added, 'Which goes some way to explain why he was hanging around there all day.'

'If you do locate him, go easy. He was pretty spooked,' Rhona said, remembering the moment when the skittish boy realized that Chrissy was actually interrogating him.

McNab didn't respond to her request, but said instead, 'I take it you're staying until the bitter end?'

'I am,' Rhona confirmed. 'I'd like to know how he died,' she told him.

McNab gave her a sideways glance as he pulled on his outer jacket. 'If he survived what happened in that room and the fall, then it was the cold that got him,' he told her.

Rhona didn't argue, aware that McNab had a better handle on the torture aspect of the incarceration than she did. 'Are you coming to the jazz club for a drink tonight?' she said instead.

McNab's expression softened. 'If you're going to be there, Dr MacLeod, then I most certainly am. But I promise to have a shower first.'

Rhona watched him go, relieved to see him returned to his normal, if annoying self, before she re-entered the room now filled with the high whine of an electric saw.

12

Glad to see the hospital retreat in his rear-view mirror, McNab opened his window a little to let the cold air dispel any remaining smell of the mortuary.

His reaction to the image of the tortured body had unnerved him. He'd believed himself free of the flashbacks that had occurred after his own incarceration, but today had proved him wrong.

Rhona had realized what was happening, although hopefully the others had not. Thank God Chrissy had already left for the lab when it happened. He couldn't have hidden it from her either.

Turning off Govan Road into Linthouse, he drew to a halt and tried to focus his thoughts. He was here to locate the boy, who might or might not have seen something that night. That was what should be uppermost in his mind.

Doing a quick check online on opening hours at Leo's, he noted his visit to the chippie would have to wait a little. So where to now?

As he approached the park again, a thought occurred. There was a library at the far end. Might Ally be known there? It was a long shot, but worth a try.

On approach, he noted that the magnificent pillared entrance to the library was similar to that of the High Court in the Saltmarket, an edifice that he was in more often than he could wish. Entering the quiet and welcome warmth, he was instantly transported back in time to when he'd frequented Maryhill library as a boy. Before he bought the idea that libraries were for softies and decided joining a gang was the way for him.

A decision that had almost brought about his downfall as a teenager.

Walking up to the desk, he found a smiling dark-haired woman who asked if she might help him.

McNab suspected the smile would fast disappear when he produced his badge and announced himself as Detective Sergeant McNab. He was right.

'And your name, miss?' he tried.

'Maitland. Sonia Maitland,' she said, looking worried. 'Are you here about what they found at the old farmhouse?' she asked.

McNab tried a reassuring smile. 'I'm just trying to locate a youngster who we think lives somewhere in Linthouse. He's around twelve or thirteen and I wondered if he might be a library user . . . like I was at his age,' he added.

'Oh,' she said, sounding less freaked now. 'Do you have his name? I can check if he's on our user database.'

'I only have his first name and a photo,' McNab explained. 'He's called Ally, probably short for Alistair. No surname as yet.' He pulled up the photo on his phone to show her.

She studied it for a moment before turning to a young male on the other side of the desk. 'Chris, come take a look at this photograph.'

Chris came over and, with a swift look at the image, asked what this was all about.

'Detective Sergeant McNab is looking for this boy. I think it might be Ally Feeney,' she told him.

Chris nodded. 'Could be. What's he done, Detective?'

'Nothing that we know of. We just need to speak to him. Do you have an address for him on file?'

'He's not a card holder,' Chris said. 'Just comes in sometimes and reads. Never takes a book out. I suspect if he did his pals would give him grief about it.'

'His pals don't come in with him, then?' McNab said.

'Sometimes, when it's too cold to hang about in the park,' Sonia told him with a wry smile. 'They're no bother. They spend their time in the comic book section.'

'You know their names too?' McNab tried.

Sonia did. 'The wee skinny one they call Dreep. The other one's Kev or Kevin. Oh . . .' She paused for a moment. 'Ally was in here yesterday. Just briefly. He looked so cold I think he came in to warm up.'

'When was this?' McNab said.

'During the morning sometime.'

Chrissy had reported the boy as coming and going from his spot on the nearby stone portico. Probably in an effort to keep warm.

At that point the desk phone rang and Chris went to answer it.

In a low voice, Sonia said, 'I don't know Dreep's surname, but he has a big brother called Darren who he's afraid of.'

'And you know this how?' McNab asked.

'I saw him once with Dreep in the park near the pond,' she admitted. 'I wanted to intervene but . . .'

McNab nodded. 'I understand. And you have no idea where any of the boys live?'

'In Linthouse definitely. They have bikes and race them in the tunnel. There's no harm in them, Detective. That's what I think anyway,' she added firmly.

McNab handed her his card. 'Will you get in touch with me if they come back? And see if you can find out an address.'

She took the card. 'I will, Detective McNab. Definitely.'

Outside now, McNab said a silent thank you for librarians, second only, he thought, to teachers, where the well-being of kids was concerned. Something he could vouch for himself.

Next stop Leo's, he decided. Where he would indulge in one of their recommended fish suppers and hopefully grill the staff on the subject of Ally Feeney, but first a call to his partner.

Janice answered on the third ring. 'I was just about to phone you,' she told him.

'Great minds think alike,' he said.

'And fools seldom differ.'

'Okay, my foolish friend,' McNab said. 'What did you want to tell me?'

'That our TikTok sensation is still missing and the guys at the Hidden Lane are freaking out and say something must have happened to him. They're apparently due to shift the filming to the Merchant City tomorrow.'

'So they've finally decided they want to advertise the fact that their star is missing?' McNab checked.

'Yeah, on TikTok and social media,' Janice told him in the tone she used when highly suspicious of someone's actions. Including his own.

'You suspect this might all be a ruse to get him trending?' McNab asked.

'It's a possibility, don't you think? Star goes missing in his old hometown of Glasgow. Anyway, just checking there isn't a chance he's our farmhouse victim?'

'No way to visually confirm, even with the stitches out,' McNab said, trying not to conjure up that face again.

'So do we ask to sample some of Jason's DNA for comparison?' Janice said.

'Definitely,' McNab said. 'For elimination purposes, at least.'

'Right. I'll organize that and put the call out on his missing status. How's it going with the search for the boy in the park?'

'Progressing. I have the surname Feeney, courtesy of Elder Park library. No address as yet. I'm heading to Leo's chip shop now to see if they can help, where I'll also be sampling the goods.'

Janice made a sound that suggested hunger. 'Lucky bugger.'

'After which I'll check in with IT about the mobile. Then go for a drink at the jazz club.'

'Definitely living the dream,' Janice said and rang off.

Leo's was now open, the delicious smell of frying assaulting McNab's nostrils as soon as he opened the car door. Before entering, he decided how he was going to play this. Order a fish supper and while awaiting it being freshly cooked, engage the proprietor in conversation, maybe mentioning Ally's name as a recommendation, he decided.

The guy behind the counter welcomed him with a smile. 'What can I do you for, sir?'

'A fish supper, please,' McNab said.

'Double fish?'

'Why not?' McNab smiled.

'We cook fresh so it'll take a wee while?'

'No bother,' McNab assured him. 'I have it on good authority you're the place to go round here.'

That pleased him so McNab continued. 'A young lad in the park recommended you. Name of Ally Feeney?'

'Ah,' the guy nodded. 'Him and his two mates come here quite often.'

'They live nearby, then?' McNab said innocently.

'Naw, they're over in Linthouse. They race in the pedestrian tunnel with their bikes. Always talking about it.' The guy gave him a look that suggested he might have been sussed. 'They in trouble with the law?'

McNab decided to come clean. 'No. We just need a word with Ally.' He showed his badge.

The guy who he assumed to be Leo dipped a large fish into a container of thick batter; then, shaking the excess off, he dropped it with an explosive sizzle into the hot fat fryer. When the noise abated he did the same with the second fish.

'Funny,' he said as McNab savoured the smell of cooking. 'You're not the first one to come in asking about Ally today.'

McNab's ears pricked up. 'Another police officer's been here?' he said.

'Didn't show me a badge but he wanted to know where Ally Feeney lived. I told him somewhere near Govan Cross. Sent him on a wild goose chase.'

'Can I ask why?' McNab said.

'Didn't like the look of him or his attitude . . . you want salt and vinegar?'

McNab nodded. 'Don't hold back on the vinegar. Can you describe this guy?'

'About five ten with short dark hair. Mid-thirties maybe. A dark stubble beard. Looked like he worked out. Local accent.'

He pushed the boxed supper with the Leo logo across the counter and McNab handed him a tenner and his card. 'Keep the change.'

The man glanced at the card. 'Good luck locating Ally, Detective Sergeant. And I hope you find whoever killed that bloke in the park. Heard it was really nasty.'

McNab gave a nod. 'If you hear anything about that or Ally, just call me.'

He ate his fish supper in the car, while he considered who the other seeker of Ally might be, and why he was looking for the boy. The worrying answer he kept returning to was that the bloke knew Ally and his mates had been using that room in the farmhouse and had possibly seen something they shouldn't have.

Having demolished his fish supper, McNab tossed the empty box into the back seat and, making a U-turn on Govan Road, headed back towards Linthouse.

There were a lot of houses in Linthouse, all of them within easy cycling distance of the Clyde Tunnel. Skipness Drive alone curved right round the dual carriageway that led into the main tunnel itself. Plus there were all the side roads leading from there back to the park.

Added to that, he had no idea whether Ally lived in a house with a garden or up a close.

He tried a few houses on Skipness Drive with no luck. Either the occupants didn't know the Feeneys or didn't want to rat on Ally to the police. Or maybe they didn't like this police officer in particular.

The hunt for Ally Feeney wasn't going to be that easy,

McNab decided, and would have to follow a more structured method, which would involve his partner, who was much better in that department than he was. At least his own quick reconnaissance had given them a name and location for the boy. Resorting to finding the Feeney family by other means would now apply. Plus he might yet get a call from the library from Miss Maitland . . . Sonia.

He'd recognized that Sonia was on the boys' side. And she'd seemed genuinely concerned about Ally's welfare and whereabouts. She'd also indicated that Dreep's big brother, Darren, had been pretty violent towards him.

It was a pity she hadn't known Dreep's surname, then he could have done a police search on Darren himself. See if his behaviour towards his wee brother had been replicated elsewhere, and perhaps got him in trouble with the law.

These musings saw him through the tunnel and back to headquarters. Trying with a quick sniff to gauge if he still harboured the smell of decay and disinfectant on his clothes, McNab entered the police station and headed for IT, stopping at the cafeteria on his way to buy two large coffees and a bag of mini sugared doughnuts.

If Ollie was sticking to his diet, then McNab planned to consume all the doughnuts himself.

Weaving his way through the multiple cubicles, he found Ollie in his usual location, eyes intently on a trio of screens. Setting Ollie's coffee down, he waggled the cellophane bag in front of his face.

'We can split these small but sweet things between us or I can eat them all. What do you think?'

McNab watched as, behind the round spectacles, desire flitted across Ollie's eyes, followed by a try at resolve, then eventually submission.

'Just one,' he said.

'One can be eaten in a single bite,' McNab warned him.

Ollie didn't respond to the goading but, carefully extracting a single miniature doughnut from the bag, popped it in his mouth. Once consumed, he said, 'You've come about the mobile phone found at the crime scene?'

'I have,' McNab confirmed between munches.

'Then you're going to be pleased,' Ollie assured him. 'First up, this. The last photo taken by the mobile's owner.'

He selected one of the files on his screen and opened it.

McNab, seated next to him, had to crane a little to see it properly, but as he began to work out what he was looking at, he felt again the nausea he'd experienced at the autopsy and just as suddenly the sweetness of the sugar in his mouth turn to bile.

'It's what I think?' Ollie said, noting McNab's expression.

McNab nodded. 'It's the body from Elder Park,' he confirmed.

'A burner phone like this doesn't have a great camera,' Ollie told him, 'hence the quality.'

'There's no doubt it's him. Chair and all.'

'So whoever took the picture dropped the phone as they left?' Ollie said. 'A bit careless for a killer, don't you think?'

'Anything on it to give us a clue as to its owner?' McNab said without answering the question. 'I don't need to know the tech details,' he added quickly, having been in one of Ollie's tech jargon conversations before now.

'We're working on it,' Ollie said with a raised eyebrow. 'However, if you were to ask me if I thought the owner didn't want to be known, I would say that was true. Otherwise why not have a smartphone?'

McNab thought for a moment. 'If I said I thought the

mobile might belong to a twelve- or thirteen-year-old boy . . . what would you say?'

'Like one for his mum to call him on when it was time to come home?'

'Maybe,' McNab ventured.

'Give me a little more time and I'll tell you,' Ollie assured him. 'Anyway, whoever dropped it was at that crime scene, before, during or after, which makes him a witness.'

That was what McNab didn't want to hear. Especially if his theory was correct and either Ally or one of his gang had been the one to drop it there.

13

His notes were copious and had, Magnus believed, fully captured his talks with Marnie. Yet, reading them over again in preparation for his meeting with her, Magnus had to acknowledge that something very important was still missing from them.

Marnie had willingly and almost robotically told him of her childhood, which had been a dark and difficult story to hear. Her mother had died when she was ten years old and her father, free then from her mother's watchful eyes, had routinely sexually abused her.

Eventually taken into care, she'd gone through numerous foster parents, because, she said, they didn't like her. Or she didn't like them. Released from the system at sixteen, she'd fallen under the influence of various controlling men and had worked as a prostitute.

What saved her in the end, she'd told him, was having her daughter, Tizzy, or Elizabeth Mhairi to use her full name.

It was then she'd returned to what had been her mother's childhood home, not far from Kilcreggan on the Rosneath Peninsula.

That had been a good time, she'd said, because Tizzy had

made the world a better place. She'd happily talk about her daughter with no indication either that Tizzy was no longer alive or that she had admitted in court to being responsible for her death.

If Magnus ever tried to press her on this point, her body would become motionless, her face completely blank, so that she resembled a mummified creature, fully intact but dead inside.

Women found guilty of murder or manslaughter were rare. Most women in prison had spent their lives being misused or abused, not being the abuser. They had drug and mental health problems. Many exhibited signs of repetitive head injury syndrome, now known as chronic traumatic encephalopathy or CTE, because of repeated beatings by male partners.

On one occasion when she'd appeared to be high on some substance smuggled into the prison, she'd told Magnus that Tizzy's father had been a violent criminal, which is why she'd taken her daughter away. In the next meeting when Magnus brought the subject up, she'd denied she'd ever said this and was adamant that she never knew who Tizzy's father was because she'd been a victim of rape.

Magnus suspected both stories were likely true and interwoven. He also believed Marnie was trying to save her daughter by leaving Glasgow and her violent father behind.

So how had it come to be that a woman so intent on protecting her young daughter should end up being convicted for her manslaughter?

That was the question he had, as yet, no answer to.

The hostel where Marnie was now living bore little resemblance to the new women's unit she'd been released from.

One of Glasgow many red sandstone buildings, it looked on the outside, Magnus thought, like a Victorian poorhouse. He could only hope the inside was less imposing and more suited to the needs of the women currently living there. The social work department had indicated that the placement was temporary, and that they were trying to find Marnie a place of her own. He could only hope that would happen soon.

Composing himself, Magnus headed inside to a small reception desk, unmanned at present. He'd texted Marnie to say he would be with her shortly, but as yet had had no reply. He decided to try calling her to tell her he was already in the building.

As he did so, a woman appeared, asking if she might help him. Cutting the call, Magnus introduced himself and said he was here for a meeting with Marnie Aitken.

'She's on the second floor, room twenty-three,' the woman told him. 'You can go on up.'

'Is there somewhere down here where I might talk to Marnie in private?' he asked her.

She shook her head. 'Sorry, the only private place is in her room.'

Somewhat disquieted by this, Magnus thanked her and headed for the stairs, deciding to suggest to Marnie that they go out somewhere. Perhaps a quiet café. He would stress he only intended a quick catch-up today. On subsequent meetings he would organize somewhere more suitable.

Reaching her door, he stood for a moment before knocking softly and saying, 'It's Magnus, Marnie. May I come in?'

When there was no response, he tried again, the knock and his voice louder this time.

Still met with silence, he wondered if Marnie had decided

she no longer wanted to meet him and had simply gone out. Considering this, he decided that, though he didn't want to pester her, he had to be certain that was the case.

Pulling out his mobile, Magnus tried it again, only to hear her phone ring inside the room.

Feeling instinctively that something was wrong, and with a rising fear for Marnie's possible state of mind, he tried the door. Fully expecting to find it locked, he was surprised when the handle turned freely and the door swung open.

The room held a single bed, carefully made up. A cupboard, the door lying open, with nothing inside. A view to the small bathroom, which also appeared empty. In fact, there was nothing in the small room to suggest Marnie had ever been there except for the still-ringing mobile on the table by the window and, next to it, a parcel wrapped in brightly coloured Christmas paper.

Ending the call, Magnus approached the table. The parcel was maybe a foot long and half as broad. The paper was crumpled and a little torn in places, as though it had been used before.

A red felt-tip pen had been used to write a name on the front in capital letters.

That name was DR MacLEOD.

14

When Rhona returned to the lab, she found Chrissy carefully unpacking one of the three black bags they'd removed from the upstairs room at the farmhouse. The forensic task ahead in examining trace evidence from the crime scene would take time and a great deal of effort, but could shine a light on who'd been there and what had happened.

'Anything interesting?' Rhona said.

'A T-shirt and hoodie with blood splatters, which suggests they were worn or were discarded in or near the attack zone.' Chrissy pointed to the table where these had already been laid out.

Rhona went for a look. 'These wouldn't fit an adult,' she said.

'No, they wouldn't,' Chrissy agreed. 'More likely they belong to whoever was using that place as a hang-out before it became a torture chamber.'

'No wonder Ally was watching us yesterday,' Rhona said. 'We thought he might be after the mobile we found, but he must have been worried about what we would find belonging to them in that room.'

'So,' Chrissy said, 'what was the conclusion at the PM?'

'Sissons thought the victim most probably died as a result of the fall from the window. His neck was broken as were multiple other bones. As for the perforated eardrums, the burns and pliers likely applied to the genitals, plus the stitched eyes and mouth, that was all done before.'

Chrissy was silent for a moment before saying, 'How did McNab manage after I left?'

Rhona was honest in her reply. 'Not good, but he covered it well, although you would have spotted it if you'd been there. He departed before the end. I told him we'd meet for a drink later. Are you up for that?'

'Definitely,' Chrissy declared. 'Oh and Magnus called. Said he was coming over. Something about a parcel for you from Marnie Aitken.'

'That's the woman I met in the Lilias Centre,' Rhona said, puzzled by the idea of the parcel. 'She was the one who asked how, if there's no body, the law can decide that someone is dead.'

'A reasonable-enough question,' Chrissy said. 'Folk who are supposedly dead have been known to turn up alive years later.'

'She was referring to her daughter, who was only four when she went missing, presumed drowned. Plus she pled guilty to her manslaughter. She was released from prison yesterday after serving a six-year sentence.'

Rhona could read in Chrissy's expression her horror at the thought of a mother killing her own child.

'I can't imagine what must drive a woman to do such a thing,' Chrissy said. 'Wee Michael's a handful a lot of the time but . . .' She tailed off.

By mutual agreement they left it at that and got back to

work, Rhona trying to imagine what Marnie Aitken might have gifted her.

The answer came late in the afternoon with the arrival of Magnus and the said parcel. Disrobed and showered, she and Chrissy were preparing to leave for the jazz club.

Magnus, looking more agitated than was the norm for the professor of criminal psychology, explained what had happened when he had gone to meet with Marnie.

'I was worried about her state of mind. Women like Marnie, when leaving prison, a place they call the "concrete mother", are very vulnerable when they first rejoin the outside world. Anyway, she wasn't at the hostel and her room was empty of her belongings apart from the mobile she was supplied with and this.' He placed a package wrapped in crumpled Christmas paper on the table. 'Addressed to Dr MacLeod.'

'You've alerted the authorities to the fact she's missing?' Rhona said worriedly.

'I called her social worker and explained what I've just told you. Although Marnie's essentially a free woman and can go where she likes, she would normally be under supervision initially. Mainly for her own safety.'

Rhona pulled the parcel towards her. The ends, she noted, had been scrunched together to keep them from opening, suggesting there had been no Sellotape available. Turning it over in her hands, she was suddenly reminded of the intent look on Marnie's expression when she'd posed her question regarding how missing people might be presumed dead, when no body had ever been found.

Loosening the paper from its folds, she spread it open.

'It's a doll,' Chrissy said in surprise.

It was indeed a doll. In fact, it was the Highland dancer

doll that had been the centrepiece of the Fine Cell Work display, with its blue velvet jacket, tartan kilt and yellow blonde hair.

Except now, it was barely recognizable as such.

Someone, presumably Marnie, had used thick black twine to deface both the eyes and mouth of the doll with large cross stitches.

The image was so shocking that Rhona heard Chrissy's gasp of horror and, glancing at Magnus's expression, registered what the significance of the mutilation of the doll might mean to him.

Aware that he had no knowledge as yet about a similar stitch pattern on the farmhouse victim, Rhona asked him why he thought Marnie might have defaced the doll she'd so lovingly created.

He shook his head, indicating his puzzlement. 'I thought the Highland doll was a depiction of her daughter. I don't understand why she would desecrate it. And why then send it on to you?'

Rhona had already been trying to work that out for herself. It must, she thought, have something to do with their exchange at the Lilias Centre.

'When she brought up the subject of declaring someone dead even if no body was found, I assumed it was because of what happened with her daughter.'

'I did too,' Magnus admitted.

'Did Marnie ever give you the impression when you were working with her that she was being prevented from speaking out?' Rhona asked.

'I encouraged her to try to explain the circumstances surrounding her conviction and imprisonment but she never would. It's the main thing missing from my notes of our meetings. She would become mute if I asked. Almost catatonic.'

'So you never learned the full story, from her at least?' Rhona asked.

'She didn't reveal it to me or to Dr Masters. Nor did she dispute the evidence against her.'

Rhona contemplated all of this. 'I think she wants me to examine the forensic evidence used to convict her. I believe that's why she challenged me in the meeting at the centre.'

'It's what I was going to ask you to do, when we eventually met up to discuss Marnie,' Magnus said.

'And you never suggested this to her at any point?' Rhona checked.

He indicated not. 'It wasn't until you came to the centre and Marnie made a point of challenging you that I even considered it.'

Chrissy came in then. 'If that's what you think the reason is for the doll turning up here, why would Marnie choose to disappear at this precise moment? Wouldn't she want to wait to see if you accepted her challenge?'

'Chrissy's right,' Rhona said. 'Her sudden disappearance doesn't blend well with our interpretation of this.' She stared down at the doll, seeing again the face of the torture victim in the farmhouse grounds.

'What is it?' Magnus said, sensing something flow between Rhona and Chrissy.

'Just a strange coincidence,' Rhona admitted. 'The stitching shut of the eyes and mouth mirrors what was done to the victim we attended yesterday in Elder Park.'

Magnus looked taken aback by this. 'Has that been released to the press?' he asked.

'I don't believe so,' Rhona said.

'Then Marnie must have had her own reasons for defacing the doll,' Magnus said. 'But I have no idea what they might be.'

15

They were back in their usual spot at the entrance to the tunnel, although in truth Ally no longer felt safe there.

'You told me Darren *gave* you the mobile,' he said, emphasizing the word.

Dreep seemed to shrink into himself. 'He had a collection of them in a box under his bed. I didn't think he'd miss one.' His face in the tunnel light had blanched of all colour.

Ally looked to Kev. 'Are you thinking what I'm thinking?'

Kev nodded. 'He doesn't have them for fun.'

Dreep was studying the ground, making a circle with his foot, fear flooding his face.

Despite his anger, Ally felt sorry for Dreep. His friend's home life was shite. And likely to get shittier if the mobile didn't turn up. To get out of his own fix, he only had to tell Darren that Dreep was the one to drop his mobile in the farmhouse grounds.

Something he couldn't do. So what to do instead?

It had gone round and round in his head last night in bed, and that was before he'd found out that Darren hadn't given Dreep the mobile at all. That Dreep had just taken it from a cache of them. No wonder Darren had been so angry when he'd come to the house.

He'd managed, he hoped, to keep his mum off the scent when he'd come back in after Darren had threatened him using the naked dead guy in the park.

The memory of Darren's face shoved into his. His spittle as he mouthed the words '. . . you're a dead man. Do . . . you . . . understand? Just like that naked dead guy they found.'

It hadn't occurred to him until this moment, but how the hell did Darren know the dead guy was naked? Neither the papers nor the news had said anything about the body being naked. Just that a man's body had been found in suspicious circumstances and enquiries were proceeding.

Did that mean Darren might have had something to do with the naked guy's death?

This new possibility must have shown on his face because Kev said, 'What's wrong? You look like you're going to puke.'

Ally was saved from responding by the sudden whirring of bike wheels as a cyclist came flying down the runway. Watching him speed away into the tunnel, Ally had a strong desire to get on his own bike and do the same.

As he tried to work out a way to tell them what he'd only just realized, Kev said, 'We're not safe here any more. We need to hang out somewhere else.'

Dreep was shivering, his teeth clacking together, either from fright or cold or a mixture of both.

'I vote we go to the library and read the comic books,' Kev said. 'Darren won't come near us there.' He looked to Dreep. 'Agreed?'

Dreep gave a little nod.

'Okay,' Ally said, thinking he would keep the next horror for when they got to the library. 'Let's go.'

They avoided taking the short cut through the park, going the long way round via Drive Road instead. Even then Ally couldn't stop himself from glancing across the park towards the farmhouse, wondering if the police were still there, looking for things.

Things like a mobile phone.

But what if they did find the phone? *There was no way they could trace it to them*, he repeated in his head as he pedalled.

They'll see the photo of the dead guy, a voice reminded him, *and maybe think whoever took that photo killed him*. Could the mobile be traced back to Darren? No way. That's why Darren used that type of phone in the first place.

Arriving at the library, he was about to dismount and chain his bike to the railings when he saw a parked car nearby. One he thought he recognized.

He stood for a moment, puzzled as to where he might have seen it before. Then he remembered. It was when he'd run away from the two forensic women. It looked like the car that had followed him out of the park and along Govan Road. It wasn't a marked police car, but detectives didn't use those, so no one knew they were police officers.

He'd eventually escaped by going down the pedestrian slipway and into the tunnel. Afterwards he'd convinced himself he was being paranoid, freaked out as he had been by the questioning of the pink-haired woman. Now, he wasn't so sure.

Ally glanced from the car to the library entrance and back again. If it was the car that had followed him, might the driver be in the library? He felt sick. The library folk knew him. Sonia knew their names. Plus he'd been in there yesterday. She would remember that.

Heart thumping wildly, Ally got back on his bike and, shouting to the others to follow, took off again, this time heading south towards the recreation ground. Despite the cold, the playground always had kids, some accompanied by adults. The presence of adults, he had to admit, would make him feel easier.

When the other two caught up, he explained the reason for his sudden departure.

'You think the police know we go to the library?' Dreep said, as though his last safe haven had just gone up in smoke.

'It looked like the same car that followed me along Govan Road,' Ally said, not sounding altogether certain.

'Jeez,' offered Dreep.

'You should have stayed hidden and not spoken to those forensic women,' Kev said.

'You think I don't know that?' Ally answered testily. 'Anyway, there's much worse things to worry about than that police car.' As both faces turned worriedly towards him, he took a deep breath. 'When Darren came to the house to threaten me about his mobile, he told me if I didn't find it and give it back I'd end up like the dead naked guy in the park.'

He watched as the significance of that began to sink in.

It hit Kev first. Staring goggle-eyed at Ally, he said, 'Darren knew that the dead guy was naked?'

'Which definitely wasn't on the news.' Ally could confirm this because he'd read everything online and watched every news on the TV. 'It just said the body of a male had been found. That's all.'

'If we thought we were fucked before,' Kev offered, 'we're doubly fucked now.'

Ally was about to point out that it was him that Darren had threatened, when Dreep's voice cut in.

'I'll tell Darren it was me who dropped the phone,' he said in a small but firm voice.

16

Rhona had risen in the dark December dawn, almost wishing to discover the blanket of snow had returned. Instead, she'd found rain beating the kitchen windows and a raw feel to the air despite the heating having clicked on half an hour before her alarm rang out.

Dressed now and considering a second coffee, she remembered she wasn't going into the lab first thing, so wouldn't have a breakfast of filled rolls provided courtesy of Chrissy. A pang of hunger sent her to the fridge to try to find a replacement. The fridge was emptier than usual, she acknowledged. Had Sean been around, there would no doubt have been the ingredients for a cooked breakfast or even tonight's meal.

But Sean wasn't here and she wasn't yet certain when, *or even if*, he would be here again.

Dismissing that thought, she decided to hang on and get something at the police canteen before the strategy meeting, perhaps even message McNab to meet her there.

Although promising he would come for a drink last night, he hadn't shown up at the club. So she, Chrissy and Magnus had continued with their discussion regarding the doll Magnus had delivered from Marnie Aitken.

On her return to the flat later, she'd done some research on the background to Marnie's story from six years ago. There was plenty of it freely available online, most of it, she thought, a mishmash of conjecture and gory details masquerading as truth. Nonetheless, the bare bones told the story of a neglectful mother who was responsible for her four-year-old daughter's death, probably by drowning, although a body had never been found. It was, of course, Marnie's confession that had convinced the jury of her guilt.

'I think Marnie didn't tell the whole truth back then,' Magnus had stressed the previous evening. 'Perhaps through fear. Perhaps because she really did blame herself for her child's death. Maybe, having served her sentence, she now wants the full story to emerge. Hence the present of the doll after she'd challenged you in the Lilias Centre.'

'Believing you were responsible for your child's death is a terrible burden to bear,' Chrissy had said at this point. 'It's enough to make a mother lose her mind.' The brief look Chrissy had given her then had only served to remind Rhona how true that was from her own experience.

To dispel that particular memory, Rhona checked that Tom's automatic feeder was full; then, with an envious glance at him still asleep on her bed, she let herself out.

The rain persisted all the way to the police station. Windscreen wipers at full pelt, Rhona became one with all the other drivers who had no choice but to brave the deluge. Drawing up outside the station, she suddenly remembered Chrissy's tale of McNab's stolen Harley.

'The desk sergeant thought it was a woman,' Chrissy had told her with glee. 'Whoever it was had balls, I'll say that.'

Chrissy's remark had Rhona immediately thinking of Ellie, McNab's former girlfriend, a Harley rider herself, who was game enough to do such a thing. The question would be why. If Ellie wanted to get McNab's attention, all she had to do was text him and he'd been there in an instant.

The call from Dr Sissons came as she was about to get out of the car.

'Dr MacLeod. I was hoping to catch you prior to the strategy meeting. It's about our study of the stomach contents, which has revealed something rather surprising. I'm sending you photographs of the said item for inclusion in your report. They should be with you imminently.'

'Thank you,' Rhona said, somewhat mystified at not being told what the item was.

Locking her car, she entered reception, registered her arrival for the meeting and headed for the cafeteria. She'd had no response to her text to McNab, but was more intent on getting something to eat than sharing his company.

Ordering a roll with square sausage and black pudding, she carried her breakfast over to a table in the corner and settled down to take a look at the mysterious object discovered in the victim's stomach. The surprising image that appeared on the screen caused her to return the roll to her plate.

At that moment, McNab arrived. 'You beat me to it,' he said, eyeing her roll.

'I'm planning on eating that,' Rhona told him firmly. 'Go get your own.'

When McNab went to place his order, Rhona had a quick read of Dr Sissons' notes confirming that what she thought she saw in the image was indeed correct. Something Bill would have to be made aware of before the strategy meeting.

Slipping her mobile back in her bag, she got back to her breakfast.

Minutes later, McNab arrived with two impressively stacked rolls of his own, which he set about demolishing, eventually downing his coffee and sitting back with a sigh.

'So what happened to you last night?' Rhona asked.

He appeared puzzled by her question at first; then, as though a light bulb had been switched on, he said, 'You mean why wasn't I at the jazz club?' He gave her a cheeky grin. 'You missed me, Dr MacLeod?'

Rhona didn't rise to the bait. 'Did you have any luck locating our runaway, Ally?'

'No, but I did find out his surname, which is Feeney, and the area where he lives, which is Linthouse, as we suspected. Also, Sonia in the library knows him and his chums, as does Leo in the chippie. All of whom seem to like your runaway. As for his family's address, Janice is on to that today.'

Rhona was relieved to hear all of this. The more she thought about Ally, the more convinced she'd become that he might in some fashion be linked to the mobile they'd found. Which put him in or very near the crime scene.

'Anything more on your missing actor?' she checked.

'He's still very much missing and his mates are getting increasingly worried,' McNab told her. 'Seems they're on the clock with the filming, which is due to shift to the Merchant City as of today.'

'So they've agreed to put his disappearance up on social media?'

'They have. Although Janice wonders if the whole thing might be a ruse for publicity purposes,' McNab said. '*TikTok star goes missing in his home city of Glasgow. Can you find him?*'

'Is that what you think?' Rhona asked.

'I just want to know for definite that he's not our dead guy in the park.'

'Janice sent through a DNA sample from your missing star,' she said. 'So you should have your answer to that soon.'

As they rose to leave for the meeting, Rhona had a sudden urge to ask McNab if he had any knowledge of the Marnie Aitken case. 'It was six years ago on the Rosneath Peninsula,' she began. 'A woman called Marnie Aitken was convicted of causing her daughter's death by drowning—'

McNab, suddenly stopping in his tracks, turned to glare at her. 'Why are you asking me about that?' he said sharply.

Rhona wasn't sure how to respond to his dark-eyed stare. 'I wondered if you were involved with the investigation?'

'No, I was not,' he stated firmly and began to walk on.

She caught up with him. 'But you knew about it?' she tried.

'Who didn't? It was all over the news. The wee girl was due to take part in a dancing competition in the local Highland games. She disappeared. As did the mother. When she was found, she said she'd killed her child. Drowned her.'

Rhona was taken aback at this bare recital of facts and McNab's angry manner when delivering them.

'So you think she did it?'

He threw her a look she couldn't interpret. 'She said she did and was convicted. That's the way the law works,' he said abruptly.

They'd arrived. McNab opened the door and, entering, immediately took himself off to the far side of the room. Receiving his message loud and clear, Rhona didn't follow. Instead, she scanned the assembling group and, noting that DI Wilson had not yet emerged from his office, headed there to update him on Dr Sissons' message.

Her quiet knock on the door brought a request to enter.

Bill Wilson had been her friend and advocate since she'd first started in the job. In fact, he'd been the one in attendance when she'd been called in the middle of the night to conduct the forensic examination of a murdered teenage boy. A boy who looked so like her, she'd thought he might be the son she'd given up for adoption seventeen years before.

He'd supported her back then and been the one she'd turned to in all times of doubt and trouble since.

'Dr MacLeod, Rhona.' Bill rose from his desk to welcome her. 'You're here to throw some light on what happened at Elder Park?' he said.

'I can explain the scene in more detail and what's been established so far from the post-mortem,' Rhona offered. 'Plus I had a call from Dr Sissons early this morning regarding his examination of the stomach contents.'

'And?'

Rhona handed her mobile to Bill, who studied the image intently. 'A symbol of a gang reprisal?' he said. 'Someone who betrayed them, which might also account for the eyes and mouth being sewn shut. Have you seen anything like that before?'

Rhona was about to answer in the negative, but then hesitated, because it wasn't strictly true. Not if you included the doll.

'What?' Bill said, noting her reticence.

'I'm assuming the press weren't made aware of that?'

'They weren't. Not officially,' Bill told her. 'However, not all police personnel can be relied upon not to give out such information for a price. Why do you ask?'

Rhona decided to explain. 'It's probably nothing to do

with this case, but a former inmate at the Lilias Centre sent me a parcel via Professor Pirie. She was recently released and has now disappeared from the hostel she was placed in. This was in the parcel.'

She watched as Bill studied the image of the defaced doll, trying to read his thoughts.

'And the name of this woman?' he asked.

'Marnie—' she began.

'Aitken,' he finished for her. 'I thought as much. Marnie Aitken. Her wee girl was a Highland dancer.' He nodded as though remembering. 'How did she come to know you?' he asked.

Rhona explained about the online forensic course and her visit to the Lilias Centre to award the certificates. 'The women were asking how I felt about dealing with dead bodies. She asked me how the police could decide someone was dead if they never found a body.'

He contemplated this for a moment before responding.

'I don't think the defaced doll is linked in any way with the Elder Park attack, if that's what you're concerned about. However, I do think it's of concern if we've lost sight of Marnie Aitken so soon after her release from custody. She was very vulnerable six years ago and I can't believe she's less so now.'

Rhona was about to ask Bill if he'd believed in Marnie's guilt and maybe why McNab had reacted so badly to her questioning him, but she didn't get the opportunity.

'They're ready for you now, sir,' a voice called from the doorway.

'Right,' Bill said. 'It's time to tell us everything you've learned from the locus and the victim, Dr MacLeod. Including what was found in the stomach contents.'

17

McNab was thinking about Marnie Aitken as he walked away from Rhona, hoping she wouldn't follow. He'd lied when she'd asked if he'd been involved with the case, and she would discover that if or when she brought the subject up with the boss. Which he was pretty sure she would, and probably because of his reaction.

Then she would likely be told the whole sorry story.

His next thought was why Rhona was even interested in the Aitken case. A case he had tried hard to forget and never succeeded. The missing girl had been four at the time of her disappearance.

Like the flashback he'd had on seeing the farmhouse victim, he now had an image of Tizzy Aitken appear in his brain. She was standing outside the judges' tent, dressed in her kilt and blue jacket, waiting for her turn to climb onto the platform and perform her dance. Someone had produced that photograph when she'd gone missing at the games. The search party that had been quickly assembled had all had a copy sent to their phones.

The games field had been mobbed with spectators and competitors, easily doubling, maybe even trebling the local population of the Rosneath Peninsula, which lay between Loch Long and Gare Loch, where two of the Ministry of Defence's biggest accumulations of weaponry in the UK were housed.

On the Loch Long side was Coulport, home to a Royal Navy Armaments Depot. A mountain full of death. On the Gare Loch side was Faslane, home to His Majesty's Naval Base and all the United Kingdom's nuclear submarines. He recalled driving past Faslane that first time, on and on past the high wire fences that encircled the place like a concentration camp. Except they were there to keep the public and anti-nuclear demonstrators out, not the other way round.

He remembered thinking at the time that the peninsula, tranquil though it seemed, sat between two centres of possible world death and destruction.

When he'd eventually arrived at the games ground, he found himself deciding that death never felt more terrible than when it centred on one small missing child.

It was said that every detective had a case that haunted them even to retirement and death. The one that had not been solved. Or never to their satisfaction. The perpetrator who'd never been identified. Or who'd simply got away with it.

The haunting of Marnie Aitken and her missing child was his.

He'd told Rhona he hadn't been involved because he didn't trust himself to speak about it. That's why he'd been so angry about suddenly being asked.

At this point in his deliberations, Janice appeared, threading her way through the group to his side.

'Anything new on our missing Yank?' he asked, relieved to turn his thoughts elsewhere.

She indicated not. 'But it's all over social media so they're getting his name up in lights.'

'Just like in the movies,' McNab said. 'Any idea what the film is he's starring in?'

'Some American gangster thing, I think,' Janice told him. 'Glasgow playing Chicago.'

'Very apt,' he said as they both turned their attention to DI Wilson, who was exiting his office followed by Rhona.

So she did go straight to the boss, McNab thought. He'd been so absorbed in his thoughts on Marnie Aitken, he hadn't noticed that. *But she usually goes in there before the meeting*, he reminded himself, *to tell the boss anything he needs to know in advance*.

Attempting to quell his self-induced paranoia, he focused on the boss's brief introduction on where they were with the investigation so far – which wasn't far at all, McNab thought, since they hadn't even established who their victim was – before the boss asked Dr MacLeod to talk them through what she'd learned from the locus and the post-mortem examination.

Having already viewed the victim's injuries in person, both in the forensic tent and on the slab in the mortuary, McNab wasn't eager to look at them again, although he did want to hear anything new the team had learned from opening up the body.

Once Rhona had led them briefly through the list of injuries before and after the victim had been ejected from the upper storey of the farmhouse, she addressed what the pathologist had concluded had been the likely cause of death.

'We can't say how long our victim was held in the farmhouse,' she said. 'However, we do think that, despite his injuries, he was most likely alive when pushed through the window, and it was the fall that broke his neck.

'In addition, we know from the contents of his stomach that his last meal of steak, potatoes and salad was around five hours prior to his death. However, that wasn't all that was found in his stomach.' She indicated the screen as another photograph appeared.

McNab stared at the new image, aware of what he was looking at while not quite believing it.

'What the hell . . .' He tailed off as the noise of consternation rose around him.

'What you see is a bullet, which has been swallowed either by choice or more likely under duress.' She enlarged the image and continued. 'In most cases, a bullet would pass into the intestines relatively quickly. Say within four hours, depending on circumstances and the amount of foodstuffs in the stomach. So we can assume this one was likely swallowed during the victim's time in the farmhouse.'

She paused, as though giving them all a chance to consider the implications of what they'd just learned.

'And before anyone asks, there's no chance of getting fingerprints from it – stomach acid, as you're probably aware, is in fact strong hydrochloric acid.'

McNab raised his hand. When Rhona indicated he should ask his question, he said, 'That looks like a symbol scratched on the surface.'

'It is,' she confirmed.

She enlarged the image still further to reveal an engraved shape that looked to McNab like the head of a snake with its forked tongue curling out.

The boss came in then. 'Anyone recognize this symbol?' There were plenty of murmurs, but no one raised a hand.

'Right, one more thing we need to check out. Let's get to it.'

As the assembled team began to disperse, DI Wilson said a few words of thanks to Rhona, then as she left, he motioned to McNab and Janice to follow him into his office.

'What's up?' Janice said quietly when she spotted McNab's reaction to the summons.

McNab immediately tried to adapt his expression to something more suitable. 'Just thinking about the boy, Ally, and his mates,' he offered. 'If this is a gangland killing and they've spotted something . . .'

'Then the sooner we find them the better,' Janice said. 'Agreed?'

'Agreed.'

Once inside the office, DI Wilson shut the door and took his place behind the desk.

McNab always felt ill at ease in this position, tall and therefore more exposed to scrutiny from the boss. He was also aware that Janice didn't appear to feel the same way. Mainly because DS Clark, to his knowledge, had fewer misdemeanours to hide.

He, on the other hand, was trying not to think that his summons might relate in some way to his reaction when Rhona mentioned the Marnie Aitken case to him. Something Janice would be blissfully unaware of, since she hadn't been in the job back then.

Eventually the boss said, 'I don't believe our victim chose to swallow that bullet, so we must assume it did play a role in the assault. Which suggests, as the reaction out there indicates, together with the sewn-up mouth and eyes, that we may have a gangland vendetta being played out here on our turf.'

He looked to them for confirmation.

McNab, relieved that this was to be the topic under discussion, immediately agreed. 'Also, IT confirmed that the mobile found by Chrissy in the roots of a tree by the fence has a close-up of the victim taken in the garden.'

'Do we know the owner of this mobile?' DI Wilson said.

'It's a burner, sir.' With a quick glance at Janice, he added, 'We think it may belong to a boy aged around twelve or thirteen spotted hanging about the scene and spoken to by Chrissy and Dr MacLeod. I've followed up the lead and believe his name to be Ally Feeney, who lives in Linthouse somewhere. We also have a photograph of him taken by Chrissy.'

DI Wilson obviously didn't like the sound of this. 'So this boy was likely at the locus around the time the victim was pushed from the window?'

'If it is his mobile, then yes, sir,' McNab confirmed.

The boss's concern visibly deepened. 'Might he have connections to this possible gang?'

'I don't think so, sir. I spoke to Elder Park library assistant Sonia Maitland. She knows Ally Feeney. He comes into the library regularly with two pals, called Kev and Dreep. They read the comic books there. She champions them, sir, and I'm inclined to believe her. There was also a good CV from Leo at his fish and chip shop on Govan Road, where the boys go. However, Leo said someone else came looking for Ally. He didn't like him and gave him short shift. Sent him on a wild goose chase. He also supplied me with a description of the guy.'

'Right,' DI Wilson said. 'We need to locate and talk to Ally Feeney as soon as possible.'

18

She hadn't seen the sea in six years, let alone sailed across it. Standing on the upper deck of the ferry, Marnie watched in awe as the metal bow sliced the water, the throb of the engine feeling like a giant heartbeat.

And the sky. She could see the whole of the sky instead of just a patch.

How she had missed this.

Marnie felt her face break into a smile, something she hadn't experienced since . . .

She stopped her thoughts there, not yet ready to travel that path.

Instead she focused on drawing other earlier and more welcome memories to mind. Tizzy not yet walking, Marnie holding her small daughter in her arms, going down to the beach near the house to swish her tiny feet back and forth in the water.

A water baby, folk had said, smiling when they saw Tizzy paddling, then learning to float, then beginning to learn to swim. That's when she'd started taking her over to Gourock on the ferry to visit the heated outdoor pool there where she could learn properly.

How Tizzy had loved that. Especially the mother-and-toddler swim group.

They'd been happy back then. Perhaps the first time Marnie ever remembered being truly happy, because she'd believed she would be able to give Tizzy the childhood *she'd* never had.

Despite her attempts to subdue the next thought, it rose to the surface of her mind like scum on water.

If you hadn't gone to Gourock, Tizzy might still be here now.

This thought produced a moment of such sheer horror that she felt her legs crumple and she had to grab the railing to keep herself upright. She forced herself to breathe in for three and out for three, as Dr Masters had taught her. *Calm your thoughts, Marnie. What is past, is past. You are in charge of your own future now.*

'I am in charge of my own future,' she said under her breath. Letting go of the railing, she stood upright and steady. 'I might not be free to speak the truth but perhaps Dr MacLeod can do that for me?'

A short while later, walking up from the pier, Marnie noted that little had changed in Kilcreggan in her years away.

The pub was still there, the shop and the café she'd taken Tizzy to because she loved their ice cream and their home-made tablet even more. The sudden memory of her daughter's smile of delight when emerging with her bag of tablet seared Marnie's heart like a hot flame.

She halted for a moment and took another deep breath to exhale slowly. Stepping back into her life here would take every ounce of courage she could muster. But, she reminded herself, it was the only choice she had. She certainly couldn't have stayed in Glasgow.

Pulling the warm woolly hat down over her ears, she

slung the small rucksack containing all her worldly goods over her shoulder and, head down against the smirr of rain, she began her walk home.

The last time she'd been here, it had been summer and the sun had been shining. But she knew the winter here too, the constant drizzle that fell on days such as this. Though neither the rain nor the cold had ever kept them imprisoned inside.

Back then, Tizzy would keep on at her until the welly boots and raincoats were put on and then they would march together down to the pebbly beach to choose the best and bluest of the stones for their collection.

Wet and tired, she would eventually persuade her small daughter to return home, where they would hang up their wet coats to dry in the warmth of the stove.

Memories such as these had helped keep her sane throughout her imprisonment. That and the Fine Cell Work class. It was the one and only class she'd taken while in prison and it was Dr Sara that had persuaded her to go.

Being in prison for killing her own child had made her an outcast. *What woman would do that?* whispered the voices that surrounded her. And all the time she'd told herself, *Not me.*

Hugging the shore road, she marched on, head down, not looking up whenever she heard a car approach from either direction. Once she turned off the main road, she could relax. There would be no one on the track to the cottage. No one to stop to offer her a lift. No one to recognize her.

The cottage wasn't visible from the shore road. Tucked below a bank and sheltered by trees, it was only clearly visible from the sea.

Realizing she had reached the spot, she checked for any cars before turning onto the track and, in a few steps, was hidden from the road by a thick and overgrown hedge.

Her heart almost skipping now, she increased her speed, stumbling over the muddy ruts and scattering of stones until at last she saw the cottage roof.

It was there she stopped, the intensity of her feelings threatening to overwhelm her. All her doubts about being here came crashing in again. Her fear at what she might or could do.

Marnie stood for a moment, trying to quell her tortured thoughts. Then, forcing herself to be brave, she walked on to eventually push open the small gate and take the short path to the front door. Extracting the key from her backpack, she shipped it in the lock, knowing that getting this far had been difficult, but that it was nothing to what she would have to endure once she stepped inside.

The wooden door, swollen and warped by damp, groaned in protest as she pushed it open. She could keep her eyes shut until she was ready to look, but what she couldn't avoid was the familiar smell of the place. It hit her in a wave, threatening to drown her with the horror of the recall. Floundering in the semi-darkness, she found the kitchen table, then a chair, and sank down on it as the swell of memories continued to break over her.

Tizzy getting dressed in her kilt, already dancing in her excitement. Herself shouting at her daughter to keep still until she'd wound her long strawberry blonde hair up into its knot on top of her head.

Then heading out into the garden, where the scent of summer flowers met them, Tizzy's small hand clasping hers as they walked to the main road to catch the bus to the park.

Marnie made herself pause there. One step at a time, she reminded herself. Just one.

As her heart began to slow, she finally opened her eyes. Becoming accustomed to the faint light from the open door, she absorbed the familiar shadowy shape of the kitchen–living room and its contents.

Heading for the light switch, she flicked it on . . . to nothing.

Of course she'd turned the power off, aware they would be coming for her. Knowing she wouldn't be back here for a long time, if ever. She thought briefly of switching it back on, then decided against it. The Tilley lamp, kept for winter emergencies, would be less likely to alert anyone to her presence here until she was ready to face them.

With the help of her small torch, she set herself the task of locating the lamp and getting it lit. After which she fetched wood from the shed and lit the stove. Once it was going well, she filled the kettle and sat it on the hotplate.

Buoyed by these small successes, she began her walk round the rest of the three-roomed cottage. Her bedroom first. Would she be able to sleep in that bed ever again?

She felt revulsion at the thought.

Turning abruptly away, she entered Tizzy's room and stood, breathing in the sight and smell, looking for her daughter in the scattering of her favourite things. She could sleep in here, she decided. Or, better still, take Tizzy's duvet and pillow through to the couch.

As she retraced her steps to the main room, she acknowledged that the police and forensic services had left their mark on the place. Black fingerprint powder. Some discarded blue gloves. As she made note of this, she thought again of the woman, Dr MacLeod, who would likely have received the doll by now, assuming Magnus had delivered it.

What would she do, if anything?

After defacing the doll, she'd almost changed her mind and taken it with her, but then she'd remembered what Dr MacLeod had said, and her kind expression when she'd said it.

'She'll want to know why I sent the doll. She'll want to know what really happened back then.'

She said the words out loud so that the cottage might hear her. So that Tizzy might hear her, wherever her darling one was.

19

'Why do you want to visit your gran now?' His mum was staring at him in disbelief. That look was swiftly replaced by suspicion. 'Well, Alistair James?'

Next thing she'd be using his surname as well. They were halfway there already. A perfect indication of her annoyance.

'She's coming here for Christmas soon,' she said.

The thought of Christmas appeared to distract her for a moment, so Ally came back in.

'I thought Gran might like some company, that's all,' he said, trying to look innocent and fearing he was failing.

Her eyes narrowed, then relaxed a bit. 'Well, you're not to eat her out of house and home. D'you hear me? And don't accept money from her. She only has her pension.'

'I won't, Mum,' he promised.

As he made to leave, she suddenly held up her hand to stop him. 'This hasn't got anything to do with Darren McGowan's mobile, has it?'

God, his mother had the nose of a police dog, he thought.

'No, that's all sorted,' he said dismissively. It was such a bare-faced lie, he knew he had to get out of there before his face gave the game away.

Pulling on his jacket, he headed out the front door, hoping she wouldn't shout at him to come back, because his mum had a habit of doing that, as though double-checking on him.

Once he took off along the road, he began to relax.

According to Dreep, Darren hadn't been home for a couple of days, which wasn't unusual.

Ally knew Darren had been in trouble with the police already. He didn't know exactly why, but suspected drugs had something to do with it. The cache of phones seemed like a sign. What he knew for certain was that Darren McGowan was a mean bastard to Dreep and their mum. His own mum was always extra nice to Dreep, feeding him whenever he came round. So she knew things weren't good in that house too.

'He'll come back when he runs out of money,' Dreep had said. 'Then I'll tell him it was me that lost the phone.'

Out of sight of the house now, he stopped to make the call. Kev answered so swiftly he must have had the phone in his hand.

'What's the plan, then?' Kev asked.

'Can you and Dreep meet me at the tunnel? We're going through to my gran's in Partick.' He didn't add that he wanted the River Clyde between him and Darren.

Thankfully, Kev didn't look for further information, just said 'Right' and rang off.

Turning towards the park, Ally decided to take a quick look to see if the police were gone from there. Since he'd been chased by what he thought was a cop car, he'd avoided Elder Park like the plague. Now he felt himself inexplicably drawn back, despite his misgivings. A sort of death wish, like in a horror film.

An icy rain began as he entered by the west gate and, in

his weird state, he thought it might be an omen. A bad one. Yet still he cycled on, his face being pinged by a shower of tiny hailstones.

Looking ahead to the boating pond, he noted that the supermarket trolley was still stranded in the middle, a couple of wee guys doing their best to hit it just like Dreep had been doing that terrible night when things started to go so wrong.

Reaching the portico, he cycled behind it, so that he might climb up for a look at the farmhouse and its grounds without being spotted.

There was nothing to see anyway. No vehicles or officers. Just a straggle of police tape on the surrounding fence fluttering in the icy wind and the dark shadow of the farmhouse roof with that one broken window upstairs. Ally wondered if they would ever be brave enough to go back up there. And if they did, what would they find?

The hail had grown heavier, bouncing on the stone of the portico, deafening him. He had no idea there was someone behind him until he felt something sharp stab him just below his ribcage.

'We need a few words with you, Feeney, so walk,' a voice ordered, turning him by the shoulder and urging him down the steps.

Ally did as bid, unable to speak, let alone try to run.

They walked like this to the gate, where a dark van stood, hardly visible through the rain. Ally made one try at getting away. The result was a stab to his side that made him drop to his knees.

The hand from his shoulder dragged him to his feet and, the sliding door now open, he was thrust inside to sprawl, gasping in pain and terror, on the floor.

As the van took off, a foot kicked him in the ribs.

'Not a sound. D'you hear me?' A different voice this time. 'Do you hear me?' he repeated.

Ally didn't want to make a sound, but the wail that rose in his throat was threatening to escape anyway, because the only image he had now in his brain was the dead guy in the park. The pale sheen of him, the blood, the marks on his face and body. The horrible eyes and mouth stitched shut.

Is that what they planned to do to him?

20

As she'd made her way to the university, the earlier deluge had been replaced by hailstones. Concentrating on driving in these conditions kept her mind off both the strategy meeting and her earlier conversation with McNab.

Now, walking through the sheltered university cloisters, Rhona replayed both scenes in her head. The bullet revelation and McNab's reaction to what she'd thought was a simple question regarding any involvement he may have had with the Marnie Aitken case.

It was common knowledge that McNab had experience of presenting what he believed to be clear evidence of guilt in court, only to watch a defendant walk free on a 'not proven' verdict. She recalled the way he'd spoken of Marnie Aitken pleading guilty and the jury believing her. *That's the way the law works* had been his parting caustic comment.

If McNab believed the outcome of the trial was wrong, that might explain his anger, Rhona decided.

Entering the lab, she found Chrissy eagerly awaiting her arrival. 'How'd it go?' she said, pouring them both a coffee.

'Much as planned with the added extra of Sissons' report on the bullet, which I'm assuming you've seen?' Rhona said.

Chrissy nodded. 'That was unexpected. And the weird symbol scratched on the surface. Like in some American gangster movie.' She paused. 'And talking about Americans, there's something you should see.' She fetched a paper and handed it to Rhona. 'The results of the DNA samples we sent from the victim and the missing actor.'

By Chrissy's expression, Rhona gauged they were interesting, to say the least. Reading through them, she soon realized why.

'So,' she eventually said, 'the missing actor Jason Endeavour, or his Scottish equivalent, Lewis McLean, is not in fact our victim.'

'But he is a person of interest,' Chrissy said, eyebrows raised.

'He is indeed,' Rhona acknowledged. 'Since he and the victim share fifty per cent of their DNA . . .'

'Which points to them being either brothers or perhaps fraternal twins,' Chrissy finished for her. 'So connected by birth definitely, but . . .' She looked to Rhona.

'Not necessarily known to one another as not all siblings grow up with their birth parents or even in the same household. Has McNab seen these?' she said, remembering his desire to know for definite if the victim was his missing actor.

'Not yet. I wanted you to see them first,' Chrissy confirmed.

'Okay. I'll send them now,' Rhona said, draining her coffee. 'Then you can show me your progress on the material from the PM.'

As she forwarded the result, she registered that Chrissy hadn't yet checked whether she'd spoken to McNab about the Marnie case and the arrival of the defaced doll. Something they'd decided on doing last night in the club.

When she *was* asked, and she would be, Rhona wondered how much she should say about his reaction and obvious anger. If she underplayed it, Chrissy the terrier would sniff that out right away. So the whole truth it would have to be.

Her mobile rang as she was donning her forensic suit. Seeing McNab's name on the screen, she answered.

'So it's not our guy, but his brother?' he checked, following her summary.

'Or a fraternal twin,' she said.

A pregnant silence followed this, so she explained. 'When two sperm fertilize two eggs at the same time, you have fraternal twins. They can be male or female, or one of each. They are not identical.'

'But in this case they did look very much alike,' McNab said, almost to himself. 'So there's another McLean brother and he's the dead one we found in the farmhouse?' he asked for confirmation.

'Yes,' Rhona agreed.

A brief silence followed before McNab said, 'Don't you think it's a bit of a coincidence that the actor brother, just returned to Glasgow after six years, goes missing around the same time that our guy gets murdered?'

'I thought you didn't believe in coincidences?' Rhona reminded him.

'I don't,' McNab confirmed.

'I take it there have been no sightings of Jason Endeavour?' Rhona said.

'Correct. Despite the fact the TikTok police have been working overtime. And now we know he's related to the victim . . .' He halted there.

'You're wondering about the possibility of mistaken identity?' Rhona said.

'I'm wondering about a lot of things,' McNab said. 'Including why our victim was made to swallow a bullet. That's like a gang retribution thing, but unlike anything we've seen here as yet in Glasgow. Our actor, on the other hand, is a self-styled American movie star.' He paused. 'You'll let us know if you come up with anything else regarding the body?'

Rhona agreed she would, then remembered there was something else she wanted to ask.

'Any luck locating our runaway, Ally?' she said hopefully.

'I can report we have been given an address via the local priest, Father Ignatius. Janice and I are about to head there now.' He hesitated, as though he might have something else to say. As before, Rhona waited long enough to allow this, but when nothing was forthcoming, she ended the call.

Zipping up and donning her mask, she told herself that McNab would talk about Marnie Aitken when ready, and not before. Not unless Chrissy managed to wheedle it out of him first.

'Come see what I've got so far!' Chrissy said, excitement in her voice. She gestured to the table where the carefully removed ankle and wrist bindings were laid out.

'First of all, all four sections of tape removed from the victim's ankles and wrists were of the same common make, which can be bought at any hardware store. A close examination of the ankle bindings revealed detritus from the room and the garden, shavings, dust, soil and vegetation, but also blood deposits. The blood is confirmed as that of the victim. So nothing useful there.'

At this point, her bright eyes met Rhona's above the mask. 'However, on the wrist sections, I struck it lucky. I can report that I have lifted one full print from the left wrist binding and one partial from the right. So whoever fastened that section of tape wasn't wearing gloves.'

It was a good start and Rhona said so.

'I heard you on the phone. Was that McNab?' Chrissy asked.

'It was,' Rhona told her. 'The good news is they have an address for Ally and are about to go there now.'

'And the bad news?' Chrissy said.

'I explained about the DNA findings. So he now knows the victim definitely isn't his missing actor . . .' When she paused, Chrissy came in.

'But it's weird that one of the brothers goes missing and the other one's found dead. Right?'

'That about sums it up,' Rhona told her.

'And Marnie Aitken? Did you get a chance to ask about her?'

Rhona decided to come clean. 'I tried before the strategy meeting. He seemed very angry at being asked and didn't want to discuss it at all. Said he hadn't been involved in the case and only knew about it second-hand.'

'Well, he was telling porkie pies,' Chrissy said. 'I've already checked. He was part of the investigation team, initially at least. In fact, he was one of the ones sent up there when the kid first went missing. Seems he rubbed some folk up the wrong way about Marnie's confession and was taken off the case.'

'You have been busy,' Rhona told her, impressed.

'I have my sources, as you know,' Chrissy said. 'If McNab won't give us the background, you could ask DI Wilson.'

Rhona explained that she'd already broached the subject of the doll with Bill. 'He didn't think there was any link between the defaced doll and the farmhouse victim's injuries.

Although he was concerned that Marnie had dropped out of sight of social services so soon after her release. Bill said she was mentally fragile at the time of the trial and probably even more so now.'

'Talking about stitched eyes.' Chrissy beckoned her over to the neighbouring table. 'The thread we removed from the victim's eyes and mouth.'

The careful extraction at the post-mortem had resulted in one length of thread for each of the eyes and a further length for the mouth. All three of which had been laid out for inspection.

'No gloves used here either,' Chrissy said. 'So we have skin flakes from whoever did the cross-stitching.'

Rhona contemplated the time and effort taken in the torture and eventual dispatch of the victim. What crime had they committed that warranted such a degree of cruelty and precision?

'I don't see this as a one-off by some psycho nutcase.' Chrissy seemed to be thinking the same way. 'This has to be a gangland execution. But which gang and from where?'

'My question exactly,' Rhona told her.

21

The street wasn't tenement-lined like the street of his youth, but it still reminded McNab of it. The nearby chapel whose resident priest had known where the Feeney family lived and how twelve-year-old Alistair was a good son to his mother. 'There's no man around,' Father Ignatius had told them with a shake of his head. 'I believe he wasn't up to the task of being a father and deserted his post early in Alistair's life,' he'd added.

All of which sounded similar to McNab's own childhood.

'Mrs Feeney is a force to be reckoned with,' the priest had told them. 'Ally would have her to deal with if he ever got into trouble.'

'And Ally's mates? One called Dreep, the other Kev?' McNab had asked.

Father Ignatius, who appeared much too youthful to have encountered many of the troubles of humankind, had nodded at this. 'Dreep, I have to say, is not as fortunate in family as Ally. Kev, I don't know well at all. They're not churchgoers.'

Walking away, Janice had asked him why he always acted weird around priests.

'I don't,' McNab had countered.

At this she'd given him a dismissive look, which forced him to say, 'You have no idea the power they used to wield when I was a boy.'

She'd laughed at that, which made McNab feel ancient.

They'd parked up the street, in case Ally spotted the car and bolted again. Despite the fact that neither of them were in uniform, McNab was well aware that a man and woman like them walking the length of the street together would have curtains twitching. Especially when they weren't recognized as coming from around here.

Reaching number thirty-three, he stood back, allowing Janice to be the first face Mrs Feeney encountered when she answered the doorbell.

She was so swift to arrive, McNab wondered if she'd already seen them coming.

'Mrs Feeney?' Janice said with a pleasant smile.

'Who's asking?' the woman said.

Janice held out her identification. 'Detective Sergeant Clark and my colleague Detective Sergeant McNab.'

Giving McNab a quick up-and-down, the woman said briskly, 'Come in first, then you can tell me what this is about.'

She didn't seem flustered or guilty. *She's a woman*, McNab thought, *with nothing to hide*.

They were shown into a small sitting room with a Christmas tree, its lights switched on. McNab, who hadn't registered how cold it had been outside, suddenly found himself enveloped in warmth and a memory of Christmases past when he'd been Ally's age.

Mrs Feeney asked them to sit, then said, 'So why are the police at my door?'

'Is your son Ally at home?' McNab asked.

'No. Alistair is not at home.' Her reply was swift and, he thought, truthful. 'Why do you ask?' she added.

'We need a word with him,' Janice said.

'About what exactly?'

The priest was right. She was formidable, much like his own mum had been, McNab thought.

Janice nodded at him to explain, but before he could, Mrs Feeney said, 'This hasn't got anything to do with Darren McGowan's mobile phone, has it?'

Taken aback by this and already searching for the name Darren McGowan in his stored list of reprobates, McNab responded with, 'It might be. Why?'

She made a *mmmm* sound. 'Darren came round here looking for a mobile he said his wee brother Brian had loaned to my Alistair. Which was odd because Alistair's got his own mobile. Anyway, Alistair said he'd dropped it in Elder Park somewhere and had gone back to look for it but you, the police, were there, so he abandoned his search.' She waited for his response to this.

'Where exactly did he drop it?' Janice said.

'I presume near the boating pond. That's usually where they ride their bikes.'

'We do need to speak to Ally . . . Alistair,' Janice said. 'Will he be back soon?'

Mrs Feeney looked perplexed. 'He decided to cycle through the tunnel to Partick to his gran's. I thought it odd, because she's coming through for Christmas. But he said he thought she might like some company.'

'And when's he due back?' McNab said.

'By nine o'clock.'

'Might you perhaps call him and ask him to come back

now?' Janice suggested. 'It wouldn't take long through the tunnel,' she added.

Reading her expression, Mrs Feeney nodded. 'I'll do that.'

She left the room and he and Janice exchanged glances. 'Did you recognize the brother's name?' Janice said.

McNab nodded. 'I had to search for a while, then it came to me. Darren McGowan was peddling drugs around Govan. Got off with a misdemeanour. Went quiet after that. Probably because he's been shifted up the chain. So it's his mobile that was found with the pic of the dead guy.' He gave her a look that spoke volumes.

At this point, Mrs Feeney came back in, a worried look on her face. 'Alistair's not answering his mobile so I checked with Mum. She says she hasn't seen him.'

For a moment McNab thought she might crumple, but suddenly Janice was there beside her, helping her to a chair.

'I'll make us a cup of tea, if that's all right, Mrs Feeney?' Janice said. 'What do you take in yours?'

'Just milk, and my name's Cathy,' she said quietly.

'Well, mine's Janice and that's Michael,' she added as she made for the kitchen.

Left alone with McNab, Cathy seemed to regain her composure. 'Right,' she said. 'I want to know exactly why you're looking for my son, Detective Sergeant McNab. And I don't need it sugar-coated.'

McNab decided Father Ignatius was right and Ally's formidable mother should be told the truth – at least what they suspected might be the truth.

'Alistair was seen hanging about the crime scene in Elder Park by two of our forensic colleagues. They spoke to him and he seemed to take fright at their questions and ran off. The phone I think he was looking for was subsequently discovered near the victim.' He stopped there to see if she was following his line of thought.

It appeared she was for she said, 'You think the three of them were in the farmhouse grounds and Dreep dropped the phone?'

'That's the way I read it too,' McNab told her. He waited while she contemplated what that might mean exactly.

'They may have seen something?' she tried.

'Yes.' McNab waited before saying the hard part as Janice appeared with the teas. Placing the tray on the coffee table, she let them help themselves. As McNab did so, Janice caught his eye and he indicated with a nod that he'd done as discussed.

'So my boy's maybe in danger?' Cathy said finally.

'I spoke to Leo at the chip shop and he obviously had a lot of time for the boys. He also said a stranger had been in asking about Ally and he'd sent him on a wild goose chase in Govan.'

Cathy almost smiled at that.

'However, that got us worrying, which is why we're here.'

'So you came to protect Alistair? Not accuse him?'

'Yes,' Janice said.

'And what about Darren? How does he fit into all of this?' Cathy said.

It was a question McNab couldn't answer, so he didn't try. 'We're more interested in seeing Ally home safe. But we do need to visit both Dreep and Kevin's homes. See if they can help us locate your son.'

She nodded. 'I'll write down the addresses for you.' She rose and exited the room.

Glancing at Janice, he noted her worried expression.

'It's not good, is it?' she said.

'He might be with his mates. We'll check their houses, then the pedestrian tunnel where they hang out on their bikes.'

Cathy came back in then and handed McNab the addresses. 'Dreep's mum . . .' She halted there, trying, he thought, to choose her words carefully. 'Brian's a nice wee boy. His big brother Darren's trouble. Don't be hard on their mum. She's frightened enough.' She paused there. 'Kevin's very quiet, but a good pal to the others.'

'Thank you,' McNab said, rising. 'I see you've added your number too.' He handed her his own card. 'We'll keep you up to date, I promise. Most kids reappear within twelve hours. Alistair wouldn't be officially missing as yet under normal circumstances,' he said, trying to reassure her.

'These aren't normal circumstances,' she said with a shake of her head.

'She's right,' Janice said when they'd exited. 'These aren't normal circumstances.'

McNab showed her the paper. 'You check Kevin's place. I'll take Dreep's.'

She shook her head. 'Better I do Dreep's. If Darren's there, he might recognize you.'

McNab wasn't keen on exposing Janice to Darren McGowan, not after what Sonia at the library had said about him, but her expression was so adamant, he didn't argue. Besides, he told himself as he headed to Kevin's address, she would likely be better with Dreep's mum than he might prove to be.

He found Kevin's house easily enough, but despite being late afternoon and the street lamps already lit, there were no lights visible in the Docherty household. He realized then that he'd been hoping to find all three boys in there together, watching a film or playing games.

When he knocked on the door, he didn't anticipate an answer and didn't get one. At that point he decided to check round the back, in case there might be a light visible round there. There wasn't.

On reappearing, he found a neighbour waiting for him. The man was in his fifties and didn't look happy.

'Who are you?' he demanded. 'And why are you looking round the Docherty house?'

McNab produced his ID. 'I wanted a word with them,' he said.

A cursory glance at the ID was followed by, 'What about, exactly?'

McNab ignored the question. 'Any idea when they'll be back?'

'None,' said the man.

'And Kevin, their son. Any idea where he might be?'

The unfriendly stare he got in return suggested he either didn't have a clue where Kevin was or, if he did, it would not be forthcoming.

McNab decided to change tactics. 'I've just been at Alistair Feeney's house and spoken with Ally's mum, Cathy, who's worried about him. He was supposed to have gone to his gran's in Partick, but didn't turn up.'

The man's expression changed completely. 'Ally's missing?' he said, shocked.

'That's why we're checking with his friends.'

The man looked sorry, but didn't apologize. Instead, he said, 'Those three including wee Dreep McGowan are as thick as thieves. They'll be in the park on their bikes or down the pedestrian tunnel. Kev's parents will still be at work.'

McNab passed the man his card. 'Can you give them this and ask them to call me when they get home, please.'

'Sure thing, Officer,' the man said, his tone now a mix of worry and cooperation.

When he got back to their car, Janice was already there. 'Anything?' he said, climbing in.

She shook her head. 'Mrs McGowan was there. She was very scared. Could hardly speak. She thought I'd come looking for Darren, who she says hasn't been home for a couple of days, which apparently isn't unusual. She thought Dreep was with his pals and would be home later. She told me to try the tunnel, if they're not in the park. Dreep set off on his bike earlier today to meet them.'

'So all three are likely to be together.' McNab voiced his wishes, rather than his worries.

'Let's hope so,' Janice said. 'I gave her my card and asked her to call me when Dreep arrived home.'

'I used to stay out when I was their age,' McNab volunteered. 'Worried my mum something daft.'

'Well, let's hope they're just being daft like you,' Janice offered. 'We'll check the tunnel and the park. If they're not hanging out there, we put out an APB.'

22

She had turned off the Tilley lamp and now the firelight was her only companion. In truth, she found the enveloping darkness comforting. A shield, in fact. In it, she felt safe. She could not see or be seen.

That there was life in the cottage would eventually be noticed. The Rosneath Peninsula wasn't an island, although it was like one. You either arrived by ferry from Gourock, like her, and were noted. Or you drove the long way round and your car was spotted coming through Kilcreggan.

She found it easy to imagine someone had perhaps recognized her either on the ferry or disembarking from it. After all, she'd passed the pub, the shop, the café and the post office.

The cottage might not be visible from the road, but during daylight hours, at least, smoke rising from its chimney would be. Also, although she had some tinned food in the store, she would eventually have to venture out to buy more.

What would the reaction to her be then?

Whatever it was, it wouldn't be violent, she thought. Which is why she'd come here and not stayed in Glasgow. Folk might well ignore her or tell her to go away, but they wouldn't physically harm her.

Throwing another log in the stove, she fetched the pillow and duvet from Tizzy's bed and lay down on the couch. She didn't expect to sleep, but if she did, then perhaps she would dream of her daughter.

The dream when it came was a replay of six years ago.

How she'd dressed an excited Tizzy in her kilt and blue jacket. How she'd brushed her hair with long strokes until it shone, a coppery gold, then made the bun and fastened it with kirby grips. Tizzy didn't like the tightness, but didn't complain because that's the way it had to be when she danced.

'I want to win,' she'd said, her face full of determination.

Marnie had wished she could say, 'You will,' but she thought it unlikely. Tizzy was good but there were others who'd been dancing for longer than her. Including two young sisters from Newcastle whose father had brought them to Glasgow every weekend to be taught by a former world champion. Something she couldn't do for her daughter.

The image of Tizzy having one last practice before they caught the bus to Rosneath was something she'd replayed countless times in prison. And she did it again now. In it, her daughter was alive and happy. What happened after that was entirely her fault.

She'd pled guilty because she was. It had been her job to keep Tizzy safe and she'd failed.

23

She'd come straight home, stopping only to buy a ready meal on the way. Her choice of macaroni cheese was now in the microwave and she was awaiting the desired ping to herald its readiness.

A guilty glance at the slow cooker, which Sean had always made good use of before their recent parting, reminded her of the welcome scent of what Sean called *real food* that had often met her when she'd entered the flat.

Now she could only anticipate the ping of the microwave or the sound of the door buzzer when she ordered online.

In truth, there were plenty of good eateries within easy walking or ordering distance. Great curries, seafood restaurants, tasty Greek and Italian places. Tonight, however, she'd settled for a ready meal with no doubt a list of additives that even she as a scientist didn't fully comprehend.

Sean's slow-cooked macaroni cheese, on the other hand, had consisted of simply three cheeses of choice, plus milk and macaroni, and was delicious. He'd even noted the ingredients on the board so she might put them all in the slow cooker herself and enjoy the result an hour and a half later. Something she had no patience for, which was odd for someone who had endless patience for the minutiae of forensic work.

With that thought, the ping sounded. Rhona, opening the door, caught an aroma of something resembling hot cheese, which would suffice, she decided. Extracting the meal, she spooned the contents into a bowl and, adding a chunk of the sourdough loaf she'd also bought in the supermarket, she grabbed a spoon and her wine glass and made for the sitting room and the gas fire.

Tom the cat was currently out on the roof, which was his playground and accessible from her top-floor flat. Aware he would require entry shortly via the kitchen window, she'd left it open just enough to allow that. Even then it rendered the kitchen chilly despite the heating being on.

In here was much warmer and the scent of food would likely cause Tom's appearance soon.

Settled on the couch, she ate with relish, after which she topped up her glass of wine and, welcoming Tom back indoors, shut the window. Peeved that the delicious smell that had brought him home appeared to have been eaten, Tom set about weaving between her legs in protest.

Laughing, Rhona scooped him up and set him beside his own food dish, automatically replenished and also likely full of additives. It, however, did not emit a smell of delight.

Back now on the couch, a disgruntled cat lying on the opposite sofa, giving her the evil eye, Rhona opened her laptop, intent on reading through today's work regarding the material they'd removed from the body.

The prints and DNA retrieval belonging to the perpetrator were a good start. Although, if not already on file, they could not be used to identify the killer. The victim had been a young fit man who would no doubt have fought his attacker. If there was more than one, or drugs were involved, he would have been more easily subdued.

If the victim knew and trusted his attacker, he would have gone with them willingly. But who would be willing to go into the old farmhouse and why? As she circled that question, she kept returning to the thought that the location held some significance in the story, or why should the torture happen there?

Which led her back to the DNA profile of the victim and his filial link with the missing actor, who'd gone stateside six years before. If they could only locate Lewis McLean, aka Jason Endeavour, that puzzle at least would be solved.

Her musings were interrupted by the sharp sound of the entry phone buzzer. Laying her laptop aside, she went to answer it.

'Can I come up?' McNab's voice sounded gruff, as though he expected her to say no.

Pressing the release button, Rhona went to open her own door to this unexpected visitor.

'I thought you might be at the club after work,' he said, following her through to the sitting room.

'Chrissy and I worked late at the lab, so I came straight back here,' she told him.

He looked around the room as though expecting someone else to be there. 'I didn't see Sean at the club.' It sounded like a statement but she knew it was a question.

'He's out of town,' she said, making her voice as bland as possible.

McNab, forever the detective, gave her a look that suggested her answer hadn't worked on him. However, he didn't pursue it.

'I'd like to talk to you about Marnie Aitken,' he said.

Rhona nodded. 'Okay. Can I get you something first? A coffee or something stronger, assuming you're off duty.'

He glanced at her wine glass. 'I know where you keep the whisky, I could help myself? I'm not driving.'

'I heard about your Harley being stolen by a mysterious leather-clad female,' she called after him.

There was no response to this until he reappeared. 'Chrissy told you?' he said with the half-semblance of a smile.

'That's Chrissy,' Rhona said, 'always first with the news.' Hoping the tension between them had been eased, she waved him to the seat opposite, which Tom obligingly gave up to return to his usual spot on the back of her couch.

'I think Mary Grant took it back,' he said with a shrug. 'She doesn't ride, but she could hire someone who did.'

'Why would she do that? I thought you two were friends from way back,' Rhona said.

'We were. I guess she felt neglected recently and wanted to remind me of that.'

Rhona was already working out the underlying story and had come to the conclusion that the friendship had been interrupted by Ellie Macmillan's arrival in McNab's life. Now that he and Ellie were no more, perhaps Mary had expected him to renew their friendship.

'Anyway, that's not what I came here to talk about,' he said firmly. 'When you asked me about Marnie Aitken I lied when I said I wasn't involved in the case.'

'I know,' Rhona said, deciding if McNab could be honest then so could she.

'How—' he began.

When Rhona smiled, he said, 'Chrissy McInsh again?'

'Who else?'

'So how much do you know?' he asked.

'That you were one of the first to arrive at Rosneath after the child, Elizabeth Aitken, went missing. That something happened that put you at odds with the investigative team and you were taken off the case.'

'That pretty well sums it up,' he admitted.

'Can you tell me what that was?' Rhona said.

'I didn't trust the story that Marnie Aitken killed her daughter. I believe she confessed because she was a traumatized woman who blamed herself for her daughter's disappearance. The body has never been found either on land or in the sea.' Anger laced his voice. 'Something happened that day. Something, I think, relating to her former life, which resulted in the kid disappearing,' he said firmly. 'Something she refused to divulge.'

McNab looked straight at her. 'If you think a woman will not kill, think again.' He spoke the words as though quoting someone, then said, 'However, very few of them do, despite often being victims of male violence on an industrial scale. Whenever I spoke to Marnie, she seemed completely disengaged from herself. As though she was already dead.' He searched Rhona's face. 'Anyway, why the current interest in Marnie's case?'

'I met Marnie at the Lilias Centre just before she was released,' Rhona told him.

'She's out now?' McNab looked perturbed by that. 'I don't think she'll cope well with freedom.'

'She's already disappeared from the hostel. She was supposed to meet with Magnus, who was working with her in prison. She didn't turn up, then I received this from her. She'd left it in her room at the hostel for me.' Rhona brought up the photo on her screen and, placing the laptop on the coffee table, turned it to face McNab.

She watched as he absorbed the macabre image of the blinded and silenced doll, reading both distress and anger in his expression.

'That's what Tizzy was wearing when she disappeared from the games field. Why would she send this to you now?'

Rhona explained about her talk and how Marnie had asked how they could know for sure that someone was dead if there wasn't a body.

'She hopes or even thinks her daughter might still be alive,' he said, almost to himself.

'I believe she wants me to look at the forensic evidence that supported the charges brought against her,' she told him.

'And you plan to do that?' he said.

'Magnus thinks I should, and now, after speaking to you . . .'

He took a moment to consider this. McNab wasn't a big fan of Magnus or of criminal psychology being used in the justice system, but more recently he'd appeared to adjust his stance on that.

'This disfigured doll,' McNab said. 'Might it suggest Marnie was prevented from telling the truth back then?'

'That's the way Magnus and I read it too,' Rhona told him.

'Weird, too, the stitched mouth and eyes like our Elder Park victim.' He made a face.

'I mentioned that to DI Wilson,' Rhona admitted. 'He pointed out that the general public has no knowledge of that. He thought she did it for personal reasons.'

'Okay,' McNab nodded. 'There'll be no problem getting access to the files. You only have to ask the boss. But we also have to find out where Marnie's gone *as soon as possible*,' he stressed. 'If someone managed to shut her up before, they could still be around.'

They sat in silence for a moment, before Rhona eventually broached the other subject on her mind. 'I gather you haven't located Ally as yet?' she said.

McNab shook his head. 'We think – or hope – he's hiding from us, or whoever else is looking for him.'

'And the other two boys?'

'Kevin's parents phoned. Said he was home, as was Dreep. It seems they'd arranged to meet Ally at the tunnel and go with him to his gran's in Partick, but he never turned up. They expected him to phone but he never did. There's an APB out on him now and a call-out via social media.' He gave her a rueful glance. 'So that's three folk we need to urgently locate. One of them a minor.'

'Have you any idea why Ally ran?'

'We're speaking to his pals tomorrow. I suspect it's all to do with that mobile we found at the scene. We'll no doubt find out how that came to be there.'

He rose, making ready to go.

'Thanks for coming round,' Rhona told him. 'And for explaining about the Marnie case.'

He gave a shrug. 'You bring out the best in me, Dr MacLeod. Which I'm sure you already know.'

Closing the door behind him, Rhona heard her mobile start to ring. At first, she couldn't remember where she'd left it and had to try to follow the sound. She located the phone in the kitchen, where the call promptly ended as she reached to pick it up.

It had been Sean, she noted. His first call since they'd parted company.

Rhona stared at the screen, wondering what she could

or should do. Eventually a ping told her that he'd left a message on her voicemail.

What would he have said? She realized she had no clear idea.

What she did know was that she had no desire, at this moment at least, to find out.

24

He'd been told that the night set would be at work, despite the late hour and their missing actor. McNab wondered what part the former Glasgow boy had in the movie and what the movie was actually about.

It was weird, he thought, the way Glasgow city centre had recently become the go-to place to shoot big action movies. Although, according to his late mother, Glasgow folk had always been big on going to the pictures. She'd told him Glasgow at one time had more cinemas than any other city outside of America. One hundred and thirty picture palaces, holding 175,000 people at a time, had given it the title Cinema City.

Not so many now, though.

Turning another grid-like corner, he was met by the wind and what might be a flurry of real snowflakes or some fake kind for effect. As he approached the barrier, he showed his ID to a burly individual, whose stone-like expression didn't alter at the sight of a police officer.

'Here to see Jerry Borstein or Ragnar Ryan. Whoever is available, please?' Why he stuck a please on the end, he had no idea. Maybe because the security guard had the build of a superhero.

Immediately on his radio, the guard barked something that didn't sound like any language McNab knew. Shortly after this, a young, skinny bloke appeared, buried within a black puffa jacket.

'Right, mate, this way.'

His guide was definitely from Glasgow, McNab thought, as he followed him into the melee. The voice being the giveaway.

'You're here about Jason?' his guide said as they threaded their way through a set crowded with folk awaiting their instructions.

'I take it he's not reappeared, then?' McNab tried.

'Nope, and not likely to, I hear.' He made a face.

McNab caught his arm to bring him to a halt. 'If you lot are wasting police time, that's a serious matter.'

The guy gave him a big-eyed stare. 'That's only my opinion, mind.'

'Based on what?' McNab demanded.

'Jason, not his real name, comes from here. And you lot aren't the only ones looking for him.'

'Someone else came looking for him? Was this before or after he was reported missing?' McNab said.

'Before. I saw them talking together. Looked pretty intense, but hey, actors are like that.' He gave a shake of the head.

'Are we talking family or . . .' McNab left the alternative blank.

His guide shrugged. 'Could be, or . . . maybe a former friend or business associate?'

'Why wasn't I told this before?' McNab demanded.

'Because you only talked to the Yanks, who know nothing.' He gave a dismissive shrug.

They'd reached the mobile home, which had been recently parked at the Hidden Lane. Whoever was inside must have heard them coming, because the door swung open and Ragnar Ryan's face appeared.

'You've found him?' he said, eyes alight.

McNab, shaking his head, caught the puffa jacket by the arm as he attempted his getaway.

'We need to talk,' he told him. 'What's your name? Real name?'

'He's a runner, Kenny something or other,' Ragnar offered.

As he said this, the runner's radio crackled and he answered.

'I have to go,' he told McNab. 'We're ready to shoot.'

McNab handed him a card. 'Make sure you call me,' he said, his tone threatening.

Kenny, checking the card, smiled. 'Sure thing, Detective Sergeant McNab.'

Now ensconced in the warmth of the camper-van, McNab took a look round at the star's quarters. That's if Jason Endeavour was indeed a star. Although, if that were true, he couldn't fathom how the movie could continue to shoot without him.

As though reading his mind, Ragnar said, 'We're using a double.'

'He has one?' McNab asked.

'It works okay in some of the action and crowd scenes,' Ragnar explained, sounding despondent. He waved McNab to a seat.

'Kenny the runner says someone else has been around here looking for Jason. Someone maybe from his former life in Glasgow?'

Ragnar pulled a face. 'Really? I know nothing about that.'

'What *do* you know of Lewis McLean's background here in Glasgow?' McNab tried.

The man shook his head decisively. 'Nothing whatsoever, apart from the fact he went to the Royal Conservatoire.'

'Did he ever mention having a brother or a twin?' McNab said.

'Jason has a twin?' Ragnar's eyes lit up as though he'd just heard of a perfect double for his missing actor.

'We have reason to believe that a murder victim recently discovered in a Glasgow park is Lewis McLean's brother.'

Ragnar's face blanched white beneath the Californian tan. 'You're certain it isn't Lewis?'

'We're certain,' McNab assured him. 'The DNA from the item you gave us had a fifty per cent match with the murdered man. Which means they shared both parents.'

Ragnar looked puzzled. 'Jason never mentioned he had a brother. In fact, he never mentioned any family at all.'

It looked like Kenny was right. The Yanks knew nothing about the background of their missing actor.

McNab decided to sidetrack a bit. 'Can you tell me what this film is about?'

'It's about an international crime syndicate operating out of Glasgow and Chicago,' Ragnar told him. 'In fact, Jason co-wrote the script.'

An explosion of thoughts collided in McNab's brain. One in particular struck home.

'And the other writer's name?' he said. 'I take it he's from the States?'

'Steven John Jarvis, SJ we call him,' Ragnar said with a smile. 'Big guy in the business.'

'I'll need to speak with him,' McNab said.

'I'm sorry. He's back in LA. Only communicates about the script via Zoom, and since Jason's here . . .' He tailed off.

'But he's not, is he?' McNab said.

Ragnar nodded. 'Of course. I can set up a meeting for you.'

'First thing tomorrow morning,' McNab said. 'Without fail.'

'There's an eight-hour time difference,' he said, making a face. 'It would be midnight in LA.'

'This is a murder enquiry possibly involving your missing actor. I'm sure he can stay up for that,' McNab said firmly.

When Ragnar didn't look keen to be given that job, McNab said, 'Who exactly is in charge around here?'

'The director, of course.' Ragnar looked as though he'd just said 'God'. 'Burt Carter.'

'Can I speak to him, then?' McNab asked.

'Not while he's filming.' Ragnar appeared shocked at having to say that.

'Then I'll speak to *him* first thing tomorrow. And you might like to remind him that here in Glasgow, Police Scotland is in charge, particularly when it involves murder.'

As he rose to go, Ragnar said, 'I'll have to see you out the long way. We can't disturb the shoot.'

McNab curbed his tongue and followed the curly black head as it threaded its way around the brightly lit set.

Once back on free and familiar ground, McNab hailed a taxi for home. When he'd asked what the movie was about, he hadn't expected the answer he'd got. So Lewis, aka Jason Endeavour, had co-written a script about a Glasgow–Chicago crime syndicate.

McNab was beginning to wonder how close it had come to the truth.

25

Photographed, swabbed, sampled and examined under the microscope, the engraved bullet was now being discussed with great interest by herself and Chrissy.

'Why do snakes have forked tongues anyway?' her assistant suddenly asked, as though the thought had just occurred to her.

Rhona found herself able to answer that question.

'The tongue ends are called tines. When it flicks its tongue in the air, the tines collect odour particles, which are delivered to a sensory organ in its mouth.'

'Mmmm,' Chrissy responded. 'I don't think that's important here. We're more in the Garden of Eden interpretation, or "he speaks with forked tongue" brigade.'

The bullet was a 9mm from a Glock 17, a favourite of both police and military personnel. Under the microscope, it did not display evidence of having been fired, merely swallowed – suggesting payback for what?

'Lying or cheating? Saying too much?' Chrissy tried.

'Or betrayal,' Rhona said. 'So who did the victim betray?'

They'd had an earlier call from McNab to inform them of a trip he'd made last evening to the film set in central

Glasgow. 'I'm back here now,' he'd told them, 'waiting to speak to God, aka the movie's director. Also half the duo who wrote the script for the Glasgow–Chicago gang movie.'

Listening to this on speaker, Chrissy had made a big *ooh* sound, despite her mouth being full of roll.

'The other half of the duo was or is our missing man Jason,' he'd informed them.

'And you think this movie may have something to do with Jason's brother's death?' Rhona had said.

'I'm in the land of make believe here, so who knows?' had been McNab's response. 'However, I do have the other half of my own duo here, who is infinitely more grounded than me. Let's see what DS Clark reads from this set-up.'

When he'd rung off, Rhona had told Chrissy about his late-night visit and what he'd had to say about the Marnie Aitken case. 'The way he spoke suggested he was pretty cut up about her confession and imprisonment,' she said.

'So he thought her innocent?' Chrissy asked.

'He believes she confessed because she blamed herself for whatever happened. Or someone from her past life threatened or convinced her to do that,' Rhona said.

'Hence the mutilated doll?' Chrissy said softly.

'I showed him an image of that,' Rhona told her. 'He said the doll is dressed like her daughter when she disappeared. Blue velvet jacket. Same tartan for the kilt. Hair colour. Everything.'

The image planted in their heads by this was both poignant and horrific.

'Anyway,' Rhona continued, 'McNab seemed keen that we review the case. And was certain Bill would okay us to take a look at the files. I'll contact Bill after this and ask.'

They'd paused for coffee plus a chocolate éclair Chrissy

had miraculously produced. Curling her tongue round the cream oozing from beneath the chocolate coating, Rhona emitted a murmur of delight.

'So what's your diet like now that Sean's no longer cooking for you?' Chrissy said, licking the final drops of cream from her fingers.

Rhona, a little startled by the question because she hadn't discussed this with anyone as yet, took a moment to compose her answer.

'Unhealthy,' she tried. 'Much like this.'

'So when will Sean be back?'

It seemed Chrissy wasn't about to give up without a full answer, so Rhona gave her one.

'Back at the club or back with me?' she said.

'You broke up with Sean Maguire?' Chrissy sounded incredulous.

Chrissy was a fan of the Irish saxophonist with whom Rhona shared a chequered relationship, but the look Chrissy was currently bestowing on her suggested more than just surprise.

Rising, Chrissy threw the cake box in the bin while muttering something under her breath.

'What?' Rhona demanded.

'I assume he was screwing someone else?' Chrissy said. 'Or else why would you ditch him?'

Rhona was reminded of a pointed conversation she'd once had with Sean when things were still new between them. Sean Maguire had plenty of female admirers, which was evident every time he played at the jazz club. Once upon a time, after noting him talking to one such female, she'd asked him outright if he was sleeping with her.

He'd looked perturbed by the question, then smiled and

said in his Irish voice, 'I may sleep with her, but I'll never cook for her.'

'Well?' Chrissy interrupted her thoughts, seemingly intent on an answer.

'We're on a break,' Rhona offered.

Chrissy adopted a disbelieving expression. 'You're on a break from good food and sex? More fool you, then,' she said firmly, before raising her mask.

Thankful that her interrogation was over for the moment at least, Rhona rose and said firmly, 'But not from work. Never from work.'

Later, when she fulfilled her pledge to contact Bill, she found him responsive to her request regarding the Marnie Aitken files.

'I can understand your desire to take a look. Especially now that Marnie has dropped off the radar,' he said. 'I take it you've had a conversation with DS McNab about her?'

'I have and he seems pretty certain they got it wrong and she did not drown her daughter.'

There was a short silence before Bill said, 'I wasn't part of the case. They needed help and McNab was assigned to the team. It didn't go well, and he had to be pulled off it.'

'Can you tell me why?' Rhona said.

'Sometimes, a detective reads evidence differently from his superior officer. In truth, I think McNab was working a hunch, which didn't match the evidence. Plus Marnie insisted she had killed her daughter. He didn't believe her or didn't want to,' he explained. 'But if she didn't in fact harm her daughter, what happened to her? I think that's the question McNab can't answer.'

There were cases going way back over decades that police

had failed to solve. In some, they believed they knew who the perpetrator had been, but the evidence hadn't been there to secure a conviction. Sometimes, such as in the famous World's End Murders in Edinburgh, advances in forensic soil science had led to a conviction years after.

Had anything been missed in Marnie's case? Or had her insistence that she was to blame led to her conviction despite a lack of evidence?

Rhona returned to the lab, where Chrissy was giving the doll as much scrutiny as any item that found its way there as evidence in a crime.

'Anything?' Rhona said on approach.

'Nothing obvious,' Chrissy said. 'So I decided to take a look inside and found this.'

It was a lock of hair, tied with a plaited blue thread. Blonde with warm tints, it still gleamed in the bright light of the lab. This treasured possession, which Marnie had chosen to give to them – for surely she would know that they would forensically examine the doll – seemed significant.

'Looks like we have a lock of Tizzy's hair,' Chrissy said. 'Why would she include this?'

'So that we might test it?' Rhona suggested.

'But the child's DNA must be among the evidence collected at the time,' Chrissy said.

Rhona tried to think back to the event at the Lilias Centre and all the questions the women had asked. DNA had been a topic much discussed. Where it might be detected. What it told about the person and their parents. Especially the father. There had even been laughter at that point, as one woman had said, 'There's no hiding who the real daddy is any more.'

Through it all, Marnie had remained silent, but obviously listening. She hadn't enrolled in the course, so most or all of it had been likely new to her.

'What are you thinking?' Chrissy said.

'That she wants to be sure we know who we're looking for,' Rhona told her.

'But since she didn't do the course, she wouldn't know about the hair roots,' Chrissy said.

Chrissy was right. The strand of hair had been cut from the hair ends. So no root follicles for ease of DNA extraction. They could retrieve mitochondrial DNA, but that would only lead them to the mother, whom they already knew.

'What colour hair does Marnie have?' Chrissy said.

'Brown,' Rhona told her.

'Her daughter must have inherited her father's colouring, then,' Chrissy said. 'It's also got a reddish tinge to it. Or is that from its age?'

Hair colour came from a mix of eumelanin, which was yellow-brown-black, and pheomelanin, which was red. Pheomelanin, being the more stable, lasted the longest. Hence the reason Egyptian mummies all seemed to have red hair.

'I don't think its age is giving it that colour. I think Tizzy was likely reddish blonde,' Rhona said.

'What d'you want to do with all of this?' Chrissy asked.

'I'll go through Marnie's case file first. See what was used in evidence against her. Then we'll decide.'

26

Sleep had been like a ghost flitting around her, unwilling to settle and give her peace.

At times she'd thought she was asleep, only to find herself standing in Tizzy's bedroom staring at the empty bed.

Regret at coming back here to the scene of the crime, knowing it would be like reliving the horror, retreated when she realized there had been nowhere else she could go.

At least here she could feel Tizzy's presence, imagine her next door or in the garden. Hear her laughter. Hum the music and watch her dance her Highland Fling.

As she rose more exhausted than when she'd gone to bed, she saw that it had snowed a little overnight. White flakes clung to the bare branches of the overgrown garden, reminding her of Christmases past when Tizzy and she had made a snowman and hung coloured lights round the eaves of the cottage.

The lights will still be here, she thought. *I can't switch them on, but I can pretend.*

But what about the tree? Tizzy's voice asked. *We always have a tree.*

Hearing her daughter's voice so clearly in her head was

as powerful as the image she'd seen from her prison room that night in the snow. The waking dream. One in which Tizzy could laugh and sing and dance.

Maybe I could have this last Christmas with her, Marnie thought. Do all the things she loved. Walking on the beach. Gathering the bluest of stones. Maybe even get the tree out of its box and put it up. Decorate it.

But what about presents?

What present might she gift her child at Christmas?

The biggest Christmas present would be if the forensic woman, Dr MacLeod, could discover the truth of where her daughter had gone, and what had happened to her.

27

The few folk wandering about at this hour looked as though they'd been out on an all-night drinking session.

'Maybe they have?' Janice said, when McNab remarked upon it.

'When I left they were in the middle of a night shoot,' he told her. 'Pretty hectic it looked too.'

Janice laughed. 'So you're the movie-making expert now?'

'I know that the director is God on set,' McNab told her. 'And we're about to meet him in person.'

Approaching the familiar trailer, he announced their eight a.m. arrival with a sharp rap on the door. When this produced no response, he knocked again, more loudly this time.

A muffled 'coming' followed, then stumbling footsteps, and the door was flung open to reveal Jerry Borstein in T-shirt and boxers, who looked at them through bleary eyes.

'Where's Ragnar?' McNab demanded.

Jerry shrugged. 'He went out early. Something he had to do. I went back to sleep. We were filming late last night,' he added through a yawn.

'I know, I was here,' McNab told him firmly. 'And I'm here again this morning with my partner DS Clark to speak to your director, Burt Carter, and also the scriptwriter Steven Jarvis.'

Jerry assumed a bemused look. 'Burt won't be up yet, and SJ's—'

'In LA,' McNab finished for him. 'Where is Mr Carter staying? I assume he isn't in a trailer?'

Jerry, picking up on McNab's serious manner, marshalled himself. 'He's staying at the Millennium Hotel on George Square. If you give me a minute, I'll put on some clothes and take you there.'

'That won't be necessary,' McNab told him. 'We know where the Millennium is.'

'I can call ahead and warn him you're coming?' Jerry tried, his expression becoming more desperate by the moment.

McNab didn't respond to that suggestion and, giving his partner the nod, left Jerry there to ponder what he should or shouldn't do next.

'I guess Ragnar hadn't spoken to his boss about your impending arrival, so made himself scarce before you turned up?' Janice said as they departed the set and headed for George Square.

'Maybe. Or BC informed him he didn't want to be disturbed this morning. Even – or perhaps especially – by us,' McNab said.

'Personally, I'm looking forward to meeting this God of film,' Janice said as they approached the imposing white frontage of the Millennium Hotel.

'Me too,' McNab confirmed.

Reception was busy with a line of folk waiting to check

out. McNab walked to the front of the queue and, showing his ID, asked which room Mr Burt Carter was in.

The young male looked askance at such a request and glanced about him as though searching for a superior to check with first.

McNab read the name tag and said, 'Ronnie, myself – DS McNab – and my associate, DS Clark, require to speak with him *right away*. His room number is?'

Quailing a little under McNab's direct gaze, Ronnie produced a piece of paper, wrote something swiftly on it, then slid it over the counter.

It was Janice who scooped it up and, giving Ronnie a big smile, offered her thanks.

Checking the paper, she said, 'Looks like he's in one of the five suites on the top floor.'

McNab threw her a look as she pressed the button for the lift. 'How do you know about the suites on the top floor?' he said with interest.

'What do *you* think?' Janice offered with a knowing smile.

McNab wasn't going to reveal his thoughts on that. Not at the moment, anyway.

Alighting from the lift a few minutes later, Janice led him straight to the door, which may have been the result of luck or familiarity, whereupon McNab knocked as firmly as before.

'Police Scotland, DS McNab and DS Clark here to speak to Burt Carter.'

Even as he said this, he heard the internal phone ring out, accompanied by the vibrating buzz of a mobile. It seemed likely that both Jerry and Ronnie were keen to forewarn Carter of their arrival.

A few moments' silence, then they heard footsteps approach.

'Here goes,' Janice whispered. 'Let's see if BC looks like his photo.'

'You've checked him out online?' McNab said, both impressed and a little put out by this.

The door swung open to reveal a young bearded guy McNab's height, or maybe a bit taller, if he was honest. He wore a white T-shirt and tracksuit bottoms and his dark hair glistened as though he'd recently been in the shower.

'Mr Carter?' McNab said.

'Please, call me Burt. Apologies,' he said with a white-toothed smile. 'Everyone phoned at once. Come in, please, DS McNab and DS Clark, I believe?'

Janice shot McNab a swift look of success as they were shown to a red settee that looked out over the spread of George Square.

'I had hoped you were bringing news of Jason's whereabouts, but I understand that's not the reason for your visit?'

'Who have you spoken to?' McNab asked.

'Ragnar texted this morning, then Jerry called, plus a rather flustered guy named Ronnie from reception, who didn't know why you were here.'

'We are becoming increasingly worried about Jason,' McNab said. 'Especially since we've now established that the body of a male who died in the city recently under suspicious and violent circumstances is related to your missing actor.'

For the first time, albeit fleetingly, McNab saw a worried shadow cross the handsome features.

McNab continued. 'Were you aware that Jason's real name is Lewis McLean and that Glasgow is his home city?'

Carter had already collected himself and answered

immediately. 'I was aware of that, yes. Which is why his role on advising our writer Steven Jarvis was so important.'

Janice came in then. 'We understand the film recounts the story of a crime syndicate operating between Chicago and Glasgow?'

He nodded, cautious now. 'It does, but it's completely fictional, if that's what you're suggesting?'

'Despite the time difference with LA, we'd like to speak with your screenwriter via Zoom. Ragnar assured us that would be possible,' McNab added.

'Of course, if you think it will help,' Carter said with a nod. 'I could order some coffee to be sent up while I organize a call?'

'Double espresso for me.' McNab looked to Janice.

'Latte, please,' she responded.

Carter left them there and, going through to the bedroom, closed the door behind him.

'What d'you think?' Janice said under her breath.

'He's very handsome,' McNab conceded.

When Janice elbowed him, he added, 'He's worried his actor's in deep shit. Possibly in hiding or even dead. Which means the movie will be too. Hope it's not funded by Russian money. As for me, I think someone's definitely got to our boy Lewis. The runner Kenny told me last night he saw Lewis having angry words with an unknown Weegie on set. I'm hoping he's gone to ground and is still breathing.'

A knock at the door heralded the arrival of the coffee.

Taking the tray from the porter, McNab handed Janice her latte, then swiftly downed his espresso.

'You didn't even taste that,' she said accusingly.

'It's not about the taste,' he told her firmly.

They fell silent as Carter re-entered and, pointing the

remote at the screen on the opposite wall, brought up an image of a nervous-looking guy at a desk.

'Steven. Thanks for joining us. These are Detectives McNab and Clark from Police Scotland who are looking for Jason. They wanted a word with you.'

Steven Jarvis blinked a bit, then nodded. 'Of course. Anything I can do to help.'

McNab turned to Carter. 'We'd prefer to speak to Mr Jarvis alone,' he said.

'Sure thing. I'll head down to breakfast. How long do you need?'

'We'll be down when we're finished,' McNab told him.

Was it his imagination or did Steven visibly relax when he saw his boss depart?

As the door closed behind the director, it was clear McNab was right on that score.

'I'm worried Jason could be in trouble,' Steven immediately said. 'I didn't want to say in front of the boss, but I think the script's maybe the reason.'

'How's that?' Janice asked.

'Jason was adamant it was entirely fictional, but it sounded very real to me. Then again, good crime fiction usually does. But when Jason disappeared . . .' He tailed off. 'Then that body was found. The description of the victim . . .' He halted there.

'You thought it might be Jason?' McNab said.

Steven nodded, his face pale, despite the tan. 'I'm sure glad I'm in LA and not in Glasgow right now.'

'We'll need to see a copy of the current script,' McNab told him. 'I'd like you to send one through now.'

Steven looked worried by this. 'The boss would be the one to ask for that.'

'This isn't a request,' McNab said firmly. 'Here's the email address to send it to.'

After a moment's hesitation, Steven said, 'Okay. I'll send a PDF through now.'

A few moments later Janice's phone pinged with the incoming message.

As Steven showed his relief at his interrogation being over, McNab said, 'One more thing, Mr Jarvis. Does a bullet engraved with a snake feature anywhere in this script?'

Steven looked incredulous. 'It does. Why?'

'That's all for now, Mr Jarvis, but we'll speak again soon.'

As Jarvis disappeared off the screen, McNab looked to Janice.

'Now's your chance to read a movie script that may well reflect the real-life crime being played out here in Glasgow.'

28

On leaving the Lilias Centre, she'd been given £82.39 discharge grant. She wondered at the odd amount and how it had been calculated. Why wasn't it a round £80? What was the extra £2.39 for exactly?

She'd also been given a travel allowance. Of course, they'd believed that was for Glasgow but she had used it to come here.

Would the authorities try to find out where she'd gone? Would *he* know she was out?

She stopped herself there.

Better to think of the upcoming Christmas, which, due to Tizzy's increasing internal demands, she had promised to celebrate.

The weather was in on the task. The continuing intermittent snow had accumulated in the garden and its surrounds. She'd spotted a small baby pine that she'd decided was suitable to replace the fake version from the loft, whose plastic needles had fallen off in its unpacking to leave only bare branches.

Something Tizzy didn't like and had told her so.

I want a real tree. Small like me.

She'd also looked in the tiny loft for the decorations. The fusty smell that met her as she'd opened the hatch made her think again of death.

Her own and her child's.

And yet . . .

Things had changed during the six years she'd been in prison. Now, her mind – less tortured by her trauma – understood why she'd said what she had. The police had been keen that she confess. It made things so neat and clean.

A mother's fault is never done.

She gave a little laugh as she unpacked the ornaments from their box and hung them on the tree.

'Well, Tizzy, we can't have lights, but will this do?' she asked out loud.

She imagined her daughter's laughter, and her excited *Yes* in reply.

That task now over, she found herself approaching her old bedroom to open the door and stare in at the rumpled bed, remembering the last time she'd lain there.

In that moment, self-hate returned with a vengeance, threatening to drown her. As did the voice that told her she was to blame for everything and six years inside wasn't and never could be long enough to punish her.

29

They'd decided not to interview the boys at the station, but separately, at each of their homes.

A station interview might prove necessary later. If so, McNab believed Kevin Docherty's parents would cope with that. As for Dreep's mum, he thought that might be the final straw for the poor woman, who currently sat close to Dreep on the sofa as though she feared they might snatch her youngest son away from her, never to return.

McNab wanted to speak to the boy alone, and had hopes he yet might, should Janice manage to persuade his mother into the kitchen to make some tea.

Staring at the skinny wee body, whose stick legs didn't look as though they could hold him up, McNab was reminded of himself at the same age. Back then, facing the world and those in it, especially the teenage gang members who ruled his neighbourhood, had seen him take to carrying a knife. Not to hurt anyone, he remembered telling himself, but for protection. And it had worked. He'd felt less skinny and terrified. Until his mother had found out about it.

McNab couldn't see Dreep's own mother having the same

effect on either of her sons. Life had dealt her too many blows already.

He gave the nod to Janice, who immediately stood up.

'Mrs McGowan, how about you and I have a chat in the kitchen and maybe make some tea? Brian'll be fine here with Michael.'

The woman rose as though used to following orders and nodded her agreement.

Was it his imagination or did Dreep look relieved to see his mum depart? Maybe their relationship wasn't that different from him and his own mum, McNab thought.

'Can I call you Dreep?' he said when the women had left the room. 'Didn't like to do that with your mum around.' He smiled. 'Want to know my nickname at your age?'

The thin face perked up and the boy nodded.

'I guess you got yours because you're good at dreeping off walls?' McNab said.

'And climbing over them,' Dreep answered with the hint of a grin.

'Well, take a guess at mine,' McNab said, glancing upwards.

'Were you tall?' Dreep asked.

'Yes, but that wasn't it,' McNab told him. 'More colourful,' he encouraged.

'Ginger?' Dreep tried, focusing on McNab's auburn hair.

'Worse,' McNab egged him on.

'Carrot heid?' Dreep was really into the game now. When McNab shook his head again, he said, 'What was it, mister?'

'Beamer,' McNab told him. 'My face was always trying to outdo my hair.'

Dreep laughed. 'That's a bummer.'

'It was,' McNab said, remembering yet the sting of it. 'So back to yours. You're good at climbing. Trees as well as walls, I take it. So you used to help get your pals Ally and Kev into the old farmhouse. Am I right?'

Dreep knew when he'd been collared, so he just nodded.

'That night in the snow, you went to hang out at the den and found a body?' McNab asked the million-dollar question.

It was as though Dreep had been waiting for it, because the answer came tumbling out of him.

'Aw, mister, it was awful. I nearly fell over him. He was bollock naked and on his back, tied to a chair.'

'And that's when you took the photo,' McNab said.

Dreep's eyes widened as he realized the significance of that statement. 'You found my phone?' he said.

'Your brother's phone.' McNab didn't make it a question.

'I told him I loaned it to Ally.' Dreep shook his head. 'I shouldn't have done that. Darren went to Ally's house looking for it.'

Registering the significance of this, McNab steered him back to that night. 'Tell me, when you got to the guy in the chair, was he alive?'

'Ally asked if I'd checked if he was still breathing.' Dreep looked haunted by the memory. 'No way. So Ally touched his neck. Said he was looking for a pulse, like we were taught in First Aid. Maybe left his fingerprints on him. He was worried about that,' he added.

'So next day, Ally went back looking for the phone?' McNab confirmed.

Tears glistened in Dreep's eyes. 'Ally always looks out for me. For us.'

Seeing the state of the boy, McNab halted there and, rummaging in the bag he'd brought with him, extracted two cans, one of Coke, the other Irn-Bru, plus a packet of Caramel Logs.

'Help yourself,' he said, unwrapping one for himself.

Giving the boy time to consume some Irn-Bru and the biscuit, McNab sat in silence until the munching stopped. The sugar rush had brought some colour back into Dreep's cheeks, so he started in again.

'The most important thing now is for us to bring Ally home. For that we need you and Kevin's help.' He waited until Dreep nodded. 'So first thing is . . . if Ally's in hiding, you have to tell us where.'

The words came out in a rush. 'Me and Kev have looked everywhere he could be and Ally promised to meet us at the tunnel. Ally always keeps his promises.'

It wasn't what McNab wanted to hear. He realized in that moment that he'd had a small hope that the two boys were keeping something back, but seeing the look on Dreep's face, with the flecks of toasted coconut still sprinkling his mouth, he knew that wasn't the case.

Reverting back to what Dreep had said earlier about the mobile, McNab asked, 'What about Darren? Might he be holding Ally somewhere?'

The change in Dreep's expression suggested the boy was concerned about that.

'Our Darren knew about the dead body, mister,' the boy said in a scared voice. 'He knew it was naked.'

So Darren had seen the body before the police got there? Maybe even before the three boys had seen it?

'You're sure about this, Dreep?' McNab asked firmly.

Dreep nodded. 'When he went to see Ally, he told him he would end up like the dead naked guy, if he didn't get his mobile back. If it's true that you've got it, mister . . .' The frightened boy looked into McNab's eyes for confirmation.

'We definitely have it, Dreep,' McNab told him. 'So, if there's a chance Darren might have snatched Ally, where would he take him?'

Dreep shook his head. 'I don't know where he goes or what he does when he's not here.'

'What about his mates? Do they come round?' McNab tried.

'Naw, except when they pick him up.'

'They pick him up?' McNab said. 'In a car or . . . ?'

'A van mostly,' Dreep said.

'Can you tell me anything about this van?' McNab said.

'It's black. No markings. No windows,' Dreep offered.

'Anything else? Make maybe?' McNab tried.

'Sorry, mister, don't know the make.' He paused, face screwed up, thinking. 'But,' he said, brightening a little, 'I might remember a bit of the number plate.'

At this, McNab could have hugged the skinny wee body, but maintaining his calm said, 'That would be good, Dreep. Tell you what, type what you remember of it into my phone for me.'

'Sure thing.' Dreep accepted the mobile and began typing. 'That's not all of it, though,' he added, worried.

'It's still a help,' McNab said with a nod. 'The mobile you took from Darren. Where did you find it exactly?'

'That's easy, mister. Under his bed, in a box. There's plenty more in it. That's why I didn't think he would miss one.'

McNab tried not to show his delight at the news. 'Is the box still there?'

'I think so,' Dreep said, looking frightened.

'Can you go fetch this box for me?'

When the boy hesitated, McNab added, 'It might help me find Ally.'

Dreep nodded and headed out and up the stairs. Minutes later he came back with an Adidas box and handed it to McNab. A quick glance inside confirmed the presence of maybe ten burner phones.

'My big brother's in trouble, isn't he?' Dreep said, perhaps sensing the enormity of what had just happened.

'It's Ally that's in trouble, Dreep, and we have to find him.'

'So we have Darren's stash of drug mobiles,' Janice said as they headed along the road towards the Docherty household.

'Plus we have a partial on the registration number for the van that picks him up at home, which I've already sent in,' McNab told her. 'Dreep also said that Darren knew the victim was naked.'

Janice looked askance at this. 'Wow. He told you that?'

'He said that Darren told Ally he would end up like the naked guy if he didn't get his mobile back.'

'So Darren knew about the state of the body,' Janice said. 'Either before or after the boys were there.'

'Exactly. All the more reason to find him and bring him in.'

'And Ally?'

'Dreep suspects his brother may have him. As do I.'

They'd arrived at the Docherty house, where, by the figures at the window, they were expected.

'How d'you want to play this?' Janice said.

'I'll talk to the parents this time while you speak to Kevin,' McNab said. 'I suspect his story will be the same as Dreep's. Plus Kev doesn't have a brother like Darren to deal with.'

The Docherty living room contained a real Christmas tree festooned in lights. McNab could smell its scent when he entered, which reminded him that in the McGowan house there hadn't been a hint of Christmas at all.

The Docherty parents exhibited a united front, just as McNab thought they would. Obviously worried by Ally's disappearance, they were more than keen to help.

'Kevin has told us what happened that night,' his father said. 'He knows that it should have been reported to the police right away. If Dreep hadn't dropped the mobile . . .' Mr Docherty shook his head. 'Dreep's not got it easy, and he tries to look out for his mum.'

'You'll find Ally, won't you?' Mrs Docherty said as McNab and Janice departed.

'We'll find him,' McNab told her, hoping that was true.

As they walked back to the car, Janice told him that Kevin had basically repeated what Dreep had already said to McNab. That they'd arranged to meet Ally at the tunnel entrance, because he was taking them to visit his gran in Partick.

'When he didn't turn up, they searched everywhere they could think of that he might have gone,' she said. 'It seems Ally always kept his promises, except this time he didn't.'

'Because he couldn't,' McNab said.

The only difference between the boys' stories was the existence of the black van.

'I think Dreep probably didn't like talking about what his big brother might be up to,' McNab said. 'Even to his pals.'

'What is it?' Janice said, reading his troubled expression.

'What if Darren isn't involved?' McNab said. 'What about the other guy who came looking for Ally at Leo's chip shop? He didn't know where Ally or the others lived, so obviously had no connection with Darren McGowan.'

'You think he saw Ally and the others in the park?' Janice said.

McNab nodded. 'I also think he'd been inside the farmhouse and made note of Leo's boxes,' he said, his mind churning.

The victim's death had all the hallmarks of a gang reprisal killing, including the engraved bullet. If anyone was thought to have seen what happened that night, they would have to be dealt with.

30

Rhona checked the time on the wall clock, aware that she should have departed the lab two hours ago at least. Chrissy had long since left and by now would have settled her small son in bed and read him a story.

Wee Michael was named after McNab, because he'd saved the lives of Chrissy and her unborn son by shielding her from a Russian bullet.

Rhona thought back to McNab's haunted expression at the locus in Elder Park and again at the post-mortem. Folk thought only soldiers had PTSD. Not true. Anyone on the front line was in danger of reliving the horrors they'd faced there.

Including herself.

And what of Marnie Aitken?

Once they'd finished for the day in the lab, she'd settled down to read through the recently arrived folder of documents relating to Marnie's trial and conviction. The Scottish verdict of culpable homicide, in which Marnie's confession had played a big role, appeared to match the crime and the sentence, begging the question as to why Marnie should now wish to have it revisited.

It had begun with her question to Rhona during the forensic event at the prison. Then the delivery of the doll, with its mouth and eyes sewn shut, suggesting there were things the police did not see at the time, or that she had not told them.

Or had been too afraid to tell them?

The forensic report had also played a role in the guilty verdict. No forensic evidence of anyone other than the mother and daughter had been found in their home. Nor had there been an indication of a struggle of any kind. However, the forensic team had discovered evidence of illegal drug-taking in the cottage. When questioned about this, Marnie would only nod in agreement with whatever was suggested.

Witness statements concentrated on the presence of Tizzy at the games. What she had been wearing. How she'd never got to perform, because she'd disappeared by the time her name had been called.

A preliminary search was conducted for the four-year-old girl by those in charge of the junior dancing. When she couldn't be found, panic had set in, especially when they couldn't get her mother on the phone.

Eventually the local police were called and they set about a wider search in the surrounding fields and woods.

Someone had spoken about Tizzy's love of swimming. How she'd learned very young. Might she have gone to the shore? It had been a sunny, warm summer's day.

That's where they'd found Marnie, soaking wet and wandering about as though in a daze.

Her first words had been, 'She's gone. Tizzy's gone. She's drowned. It's all my fault.'

While the search went on for Tizzy, Marnie had been

taken to the Kilcreggan medical centre where she'd continued to talk in an agitated fashion about Tizzy being dead.

No recordings were taken of what she'd said there, although staff reported that they believed she may have been under the influence of drugs. During that time, Marnie continued to say: 'I should never have taken her to Gourock. I should never have taught her to swim.'

Marnie's statement, when she was eventually interviewed at Helensburgh police station, had been short and concise.

I am responsible for my daughter Tizzy's disappearance and death by drowning.

After which she would say no more, despite further questioning by officers and an assessment by psychiatric services.

Background checks had been made and had revealed Marnie's life, prior to coming to live in Rosneath, to have involved drugs and prostitution in Glasgow. In the early days of the baby's birth, there had been checks on mother and baby for fear of possible child neglect.

Eventually social services were assured all was well and had left them alone.

The crossover between what Dr Sara Masters had said regarding Marnie's state of mind then and now was yet another piece of the puzzle.

Marnie had blamed herself at the beginning of her incarceration for her daughter's death, but in recent days no longer seemed willing to do so.

As she'd read through the notes, Rhona had highlighted the sections that brought a question for her, the most pertinent one being the words uttered by Marnie during her visit to the Lilias Centre.

'What if the police don't find a body to examine?'

Bodies didn't always come ashore. Or get caught in fishing

nets. Or get sliced through by nuclear submarines patrolling from Faslane.

Rhona recalled other investigations she'd been involved with, including one in Raasay Sound between the islands of Raasay and Skye, when the body parts of a male had come ashore. Back then, the Ministry of Defence had denied any involvement in the said fisherman's death. Yet they'd removed the body parts from her lab fridge and taken them south anyway.

Might something similar have happened here?

Another item of evidence had interested her. Samples of sand and soil had been retrieved from the cottage. As far as she was aware from the notes, because Marnie had admitted guilt, neither the soil nor sand had been analysed by a forensic soil scientist.

Rhona knew from a case on the Orkney Island of Sanday that sand differed from beach to beach. Had the sand found in the cottage come from the beach they'd found Marnie wandering on or not?

And what about the soil? Where exactly on the peninsula had it come from?

If she sent the samples still in storage to her forensic soil scientist colleague, Dr Jen Mackie, what might she make of them?

Rhona couldn't help but wonder if Tizzy's body had never washed up onshore, whole or in parts, or been pulled up in a fisherman's net in the Firth of Clyde . . . it might never have reached the water at all.

An hour later, she finally departed the university. While shut up in the lab she'd missed the return of the snow, now softly falling as she left the cloisters to take the path downhill to the park below. It was a magical evening. Even Rhona, her mind filled with her thoughts on the Elder Park victim, plus the Marnie notes, could appreciate that.

At the foot of the hill she stopped to breathe in the cold night air and admire a scene reminiscent of her childhood and the magic of Christmas. Turning homewards, she walked between the snow-touched trees of Kelvingrove Park, thinking how many times she'd taken this path and wished for some good, somewhere.

As she climbed the steep stairs that led to Park Circus and her flat, she realized that the light in the sitting room was shining out. Had she left it on, in the darkness of a midwinter morning? Or had Sean reappeared in her life once again?

Sean, of course, wasn't the only person who held a key for emergencies. Chrissy did. As did her own son, Liam, but he was still roaming the world.

'I shouldn't be so free with my keys,' she muttered to herself.

It comes from being brought up on Skye, she thought. *You either leave your door open for visitors, or you tell them where they can find a key, if they should ever come to call and you're out.*

Slipping her own key in the lock, she caught the sound of Sean's voice talking to someone. She stood for a few seconds, considering who might be in there with him. Certainly not Chrissy, who would be home by now. McNab maybe?

She hadn't got round to playing Sean's voicemail so had no idea how she should greet him.

At this moment Tom, her cat, poked his head round the partly open door and with a loud meow demanded she enter.

Rhona did so, making a point of firmly closing the door behind her. Whoever was here now knew she was back.

The kitchen door stood half open, and it was then she caught the pleasurable scent of something cooking. Since she hadn't stopped to buy food on the way home, she found herself happy about that, despite the circumstances.

Entering, she found Sean and her other visitor seated at the kitchen table, a bottle of whisky and two glasses uniting them.

The two men rose to greet her.

'You have a visitor from Skye,' Sean said with a smile. 'And dinner's ready.'

31

She rose in darkness and headed for the shower, keen to escape to the lab.

She'd explained about her busy work schedule before going to bed and had apologized to Jamie that she couldn't spend time with him on his visit to Glasgow. He'd been sanguine about this, apologizing himself for arriving without notice. He was only in town for another night, then he would be heading back to Skye.

'I'm happy to find a hotel,' he'd offered.

'Not at all,' she'd told him. 'I said you were always welcome to stay here whenever you came to town,' she'd added. 'Although if Sean hadn't been around, the food wouldn't have been this good.'

Earlier, while Sean had served up the meal, she and Jamie had talked of Skye. Rhona had asked after friends there, in particular the guys out at Ace Target Sports and Blaze, her erstwhile forensic canine assistant.

They'd also chatted about the hills they'd climbed and the cliff walks taken together during her summer visit earlier in the year.

'You're not a climber, I take it?' Jamie had asked Sean at this point.

'I am not,' Sean had agreed. 'Anyway, I was touring in the States when Rhona was last on Skye.'

Rhona, hearing the easy tone of Sean's voice, suspected he thought things were back to normal between them. Either that or he'd assumed she'd listened to whatever message he'd left for her and was happy with it.

It certainly seemed that finding Jamie McColl from Skye at her door hadn't phased Sean Maguire one little bit. She'd found herself mildly perturbed by this, while at the same time glad she hadn't entered her kitchen to find two stags at bay.

Sean had left for his own flat after the meal, which meant there had been no worries about who was sleeping where. After which, she and Jamie had shared a nightcap before she'd shown him to the spare room and headed for her own bed. Alone.

Despite the success of what could have been a difficult situation, sleep had still eluded her, and instead her brain had focused on everything she'd read regarding Marnie Aitken and her daughter Tizzy, playing it out in Marnie's voice to add to the drama.

Eventually she must have slept, but when she awakened to the early alarm, she certainly didn't feel as though she had.

Dressed now, she decided not to have anything to eat but to rely on Chrissy to appear with filled rolls as usual. She had almost made her getaway when Tom arrived to wind himself round her legs, reminding her that she hadn't refilled his automated food dispenser.

Swearing under her breath, she was heading for the

kitchen to do just that when the spare room door opened and Jamie appeared, dressed for a run.

As apparently surprised by their sudden encounter as she was, they stood in silence for a moment, before he said, 'Sorry, I thought I could head out without disturbing you.'

'And I thought the same,' Rhona admitted. 'You're going for a run?'

'You live so near Kelvingrove Park, it seemed too good an opportunity to miss.'

The previous evening, they'd managed to cover their awkwardness by chatting about Skye. She'd known Jamie McColl since her childhood spent there with her adoptive parents. They'd passed many teenage summers together too and never been more than just friends, although she'd suspected, after her most recent visit, that things might have changed in that respect. For Jamie anyway.

Observing his manner now, she realized that might be true.

'Right, I'd better feed Tom and be on my way,' she said, making for the kitchen.

'And I'll head off and see you later,' Jamie said in return. 'My turn to cook tonight. Or I could treat you to a curry in that place you talk about in Ashton Lane?'

Her first thought when he suggested this was that a meal out could be better than being at home.

'Ashoka it is, then,' Rhona said. 'But I might be late finishing?'

'No worries.' Jamie sounded and looked more cheerful now. 'Just let me know when.'

Rhona waited until she heard the front door close behind him before she ventured back into the hall. Muttering a few curses under her breath, laced with the names of Jamie McColl and Sean Maguire, she then set off herself.

The light covering of snow had crisped overnight and the white veil that covered the hill gave the university building itself the look of a medieval palace.

Hoping she wouldn't encounter Jamie on his run, she swiftly crossed the park and headed up the path, for the most part alone. The university term being over, the majority of the students had dispersed for the Christmas break.

Rhona liked the university teeming with students during term time and also as it was now, the cloisters wound in a web of white fairy lights, the only sound being the echo of her own footsteps.

Assuming she would be first in, she was surprised to smell fresh coffee on entry. Plus the even more welcome scent of cooked bacon.

Chrissy turned as she came in and gave her a surprised look.

'It's my job to be first here of a morning, but if you want to swap?' she said quizzically.

Rhona shook her head. 'I was escaping a visitor,' she admitted.

Chrissy's eyes immediately lit up. 'Who?' she demanded. 'You haven't replaced Sean already?' she added.

Rhona took off her coat and accepted a mug of coffee before answering. 'When I got back late from work last night, I found two men in my kitchen.'

'Lucky you,' Chrissy said. 'Let me guess – Sean's back from wherever he was and . . .' She examined Rhona's expression before saying, 'Let me guess – the guy on Skye.'

'How on earth?' Rhona said, mouth open.

'I can read minds. Yours in particular,' Chrissy told her. 'And?' she encouraged.

'They were seated at my kitchen table drinking my

whisky.' Saying it out loud reminded Rhona how weird the image of that had been.

'Awkward,' Chrissy said. 'So?'

'We ate Sean's casserole. Sean went home and . . .' She drew to a halt.

'And what exactly?' Chrissy said.

'Jamie slept in the spare room. I left early to come here.' Rhona fell silent, remembering the uncomfortable scene in the hall.

Chrissy handed Rhona a bacon roll. 'So why is Skye man here in Glasgow exactly?'

Rhona didn't know and said so. 'But I did say if he ever came to Glasgow he could stay at my place.'

'So when he arrived at your place, Sean let him in?' Chrissy laughed. 'Wish I'd seen that.'

Rhona was glad she hadn't. 'Although Sean seemed very relaxed about it,' she added.

'Well, he puts up with McNab's nocturnal visits,' Chrissy reminded her.

'Sean doesn't tell me what to do,' Rhona said.

'Which is why he's been allowed to hang around as long as he has,' Chrissy said, rising. 'So is Skye man gone now?'

'We're having curry later at Ashoka. Fancy coming along?' Rhona tried.

Chrissy laughed. 'As your chaperone?'

'Jamie met you on Skye, so it wouldn't be weird if you joined us.'

'Not weird,' Chrissy said, managing a straight face. 'Not weird at all.'

Thinking back to that conversation, Rhona was embarrassed at herself. Although a small hope still lingered hours later that Chrissy might concede to her request (if only out of nosiness) and call her mum to ask her to babysit wee Michael.

Glancing across the room at Chrissy's suited figure busy at work, Rhona chastised herself for being ridiculous. She would eat with Jamie and make it clear during their time together that nothing had changed between them. They were pals from way back. That was all.

Besides, he knew about her relationship with Sean and finding him in her flat cooking for her must have reinforced that. A brief thought crossed her mind that she could always ask McNab to join them. Ashoka was a favourite haunt of his and he would definitely accept.

Glancing up, she met Chrissy's eyes and knew her assistant was likely reading her mind again. In fact, she heard what she thought might be a laugh barely smothered by the mask.

The call from Jen Mackie spared her from further ruminations on what the evening might bring.

'I'm calling about the soil samples you wanted me to take a look at,' she said. 'I'm intrigued as to why?'

Rhona gave her a fuller picture than she'd outlined in the email.

'I wasn't involved six years ago,' Jen confirmed. 'I assume the samples didn't appear significant in the case back then?'

'The woman, Marnie Aitken, confessed to killing her daughter by drowning and served her time.'

'Why are you interested, then?' Jen said.

Rhona gave her a brief résumé of her visit to the Lilias Centre and Magnus's concerns regarding Marnie, but it was the delivery of the defaced doll that hit home.

'So Magnus thinks she was hiding the truth of what really happened back then?' Jen said. 'Or maybe even the whereabouts of the body?'

'Which has also crossed my mind,' Rhona said. 'Or she was too frightened to tell the truth, despite the consequences.'

'And this all happened on the Rosneath Peninsula?' Jen said.

Rhona confirmed this. 'She lived alone with her daughter near Kilcreggan, close to the beach. No car. The child could swim apparently. Marnie had a history of drug abuse and prostitution, which ended with her pregnancy. But all was well, according to Magnus, until the child disappeared.'

'And you want to know if the soil samples match her last known location?' Jen said. 'Which, as I understand it, was at the Rosneath games.'

'That's the last place the child was seen,' Rhona confirmed.

'Then again, if they come from elsewhere on the peninsula . . .' Jen didn't say it might point to where the child was possibly buried, or the actual location of her drowning, but Rhona knew that's exactly what she meant.

32

As the last officer entered the room, DI Wilson signalled to McNab to turn on the big screen.

Without an explanation as to what they were about to see, McNab did as commanded.

The words of the movie script sent to Janice's phone by Steven John Jarvis now appeared against a blue background.

McNab studied the assembled faces as they registered that they were required to read them, aware that none of those present would likely have seen a movie script laid out on paper before.

```
                EXT. GLASGOW. ALLEY
```
The BEAT of MUSIC swells as DS Boyd moves over slick cobbles to a graffiti-daubed door buried in thick stone walls.

With one swing, 16 kg of hardened steel hits the door, springing multiple locks.

THUMPING RAP MUSIC explodes around them as the door crashes open.

Boyd produces a gun and enters. Behind Boyd are two helmeted marksmen, the red dots of their laser sights playing Boyd's back.

CUT TO:

The POUNDING MUSIC drowns their entry as Boyd moves swiftly down the narrow, dark tunnel, towards a door at the end framed by light.

Boyd throws open the door.

CUT TO:
INT. CLUB. ROOM

The red laser dots fix on the bare backs of two MEN who are having sex with two YOUNG WOMEN on red-cushioned couches, while a BLONDE WOMAN looks on.

All eyes dart to the door where Boyd stands flanked by two armed officers. Behind him the dog strains on its leash.

BOYD (shouts) Down on the ground.

One of the men breaks free, runs for the bar counter. Throws himself over. FEMALE SCREAMS as the now-released BARKING dog plunges into the melee of scrambling bodies. The dog makes for a rear door and SCRABBLES against it.

Boyd follows, gun in hand, and shoulders open the door.

CUT TO:
INT. CLUB. BACK ROOM

To reveal a brightly lit room stocked with equipment to process and package cocaine. At first it seems empty, then a SHOT rings out and thuds into the wall near Boyd, who dives for the floor.

A face inches above a metal table piled with cocaine bundles. It belongs to LENNY HARRIS (20s), thin as a stick, spaced-out eyes wide with fear, a snake tattoo curling up his neck, its forked tongue licking his ear.

A muscled arm, belonging to older brother MAXIE HARRIS (30s) yanks him back down.

BOYD (to dog) Go!

The dog launches itself up and over the table, scattering packets and loose cocaine in its path in a white cloud.

A YELP from the dog as Maxie HURLS it to THUMP against the wall. The dog falls stunned and winded just as –

A second SHOT hits Boyd, slicing his left arm. Furious, in pain, Boyd RETURNS FIRE as both men scramble towards a rear exit, Maxie in front.

Boyd's bullet SLAMS into Lenny's shoulder.

Lenny staggers and falls, sending more cocaine packets flying, spraying white powder to add to the cloud.

Maxie exits. SLAMS the door behind him.

Boyd scrambles over Lenny's writhing GROANING body and is enveloped in the cocaine cloud.

McNab watched as the silent read was replaced by a babble of voices. Eventually DI Wilson signalled them to quieten down.

'What you've just read is from the movie Jason Endeavour, aka Lewis McLean, was co-writing and acting in before he went missing,' he said. 'Some in the room might recognize the resemblance to a raid by Police Scotland three years back on an international drug cartel run by the Jamesie brothers, whose home ground was Glasgow.

'The brothers, Mark and Luke, got away in a not dissimilar manner to that depicted in the scene and are rumoured to be currently in Venezuela. Their business we believe is still operational although who is currently in charge here in the UK has not been established.'

He continued.

'As far as we know, the snake tattoo visible on the younger brother in the script wasn't an identifier of the cartel back then. However, the bullets used by the head of the cartel in the movie do have a snake engraved on them.'

Silence followed this announcement as those in the room absorbed the importance of the link.

DI Wilson turned to McNab. 'Bring them up to date, Sergeant.'

'As DI Wilson says, the similarities between the real and fictional raids are striking. Even to the point of the cocaine cloud at the end of the scene.'

At this point, a voice shouted, 'DS Boyd's you, isn't he?'

When the place erupted in laughter, McNab said, 'And I can confirm that I was high for a week afterwards.'

As DI Wilson quietened them down, McNab went on. 'The other scriptwriter, Steven Jarvis, confirmed that he wondered if Jason was writing about something he had real knowledge of, although Jason apparently denied this. But when he disappeared, and then our victim was found who closely resembled Jason, SJ got scared and said he was very happy to be in LA and not Glasgow. I should stress that at no time did Jason mention to SJ that he had a brother back home and we're working on the assumption that he may not have known about him.

'Now that we have forensic evidence to prove the dead man isn't in fact Jason, or Lewis as he was known here before his fame, there's a chance his killer was going after Jason because of the script and got the wrong guy.'

'How did they know what was in the script?' someone asked.

'The set is full of Weegies working at various levels. One of them, Kenny, a runner on set, saw and heard an altercation between Jason and a male Glaswegian shortly before he disappeared,' he explained. 'Kenny has made contact recently and is coming in for interview and hopefully will give us a fuller description of this man.'

When Kenny had called him, he hadn't been anxious to visit the station, citing previous brushes with the law when a teenager, but McNab had succeeded, he hoped, in allaying his fears.

'Now, to the missing boy, Alistair Feeney . . . who may have been snatched as a possible witness to what went down that night at the old farmhouse.' He paused there for a moment.

'When I visited Leo's chippy where Ally and his two pals Dreep and Kev were regular customers, evidenced by empty boxes found at the locus, Leo told me that another guy had been in looking for them. The description Leo gave of this man sounds very similar to that given by runner Kenny.

'If both men can confirm this via identikit images, then we have a possible link between the movie being made here and the farmhouse killing.'

At this point, Janice came in to express the fear that everyone in the room was experiencing.

'Which means we must locate Ally Feeney's whereabouts as quickly as possible.'

33

Chrissy had been right, of course. Samples of Tizzy's DNA were on file, so they didn't need to work on the clip of hair Marnie had sent them.

What that must have cost her, Rhona thought. To give up such a precious memento of the child she'd either lost, or perhaps killed?

Magnus had said that Marnie's story of Tizzy's conception was of being raped by a man she didn't know. That had been later contradicted and replaced by a story of a former partner. A man who'd beaten and abused her.

She'd left him because she wanted the child to live free of his abuse, moving back to the place where her own mother had lived as a child. There, she'd tried to build a life with her baby daughter. And she'd succeeded. Social services, at first concerned about her, eventually decided that mother and daughter were both well.

Tizzy had become both a dancer and a swimmer under her mother's watchful eye. It seemed they'd been happy together.

So what had changed that day at the Highland games?

Marnie's own background . . . a mother she'd loved and who'd protected her had died when she wasn't much older than Tizzy. Her father, free of his wife's watchful eye, then began to sexually abuse his daughter.

Marnie, it seemed, hadn't wanted that to happen to Tizzy, so she'd escaped her abusive relationship and started afresh.

Magnus was convinced that the real story of Tizzy's conception was that Marnie had been a victim of rape, probably multiple times, by that abusive partner, and that he, whoever he was, was Tizzy's father.

Had this man re-entered her life in the lead-up to Tizzy's disappearance? Might that have triggered whatever happened that day at the Highland games?

McNab hadn't believed Marnie's confession and he thought she'd been hiding something, even though it meant her going to prison.

The doll, with its sewn-up eyes and mouth, suggested McNab was right.

As for Tizzy's origins, her DNA sample would contain her birth father's DNA, and if her father had already been in trouble with the law, they would be able to identify him on the database.

Glancing at the wall clock, Rhona registered how quickly the day had gone. Then her brain reminded her of her evening date with Jamie at Ashoka.

'Fancy a drink before your curry?' Chrissy said with a hint of glee as she passed on her way to the changing room.

'Of course,' Rhona said, trying to maintain an air of calm. After all, how awkward could it be? She and Jamie had managed to walk and climb together for a week. Eating a curry would be just as easy.

Even though she announced this internally, she already suspected it wouldn't be. However, a large glass of white wine at the jazz club beforehand might manage to still her nerves.

'Is McNab coming?' Chrissy said as she discarded her hazmat suit.

Rhona shrugged as though she didn't know.

Chrissy shot her a look. 'You're not planning on inviting him to join you and Skye man at Ashoka?'

When Rhona didn't respond, she threw her a look. 'You are,' she said.

'If he's there, I might,' Rhona admitted.

Chrissy laughed. 'And that definitely won't be weird.'

Rhona changed the subject. 'Anything back on the fingerprints you lifted from the tape?'

'Nothing as yet,' Chrissy confirmed. 'I have DNA from the skin flakes. Just waiting to see if we have a match on the database.'

'Assuming the killer is a UK citizen,' Rhona added. 'And, judging by the way the story's developing, that might not be the case.'

'I'm sure our police friends over the water will help us with that,' said Chrissy, who was now enveloped in a thick black puffa jacket, her pink flame hair hidden by a beanie with a very large pompom.

Exiting through the main gates of the university, they set off down University Avenue before cutting through University Gardens and down the back path into Ashton Lane and the jazz club.

There was a smattering of snow on the cobbles. Frosted and slippery, they were reflecting the overhead trails of multicoloured Christmas lights.

'What are you planning for Christmas?' Chrissy suddenly asked.

'I haven't thought about it,' Rhona admitted. 'I don't

really do Christmas, so I'll probably work at home and buy a dinner from M&S.'

Chrissy turned to look at her. 'Sean usually makes you Christmas dinner,' she said.

'Maybe not this year,' Rhona told her honestly.

Chrissy eyed her for a moment before saying, 'Then you should eat with us. Mum, me and wee Michael.' She halted there. 'Come to think of it, I should invite McNab too. Now that we're all sad singles.'

They'd reached the entrance to the jazz club, so Rhona was saved from having to reply.

Heading down the stairs, they met the warmth on entry. Glancing round, Rhona saw no sign of Sean, but that didn't mean he wasn't there. As co-owner of the club, he could be in the back office. She registered yet again that she hadn't listened to his recorded message, so was none the wiser about how he thought things were between them.

As for her, she preferred it to stay like that. For now anyway.

Chrissy was already in front, steering her way through the after-work crowd, mostly from the university, both staff and students.

A female pianist Rhona didn't recognize was playing on stage to accompany her voice, which was low and throaty, like a siren's song. *That must be Charlene*, Rhona thought, the club's latest acquisition, signed up by Sean Maguire, of course.

She briefly wondered if Sean cooked for her too before McNab managed to catch her eye and beckon her over.

'The usual?' he checked, before signalling her order to the barman. 'I wanted a word with you,' he said, drawing her to one side. 'About Marnie Aitken.'

'Good,' Rhona said. 'I wanted to talk to you too.'

'She's definitely left Glasgow and gone back to Kilcreggan,' McNab told her. 'I called the café there, by the pier. Joan, the owner, knows me from way back when it happened. She says Marnie came in recently and bought some homemade tablet. The kind Tizzy liked.'

'Marnie's staying in her old cottage?' Rhona asked.

'She thinks so. She saw smoke coming from the chimney, but no electric light. She hasn't gone to check yet, but I suggested she did, and to let me know if Marnie's okay,' McNab said.

'Chrissy found a lock of, we presume, Tizzy's hair inside the doll,' Rhona told him.

McNab looked distraught at this. 'She gave that up?' When Rhona nodded, he said, 'She must be desperate to do that.'

'She didn't take the forensic course so didn't know that the roots of hair are better—'

McNab interrupted her. 'She's trying to get you to identify Tizzy's father.' He ran his hand through his own auburn hair. 'I wanted to know who the father was back then, because he was without doubt a bastard. But it didn't fit with the oh-so-simple story of a troubled woman drowning her own child. Through wilful neglect or by accident.'

'That's why you left the case?' Rhona said.

'Thrown off it, more like. Some folk don't like their investigative methods being challenged.' McNab paused for a moment. 'Things are hectic with the farmhouse case, but if you'd like we might find time to go visit Marnie. See if she's willing now to say more face to face?'

'Let's try to do that,' Rhona said, wondering if getting Magnus aboard might be a good idea too.

Switching subjects, she asked if McNab had eaten. 'I'm

going for a curry at Ashoka after this,' she said. 'Meeting up with Jamie McColl from Skye, who's here in Glasgow for a couple of days.'

McNab gave her a sideways look she couldn't interpret, before saying, 'Our man in Skye, is it?' and laughed. 'Well, if you need a chaperone, I'll be more than happy to assist.'

Rhona had to smile. 'Thanks. I owe you one.'

'She got you, didn't she?' Chrissy sidled up to say. 'I didn't need to read your lips,' she told Rhona. 'Just interpret McNab's facial expressions from afar.'

'So when are we eating?' McNab said with relish.

At that moment, Rhona's mobile rang. Checking the screen, she answered. 'Hi, Jamie. I was just about to call you.'

'I'm already at Ashoka with a starter,' he told her. 'Couldn't stave off the hunger any longer.'

'We'll be there shortly. I'm bringing DS McNab with me, but I promise we won't talk shop,' Rhona said before ending the call.

McNab, she thought, looked like the cat that got the cream.

'You might not be talking shop, but that doesn't mean I won't,' he said with a grin.

34

She'd been rationing her use of the Tilley lamp at night. Relying on the firelight until she could finally fall into a fitful sleep.

She would rise as soon as the grey dawn found its way into the room and boil a kettle for tea. Black, of course, because she'd decided that milk was a luxury she couldn't afford.

She'd bought only one small luxury from the café near the pier. A Christmas present for Tizzy. Homemade tablet. Her favourite.

She'd contemplated making it again here in the cottage, remembering how much Tizzy had loved stirring the mix of sugar and condensed milk until it was just the right consistency to melt in your mouth. But the wave of emotion at that memory had convinced her to buy it instead.

She'd thought she'd managed to keep its purchase a secret from her daughter, but the tinkling laugh when she'd arrived back with the precious packet told her she hadn't.

'No peeking,' she'd said. 'You'll just have to wait until Christmas.'

This morning, as she sat sipping her tea, she heard the bells on the tree jingle and knew Tizzy had joined her.

'What shall we do today?' she said to the shadows. 'Go to the beach or visit the old church for holly?'

The expected answer didn't come and the silence that followed frightened her by its emptiness.

Rising, she went outside to stare across the water to Gourock.

She wondered if Dr MacLeod had found the lock of her daughter's hair inside the doll. She wondered what she would do with it.

She wondered if they would use it to discover who Tizzy's father was.

She turned from the water and took the path to the main road, intent on visiting the old church where there was a holly tree with bright red berries, branches of which they'd planned for the windowsills in the cottage.

Why hadn't Tizzy answered her when she'd asked where she wanted to go today, either the shore or the old church, despite both being favourite destinations? The fear that her daughter had left her again began to bloom.

'Please stay with me until Christmas at least,' she muttered as she entered between the stone gateposts of the old abandoned church.

The snow cover here was light and partially melted by the meandering burn that ran off the steep hillside behind. Sometime in the past, when the church had still been in use, the burn had been kept clear and channelled towards a drain. Neglected now, it spread like a delicate fan across the former well-kept grounds.

At that moment, Tizzy, wearing her favourite red welly

boots, appeared to splash through the surrounding puddles, shrieking with glee.

'So you haven't abandoned me . . . yet,' Marnie said thankfully.

Here, at the rear of the church, all was shadowy and overgrown. Ivy, rich and green and ignoring winter, wound its way through the dead deciduous branches as though reaching towards the holly tree.

> *The Holly and the Ivy*
> *When they are both full grown*
> *Of all the trees that are in the wood*
> *The Holly bears the crown*

She sang the words of the Christmas carol as she snipped at the trails of ivy with the kitchen scissors and broke off the holly branches with the most number of berries.

And all the time she knew that Tizzy was singing along with her in her high, birdlike voice.

At last she had enough and stopped, although she wanted to extend the magic of the moment as long as she could. As she departed the church grounds, she could still hear the splish-splashing of Tizzy's wellies as she danced through the spreading waters of the burn.

Seeing the curl of the woodsmoke from the stove as they walked down the track, she thought of the hot tea she would make to warm herself up.

The moment she pushed open the door, she knew someone was or had been in the cottage.

Standing rigid on the threshold, she felt for the scissors in her pocket, grasping them tightly, and shouted for whoever was in there to reveal themselves, all the time thinking she should turn and run.

But the smaller, higher voice of her daughter told her to stay. And so she did.

35

The runner Kenny from the movie set, whose second name turned out to be Dalglish, much to McNab's amusement, was waiting for him in the interview room.

'So I take it your dad's a Celtic fan?' were McNab's opening words.

'Ha bloody ha. If I only had a tenner for everyone that asked me that,' Kenny said. 'And yes, he is . . . was. He died a year ago. Used to frequent the Beechwood Bar back in the day where young Kenny met his future wife, Marina. Talked about it all the time. Big Jock Stein went there too. A real gent, he said.'

'You don't have a string of other players as your middle names, I hope?' McNab asked.

'Naw. Thank God. Sometimes I say I'm Kenny's grandson. Gets me free drinks in Celtic pubs at match times.' He grinned at this point. 'So you didn't bring me here to ask me that?'

McNab admitted he hadn't. 'There's a twelve-year-old boy missing, Alistair Feeney. We think the guy you saw arguing with Jason Endeavour might have something to do with that.'

Kenny looked aghast. 'What the fuck? Why would he be interested in a kid?'

McNab explained that the kid may have seen something related to the murder at the farmhouse in Elder Park.

'I saw the dead guy's description on social media. He could have passed for Jason.' He looked thoughtful. 'But it definitely wasn't him?' he checked.

'It definitely wasn't,' McNab assured him.

He watched as Kenny made a calculation. 'But maybe it was meant to be?' he said.

'Maybe,' McNab agreed.

'And the kid saw something. Or this guy thought he did?'

'It's a possibility,' McNab acknowledged.

'Fucking hell. Right, just tell me what you want me to do and I'll do it,' he said, determination in his voice.

'We'd like you to help create an identikit picture of the man you saw arguing with Jason.'

'Sure thing, but I can maybe go one better. I took a photo of the bastard.' He pulled out his mobile. 'Want to see if it's good enough?'

McNab definitely did.

After much flicking through his collection, Kenny alighted on the right one and handed the phone over.

The image definitely wasn't a close-up, but it was a clear shot of the two men in what looked like a face-off. The man had short dark hair and his height and build was similar to that of Jason. He had dark stubble and looked to be in his thirties. It wasn't an identikit picture but it would be good enough to show Leo. See if it was the guy who'd been looking for Ally.

'That's when you saw them arguing?' McNab said.

'Yes,' Kenny confirmed. 'I think he wanted Jason to go

somewhere with him and Jason was saying no, because he was due on set about then.'

'Did you think they knew one another? Maybe from before?' McNab asked.

'Not sure,' Kenny admitted.

'What about the guy's voice? From around here or maybe a Yank?'

'Definitely Glasgow. Jason had perfected an American twang that he could drop into. With this guy he was pure Glasgow.'

'Can you send this to the same number you rang me on.' It was more of an order than a request and, when his phone signalled its arrival, McNab checked it to make sure.

'Right, that's all for now,' he said, rising. 'You can go, Mr Kenny Dalglish. And thank you.'

'You'll let me know when you find the kid?' Kenny said in a determined fashion.

'I will,' McNab promised.

Leo, whose surname turned out to be Fratelli, was waiting for him in reception. Having said his goodbyes and thanks to Kenny, he then asked Leo to follow him and retraced his steps to the interview room.

The Scots Italian looked different without the white coat. He smelt different too, the mouth-watering scent of fish frying being replaced by what McNab assumed was aftershave or male cologne.

The voice, however, was the same. Plus the willingness to help in any way he could.

McNab retrieved his mobile and, bringing up the photograph taken by Kenny, slid it across the intervening table.

'Do you recognize either of these two men, Mr Fratelli?' McNab said.

Leo's dark brown eyes moved from McNab's face to the mobile. He drew it closer and, fetching a pair of glasses from an inside pocket, settled them on his nose. Only then did he lift the mobile to study the image.

McNab saw the recognition in his eyes before he voiced it.

'The dark-haired man on the right is the one who came into the shop asking after Ally Feeney,' he confirmed. 'I also recognize the man on the left with the auburn hair,' he added. 'I believe he's gone missing from a film set in the Merchant City. Police Scotland have posted his image online.'

'You're sure the dark-haired man is the one who came looking for Ally?' McNab stressed.

'Yes,' Leo said firmly.

'How did the identikit meetings go?' Janice asked as soon as McNab entered the office.

'Kenny had a photo on his mobile of the dark-haired guy arguing with Jason,' he told her.

'That's good—' She halted there when she saw his expression. 'Isn't it?'

'Leo recognized him as the guy who came looking for Ally at the chip shop,' McNab said.

'Oh, God,' Janice said, looking as worried as he felt.

McNab gathered himself. 'There's no evidence that the chip shop guy ever found Ally. Remember, Leo sent him on a wild goose chase. Darren, on the other hand, did threaten Ally. So my bet is still on Darren being behind Ally's sudden disappearance.'

Well aware he was voicing this for his own benefit as well as his partner's, he continued, 'Darren's also way down the pecking order of whatever drug gang he's working for.'

'But he knew about the naked body,' Janice reminded him.

'There's a big difference between knowing about something and doing it.'

Janice was prevented from responding by the boss's door opening and his command for both of them to come and speak to him.

Janice glanced at McNab. 'What's up?' she said.

'Something serious by the look on the boss's face,' he told her.

Heart rate rising, McNab said a brief prayer that this wasn't going to involve the body of a boy, and headed for DI Wilson's office.

On their entry, the boss motioned them over to his computer screen showing a black police officer sitting at a desk, behind which was an impressive shield with 'Chicago PD' on it.

'This is Detective Samuel Johnson from the Chicago Police Department, who has kindly joined us now despite the time difference. He's very interested in the movie being made here in Glasgow and any links it may have with organized crime here or in his city.'

'Good to meet you both, Detectives McNab and Clark,' the man said in a deep and resonant voice. 'DI Wilson and I know each other from way back when I visited your police college in Tulliallan.

'He recently sent me through the movie script currently being filmed in your city of Glasgow and explained about the likely connection with your murder enquiry. My team here have also pointed out similarities in it to both past and more recent criminal activities here in Chicago.'

'You believe Jason Endeavour may have been targeted because of those similarities?' McNab asked.

'We're assuming so,' the American detective responded. 'The fact that the victim turned out to be Jason's unknown brother suggests a possible botched job by whoever made the hit.

'We're running the DNA and fingerprints from your crime scene through our own databases. Although, if the order did come from here, it's more likely a Glasgow hitman would have been recruited to carry out the job.'

DI Wilson came in at this point. 'We've just received CCTV footage of someone resembling Jason leaving a Glasgow nightclub in the early hours of the morning following his reported disappearance, where he's approached by a man. After which they then walk together towards a dark van.'

'Was the man dark-haired and the same height and build as Jason?' McNab asked.

'It's a poor-quality image,' DI Wilson said. 'Tech are running it through their software to try to improve it.'

McNab explained about the van that Dreep had seen picking up his brother Darren, and the photograph taken by a witness of the man who'd come looking for Ally Feeney.

'This is the twelve-year-old boy you told me about who may be a witness in the murder case?' Detective Johnston asked.

DI Wilson confirmed that it was.

His American counterpart expressed his deep concern. 'The people behind this will stop at nothing to cover their tracks and accomplish their goal, which means that the boy is also in danger.'

He was only echoing what all three in the room already knew.

36

Last night's Ashoka story having been related over breakfast, Rhona now awaited Chrissy's reaction. She didn't have to wait long.

'He's what?' Chrissy said, open-mouthed.

'Getting married. In the spring,' Rhona repeated, her own laughter bubbling up to meet Chrissy's.

'And that's what he came to Glasgow to tell you?'

'Not exactly,' Rhona admitted. 'He was here on family business.'

'Jamie told you this in front of McNab?' Chrissy said.

'He waited until McNab took a trip to the Gents and then quickly explained. Said he'd felt awkward when he arrived and Sean was there. Then in the morning it was weird again so he suggested the meal out so we could chat freely.'

'And then you'd invited McNab along,' Chrissy said with a laugh. 'So why did he feel he had to tell you in person? He could have just phoned or texted you,' she suggested.

Rhona shrugged. 'We've been friends for a long time?'

'Or he thought you were becoming something else?' Chrissy said.

Rhona thought back to her week on Skye during the

summer. She'd spent a lot of time with Jamie. In fact, he'd taken time off work so they could do some walks and climbs together.

As though reading her mind, Chrissy said, 'And where was the girlfriend when you were there in the summer?'

'In New Zealand visiting relatives apparently,' Rhona told her.

McNab's return from the Gents had brought an end to the conversation, although Jamie did manage to issue an invite to the said wedding just as McNab slid back into his seat.

'Who's getting married?' he'd immediately asked.

'Jamie is,' Rhona had told him. 'Next spring,' she'd added.

McNab had offered her a look at this point that clearly indicated his thoughts surrounding this, before he offered his congratulations. Having described this particular scene in more detail to Chrissy, Rhona now joined in with her laughter.

Eventually, order restored, they disposed of the breakfast debris and got kitted up.

'The toxicology report's through for our unknown victim,' Chrissy said. 'I was wondering how they got him up there in the farmhouse. He looked fit enough to fight an attacker off.' She handed Rhona a copy of the report.

Rhona took a look. Routine tests had been performed and the presence of alcohol and cocaine found, but not in substantial quantities.

'If their intent was to torture him, they would have wanted him to feel it,' Rhona said, an image of the broken body they'd examined still sharp in her mind. 'Which suggests more than one attacker could have been involved,' she added. 'The gate on to Govan Road had been forced open, apparently. So a vehicle could have brought him in that way.'

'Once he was taken upstairs and secured, it only needed one man to do the job,' Chrissy said. 'But why take him there unless it held some significance for the killer or for the man they thought was Jason?'

'And if the killer knew Jason from his past here in Scotland,' Rhona said, 'he wouldn't have made the mistake of torturing and killing the wrong man.'

Chrissy nodded thoughtfully. 'But if he only had a photograph, it would be easy to mistake our victim for the guy all of TikTok was looking for.'

'And are still looking for,' Rhona reminded her.

Going back to their individual tasks ended their discussion. Work always brought Rhona a sense of peace, even though the circumstances that led to it were often violent.

When the woman in the Lilias Centre had asked how she could deal with dead bodies all the time, she'd replied by saying she thought of them not as bodies but as people, with stories and sometimes secrets to tell.

Their latest victim, the man they at present thought had been mistaken for a brother, perhaps one Lewis McLean never knew he had, was still a man of mystery.

He'd been in his twenties, handsome and in good health according to Dr Sissons. They'd found no clothes in the room that he might have been wearing, but Rhona suspected they would have been of good quality. His nails had been trimmed. His hair styled. No rings or watch, which they'd assumed had been taken by his assailant.

The police had issued a description of him, of course, minus a live photograph, but as yet no one had come forward. Someone, somewhere out there, knew their victim.

A lover maybe. A workmate or neighbour. And, of course, parents. One person both brothers must have shared, even if only for a short while, was their mother.

Had she raised either of the boys herself? Or had she given both up for adoption?

Just as I did with Liam.

Rhona stopped there. She no longer blamed herself for doing that and now had contact with her son, who had sought her out as a teenager, just as she'd begun to look for him. Reconciled now with one another, they met up once or twice a year, when he wasn't travelling the world.

Thinking about parentage brought Marnie Aitken and Tizzy to mind again. They hadn't made a formal request to run Tizzy's biological father's DNA through the national crime database, because as far as the police were concerned, the case was closed, and they had nothing to argue against that. Apart from Marnie's attempts to gain their interest.

We should go to Kilcreggan, as McNab suggested, she thought, *and speak to Marnie face to face, now that we know where she is.*

Perhaps she would be ready to reveal more now. Tell them the secrets she'd been keeping for the past six years.

At this point, Rhona glanced towards the doll that sat nearby. Chrissy had taken pity on the little Highland dancer and, having freed its eyes and mouth, had stitched it back up and looped the lock of hair over its right hand.

Rhona decided in that moment to return the doll to its owner.

If the doll was free to tell them her secrets now, so might Marnie be.

37

The club was called the Red Dragon and, arriving at its entrance, a thick door buried in a sandstone wall, McNab was struck by its resemblance to the sex club featured in the movie script.

This time, however, neither the fictional Detective Boyd nor himself required a battering ram to gain entry. Instead, a press on the buzzer was sufficient to bring a swift response from the manager, a tall and well-built guy in his fifties who introduced himself as Michael Russell, and suggested McNab might call him Mick.

Entering the main area of the club, he indicated that McNab should take a seat at a nearby table.

'Can I get you a coffee, Detective Sergeant? I just made some fresh for myself,' he offered.

When he received a 'yes' in reply, Russell disappeared through a swing door into what McNab assumed was the kitchen.

Meanwhile, he took in his surroundings.

The Red Dragon motif was everywhere, its scaly red presence eyeing him from behind the bar and replicas of it swirling round the walls.

The centrepiece of the large room was, of course, a rostrum with three shiny red-and-black-striped poles arising from it, their dragon heads breathing red lights like replica fires.

Around the stage were black tables with the dragon motif repeated, just like the one he currently sat at. And, finally, plush red alcoves lined the outer walls under the eyes of the dragons, where he assumed the private lap dancing offering took place.

The manager set McNab's coffee on the table in front of him. 'I saw your request on social media and I thought the TikTok guy had been in here before he went missing. We don't cover the inside for obvious reasons, but when I looked at the security footage from outside the entrance, there he was,' he said, looking quite pleased with himself.

'Is this the man you saw?' McNab said, passing over his mobile.

The manager studied it before pointing at Jason. 'Yep. That's him all right,' he confirmed. 'Had a ringside seat when Moondance was performing.'

'Moondance?' McNab repeated, thinking he recognized the name from some song or other.

'Our star pole dancer. The one most folk . . . men come to see,' Russell explained.

'And he was one of those men?' McNab asked.

'He was. Paid extra for the seat closest to her pole,' Russell told him.

'What about the other guy in the photograph?' McNab pointed at the dark-haired man.

After a moment's study, he shook his head. 'It might well be him on the security footage, but as for inside here, I couldn't say.'

'So they weren't together in here, then?' McNab checked.

'Definitely not. TikTok guy was alone and only interested in Moondance.'

'Anyone else come over and speak to him while he was here?' McNab tried.

'Not to my knowledge. After Moondance performed, the two of them went and sat in one of the alcoves and had a chat.'

'No lap dance?' McNab said.

He shook his head. 'No lap dance. That's not a Moondance thing. She's pole only.'

'So when did he leave?' McNab said.

'Not sure, but the time'll be there on the tape.'

'This lady called Moondance,' McNab said. 'I'd like a word with her.'

His request brought the first cloud to cover Russell's face. 'She's not here. We don't open until nine o'clock,' he said.

'You have her contact details?' McNab asked.

The facial storm was growing darker. 'We're not supposed to reveal those. Punters might . . . well, you know?'

'I'm not a punter,' McNab reminded him.

'It's just that the girls all have other lives they like to keep private,' he said. 'They only dance in the evening.'

McNab's studied expression seemed to change his mind.

'Okay. Her name's Karen Bell. She works as a guide at Kelvingrove Art Gallery and Museum. That's where she'll be, I expect. This is her mobile number.' He produced a card from his wallet with the name Moondance on it in red-and-gold writing and a number. 'You'll need to tell her I didn't want to give it out, but seeing as you're police . . .'

McNab didn't react to his request. 'As a matter of interest, did Ms Bell ever mention knowing Jason Endeavour before she met him in here?'

Russell shook his head. 'Not to me, no.'

Back at the car, he checked in with Janice and told her the outcome of his visit to the Red Dragon club. She listened attentively, then asked if he was heading for Kelvingrove and did he want her to meet him there.

McNab considered this for a moment. 'Can you spare the time?' he said, thinking a female officer might be a wise move when approaching Moondance.

'I'll see you there in twenty minutes,' she said and rang off.

On his way across town, McNab tried to piece together all the disparate bits of the Jason puzzle. Since the dead man definitely wasn't the actor, they had to assume, until proved otherwise, that Jason was alive and most probably hiding somewhere in Glasgow. Either that or he'd skipped the country altogether.

He knew he was consciously separating Ally's disappearance from that of Jason. Was that to save his sanity or because he was relying on his gut reading of the whole scenario, despite the fact the guy looking for Ally had also come looking for Jason?

Ollie had spent considerable time trying to identify the dark-haired bloke, but it seemed he had no prior convictions that they knew of, so wasn't known to the police.

He'd also asked Ollie to check out former Conservatoire drama school graduates from six years ago, looking for Jason and the guy seen talking to him, in case they knew each other from back then.

As for the dead brother, they'd had no luck as yet in finding a next of kin for him, or even someone looking for a missing person that matched his description. Possibly because they had no photo of him alive and well and couldn't openly promote the fact that he resembled TikTok's missing star.

Reaching Kelvingrove, McNab pulled into the rear car park. Getting out of the vehicle, he could hear the roar of the River Kelvin sweeping away the remains of the melted snow and the heavy rain that had followed in its wake.

Looking up at the university, he thought back to last night and the entertaining fiasco he'd been witness to. He was still convinced that Jamie McColl's visit had been more than just to give news of a possible wedding. In fact, he thought McColl had come to check whether Rhona felt in any way the same about him as he obviously felt about her, before he decided to marry whatever her name was.

Join the queue, McColl, McNab muttered to himself as he headed for the back entrance to the Museum and Art Gallery.

Entering the impressive main hall, he made for the café section where he planned to order a double espresso. While at the counter, however, his stomach reminded him that he hadn't as yet had breakfast, so he ordered a Caramel Log from the available biscuits, which immediately conjured up an image of Dreep's face when he'd produced the packet of biscuits and the can of Irn-Bru.

'Hey,' Janice said on approach. 'Something bad happen? Your face . . .'

He waved the remains of the Caramel Log at her. 'The wee bloke Dreep likes these. Either that or he was half starved.'

'Both may be true,' Janice told him. 'There wasn't much in the way of food in the house. I gave his mother the address of the nearest food bank, but I'm not sure she'll go. I suspect whatever money's coming in, it isn't a lot.'

'Dreep said his brother only comes home when he's run

out of money,' McNab said, remembering their conversation. 'That's probably where all her money goes,' he added.

'And I thought drug dealing paid well,' Janice said.

'Only for the ones at the top,' McNab told her. 'And I don't think Darren's up there.'

'So,' Janice said, 'tell me about this Moondance.'

McNab related what he'd learned from Russell.

'Okay, I'll go and check if she's about. Where do you want to talk to her?' Janice said. 'Maybe here over a coffee? Easy and relaxed?'

'Good idea,' McNab agreed.

When Janice went off towards reception, McNab settled down to wait and think about how they should play this. Judging by Russell's expression when he'd left, McNab suspected that he may have already warned Karen Bell that they were going to turn up here. So there was always a chance she could have bolted. Then again, Russell would know if that did happen McNab would be straight back to the Red Dragon to confront him.

As he'd related their meeting to Janice, a number of things had crossed his mind. One of them being that this was all a set-up. That Russell had sent in the footage to the police so that he was in on their search for Jason. Maybe he, or whoever he worked for, was keen to locate the TikTok star too.

Not unsurprising, if the aim was the social media promotion of the Red Dragon.

But there was an alternative interpretation.

As he began to contemplate this, he spotted the two women crossing the mosaic floor towards him. They looked, if not pals, then definitely acquaintances. God, Janice was good at this part of the job, he thought, and not for the first time. Have the interviewee on side and you get, if not the truth, then closer to it.

Then again, if Karen had been warned of their coming, she would have her story ready.

The nearer she came, the more McNab began to appreciate how a guide at the museum might at night turn into Moondance. She was tall and dark and very pretty. In fact, he would put her in the beautiful bracket. Although it was her movement that proclaimed her as a dancer.

McNab composed himself and rose to his feet. 'Ms Bell,' he said, 'good to meet you.'

She nodded and sat down.

'You're free to chat to us?' he said.

'I'm due my lunch break, so yes,' she told him, her direct gaze meeting his own unflinchingly.

'I'll get our coffees,' Janice said. 'You need another?' she asked him.

McNab found himself shaking his head.

As Janice joined the queue, he said, 'Thank you for agreeing to speak to us.'

'It's about Lewis?' she asked.

'You knew Jason Endeavour as Lewis McLean?' McNab said.

She nodded. 'We were at the Conservatoire together. I did musical theatre. He was an actor.'

'Tell me about him,' McNab said.

She took a moment. 'He was good, very good. But when we graduated, there wasn't much work here. So he headed for the US, where a lot of Scottish actors had gone. It took a while, but he made it.'

McNab wanted to ask about her but didn't have to.

'I didn't leave,' she said. 'So now I dance at night

and work here during the day, and take part in amateur musicals.'

He thought she might be sad about that, but if she was, it wasn't apparent in her voice.

'Tell me about meeting Lewis at the Red Dragon,' he said.

Janice arrived at that moment with their lattes and Karen waited until she'd sat down.

'I'd heard he was in town. I follow him on TikTok. I said "Hi" online and he turned up at the Dragon. Watched my show and then we talked,' she said simply.

Before he could urge her on, she continued herself. 'He wasn't happy. Something about the script. Wasn't sure it would work.'

'Was he afraid for any reason?' Janice said.

'More concerned, but he didn't say why exactly.'

McNab nodded at Janice to ask the next question.

'Did you know Lewis has – had a brother?' Janice corrected herself.

By Karen's reaction she obviously didn't. Either that or she was a good actor too.

'He never mentioned a brother. He told me he was brought up in care from a baby. In and out of foster homes. Really shite.' She hesitated. 'I know he was in trouble as a teenager. Got in with a bad crowd.'

She looked at McNab as she said this and he had the strange feeling she could read his own history.

'But he got out, did his degree and headed off.' She switched her look to Janice. 'You said *has*, then *had* a brother. Is he dead?'

It was McNab that responded. 'The body found in Elder Park recently was DNA'd as Lewis's brother.'

'God.' She covered her mouth in horror. 'I thought the

description sounded like Lewis, but when he was still reported missing, I realized it couldn't be.'

'We're concerned the killer might have thought it was Jason Endeavour when he was attacked,' Janice said.

'But why would anyone want to kill Lewis?' she said. 'I know TikTok stars get stalkers but . . .'

McNab came back in. 'It's imperative we find Lewis, and as soon as possible.' He held her gaze. 'If you have the slightest idea where he might be hiding, or where he might have gone, you need to tell us.'

He watched as she struggled with this and he couldn't decide if she knew something and had promised not to tell, or just wished she did.

'He gave me a mobile number and asked me to keep in touch,' she said. 'But when I texted him, the number wasn't valid.' She shook her head. 'I assumed he wasn't interested now he's a star so I just deleted the number.'

McNab brought out his mobile and showed her the photograph. 'What about this guy?' he said. 'Do you know him?' He enlarged it to focus on the dark-haired man.

She was taking the question seriously and her expression suggested she just might.

'I think I've seen him before, but I'm not sure,' she said finally. 'A lot of men come into the Red Dragon,' she added pointedly.

'What about that night with Lewis?' Janice tried.

'No, not then.' She shook her head.

'Maybe back at the Conservatoire?' McNab suggested.

Her brow puckered. 'I'm sorry, I don't know.'

'Okay,' McNab said, handing her his card. 'And thank you, Ms Bell. If you think of anything else, or Lewis makes contact, you'll let us know?'

As she walked away from them, McNab said, 'Let's go,' and headed towards the back entrance and the car park.

'You're not happy,' Janice said as they descended the steps. 'You think she's lying?'

'Not lying, exactly,' McNab said. 'Just not telling us the whole truth. My bet is that she's in contact with Lewis McLean and is intent on checking with him first, before she says anything more.'

38

Marnie didn't run away as she'd wanted to, but instead stepped inside as Tizzy had ordered.

There was no one in the room or, she knew instinctively and without checking, elsewhere in the house.

But there had been.

While in prison, she'd grown able to recognize the smell of everyone she'd shared a cell with. She'd realized that all humans have an individual scent that lies beneath the shower gel and the deodorant.

It was after she'd watched a TV programme in which a Syrian man, who'd written about human rights resulting in his imprisonment for eight years, had spoken about his seven fellow prisoners. Incarcerated in the dark for much of the time, he knew each one by their breathing, their footsteps and their scent, and did not need to hear their voices.

She'd practised this herself while in prison and had found it to be true.

Once she'd moved into the Lilias Centre she'd had her own room, but could still recall the breathing, the footsteps and the scent of all the women she'd once shared a cell with. All she had to do was close her eyes.

The scent in the room she now stood in didn't frighten her. In fact, it brought her pleasure.

Tizzy was the same. Running in, squealing with delight at what she discovered on the table.

The box held homemade tablet, of course, but other things too. Christmas sweets and biscuits, tinned food, cheese, a Christmas pudding.

There was also a note, which read . . .

> *DS McNab called the café to check if you were here and all right.*
> *This is from him.*
> *Don't be a stranger at the café.*
> *Merry Christmas when it comes.*
>   *Joan X*

Marnie stood for a moment drinking in the scents and the pleasure the parcel and note had brought.

She wasn't an outcast here. Not at the café anyway.

And DS McNab remembered and was thinking about her. She hadn't told him what had really happened back then. But she'd always thought that he knew anyway.

She wondered if he also knew about the doll and Dr MacLeod and Magnus.

She wondered and wished and hoped he did.

39

They were arguing again, something about letting him go or . . .

Or what? Ally thought. Keep him here in the dark, or kill him?

They don't want to kill me, or it would have happened by now, he tried to tell himself. How long had he been here? He had to admit he had no idea. He remembered getting bundled into the van and told to shut up. What happened after that, he didn't know, except that he must have passed out from fear or from something they'd given him.

When he came to, he was here. Wherever here was, he could hear no signs of life outside it, except when voices were raised next door.

As soon as he'd come to, the guy from the van, a ski mask over his face, had questioned him about the photo he'd taken of the dead guy.

He'd decided to be honest, because he suspected they knew the truth already, especially if Darren was involved. So he'd told them how he, Kev and Dreep were in the grounds that night in the snow and had stumbled on the body. Dreep had taken a photo of it and they'd all run away and never told anyone. Except Dreep had dropped the mobile and when he revealed it belonged to his brother, Darren, he was too scared to go back to look for it. 'So I went instead,' he'd said. 'But the police were already there. I think they might have found it.'

His story wasn't enough, though, because the guy kept on asking questions, like, 'Did you go upstairs in the farmhouse? Did you see anyone? Did you check he was dead?'

He answered all the questions, including the last one, listening to the terror in his voice as he described placing his fingers on the dead man's neck, looking for a pulse and imagining for a moment that he might have found one.

After that they'd left him alone except to toss in a burger and a can of Coke now and again, which gave him hope that maybe they didn't want him to die.

He'd spent a lot of time thinking about his mum. How frightened she would be. Knowing if only he had told her the truth, this would never have happened.

He thought about Dreep and Kev too and how the police would have questioned them and would know everything now when it was too late.

Lifting his head out of his hands, he realized all was quiet. Had they gone out? Rising, he moved towards the door and listened, but all he could hear was the thump of his own heart.

Every time they'd gone away before, he'd tried to open the door and it was always locked.

Despite this, his hand reached down of its own accord to try again.

40

Every contact leaves a trace.

Dr Edmond Locard's famous words effectively said that with contact between two items, there would be an exchange.

In this particular case, whoever had tightly bound the victim's wrists to the arms of the metal chair had not worn gloves and had left evidence of themselves in the form of skin flakes.

The single and partial fingerprints that Chrissy had also carefully lifted from the tape had not been identified. The DNA from the skin flakes, however, had been more successful. Although the route taken had been a more complex one.

Which was the reason for her assistant's beaming countenance.

'There wasn't a match on the National Database, so I did as you suggested and tried for a familial connection with the skin flake DNA,' Chrissy said.

A familial DNA search offered up names of potential relatives of an alleged perpetrator.

'How many names came up?' Rhona said, knowing it could be a lot.

'Fifty,' Chrissy admitted. 'But one in particular looked interesting.' She handed Rhona a printout. 'Jack Boyd's on our system. He's thirty-six and is from Glasgow – Govan, in fact – and has served time for violence, drug offences and running prostitutes. Nothing recent, though. And we haven't found his DNA at the scene of crime . . . yet,' she added. 'Although there's a lot of blood samples still to run.' Chrissy paused, then said, 'Isn't it just a wee bit weird that he's called Jack Boyd and the main detective in the movie script is called DS Boyd?'

'And Jason Endeavour co-wrote the script,' Rhona said. 'Maybe there are other names in there linked to the real players in whatever was or is going on here in Glasgow or in Chicago,' she added. 'Has McNab seen any of this yet?'

'I thought you could send it through,' Chrissy said. 'In time for the strategy meeting.'

'Which is later today,' Rhona said, checking the time.

Changing the subject, Chrissy said, 'Any news on Ally Feeney?'

Rhona shook her head. 'Nothing, as far as I know.'

Since they'd been the first to meet and talk to Ally in Elder Park, they both felt a measure of responsibility for what had happened to him since then. Rhona couldn't help but wonder if someone had seen Ally talking to them and that's why he'd been targeted in the first place.

Ally knew nothing, of course, and neither did his two friends. That she was certain of. The three boys had simply been in the wrong place at the wrong time.

Returning to her own desk, Rhona forwarded their latest findings to DI Wilson and McNab and checked over what she'd prepared for the strategy meeting later.

The possible familial DNA lead to Jack Boyd was key to

what would happen next. If the police could locate him and bring him in, that might help break their case wide open.

But at the moment, all she could think of was the collateral damage that was the missing Ally.

Crossing town later, Rhona suddenly registered by the myriad of coloured lights and decorated trees how near it was to Christmas. As she'd said to Chrissy, she didn't really do Christmas. In their time together, that had been Sean's thing. No longer a practising Irish Catholic, Sean had still retained a belief in the wonder of the season.

It hadn't involved a religious ceremony, unless you regarded cooking a Christmas meal as a labour of love, which it was for Sean. When they'd first met, he'd been alarmed at her attitude to food as being functional and merely necessary, and had attempted to change this, eventually realizing that his love of cooking and playing the saxophone was matched on her side by her love for her work.

She briefly considered taking up Chrissy's offer of Christmas dinner with her family and McNab, but something told her that much was likely to happen in the few days left between now and then to make that impossible.

Parked up, she made a dash for the main entrance of the police station through the seasonal sleet. Once safely inside and with time to spare, she decided to give McNab a call and suggest they get together briefly in the canteen before the meeting.

Her call was swiftly answered.

'Did you get the news about Jack Boyd?' she checked.

'We did. I'm just out of the boss's office about it,' he confirmed. 'He's well pleased and we're already looking for him.'

'Have you time for a quick word?' Rhona said.

'I'll see you in the cafeteria,' he said and rang off.

Rhona's desire to speak to McNab was to firstly ask about Ally Feeney and then to bring him up to date on where she was with the Marnie Aitken situation.

As she saw him enter the cafeteria, Rhona realized she could often read his thoughts by the manner of his approach. The fact that he gave her a quick smile and nod before asking if she needed a refill for the coffee she'd only just purchased suggested that identifying a possible familial link to at least one of the perpetrators had definitely lifted his spirits, but it wasn't the only thing on his mind.

Arriving back at her table with his espresso, he pulled out a chair and sat down.

'We'll have to stop meeting like this, Dr McLeod,' he quipped. 'It's more fun at the jazz club and the drink's better.'

'Amen to that,' Rhona said.

'So I assume you've brought me here to ask me something, or else tell me something,' he said candidly.

She acknowledged this with a nod. 'Firstly, is there any news on Ally Feeney?' she said.

He shook his head, his mood openly deflating. 'Although I cling to the hope that he's okay,' he offered.

'Have you any evidence for that?' Rhona asked.

He shook his head. 'Just a feeling.'

It was a feeling she shared, but couldn't say why, either.

'So what is it you wanted to tell me?' he said. 'Apart from familial search results?'

'I think we should make that trip to Kilcreggan you suggested. I also think we should bring Magnus along.'

Now it was McNab attempting to read her expression, obviously trying to work out why she should suggest this. Rhona told him.

'I've had nothing back yet from Dr Mackie on her analysis of the soil and sand samples retrieved from the cottage. However, I have retrieved the child's DNA sample and have analysed it to produce the father's DNA, which I think Marnie wanted us to do.'

'You've run it through our database?' McNab said.

'We have no evidence that the child's father was either there that day, or has been involved in her disappearance, or any crime before or after,' she reminded him. 'I think we need to ask her in person about the doll's mutilation and why she sent it to me before we make a request to run his DNA.'

McNab was silent for a moment, although she could almost see his thoughts regarding what she'd just said. This was not an official or sanctioned investigation. They couldn't go further with it, until it was.

'You're right,' he admitted. 'Okay, let's take a trip over on the ferry and ask Marnie those questions.'

'With Magnus,' Rhona stressed. 'He was and still is our go-between.'

He shrugged. 'Sure. If you think it will help.'

'Have you been in touch with Marnie at all?' Rhona asked.

'Not directly, no.' McNab looked a little embarrassed, if that was possible. 'Although I did ask Joan from the café to deliver some Christmas stuff, biscuits and cake, to the cottage.'

Before Rhona could make any comment about this thoughtful gesture, he quickly rose. 'Right, better get back to the real investigation. I'll go on ahead and see you there.'

Rhona let him go, aware that he wanted to walk back alone. McNab might give the impression of being a hard man, but she'd been through enough with him to know how big a heart he actually had.

Finishing her coffee, she made for the Ladies, then headed to the meeting.

The room was fast filling up and she made her way through the gathering crowd intent on checking in with DI Wilson first. She'd sent him a copy of what she planned to say, along with the reported results of the familial DNA search.

It wasn't often that Bill looked a happy man. Not unless it was outside work, that is. Although the loss of his much-loved wife Margaret, through cancer, had hollowed him out for a while. It had been his two teenage children, Lisa and Robbie, that had kept him going during that time. McNab too had played his part, especially when his boss had considered quitting the force altogether.

Rhona imagined that had DI Wilson left the force, it was likely McNab would have followed.

'Dr MacLeod. Thank you for your good news this morning. We certainly needed it. There's an APB out on this Jack Boyd and a few others from the familial list you sent through.'

'The fingerprints we lifted didn't find any match on the database,' she told him. 'But we're also trying to identify low-level DNA from them too.'

'So more than one perpetrator at the scene of the crime?' Bill said.

'The toxicology report came back with alcohol and cocaine, but only in small amounts. If he was administered a date-rape-type drug, that would have been enough to incapacitate him and allow his easy transference to the locus, with no evidence of it afterwards,' Rhona said. 'Once they got him in there and secure, one man would have been enough.'

'If he was out on the town, looking or acting like the TikTok star, it would have been easy to spike his drink thinking he was Jason Endeavour,' Bill said.

'Even easier if they used a female to set him up,' Rhona said.

'My thoughts exactly,' Bill said, checking his watch. 'Okay, let's talk to the team and try to put some pieces of this puzzle together.'

41

Ollie looks startled, McNab thought, *like a deer caught in a car's headlights*.

He'd known the IT specialist long enough to realize that Ollie was very uncomfortable in crowds. He'd often wondered if Ollie's ability as a super recognizer meant that he was analysing every face in the strategy meeting, comparing them to photos he'd examined in the past, or even more recently. This, despite the fact that the room was supposedly full of the good guys.

Glancing round the sea of faces, he remembered how wrong that assumption had been not so long ago. Since then, the rotten apples had been removed. For now, anyway.

As the boss appeared, followed by Rhona, the company fell silent, eager as they were to hear if the rumours about a possible lead through DNA were true.

McNab had expected Rhona to say her piece first, but now saw that it was to be Ollie, and he wondered if the boss was keen to let Ollie escape as soon as possible from what was obviously an uncomfortable situation for him.

When Ollie came to the front and fired up the screen, he

appeared to relax a little, as though being back in charge of an electronic device had served to ease his fear and focus his thoughts.

As a series of photographs began to appear, McNab registered that he was looking at Lewis McLean in his younger days as a drama student, then Conservatoire graduate, then playing guitar in a band. That image, he realized, also contained Karen Bell, or Moondance, as a vocalist.

So she had been telling the truth regarding her friendship with the student Lewis, back then at least.

Finally came Lewis's transformation into American actor Jason Endeavour in a photoshoot for his upcoming movie entitled *Snake House*.

So that's what the film's called, McNab thought. Funny that had never been mentioned by either the director, Burt Carter, or Jason's fellow scriptwriter, Steven John Jarvis.

McNab hadn't revisited the film set as yet, but Kenny had been of the opinion that if Jason didn't reappear imminently, the movie would have to be shut down and the team head back to Chicago. Maybe that had been the perpetrator's intention all along, he thought, to remove the star and thus close down the movie.

'As you know, I spend most of my time going through captured CCTV footage trying to identify those involved in various crimes. I also trawl social media for the same reason,' Ollie was saying. 'When we established that Jason had been at the Conservatoire in Glasgow, it was easy to find photographs of him in that capacity and in his later career. His photo also threw up matches against other guys who looked like him. Once forensics established that the victim was in fact Jason's brother, I went back to these and investigated them further.

'The closest resemblance was to this guy, Robert Forbes, who I believe is our victim. He also had a presence online that gave some details of his upbringing in Glasgow, including the fact he had a brother.

'Social services department records show that their mother, Amy Forbes, died of a drug overdose when the boys were aged three and two, at which time Lewis and Robert were taken into care. Robert kept his mother's surname, Lewis did not. His last foster family was called McLean.

'They obviously shared a father by their DNA but he isn't registered anywhere that I can find.'

'Have we put this information out in the public domain yet?' McNab asked.

'The name and photograph of the victim will be on the news tonight, plus social media,' DI Wilson said. 'Hopefully someone will come forward either from family or friends.'

McNab wasn't so sure of that. Anyone close to the victim might well not want to make themselves known to the police, especially since the killing had the hallmarks of a gang reprisal.

But by which gang? A Glasgow-based outfit or a Chicago one?

Ollie, having related his tale, now left, with a quick nod to McNab on exit.

It was Rhona's turn and she too used the screen to explain the DNA trail that had led them via skin flakes and a familial DNA search for the perpetrator to a number of potential family members, including one Jack Boyd, thirty-six years of age, with multiple convictions for violent assault, drug offences and running prostitutes.

However, what the familial search hadn't helped with was

his current whereabouts. Boyd hadn't apparently registered on the police radar for the past five years. That didn't mean he wasn't still plying one of his various trades, just that they hadn't caught him doing so.

Bill took over now, thanking Dr MacLeod, who moved to join the audience.

McNab mouthed over to Rhona that they would speak later about the Kilcreggan trip, and she nodded in response.

Seeing Janice enter, McNab crossed the room to join her.

'Any word on Ally?' he said as soon as he was close enough.

'Nothing,' she replied. 'His mother is sick with worry.'

How can a street-savvy kid like that just disappear, McNab was about to say, before the image of a four-year-old girl in Highland dress crossed his mind. Kids' disappearances were rare and they or their bodies were usually discovered not long afterwards. The first twelve hours of the search were crucial, and they were well past that now.

'Anything further on Darren's whereabouts?' he checked.

'Nothing, and nothing on the van either.'

'It'll be in a garage somewhere, getting a paint job and new plates,' McNab said. A constant stream of vehicle changes were essential to keeping the drug distribution ongoing and below the radar.

The boss was back on stage now, with a new image on the screen. It appeared the team were about to meet their Chicago counterparts, who were presently six hours behind them. McNab hoped the opposite might be true regarding the investigation.

Detective Samuel Johnson appeared to greet them, together with two senior officers, Hindel and Kwiatkowski.

The conversation focused firstly on the *Snake House*

script, which had apparently gone through a number of rewrites in an effort to tone down the original by Jason Endeavour.

'According to SJ,' Johnson told them, 'it sounded too near the truth, especially the Chicago gang connections with Glasgow, which we are aware of.'

McNab raised his hand at this point. When given the go-ahead by the boss, he said, 'The DS in the movie script is called Boyd. We now have a familial link from the crime scene locus to one Jack Boyd. Our Boyd has a string of convictions this side of the pond, although he's been off our radar now for five years. Is this merely a coincidence or was Jason pointing up a connection?'

They all waited as the three from Chicago had a brief confab.

'We're still studying the script for insights into what may have happened because of its contents,' Detective Johnson eventually said. 'We'll make a note of that possible connection and get back to you on that. Thank you, DS McNab.'

'What happened here in Glasgow has all the hallmarks of a gang reprisal,' DI Wilson offered now. 'Any thoughts on that?'

'Probably exactly the same as your own,' Detective Johnson said. 'That whoever is running the Jamesie Brothers' worldwide operation doesn't like the movie script, its writer or its main lead.'

'Jack Boyd went off our radar five years ago. We wondered if he might have turned up on your shores,' DI Wilson said.

'We'll check if you send everything you have on him through.'

'Will do,' the boss assured him. 'One other thing . . . the signature sewing of the eyes and mouth. Is that something you are familiar with in your local crime syndicates?'

'Let's say it's a thing in certain gangs, both here and in South America, usually associated with someone who couldn't keep their mouth shut,' Johnson said.

They signed off then and, after a few words of continued encouragement, DI Wilson sent his team back to work.

'What's wrong with your face?' Janice said as they headed back to their desks.

He was disgruntled and it obviously showed, so McNab decided to tell her why.

'Robert Forbes or McLean or whatever you want to call him died on our patch, i.e. Glasgow. It's our job to find the bastard that sewed up his mouth and eyes and pushed him to his death. Not Chicago PD.'

'It's called trans-Atlantic cooperation,' Janice tried.

'It's called fucking failure,' McNab said. 'I'm off out. Call me if Ally turns up, dead or alive,' he said sharply.

Janice caught his sleeve as he turned to go. 'Where exactly are you going?'

'Where the gangs of Chicago meet the gangs of Glasgow,' he told her.

The set hadn't been disbanded, although there was little evidence of the bustle of his previous visits. It looked like Kenny had been right. Without their star, they couldn't keep paying the crew for work that wasn't happening.

He wondered about the director, Burt Carter, and Jason's two sidekicks, Jerry Borstein and Ragnar Ryan. Were they still here waiting for their star to return or had they already headed back stateside?

He had no experience or knowledge of how this world of movie-making worked. It took a lot of money, that he did know. And it aimed to make even more back.

After they'd finished their interview, Kenny had told him a story to explain how that worked. His tale had involved a Scottish script at the Cannes Film Festival being taken up by a supposed Italian company. It was only when the Swedish producer had been flown to Italy to talk to the interested investors that he'd discovered it had been Russian money that had been on offer, and he would be required to open a British bank account for the money to be deposited therein.

If the film failed to make a profit, he'd feared he would be kneecapped or worse.

McNab had laughed when Kenny had regaled him with this tale, but Kenny didn't remember it as funny at the time, since the producer had been a mate of his.

Had that story been a subtle way of telling him what was really going on with the *Snake House* film? Just like the Chicago police had thought?

Having walked past the now unmanned security barrier, McNab found his way back through an almost-deserted lot to the camper-van he'd first encountered at the Hidden Lane. There were no sounds from inside, and his first knock went unanswered. The second one was much louder and accompanied by a demand to open up.

This time he heard some muttered fucks from inside, before the door was flung open by a bleary-eyed Ragnar smelling strongly of marijuana. A sudden realization as to who his visitor was brought a brief moment of clarity in which Ragnar rid himself of the joint and promptly stood on it.

'Can I come in?' McNab said, already doing so and taking a quick look round through the lingering smoke. 'So where's your mate Jerry?' he said.

'Gone,' Ragnar managed.

'Gone where exactly?'

'Back to the States, to LA,' he said, his expression suggesting he wished he'd gone with him. 'With Jason still missing, we had to call a halt to our shoot here in Glasgow,' he explained.

'So the movie's cancelled?' McNab said.

Ragnar shrugged. 'As a mere production assistant, that decision's way above my pay grade.'

'So who else has gone?' McNab said.

'All the big boys, the director and producer, the other American actors.' He looked bereft at that.

'Why not you?' McNab asked.

'I've to wait another week.' He gave a sigh. 'Just in case.'

There was something in the way he said this that alerted McNab to – what exactly?

'You still expect Jason to turn up?' he said, before pausing for a moment. 'Or you know he will?'

Something crossed Ragnar's face, so that McNab saw the lie coming and held up his hand to stop it.

'When did you last speak to him?' he demanded. 'And before you check your memory, remember who you're talking to. I can remove your mobile. I can keep you in Scotland indefinitely. I can charge you for withholding information in a murder enquiry.'

The bleary eyes from before were now doing a merry dance.

'Well?' McNab said.

The words finally appeared. 'He called me yesterday. He

doesn't think it's safe to come out yet. They killed his brother because they thought it was him. Now they know it wasn't.'

McNab, trying to control his fury, held out his hand. 'Mobile,' he demanded.

42

They'd eaten a few of the goodies DS McNab had sent. She'd chosen the Christmas biscuits. Tizzy, the homemade tablet. After which she'd finished stitching the Christmas stocking for Tizzy to hang up on Christmas Eve.

She'd slept well afterwards and woke up, if not happy, then not in despair.

Tizzy was still with her so it seemed she intended to stay for Christmas. Their last one together. That thought made her sad, but she knew she shouldn't show it or Tizzy might take fright and leave too soon.

Opening her eyes in the dawn light, the first sight she'd seen was the waxy green holly on the windowsill, its red berries glowing.

She'd lain there remembering her first Christmas in the cottage. Her flight here when she knew for definite she was pregnant. She'd been terrified that he would discover where she'd gone and come looking for her.

For a while she'd watched the ferry, but if he did locate her, he would never come by passenger ferry. She knew that. He would come by car, and she couldn't watch every car that arrived by the long and winding road from Glasgow.

Back then she'd had to keep reminding herself that she had never spoken of her childhood here. Never mentioned her own dead mother. Or her father either. If she had, he wouldn't have listened anyway. She was his now, he'd told her. To do with as he pleased.

She rose then to end that train of thought and got the stove going again and boiled the water and had her mug of tea. And all the time she imagined she could hear Tizzy playing round and about her. Chatting and singing and sometimes practising her dance steps.

Today would be the day, she decided. It was the last thing she had to do before they celebrated Christmas properly together.

She had to tell Tizzy the truth of that day six years ago.

Making sure they were both wrapped up warmly, she led the way up the track and on to the main road. Passing the café, she considered Joan's kindness in delivering DS McNab's Christmas parcel and thought briefly about going inside to thank her.

Don't be a stranger, she'd written on the note. And *Merry Christmas*.

Turning on to the Fort Road, Tizzy ran ahead, skipping and jumping. Earlier rain had made puddles and she splashed through them in her red wellies.

The water baby, they'd called her.

Eventually they left the curve of the road and moved onto the beach at Portkil Bay.

'I know where we're going,' Tizzy sang in her childlike voice.

But her voice would be older now. Her red wellies wouldn't fit. Neither would her dancing pumps and her kilt.

Marnie waved such thoughts aside. As long as Tizzy was here with her. That's all that mattered.

She felt a cold dread sweep up and over her the closer they got to the ancient sea cliffs with their shallow fissures and overhangs. In the summer the entrances were hidden behind ferns and wild flowers and clumps of heather.

She could still remember their scent as it was in the warm summer air.

She began to count the crevices, Tizzy's voice repeating the numbers behind her as they picked their way across the slippery stones.

Then they were there.

'We've reached the place,' Marnie told Tizzy. 'Let's go inside.'

43

The ferry from Gourock was passenger only. To go to Kilcreggan by car would have involved a long trip by Gareloch and Faslane. Something no one wanted or could afford the time to do.

So they took the fast road to the pier at Gourock. McNab alone in his vehicle. Rhona with Magnus.

The trip had finally been arranged when they'd met after work at the jazz club the previous evening. Few words had passed between McNab and Magnus then. Nothing unusual about that. With Rhona as go-between, the desirability of the trip had been established and the decision to go the following morning.

Magnus was keen to discover how Marnie was managing in the outside world. He also had a message to deliver to her from Dr Sara Masters. As far as they were both aware, Marnie was not in digital contact with the outside world. Nor did she have a mobile, having left the one provided for her back at the hostel.

So Sara had organized a replacement, with money registered to it and a recorded message from her. Magnus had put his number on it too. As had Rhona and McNab. All four of them trying to assure Marnie that they were still interested in her welfare.

As they boarded the ferry at Gourock, the swell from the midwinter winds frothed the surface of the estuary. Magnus, used to crossing the wild and wayward Pentland Firth to his Orkney home, was unperturbed. McNab was not so keen, and obviously glad that the trip over didn't last very long.

Rhona, standing with a view of the fast-approaching Rosneath Peninsula and the snow-topped high ground behind, wondered what Marnie must have been thinking as she'd viewed Kilcreggan getting closer.

It had been brave to come back to this small community after what had befallen her here. Most prisoners, used only to walking short distances during their incarceration, often found a simple expanse of road on the outside challenging. What must it have felt like to venture so far? To be on public transport again, train and boat? To cross this expanse of water? To arrive home after six years in prison?

She could hardly imagine.

When they docked at the small pier, McNab led them up to a row of buildings that housed a bar, a shop and the all-important café he'd made contact with.

'I suggest we get a coffee,' he said. 'I'll check with Joan if Marnie's been in recently and whether she got the Christmas delivery I organized.'

The café was gloriously warm after the bitter chill of the crossing. Rhona headed for a table at the window, Magnus following, while McNab gave their order and asked to speak to Joan.

The young girl behind the counter prepared their coffees, then went to seek out Joan. When McNab brought their drinks over, he indicated that he was going through to the back.

'It's better if Joan and I talk in private,' he explained. 'Word will get out soon enough that we're here,' he added.

When McNab had disappeared from view, Rhona asked Magnus if Marnie had ever talked about her home here.

'She spoke about Kilcreggan, yes, and the cottage,' he told her. 'When she did, she seemed to be back here in the time before it all went wrong.' He halted there for a moment. 'Her cottage isn't far from the pier going west. She said there's a track down to the beach where she taught Tizzy to swim. Before she started taking her across in the ferry to the outdoor pool in Gourock.'

He stopped again, a shadow crossing his face. 'I think something happened in Gourock. Something that frightened her, but she wouldn't say what. She stopped going there, whatever it was. Tizzy was sad about that.'

'I wonder what it was that scared her away?' Rhona said. 'Or who it was?' she added.

'My thoughts exactly,' Magnus said.

At this point, McNab reappeared to take his seat beside them.

'When Joan delivered the parcel, Marnie wasn't at the cottage, but the stove was lit and it looked like she was sleeping on the sofa,' he told them. 'She said there's no power and Marnie's been using a Tilley lamp. She goes out walking along the shore and she's been seen at a derelict church along the road. She hasn't been back to the café since that first time.'

'Three of us arriving together might be too much,' Rhona said. 'Why don't you go first?' she suggested to McNab. 'Then call us if she's okay about seeing us too.'

McNab seemed to be contemplating this and, Rhona suspected, was about to reject her suggestion. She'd sensed his discomfort at being back here from the moment he'd stepped off the short ferry crossing. He'd been convinced he'd let Marnie down six years ago, and was, she thought, reliving that now.

His reply seemed to confirm this.

'I think you should be the one to go,' he eventually said. 'It was your visit to the prison that started all of this. It was you she sent the doll to.'

'I agree,' Magnus said quietly.

'I'll walk you to the road end, you can take it from there,' McNab said. 'We'll wait back here for your call.' He stood up then as though it was decided.

She'd spoken to Marnie for only moments during the prison visit and not since. Whereas the two men had talked to her about her life in general and what had happened six years ago. Rhona wasn't convinced she should be the one to make the first approach.

Perhaps reading her concerns, Magnus said, 'There was a rapport between you two that day at the Lilias Centre. Something I don't think either myself or Sara ever managed to achieve. And she did send you the doll.'

The doll that was the beginning of everything.

'Okay, I'll go,' Rhona said and rose.

McNab was silent as he led the way along the main road. Rhona wanted to ask him questions, but knew he had no wish to answer them. He'd known Marnie six years ago in the midst of the horror of losing her daughter. He'd suspected back then she wasn't guilty of the crime she'd confessed to. He had no idea what she was like now. What he did know was that Marnie had confided in her and asked for her help.

McNab, a little ahead of her, had stopped. The track he stood alongside had nothing to indicate where it was going and it was obvious no vehicle had been down that way in quite a while.

'The track stops just short of the beach,' he said. 'You likely won't catch sight of the cottage until you reach the gate because of the height of the hedge.' He hesitated. 'Good luck.'

'I'll call you,' she said, before heading down the track.

The snow at sea level had gone and the muddy ruts were studded with puddles and the shape of footsteps leading both ways. Her forensic eye noted three in particular, ranging in size: a small childlike print, a medium one and a large one, going in both directions.

McNab had indicated that the cottage was the only dwelling down the track, but if it went almost as far as the water, then it was likely used to access the beach, she reasoned.

The gate came on her unexpectedly, hidden in a tangle of overgrown bushes and hedgerow, as McNab had suggested. It wasn't until she was through the gate that she could see the cottage properly.

It had been painted white at some point in the past, but was now stained by damp and neglect. Its red metal roof had survived the elements better, the once-blue wooden door not so much.

Rhona noted the faint curl of smoke from the single chimney, but no light from any of the small windows.

Gathering herself, she used the old brass knocker, listening to its echoing sound, which was followed by silence. She reached for the door handle and turned it. The door opened with a groan. Setting it at a few inches wide, she called out this time.

'Marnie, it's Dr MacLeod from the Lilias Centre. You sent me your Highland doll. Can I come in?'

When no one answered her request, she stepped inside the kitchen–living room. On the table sat what she believed to be the Christmas parcel McNab had ordered. Taking a closer look, she found the star-like biscuit packet open and the same with the homemade tablet, the resultant crumbs evidence of their consumption.

There was bright-berried holly on the windowsills and a tiny decorated Christmas tree in the corner minus lights. The duvet and pillow indicated that Marnie had been sleeping on the couch. On its arm lay a red-and-green-felt Christmas stocking with the name 'Tizzy' beautifully embroidered in cross stitch around the top.

Only then did Rhona register the tiny dance pumps and slippers near the still-warm stove.

In that moment, she remembered her own loss all those years ago, when she'd handed over her baby son, thinking she would never see him again.

What had happened here, six years ago?

The woman who'd embroidered that Christmas stocking, who'd made that beautiful doll – how could someone with so much love for her child cause their death by drowning?

On the surface it didn't make sense. And yet, some women did harm their children, even kill them, often because of abuse they'd suffered themselves. Or because they wanted to spare their child such abuse. Death for some women meant freedom from the horrors of their life.

But apparently Marnie had lived here happily with Tizzy for four years. Taught her to dance and swim. Something had happened six years ago to change all that.

Not wanting to be found inside the house if or when

Marnie should return, she wrote a brief note saying she was at the café and that she would really like to chat to her, and that her number along with Magnus's and DS McNab's was on the phone.

Alongside the note, she placed the doll, with the lock of Tizzy's hair and the mobile.

Then she left, closing the door quietly behind her.

44

Her mobile rang as she reached the end of the track. It was McNab to say he was on the return ferry.

He told her why. 'We've located Ally Feeney.'

'Is he okay?' she asked, dreading the answer that might follow.

'Alive and definitely okay. He got away somehow and, realizing he was in Partick, went to his gran's house. She just called me. Did you see Marnie?'

'She wasn't at the cottage so I left her a note and the mobile and told her we were at the café.'

There was a short silence before McNab said, 'Wait there as long as you can. If she doesn't call, you and the Prof try the cottage again. Last ferry back is half six.'

He didn't say 'don't miss it', but she knew that's what he meant. Without a vehicle, there was no way back tonight if they did.

Walking along the road to the café, she spotted a small, slight figure approaching and sensed almost immediately that it was Marnie Aitken.

As she drew closer, Rhona realized she was humming a tune and intermittently speaking – to whom? The sound was muffled by the distance between them, but Rhona could make out some of the words, which sounded like dance instructions.

'Head up. Point toes. *Pa de ba*.'

Rhona stood motionless, caught up in both the image and sound of this strange performance. Then Marnie suddenly looked up and saw her. Surprise filled her face, but not fear, Rhona was glad to note.

'You came,' Marnie said. 'Good.'

Buoyed up by her reaction, Rhona smiled in reply. 'I went to the cottage, but when you weren't there I left a note and a mobile with my number on it. I also brought back the doll and the lock of hair.'

Marnie considered all of this for a moment; then, looking down as before, she said, 'Dr MacLeod came. I told you she would,' and smiled.

Trying not to be nonplussed by all of this, Rhona said, 'Can we talk?'

Marnie nodded. 'Of course. Come on,' she ordered. 'We're getting cold.'

Once inside the cottage, Marnie removed the duvet and pillow from the couch. 'It's warmer sleeping in here,' she said. 'You can sit and I'll get the fire going again.'

Opening the stove door, she threw some logs on the smouldering ashes. 'The kettle's still warm so it won't take long to boil.' She pulled it onto the hot plate, then set about lighting the Tilley lamp.

'I don't have milk for the tea,' she warned as the warm light of the oil lamp began to drive away the shadows.

'I like mine black anyway,' Rhona told her.

At this point, Marnie took off her welly boots and put them on the opposite side of the stove to the tiny dance pumps.

'May I message Magnus at the café?' Rhona said. 'Tell him where I am?'

Marnie nodded. 'But tell him I want to speak to you alone.'

Rhona sent the message, then settled back in the warm glow of the fire. As the shadows receded, she noted again the items from the Christmas food parcel.

'I understand McNab sent you those,' she said as she accepted her mug of tea.

Marnie nodded. 'Would you like a Christmas star biscuit?'

'I would,' Rhona said.

'Tizzy likes the homemade tablet the best. It was always her favourite.' Marnie looked towards the tree as though someone was there.

The sudden feeling of another presence in the room transported Rhona back to the time after she'd given Liam up for adoption. In the weeks that had followed, she'd woken constantly in the night hearing his cry. She'd behaved as though he was in her arms, soothing him, talking to an empty bundle, sure he hadn't yet gone.

When she resurfaced from this memory, she found Marnie staring at her. 'You know what's happening here?' Marnie said.

'I do,' Rhona told her.

'But you don't know it all. That's why you've come.' Marnie nodded to a shadow near the small Christmas tree. 'It's time we told her, Tizzy. It's time we told Dr MacLeod the truth.'

45

The boy looked unharmed and had been in the shower recently, his hair still wet. He wore clothes that didn't quite fit, obviously supplied by his gran, who couldn't take her eyes off him, even as she addressed McNab.

'He looked a mess. Smelt bad too. When I opened the door and he was there . . .' She tailed off at that, her emotions getting the better of her.

At this point Ally put his arm around her. 'I'm okay, Gran. Can you make Detective McNab a cup of tea? I need to tell him what happened.'

'Of course, son. I'll do that,' his gran said.

Once she'd left, Ally let down his guard, his face crumpling a little.

McNab made him sit down.

'You've spoken to your mum? McNab checked.

'Yes. After Gran called you. She knows I'm telling you what happened.'

'We can wait a bit, until you're ready,' McNab offered.

'First, I need to take you to the place they kept me. I think I remember how I got here but I'm not sure.'

'Okay,' McNab told him. 'Go explain to your gran what

we're doing and we'll have the tea when we get back. And, Ally, tell her not to wash the clothes you were wearing. Just put them in a bin bag. Make sure she does that.'

Ally nodded. 'I shouldn't have had the shower,' he said apologetically. 'Gran insisted.'

'No matter,' McNab told him.

When the boy headed for the kitchen, McNab called Janice. He'd held off until now because he wanted to see Ally alone first, before the whole police machine went into action.

'He's fine,' he assured her. 'They scared him, but didn't hurt him. He's taking me to where he was kept. He's worried if he doesn't do it now, he'll forget the way. I'll call you when we find the location and you can bring the team.'

'I take it his mum knows he's okay?' Janice checked.

'She does,' McNab assured her.

Ally reappeared at this point, looking happier. 'The clothes I was wearing.' He handed McNab a bin bag, knotted at the top.

'Right. Let's go,' McNab said.

It took a while as Ally tried to retrace his route from where he'd been incarcerated to his gran's house. It had been dark when he'd got out and he'd lost all track of time while in captivity. He had no idea where in Glasgow he was and was afraid to be seen, in case they came after him. So he'd hidden in a shed in a back court until the sun had come up.

Eventually realizing that he was north of the river and to the east of the Clyde Tunnel, he decided to make for his gran's in Partick. Cold, hungry and fearful about sticking to the main road, he had zigzagged his way through the back streets, trying to take note of his route.

Even when they had to double back in the car a couple of times, McNab held his tongue, aware of how disorientated the boy must have been. He knew how that felt having escaped from captivity himself in London during a previous case. Lost, bare-footed, bloodied and stinking to high heaven, a rough sleeper had taken pity on him and summoned the Simon Community's night patrol.

Eventually they reached a boarded-up building that had once been a pub and was now destined for demolition to make way for the ever-expanding riverside flats phenomenon.

'This is it,' Ally said, his face white with tension.

'You're sure?' McNab checked.

He gave a little nod.

'Okay, where did you come out?'

'Round the back. You have to get under or over a fence,' he said, eyeing McNab speculatively.

'My name's not Dreep,' McNab said. 'But I'll manage that all right.'

His attempt at a joke brought a little colour to Ally's face.

'Right. I'm going to call this in. Then I'll take a quick look round the back while you stay in the car and wait for the cavalry. Okay?' McNab said.

'Shouldn't I show you how to get in?' Ally asked.

'You okay with doing that?' McNab said. 'Or do you just want to see me climb that fence?'

That brought a half-smile, which would do for the moment, McNab decided.

The kid was right, he thought, when he saw the height of the mesh fence. 'Okay, you said there was a way under?'

Ally nodded. 'Further on a bit.' He led the way round the perimeter, eventually stopping and shifting a sheet of corrugated metal to expose an opening.

'You'll have to squeeze through,' he offered.

'You first,' McNab said.

Ally wriggled through no bother. McNab not so much.

'Right,' he said, brushing himself down. 'Lead the way.'

The door Ally led him to was unlocked and opened easily. McNab stood for a moment, listening. When he was sure he heard nothing from inside, he said, 'I'll go first. You follow. Tell me if I have to turn right or left.'

After moving through a narrow corridor and what may have been the back kitchen, they came to the main area. There were two rooms, one leading into another, just as Ally remembered.

'I was in the back one. I heard them in here,' he said, standing on the threshold.

'Okay,' McNab said, with a quick glance round. 'Now we go back to the car and you tell me what happened in as much detail as possible.'

It was a story that had begun in Elder Park with Ally being drawn back once again to the crime scene. As he described it, McNab understood the pull the place exerted on the boy, who was no doubt still reliving the discovery of the victim, naked and bound to the chair. He hoped Ally never had to see such a thing again.

Then they moved on to the snatch, and him being pushed into the back of a black van. The fact he'd seen no one's face and didn't recognize any of the voices except that they were from Glasgow wasn't helpful.

'What about Darren?' McNab tried.

Ally shook his head. 'If he was there, he never spoke. I would have recognized his voice.'

It appeared they'd fed and watered him via burgers and Coke. Asked plenty of questions but didn't hurt him.

'Then they went and left the door open,' Ally finished up.

'Why do you think they let you go?' McNab said.

Ally thought for a moment before saying, 'I think the last one that questioned me believed my story that we'd seen nothing, except the body.' He went silent then, as though he might have remembered something else.

'What?' McNab tried.

'He had a Glasgow voice like the others, but sometimes it changed,' Ally said. 'Like he was trying to sound American. Dreep does that sometimes after he's seen a movie.'

Noting the expression on McNab's face, he added, 'Does that help?'

'It does. Very much, Ally. Thank you.'

46

They were on the open top of the Island Princess, a sharp wind whipping round them, the light beginning to fade.

'There,' Rhona said, pointing to the far right. 'Portkil Bay, about a mile along the Fort Road from the harbour. That's where Marnie said the cave is where she and Tizzy often went.'

There hadn't been time for them to take a look, but if what Marnie had said was true about the nature of the cave, Jen Mackie would likely be able to confirm it as a possible match for the material retrieved from the cottage.

Rhona had recorded Marnie's story on her phone, anxious not to miss anything in the intensity of the moment. There were still many questions to be asked, but she felt that Marnie had begun to shine a light on that day at the games and what may have happened to Tizzy because of it.

Deciding how much of it might be made up or even imagined was more in the province of a criminal psychologist like Magnus than a forensic scientist like herself.

As the lights of Kilcreggan retreated, they turned to watch the harbour at Gourock approach, each nursing their own thoughts about what had happened.

Heading to the car, Rhona suggested they might listen to the recording on their return journey to Glasgow. After which Magnus could be sent a copy to consider in more detail, perhaps together with Sara Masters. She would also send the recording to McNab, who would ultimately decide whether to progress with it further.

'What d'you think?' Rhona said as Marnie's story drew to an end.

'My first instinct is that it's the truth, as far as she's willing to reveal it,' he said quietly.

Rhona felt the same. 'And her constant referrals to an imaginary Tizzy?' She asked the question that worried her most.

'People talk to their dead loved ones all the time,' Magnus said. 'I do it, especially when I'm at home in Orkney. I feel my father's presence constantly with me. It's a great comfort.'

Rhona didn't mention her own experience with baby Liam. At the time she'd put it down to post-natal depression, but later she'd begun to analyse it differently.

'Strangely, I felt a presence in the cottage too,' she admitted. 'Maybe it was the little dance pumps, the half-eaten tablet and the shadows that seemed to form the shape of a child.'

'It's like being in old buildings – churches are a powerful example,' Magnus said. 'St Magnus Cathedral seems to me to hold all the voices, hopes and prayers uttered in there in its very stones. Especially for me at least, when I stand beside John Rae, asleep on his plinth.' He gave a little laugh. 'I can imagine him awakening in front of my eyes and standing up. Probably because he's a hero of mine, so I'd love to talk to him.'

'So you think Marnie's talking to Tizzy to keep her alive in her head?'

Magnus nodded. 'I do. Sometimes the dead feel closer than the living.'

'There are places Marnie won't go in the house,' Rhona said. 'Her bedroom, for example. The duvet and pillow are from Tizzy's bed.' She halted there. 'I think there's something still missing from her account.'

'You didn't ask her about their trips to Gourock?' Magnus said.

'I didn't question her at all. Just let her tell her story,' Rhona said. 'When she stopped, I thought she had more to say.'

'And Tizzy's father? No mention of him?'

Rhona had been saving this for the end of their discussion. 'Yes, but before I started recording. She said the reason she'd sewn the mouth shut on the doll was because he'd done that to her. Sewn her mouth shut and locked her in a dark cupboard for two days. She'd just found out she was pregnant with Tizzy.'

Magnus, his expression displaying his horror at this, said, 'Did he know she was pregnant?'

'She said she never told him, just made up her mind to escape.'

'But what if he did find out?' Magnus said.

Rhona thought back to the end of the recording. The manner in which Marnie had suddenly stopped talking and looked to the shadow beside the tree. Had the imagined Tizzy silenced her? And if so, why?

'Let's see what McNab thinks, once he listens to it,' Rhona suggested.

'Agreed,' Magnus said, looking relieved.

The rush-hour traffic having slowed them down, Rhona decided to head straight home rather than visit the lab, dropping Magnus at his riverside flat on the way.

'You don't want to get a drink?' Magnus suggested.

Seeing his expression, Rhona decided to say yes. 'We'll drop the car near my place and walk to Ashton Lane,' she said. 'I'll text Chrissy and tell her that's what we're doing.'

'And McNab?' Magnus asked.

'Him too. Although he might still be following up on things with Ally Feeney.' She'd told Magnus the good news about the boy as soon as she'd reached the café.

'But if he does make it, we can at least toast the boy's safe return,' Magnus said.

'That I would like to do,' Rhona agreed.

It's not what people say, it's what they don't say, Rhona thought as she and Magnus walked together in silence through the park and up over the hill towards Byres Road. She found herself reflecting on the silences in Marnie's recording. The moments when she had gone quiet, looking over into the corner as though being coached in what she should say next, or not say at all.

Battered women had been taught forcibly to still their tongues. None more so, it seemed, than Marnie, if her story of having her mouth sewn shut was true.

'You're thinking about the silences in the recording?' Magnus suddenly asked.

'It's that obvious?' Rhona said.

'Silences often mean more than the spoken word, psychologically speaking,' Magnus offered.

'When I was working on the thread from the victim's mouth, I checked out the tropes around lip sewing,' Rhona said.

'Me too,' Magnus told her, 'although to be honest I already knew about them, especially when they're used as a form of protest. Or in the case of women, as a form of control.'

'Like Marnie,' Rhona said. 'As for gangland victims, it's used as a message that the corpse talked too much when alive. A bit like an inversion of the Glasgow Smile, where a razor attack on both cheeks leaves a victim with scars that turn his mouth into an upward grin.'

Magnus grimaced. 'God. That's one aspect of it I hadn't thought of,' he said.

'That's because you're not from here,' Rhona told him. 'Although I think your Viking forebears had their own way of showing their displeasure regarding those who talked too much.'

They'd reached the club and, descending the stairs, were quickly enveloped in warmth, music and chattering voices. In that moment, Rhona was glad she'd not gone straight home to continue with her analysis of what Marnie had or hadn't said.

'You made it back,' Chrissy said. 'With no doubt loads to tell?'

'Yes,' Rhona said, 'but not at the moment. You've heard they found Ally, safe and well?'

'Of course I have,' Chrissy said with a grin. 'Good news travels fast.'

'I'll drink to that,' Rhona said as she was handed her glass of white wine. 'Is McNab going to make it?'

'He says he'll try to call in once he delivers Ally back to his mum. There's a SOCO team out at the place they held him north of the river,' Chrissy told her. 'The material they collect will come to us tomorrow.'

'Good,' Rhona said.

'Oh and one more bit of news,' Chrissy added. 'One of

the men who questioned Ally had a Glaswegian, sometimes American accent so—'

'McNab thinks it might have been Jason Endeavour,' Rhona finished for her.

47

He hadn't rung ahead to check if Moondance was at her day job. If she wasn't, McNab fully intended to get her address from her workplace and visit her at home. If she wasn't there either, he planned to camp outside until she returned.

If Jason Endeavour, aka plain Lewis McLean, was found to be hiding at Moondance's place, there were things he could charge her with. Obstruction and harbouring a fugitive being two of them.

His anger had grown overnight, despite the good news regarding Ally. Much as he was relieved by the boy's return home, he was furious that he'd ever been kidnapped in the first place, and possibly by a man they'd been putting all their resources into finding in order to prevent his death by his brother's killer. He didn't have definitive proof of this, of course, but Ally's convincing description of the Glaswegian voice moving into American at will pointed to the strong possibility of that being the case. If in fact it was Jason who had captured the boy and questioned him, this suggested to McNab that he wasn't trying to hide from the killer, but was perhaps trying to apprehend him himself – and do what?

Kill him, seemed the most likely possibility. And perhaps torture him first.

Had he known all along that he had a brother? Had they been mistaken when they thought the brothers had never known about one another?

No one had as yet come forward to claim Robert Forbes's body, despite their efforts to contact any family or friends online with the help of Ollie's findings. Which was odd to say the least. He was a handsome bloke who looked as though he should have had at least one woman wondering where he was.

How long had Lewis McLean known that it was his brother who'd likely died in his place? When did he realize it was meant to be him, tortured and trussed naked to a chair?

There were still too many questions and definitely not enough answers.

As McNab parked his vehicle behind the museum, he knew the only way to find those answers was to locate Lewis McLean and ask him.

And Moondance was going to help him do that.

Using the back entrance again, he went straight to Enquiries and, showing his ID, asked to speak to Karen Bell.

The man in charge gave him a worried look. 'What's wrong? Has something happened?'

McNab, curbing his tongue, repeated his request to speak with Karen without giving more details.

Catching the tone of his voice, the man said, 'If you give me a minute, I'll get her on the radio.'

'Don't mention the police,' McNab ordered.

The man's expression coloured even darker. 'Can I look at your ID again, please, Officer? I have a duty of care to our employees.'

McNab showed his warrant card again. 'Detective Sergeant McNab to see Ms Karen Bell,' he said.

'Right, Detective Sergeant, I'll call her now.'

McNab took a breath. She was in the building at least, which was a plus. In fact, he didn't have to wait long. This time on approach he noted that she didn't walk with the same grace and confidence.

She knows what's coming, he thought. *Or suspects she does.* What would her reaction be, he wondered? He supposed it would depend on the hold Jason, or Lewis, had over her.

The official made himself scarce when he spotted her imminent arrival. So much for protecting staff, McNab thought. Then again, if he suspected she was about to be arrested, it might be to save her from embarrassment.

Reaching him, she said, 'You wanted to speak to me, Detective Sergeant? I assume it's about Lewis?'

'It is, Ms Bell. I believe you know of his whereabouts and I'd like to speak to him in connection with the kidnapping of a twelve-year-old boy, Ally Feeney.' He'd kept his voice low but the tenor of it told her exactly how he felt about that.

He watched her hand rise to cover her mouth. As all colour slid from her face, he reached out in just enough time to stop her own accompanying slide to the floor.

Glancing about, he located the nearest chair, sat her down on it and waited, wondering if the collapse had been orchestrated like a dance movement, although the way all blood had departed her face had looked real enough.

Eventually she drew herself together and looked up at him.

'I have reason to believe you know where Lewis McLean, known as Jason Endeavour, is currently,' he said, 'and therefore could arrest you now. Alternatively, you take me directly to him.'

'I'd rather you arrested me,' she said. 'And take me to the station, please.'

It wasn't what McNab had expected to hear, but he wasn't going to quibble.

'Okay, let's go. My car's round the back.'

'I should tell my supervisor,' she began.

When the guy from before appeared on cue, it was apparent that he'd been listening behind the door.

'Karen,' he said, 'are you sure about this?'

'I'm sure,' she said firmly. 'If you give Shelley a call, she'll cover for me.'

It was an easy exit and a quiet drive back to the station. En route, McNab informed Janice of their imminent arrival, and that he would take Ms Bell to the interview suite.

He left her there, to stew he hoped, while he went in search of coffee.

As he waited for the machine to disgorge the required caffeine fix, he acknowledged, if only to himself, that Ms Bell had blindsided him with her desire to be arrested. Why this had been the case, he had no idea. Except, among the criminal fraternity, it usually meant they were more frightened to be in the outside world than in a cell.

Was that the case with Moondance? And if so, why?

McNab found himself eager to find out.

He discovered Janice already seated in the interview room, which, by the look on Ms Bell's face, was a positive thing.

McNab had a small and secret smile to himself. If she thought DS Clark was a soft touch, she was about to discover how wrong she was.

Janice gave him a nod as he entered and he took his seat

alongside her. After the usual formalities, he relaxed back and left his partner to it.

It was a short initial skirmish. Ms Bell admitted that Lewis McLean had visited her at home later that night after they'd met at the Red Dragon Club. They'd reminisced about old times, had sex and he'd stayed over.

Next day, he had a call that worried him. 'Quite a lot,' she said. 'He told me things were going badly on the set, some problems with the script, and that he might have to lay low for a while, and could he stay with me.' She looked pained at this. 'We were a thing back in the day, so I said yes.'

'You saw the social media request by Police Scotland for any news on his whereabouts?' Janice asked.

She gave a little embarrassed nod. 'He told me not to worry, he would get in touch with the police and his employer once he'd worked things out. Anyway, his disappearance was good publicity for the movie.'

'Did he say what the problems with the script were?' Janice asked.

She shook her head. 'Only that he'd used some of his former life in it. Then we heard about the body in Elder Park. That really freaked him. The description of the victim sounded like him.'

McNab gave Janice the nod to ask the million-dollar question.

'When did he find out that the dead guy was his brother?' she said.

There was a moment's stunned silence before Karen looked up, her face drawn. 'He said he'd spoken to someone from the film set.'

'Ragnar,' McNab said to Janice. 'I confiscated his mobile. Ollie has it.'

'So he already knew he had a brother?' Janice asked.

Karen gave a little nod. 'They found one another online before he came here to make the movie. Robert was living in London. When Lewis told him he was in Glasgow, Robert came up to see him.'

If Robert was a Londoner, that might account for the lack of response to the Police Scotland appeal, McNab thought.

He came in then. 'Did Robert ever visit the Red Dragon?' he said.

It had been a shot in the dark, but by her reaction a good one, so he added, 'So it was Robert who came to see you that night at the club and not Lewis?'

The edifice she'd set up had begun to crumble. 'I thought it was Lewis . . . at first,' she admitted. 'I hadn't seen him for years.'

'Whose idea was that?' McNab said. 'Robert or Jason's?'

She shook her head. 'I don't know. But it was definitely Jason who came back to my place later,' she added. 'I'm certain of that.'

She didn't have to explain why.

'So Lewis used his brother as a decoy,' Janice said. 'And whoever was after Lewis got Robert instead.'

Karen's expression had become one of misery and guilt. 'He said Robert liked the idea of impersonating him. He loved the attention it brought him, especially from female TikTok fans. Neither of them thought . . .' She halted there for a moment. 'Lewis was horrified when he realized what had happened,' she said. 'He went crazy. Said he would get the bastards who did it.'

'Something that we can't let happen,' McNab said. 'At the moment he's only implicated in the abduction of Alistair

Feeney. You don't want murder added to that.' He paused. 'Want to tell us what you know about Ally?'

'Lewis told me that some local boys had found the body,' she said. 'And they'd dropped a mobile at the scene. He needed to check if they'd seen anything that might help him identify his brother's killer.'

The only way Lewis could know about the mobile was via Darren, McNab thought, which suggested that the gang Lewis was involved with prior to his move to the States was still operational, and Darren was a player in it.

'So that's why he kidnapped Ally?' McNab said.

'But he let him go,' she said. 'He told me he didn't harm him.'

'So where's Lewis now?' McNab asked. 'If you have any idea, you need to tell us. Remember, they know he's alive and will be looking for him. And maybe even you.'

'That's why I asked you to arrest me,' she said. 'But I don't know where Lewis is or what he plans to do.'

'But they likely think you do,' McNab said. 'You want to help us find Lewis? Make him and you both safe?'

She nodded, unsure what he might mean.

'Then we release you without charge,' McNab said. 'And you cooperate with us in finding Lewis before they do.'

'I don't understand,' she said.

'Take time off from the museum. But not the club. You haven't missed a night there yet?'

She shook her head. 'I don't work every night anyway.'

'When's your next appearance?' McNab said.

'Tomorrow, Saturday night. That's when—'

'They all come to see Moondance,' he finished for her.

48

His call had been brief. 'We have to talk, Dr MacLeod. Have you eaten yet?'

When she indicated she hadn't, he'd told her he'd bring pizza with him. A slight pause followed, after which he'd asked, 'Is your Irishman about?'

When she'd told him 'no', he'd rung off.

She was well aware what McNab's visit was about. When she'd sent the Marnie Aitken recording, she'd also told him what Marnie had said regarding her former partner, and Tizzy's likely father. Something Rhona knew McNab hadn't been aware of at the time of the investigation into Tizzy's disappearance and Marnie's confession.

It wouldn't be the first time McNab's gut feeling was likely to be nearer the truth than the official line taken in the enquiry.

By the time he arrived, laden with two pizzas 'in case you're as hungry as me', she'd had a quick shower and replenished Tom's food dish. Checking her mobile on coming out of the shower, she registered that she still hadn't listened to Sean's voicemail.

Deciding it wasn't the moment to do so, she'd answered the buzzer and let McNab in.

'I assumed you would supply the white wine and whisky?' he said, putting the pizzas down.

Rhona pointed to the usual cupboard and, with an appreciative nod, he fetched a glass and the whisky bottle, while Rhona poured some wine and helped herself to a slice of pizza.

Eventually, their hunger abating, McNab said, 'Okay, now tell me about your Marnie visit. Take your time and don't miss anything out,' he ordered.

He listened carefully as she described how she'd met Marnie on the road. How pleased Marnie had been that she'd come. The weird little asides as though Tizzy was there with her.

At this point, McNab looked troubled. 'You think she's lost it?' he said.

'I think being back in Kilcreggan has made her feel closer to her daughter,' Rhona told him. 'It's not unusual for folk to talk to those they've loved and lost.'

'What did Magnus think about it?' McNab asked.

'Just that,' she told him. 'There was a Christmas tree up in the cottage and she'd embroidered a Christmas stocking for Tizzy.' Rhona halted there for a moment. 'And, of course, the Christmas goodies you sent were on display.' She didn't say that Tizzy's favourite, the homemade tablet, had been partially consumed.

McNab was silent in response, staring off into the middle distance, his expression unreadable.

'She didn't tell you everything,' he said at last. 'There were a lot of silences in the recording.'

'I think she got scared,' Rhona told him. 'And couldn't voice her fears.'

McNab gave a nod. 'You think the fear was about her former partner?' he asked.

'I do,' Rhona admitted. 'You heard what he did to her. That's why she sewed the mouth and eyes shut on the doll.'

'Signifying that she was too afraid to tell the truth of what happened to Tizzy?' he offered.

Rhona had begun to think that way too. 'We need to try to identify Tizzy's father from her DNA collected at the time of her disappearance,' she said. 'Running his DNA through the database would be a start. If he's on it or someone close to him is . . .'

She could tell by McNab's expression that he felt the same.

'I plan to talk to the boss about that,' he said, pouring himself another dram. 'We know Marnie was working as a prostitute. He was no doubt her pimp and drugs supplier. But maybe there's more to stitching her mouth shut than just her personal story,' he added.

Which was what Rhona had been thinking, ever since Marnie had told her about that particular abuse. 'It was what? Ten years ago,' she said, 'but all the same . . .' She tailed off.

'As we both know, old habits die hard, Dr MacLeod,' McNab said with a keen look and a wry smile.

When Rhona didn't respond to this, he added, 'Let's see if Tizzy's father is on our database and, if so, what he's been up to in the interim.'

They lapsed into silence before McNab spoke again. 'And this cave Marnie mentioned before she went silent on what happened that day. Should we be taking a look there?'

'Her silence suggests the cave is significant, but she couldn't yet voice the reason. Trauma has that effect on people. You and I both know all about that kind of silence.'

He met her eye. 'We do indeed.'

'I sent Jen Mackie the forensic soil samples from the cottage,' Rhona told him. 'If her analysis of them points to Portkil Bay, then something happened there, probably involving the cave.'

As they were toasting to that, Rhona heard the front door open.

'You said your Irishman wasn't around?' McNab reminded her.

'He wasn't,' Rhona offered. 'Until now.'

It wasn't the first time Sean had entered her kitchen to find McNab sitting at the table. As usual, he showed no surprise at her visitor, but rather gave him a welcome smile.

Glancing at the almost-empty pizza boxes, he waved a bag at them.

'So you won't be requiring my offering?' he said cheerily.

'Which is?' McNab enquired.

'Venison casserole,' Sean said. 'With mushrooms and garlic.'

Rhona watched as McNab considered this enticing prospect.

'Okay, gentlemen, I have eaten and have work to do. Feel free to have the next course without me.' She rose with a smile and, lifting her glass, departed for the sitting room, trying not to imagine what might follow.

As it was, the two main men in her life apparently ate Sean's casserole and had a conversation without her, while she shared the couch in the sitting room with a cat who purred but didn't speak, for which she was grateful.

Eventually she heard the front door open and close again, and wondered which of them had departed. When there was no other sound, she contemplated the fact that perhaps they had both left and maybe together. Either that or, with the late hour, Sean had gone to bed in the spare room, which he'd done in the past.

She went to check and saw the light still on in the kitchen. Pushing open the door, she found Sean seated at the table.

'Hey,' he said. 'McNab's gone, suitably replenished.' He gave her a wry smile. 'I'm sorry about being away for Christmas,' he added.

Rhona, realizing that may have been the message she hadn't yet listened to, chose not to respond.

'So sadly no Christmas lunch together this year,' he said.

'That's okay,' she said. 'Chrissy's asked me to her place with her mum and wee Michael,' she told him. 'I think she might have asked McNab too. Since we're all on our own,' she added.

A shadow crossed Sean's face before he gathered himself and responded. 'Good. It's better to be with friends at Christmas.'

Her sense of guilt blossomed and almost sent her to wrap her arms about his neck. Despite the strength of feeling, she didn't do so.

'It's just another day,' she said. 'I'll' – she corrected herself – 'we'll manage.'

He rose then and took her in his arms. She felt the strength of him and knew that there had been something else in his unheard message. A piece of their puzzle she didn't yet know.

49

Marnie spread the newspaper on the kitchen table so Tizzy could see it too.

She'd begun teaching Tizzy to read, back when it had happened, so she could read and understand the steps of her dances.

While she'd been in prison, she'd read a lot. And not just adult books. When she was on her own in the cell, she would read the children's books she'd borrowed from the family room. She'd read them out loud, imagining Tizzy was listening and learning.

She'd found the pile of newspapers together with a sack of logs at the front door. She knew they must be from Joan, worried whether she would be able to keep her fire going.

Tizzy had been delighted. First a Christmas food parcel. Then logs for the fire. Which had to mean that Father Christmas wouldn't forget them either.

Her daughter's joy had rubbed off on Marnie until now, when she began to read the paper.

The story of the murder in Elder Park dominated. Being a tabloid, it revelled in sensational possibilities, just like what had happened in her own case six years before.

Back then she'd been cast as a drug addict and former prostitute, who'd neglected her child so badly that she'd drowned near their home. It had been an easy task to pretend to be exactly that. To admit neglect. To confess to abandoning her child to the sea, while she got high.

'That's not what happened, Mummy,' Tizzy told her.

'But I did leave you,' Marnie said.

'You left me safe in the cave.' Tizzy's voice faded then and Marnie wondered if she'd heard it at all.

The next paragraph read like a nightmare. Her nightmare.

> The victim was found naked and tied to a chair in the garden, after being thrown from a window of the derelict farmhouse in Elder Park. He was discovered by three young boys, who took a photograph of him, showing his eyes and mouth had been sewn shut. Now, one of the boys, Ally Feeney, aged twelve, from Linthouse, has disappeared, kidnapped perhaps by the killer.

The images conjured up by this sequence of events seemed to Marnie to mirror her own horror. The incarceration. The darkness and torture. The inability to cry out or even whisper her terror.

All that was bad enough. But what of the child? The missing boy?

She'd hidden Tizzy, but it hadn't been enough to save her.

The words swam in front of her and she felt herself drowning again.

People who wrote about these things knew nothing of the horrors that some folk had to live with. The truth was always too terrible to tell. No one would want to listen to it.

She thought back to DS McNab, who had tried hard to listen. Even when she couldn't speak.

Then Dr MacLeod. She had come. She had listened.

'But I was too afraid to tell her everything,' she said out loud.

Fear. The great controller.

'Only if you let it be,' Tizzy's small voice told her. 'You promised you would tell the truth in the end.' There was a moment's silence, before her daughter added, 'This is it, Mummy. This is the end.'

50

Explaining to the boss why he was interested in an already prosecuted case from six years ago, while they had a major murder and gangland investigation going on, was never going to be easy.

He'd tried it out on his partner first and Janice hadn't been convinced, even when he'd used Dr MacLeod's support as leverage.

'I – we – just want to identify the child's father. See if he's on our books,' he'd finished by saying.

'And if he is, what then?' Janice had posed the million-dollar question. 'Marnie Aitken made a confession and was given a sentence, which she served. She's out now and home. It's over,' she'd said.

Which was true. But he hadn't believed her confession back then and believed it even less now.

When he'd told Janice this, she'd nodded and said, 'Then you have to ask at least. Maybe tag it on after you've spoken about Moondance?' she suggested. 'Which is, after all, the thing he's really interested in.'

His partner was right, as always, McNab thought as he

chapped on the boss's door at the allotted time and was told abruptly to enter.

The boss looks tired, he thought, then wondered briefly what he looked like himself. He hadn't been getting much sleep, that was true. But he had been eating well, he reminded himself, especially last night when he'd had two meals, one after the other.

The boss's barked request for an update brought him swiftly back to the present.

'As I wrote in my report, Karen Bell – or Moondance – will be at work tonight at the Red Dragon, sir. We suspect those looking for Lewis McLean will want to speak to her regarding his possible whereabouts. She is aware that we will have officers on the premises, including DS Clark, for her safety.'

'And she's the only identified link we have with Lewis McLean apart from the call he made to Ragnar Ryan?'

'There's also Ally Feeney, who we believe spoke to him in captivity, and Darren McGowan, who we think has links to the group he's with, sir.' McNab knew how thin that was, even as he said it.

'And the dark-haired guy caught on CCTV outside this club with Robert Forbes who we now know was the victim?' he demanded sharply.

McNab recognized the boss's frustration, because it made him as angry as hell too.

'Still unidentified, sir, although I've a meeting in IT shortly regarding that footage.'

'Can the boy Ally give us anything more on his captors, d'you think?' the boss said.

'DS Clark and I are scheduled to chat with all three of the boys here this afternoon, sir.'

'Okay, carry on, Detective Sergeant, and keep me up to date. I have a meeting later with our counterparts in Chicago. Let's hope they have some intel on all of this that might aid us.'

When McNab didn't shift at this point, the boss added, 'You may go.'

'There was something else, sir,' McNab said cautiously.

'What, Sergeant? And it had better be quick,' he ordered.

So McNab did his best to be swift and concise and now stood like a recalcitrant schoolboy awaiting his headmaster's wrath.

'And what has Dr MacLeod to do with all of this?' DI Wilson said.

McNab gave a potted version of Rhona's visit to Marnie in Kilcreggan and the recording she'd made, leaving out his own brief presence there.

A short but pregnant silence followed.

'You're sure this isn't you trying to settle old scores in the case, Detective Sergeant?' DI Wilson demanded.

'It is not, sir,' McNab said. 'Marnie also told Rhona off the record that her former partner had sewn her mouth shut and imprisoned her in the dark for two days. Which was why she'd defaced the doll in that manner, sir.'

That announcement definitely made an impact.

'What do we know of this man?' DI Wilson said.

'Only that he supplied Marnie and other young girls like her with drugs and pimped them out.'

'And he was the child's father?'

'She was pregnant at the time he did that to her, and that's why she ran away, sir.'

'But she wouldn't reveal his name to Dr MacLeod?'

'No, sir.'

The grim silence that followed seemed to last for ever. Then . . .

'Dr MacLeod mentioned the defaced doll back when we first found the Elder Park victim,' DI Wilson said. 'I told her then that there couldn't be a connection, because the public and press hadn't been informed of this aspect of the case. It was just a coincidence.' He paused to meet McNab's eye. 'You think I was wrong about that, Sergeant?' he asked.

McNab had no idea how to respond, since neither 'yes' or 'no' would be okay, so he remained silent.

Eventually the boss gave his decision.

'Tell Dr MacLeod to check out the father's DNA. Maybe also do a familial search as it might, just might, have a link to a current serious crime investigation.'

'Thank you, sir.' McNab didn't give a whoop, but almost felt like it.

Returning to his desk, he gave Janice the thumbs-up.

'He gave the okay?' she said, obviously surprised.

'Apparently Rhona raised the subject of the defaced doll back when we found the body. So he's decided to go with it,' McNab told her.

Janice looked pleased about that. 'And tonight at the Red Dragon?' she checked.

'All in place,' he told her.

'So what should I wear to blend in?'

Various responses flipped through his brain, such as bring your own pole, dress like a bloke or maybe a cocktail waitress. All of which, even to his mind, definitely sounded non-PC.

Obviously reading his tortured expression, Janice gave a laugh. 'I know, I'll bring my own pole,' she said.

He called Rhona around lunchtime, hoping not to have to bring her out of the lab. It was Chrissy who answered.

'McNab,' she said on hearing his voice. 'I heard you and Sean Maguire got cosy over a venison casserole last night. Are you making a point of having dinner with all of Rhona's admirers?' She laughed. 'Oh, I forgot,' she added, 'you're one too.'

McNab decided to maintain his dignity, if he had such a thing.

'Can you tell Dr MacLeod that the boss okayed her to run a check on Tizzy's father's DNA. He also suggested she run a familial search because of a possible link with a current serious crime investigation.'

A surprised silence followed. Then, 'I believe Dr MacLeod may be already on to that. So she must have had every faith in you to sell that to your boss. D'you want her to call you back later? She's busy at the moment.'

'That won't be necessary, Ms McInsh,' McNab said. 'I'm busy too.'

Seemingly unperturbed by his attempts at sarcasm, Chrissy came back in. 'Oh, before you ring off, d'you want to have Christmas dinner with me, mum, your namesake wee Michael and Rhona on Christmas Day?'

McNab, after deciphering what had just been said, was at a loss as to how to respond before Chrissy spoke again.

'No worries about confirming just now. But the offer's there. Who wants to be on their own on Christmas Day?'

As she ended the call, McNab was left staring speechlessly ahead of him.

'What?' Janice said.

'Chrissy asked me over for Christmas dinner.'

Janice smiled. 'She doesn't want you to be a sad old

bastard on Christmas Day. She's a better person than me,' she added with a laugh. 'So what's happening now?'

'I go see Ollie about that footage outside the Red Dragon. Then we talk to the boys.'

51

It looks as though he's been scrubbed, Ally thought as his wee pal came into the room. Despite his shiny appearance, Dreep was as skinny as ever, the jumper he wore drowning him. Ally wondered if it was a cast-off of Darren's.

Even thinking Darren's name brought back the fear he'd been living with since that first night in the snow.

The door now shut behind him, Dreep seemed to relax and even managed a smile that looked more like a grimace.

'Are we arrested?' he said, his eyes wide.

'I don't think so,' Ally said. 'More helping with their enquiries.'

'Where's Kev, then?' Dreep said, looking round at what they called the Family Room.

'He'll be here,' Ally offered, hoping that was true.

Kev was like their anchor in stormy seas. Didn't say much, but never panicked. Or nearly never.

'The police bloke that came to the house with the woman. He was okay,' Dreep offered.

'Detective Sergeant McNab,' Ally said. 'He couldn't climb the fence where I was held. Said he wasn't as good as you and had to roll underneath.'

Dreep liked that and his eyes lit up. 'He brought Caramel Logs and Irn-Bru with him. D'you think that'll happen again?'

Ally hoped so.

Their prayers were answered when the door opened and Kev appeared, together with a plastic bag.

'These are for us,' he said, emptying the bag to reveal the said Tunnock's Caramel Logs and a choice of Irn-Bru or Coke. Without further ado, the boys distributed the goodies and set about them.

Silence intermingled with appreciative sounds followed, before Ally said, 'Okay, what we talked about after I got away. Are we still on?' He studied the other two faces. 'They'll come in soon, so we need to be sure.'

'No more secrets,' Kev said.

When McNab opened the door to the Family Room, he noted that the goody bag he'd prepared earlier had been shared out.

Earlier, in the observation room, he and Janice had watched as each of the boys had arrived.

Ally, the leader, had been first. Just as McNab had requested. Dreep next, looking drowned in a jumper belonging to someone twice his size and weight. Kev, the third member, had been the recipient of the bag, handed over by McNab, and pretty pleased he'd looked about that.

'Bribing a witness,' Janice had said.

'All part of the grand plan,' McNab had offered in return.

'So how will a high dose of sugar and caffeine help their memories?' she'd asked.

'It works for me.' McNab smiled. 'Maybe it's just a male thing.'

After the boys had finished munching, Ally had called them to order.

'Do they know what you have planned?' Janice had asked McNab.

'I didn't know myself until after I spoke with Ollie,' McNab told her. 'Right, it's time. I'll see you after.'

The boys looked up expectantly as McNab appeared, then rose from where they'd been sitting.

'Thanks for coming in, boys.'

'What are we here for, mister?' Dreep said.

'I'd like you to help me by looking at some pictures of faces,' McNab explained. 'Can you do that?'

Dreep's eyes lit up. 'Sure thing, mister,' he said, then checked Ally for approval.

'How do we do that?' Ally said.

'In the IT department, where you'll meet Ollie, our super recognizer.'

'Is Ollie a robot?' Dreep said, open-mouthed.

McNab tried not to laugh. 'No. Ollie's a guy who can recognize faces even when there's not a good image of them.'

When all three looked impressed by this, he added, 'He's going to see how good you three are at doing that.'

'Cool,' Dreep said.

Their walk through the busy station caused a great deal of interest, which McNab knew it would. Everyone involved in the case was delighted at Ally's safe return and there was a flurry of clapping and big smiles at their presence, which both surprised and pleased the boys.

'Right,' McNab said when they reached IT. 'I take it you've all played computer games before?'

The boys nodded.

'Well, in here it's not a game. It's the real thing. So follow me through quietly.'

Reaching Ollie's station at the far side of the room, McNab did the introductions.

'So, boys, I'd like you to meet Ollie, digital expert and super recognizer,' he said. 'I plan to leave you in his capable hands, if that's okay?'

The boys exchanged glances, suggesting that was definitely okay.

'I'll be back when you're finished.'

The idea for all this had been Ollie's. When McNab had met with him earlier regarding the poor footage from outside the Red Dragon, Ollie had suggested that if the dark-haired guy they sought had seen Ally in or around the crime scene and could describe him to Leo in the chip shop, then there was a chance that Ally or one of the others might have seen him too. They just hadn't realized.

Entering the small side room where he could view Ollie's station, he saw that Ollie had already settled the boys in front of a hi-res screen. The plan was to run an official super-recognizer test and see how each of them performed. However, in this case the image tested in the collection would be that of the missing dark-haired man.

The boys were obviously keen, by the looks on their faces. Life as a game was much more fun and definitely less scary than their current reality.

The test took about ten minutes after which Ollie turned towards McNab in his booth and indicated that he should return.

When McNab mouthed a *how did it go*, he was rewarded with something he realized he'd rarely seen in all the time he'd known Ollie. And that was a smile.

'Ally got top marks,' Dreep told him. 'He spotted the guy's face in among the others every single time. It didn't matter if it was a side view or he had a hat on or a hood up or anything,' he said in amazement. 'Ally could still recognize him.'

They were back in the Family Room, still high from what they'd just done or maybe the earlier sugar rush.

Noting the serious look on Ally's face, McNab said, 'Ollie says you think you've seen that man before?'

'Yes,' Ally said. 'I remember where too.'

'Go on,' McNab urged.

'It was that night after we found the body.' Ally halted there for a moment, gathering himself. 'The guys took off for the tunnel. I was a bit behind them. I was running past the Vital Spark and banged into a man, who grabbed my hood and asked if the polis were after me. It was him. It was that man.'

'You're sure?' McNab said.

'Certain,' Ally said.

McNab remembered passing the pub en route to the cycle path entrance to the tunnel.

'Have you seen him since?'

When the boy shook his head, McNab's hopes began to fade.

'But I remembered something else,' Ally said. 'The hand that grabbed me outside the pub. There was a tattoo along the knuckle. Like a snake.'

52

When Dr Jen Mackie's call finally arrived, it confirmed Rhona's suspicions.

'So,' Jen began, 'the samples you sent did come from the south coast of the Rosneath Peninsula. They're quite unique, in fact.'

As Rhona listened intently to the experienced soil scientist, Jen continued with her explanation.

'They come from quite a famous cave in Portkil Bay, recently excavated by a local archaeological society. Their finds included evidence of the Bronze Age in the form of charcoal-enriched floor deposits. Also burnt and unburnt bone and wood fragments were preserved in the same deposit. My full analysis of the material you supplied is without a doubt from the same cave.'

So what Marnie had said regarding the cave was true. But what about the rest of it? She'd got as far as saying she'd taken Tizzy to the cave and told her to stay there. What she hadn't said was why.

'Does that help with the mystery?' Jen said.

'It confirms part of Marnie Aitken's story,' Rhona admitted.

Magnus had said the silences often held the most traumatic

part of the experience. The words that were too painful to hear yourself say.

'Anyway, I'm happy to offer evidence to that effect if it ever gets that far,' Jen told her.

'Thanks, Jen, I'll get back to you.'

'I'll send the full analysis through for you to take a look at. I hope it helps.' Jen paused there. 'How are things with the Elder Park case? Any progress on that?'

'Yes and no,' Rhona admitted. 'We collected DNA from one of the perpetrators and a familial search threw up a name, which the police are progressing with.' It sounded small even as she said it.

'I'm glad you got the boy back at least. That was very scary,' Jen said.

'One definite success. Chrissy and I are working on what was retrieved at the location where he was held, but . . .'

'It's attention to detail that gets us there in the end,' Jen said. 'If that soil you sent me had been examined before now, perhaps the outcome in the Marnie Aitken case might have been different.'

Ringing off, Rhona contemplated that thought for a moment before her mobile rang again, this time with Bill's name on the screen. She answered, immediately concerned that something else had happened.

'Is there a problem?' she said.

'I just wanted to check with you about this line of enquiry regarding Marnie Aitken. I understand from DS McNab that you've spoken to the woman and she's back in Kilcreggan?'

'Yes,' Rhona said cautiously.

'I had a résumé of your visit from McNab, the content of which reminded me of your comments regarding the doll at the beginning of the Elder Park case.'

Rhona waited, knowing there was more.

'I believe you'd like to run the father's DNA and see what comes up?' Bill added.

'That's correct,' Rhona said.

'I've sanctioned that, although I suspect McNab has already told you my decision?'

'He left a message with Chrissy,' Rhona told him, wondering where this was all going.

'I would like to hear the woman's story. Could you send me a copy of the recording?' Bill said.

'Of course. Although there are aspects of her story still missing,' she added.

'Ones I suspect we need to hear,' Bill said. 'The child was four when she disappeared six years ago and there's a probability her father was involved then with prostitution and drug running. I'd like to know if he still is.'

Chrissy appeared as they ended the conversation. 'You about ready to finish up?' Seeing Rhona's expression, she said, 'What's up?'

'I'm going to try to ring Marnie,' Rhona suddenly decided.

'Any reason in particular?' Chrissy said.

Rhona told her about Dr Mackie's phone call. 'Plus the boss is on side now and wants the whole story.'

'Good,' Chrissy said. 'You said she has no electricity in the cottage. The basic mobile you left her with will only last up to a week without recharge.'

'I had hoped she might enlist Joan at the café's help with that,' Rhona admitted.

'Better make contact, just in case,' Chrissy said.

Rhona nodded and, pulling up the number, listened to it ring out. When it finally went to voicemail, she left a message saying she'd like to speak about the soil sample and the cave at Portkil Bay and asked Marnie to call her back.

'I take it you've run the father's DNA sample?' Chrissy checked.

'I did it in anticipation of the okay from Bill,' Rhona said. 'Now we have to await the results.'

The evening sky was clear and the swiftly falling temperature had painted the pavement in a web of ice drawings. That plus the coloured lights and decorations made for a picturesque festive scene.

'Wee Michael's going mad with excitement,' Chrissy admitted. 'Every morning he wakes up, he asks if it's Christmas yet and whether Jesus has been born.' She made a face. 'Mum's been feeding him the religious angle.'

'Nothing wrong in thinking children can change the world for the better,' Rhona offered. 'Liam did for me, although it took me a while to appreciate just how much.'

'Wee Michael did it for me too,' Chrissy admitted. 'And judging from what I've heard, having Tizzy saved Marnie's life.'

'She did. For four years anyway,' Rhona said.

'D'you think her father found out about her?' Chrissy said. 'I know Sam would never harm wee Michael or take him away from me. Keeping Michael hidden from him would have been torture. I might have gone mad myself.'

In Rhona's own case, Liam's father hadn't even wanted him to be born. Then, when he was, Edward had made it very plain that his name was not to be associated with his unacknowledged son.

'Oh, I invited McNab for Christmas dinner,' Chrissy said.

'Really?' Rhona said. 'And what did he say?' she asked, intrigued.

'He went completely silent,' Chrissy told her. 'I said there was no hurry to give me an answer. I also said you'd be there.'

'But I haven't given you an answer yet,' Rhona tried.

Chrissy shrugged. 'I'm happy to wait. For both of you.'

They'd reached the lane where, it being a Saturday night, with Christmas on the horizon, it was busier than usual. The smells, which were usually dominated by the offerings of the curry houses in particular, now consisted of something fruity and hot with a hint of nutmeg.

'Mulled wine,' Chrissy said, reading Rhona's expression and pointing at an outdoor party being served from big steaming pots of the said beverage. 'Fancy some?' she suggested.

'I don't like my wine warm,' Rhona said. 'Are we expecting Janice or McNab to be here?'

'I think not. Apparently there's something going down at the Red Dragon Club tonight,' Chrissy said knowledgeably.

Rhona found herself relieved that neither of the two men who'd shared the venison casserole in her flat last night would be around here tonight, with Sean already in Dublin if he'd caught his plane in time.

As she ordered a glass of white wine, her mobile rang. A quick glance at the screen showed Marnie's name. Pleased, Rhona answered.

'Dr MacLeod. Sorry to bother you. It's Joan here from the café in Kilcreggan.'

Rhona, her stomach already flipping over, said, 'Hi, Joan. Everything okay?'

'Not sure, to be honest. I dropped round some wood and old newspapers last night. I thought I would check in again today. Anyway, Marnie had taken in the papers and she'd spread them out on the table next to the mobile, as though she'd been reading them. But she's gone. The place was freezing so she hadn't lit the stove recently. It just feels wrong.'

Rhona hadn't set a password on the simple pay-as-you-go phone, and thought it unlikely Marnie would have either.

'Has anyone rung the mobile?' Rhona tried. 'Apart from me earlier.'

'No. Just the voice message from you. I didn't listen to it, just thought since you'd tried to call her earlier, I should phone you.'

'You did the right thing,' Rhona said. 'Can I ask you what she was reading in the newspaper?'

'All about that horrible killing in the park in Glasgow. The naked man who'd been tortured. And the boy that went missing.' She stopped there for a moment. 'God, I should have thought before I gave her those newspapers. I hope the missing boy didn't bring it all back for her. She's still very fragile.'

'Can you check maybe again in the morning and let me know if she's back?' Rhona said.

'Of course. But not sure I'll sleep a wink after this,' Joan said before ringing off.

In the earlier days of the murder enquiry, no one, including the press, knew about the special circumstances of the crime in Elder Park. But eventually such details get out because they sell newspapers. The gorier the better.

As far as Rhona understood, Marnie, caught up in her own thoughts, even obsessed by them, hadn't been engaging with the outside world, except at its very edges. So Joan's worry that the delivery of the more recent papers and their contents had caused a relapse of some sort in Marnie's mind sounded like a probability.

But what would it make her do?

Rhona imagined her walking the beach with her imaginary daughter, trying to talk her way through it, like she had on the recording. Rhona had hoped she would talk more the next time they met, but what if Marnie had already had enough of the outside world, depicted in all its glory in the tabloid press?

Or, alternatively, what if what she'd read had made her wonder, just like Rhona had, at the crossover between what had happened to her in Glasgow and what had happened to the victim?

'Penny for them?' Chrissy finally said.

'That was Joan from Kilcreggan using the mobile we gave Marnie.'

'What's happened?'

'Joan gave her some recent newspapers for her fire. They were laid out on the table so it looks like she'd been reading them. Especially the stories of the torture and killing in Elder Park and Ally's disappearance,' Rhona told her.

'But Ally's okay. They let him go,' Chrissy said, looking worried.

'She may not know that, though. And even if she did, the fact that someone snatched a child would seem very close to home.'

53

The Vital Spark sat at the corner of Govan Road and Clachan Drive. It had been around a long time and the various signs suggested it was still operating as a local boozer, despite the changing face of Govan and neighbouring Linthouse.

It was also very close to Elder Park and the old farmhouse.

If the dark-haired guy was standing outside the pub having a smoke that night, he hadn't been far from the crime scene itself.

McNab pushed open the door and stepped inside. Being a Saturday night, it was busy, not with the thirst of men from the nearby and once-great shipyard, but a mixed clientele of men and women of all ages, plus a few who looked too young to be served drink in the first place.

That's not why I'm here, McNab reminded himself.

Heading for the bar, he encountered a woman in her fifties who eyed him like a suspect in an interview room.

'DS Michael McNab,' he said, reaching for his ID.

'I know who you are,' she said. 'You're the one that found Ally Feeney and brought him home to his mum.'

McNab considered pointing out that Ally had escaped by

himself, but seeing as it had bought him some standing in the community, he decided to build on that.

'What can we do you for, Sergeant?' she said.

McNab brought out his mobile with the best image they had of the dark-haired guy and handed it over.

'Ally says this man was standing outside here smoking on the night of the murder in Elder Park. He caught Ally by the hood as he was running past and asked if the polis were chasing him.'

The woman took a long hard look. 'It's not a great picture,' she said. 'Anything else you can tell us about him?'

'He's local by the voice. About five ten, dark hair, mid-thirties, works out, maybe a stubble beard.' When her expression didn't change, he added, 'And he has a snake tattoo along the knuckles of his right hand.'

'Say that again,' she demanded.

McNab obliged. 'A snake tattoo along the knuckles of his right hand.'

Her eyes narrowed. 'That bastard's back?' she said. 'We thought we'd got rid of him.' She shouted to a man serving further along the counter. 'Come and see this photo, Archie. The polis think he's something to do with wee Ally Feeney's disappearance.'

McNab chose again not to correct her, but waited while the older guy took a look.

'Was he not in here a few nights ago?' he said, rubbing his bald head.

'He has a snake tattoo along his right knuckle,' she told him.

The man's expression changed in much the same manner as hers had.

'Jesus, I thought he was in prison or gone stateside. He disappeared from here, thank God.'

'Well, he's back and Detective Sergeant McNab here wants to talk to him regarding wee Ally Feeney's abduction.'

'Who is this man?' McNab said.

'He's one of the Jamesie brothers' team,' Archie told him. 'At least, that's what we thought back then. A bad bastard, like most of them. The snake tattoo was a thing for a while, along the knuckles, usually beneath a knuckleduster.'

'How long ago was this?' McNab asked.

'Five years or more,' Archie said. 'I wouldn't have recognized him if Mags hadn't mentioned the tattoo.'

'And his name?' McNab tried.

'Daryl, that was it. Daryl Boyd. He's one of the Boyd gang,' Mags said. 'One of the younger ones. Big brother Jack was the boss around here, back in the day.'

'He's Jack Boyd's brother?' McNab checked.

'Could be a cousin,' Archie ventured. 'There was a whole clan of them lived in Govan on the other side of the park.'

'Any idea where I might find either of them now?' McNab tried.

'Well, if Daryl was drinking in here, he can't be far away,' Archie said. 'As for Jack Boyd, word was he went stateside.' He threw McNab a look. 'You think Daryl might have something to do with that murder in the park?' he said.

'It's a line of enquiry,' McNab admitted. One that just might pay off, he'd begun to think.

'That old farmhouse used to be a drug den for a while,' Angus said, nodding.

'Right,' Mags came back in. 'Folk around here, once they know one of the Boyds had something to do with taking wee Ally Feeney, will want them caught. We'll put the word out and let you know.'

McNab handed Mags his card. 'Call me any time, with

anything you hear. Anything at all,' he stressed. 'No matter how small.'

Outside now, even the sharp frost that had fallen in the interim couldn't quench the fire of hope that Mags and Archie had kindled. He thought back to Ally and the other two boys, and said a silent thank you to Ollie for engineering today's proceedings.

Checking his watch, he registered he still had an hour before he needed to turn up at the Red Dragon, which meant he could both eat and perhaps do a bit of digging around the topic of Daryl and Jack Boyd and whether they'd been sighted in their old hunting ground of Govan.

Leo's, like any good fish and chip shop, was busy at this time of night. McNab parked within sight and smell, and waited for the queue to lessen before heading inside.

There were two on behind the counter, one of whom he was pleased to see was Leo, who spotted him right away.

'Same as last time?' he asked.

McNab nodded. 'Any chance we could also have a private word?' he said under his breath.

'Double fish and chips for the gentleman,' Leo ordered his young male assistant, before ushering McNab into the back shop and closing the door.

'I don't have long,' Leo told him. 'The boy's just learning.'

'Daryl Boyd,' McNab said. 'Does the name ring a bell?'

Leo muttered something unintelligible under his breath, then said, 'The fucking Boyds. What about them?'

McNab showed him the photo again. 'Ally Feeney says he was stopped by this man outside the Vital Spark pub on the night of the murder.'

'And that's maybe the guy who was in my chip shop?' Leo said, studying the image.

'Mags at the Vital Spark realized who it was,' McNab told him, 'because Ally remembered he had a snake tattoo along his right knuckle.'

Leo's expression grew even grimmer.

'I didn't clock that when he was in here,' he said. 'If I had recognized him, I would have told you a different story. A worse one.'

'You knew the Boyd family?' McNab asked.

'Who in Govan didn't? But by reputation mostly,' he said. 'When the Jamesie brothers got busted and flew Glasgow and Scotland, the Boyds did too, or so we thought. So that's the bastard who lifted Ally?' Leo looked suitably angry.

McNab didn't enlighten him, hoping that the gold mine that was Daryl Boyd would keep on giving.

'So Mags told you Govan was their stomping ground and you want to know if he's back here?' When McNab nodded, Leo said, 'Okay. I don't know if he is, but everyone comes in here. So I'll make a point of finding out.'

They re-entered the shop as Leo's assistant lifted out McNab's freshly fried fish and sat it on top of a pile of fat chips.

'He wants salt and vinegar,' Leo told him, 'and it's on the house.'

McNab accepted the hot bundle and, giving Leo the thumbs-up, left to consume his meal in the car before he headed for the Red Dragon.

The Red Dragon doorway, now glowing like fire, looked like the gateway to hell, McNab thought.

The bouncer, obviously aware of his imminent arrival,

nodded him through, behind two middle-aged men and a couple of young bucks, who he suspected were already high on something other than drink.

Reminding himself in what capacity he was here, McNab said nothing, but headed to the alcove closest to the bar where he'd arranged to meet his partner.

She was sitting with 'Call me Mick', who, as far as McNab was concerned, was taking too big an interest in a female police officer.

Janice, looking spectacular he had to admit, glanced up with an expression that conveyed exactly how she felt about her companion.

'Moondance hasn't arrived,' she told McNab. 'And should have been here thirty minutes ago.'

Russell rose and, replacing his earlier expression with one more befitting a concerned employer, said worriedly, 'Moondance is never late.'

'Have you called her?' McNab said.

'I have, but her mobile goes to voicemail.'

'How does she get here normally?' McNab said, his concern mounting.

'An Uber or a black cab,' he said.

'Does she use one operator in particular?' McNab said.

He shook his head. 'Not to get here. But I book the return ones for the girls and it's on contract.'

'When is she due to perform?'

'Eleven o'clock. We're chock-a-block by then. If she doesn't appear, we'll have a problem. A big problem.'

'I'm not interested in your problem,' McNab said sharply. 'Call the taxi service you use and check if she asked them to pick her up.' He nodded to Janice to follow him and moved out of earshot of the manager.

'This isn't good,' he said. 'Did you try the number she gave us?'

'I did. It went to voicemail.'

'Okay,' McNab said. 'I'll request a patrol car to go by her flat.'

'I'll go and talk to the other dancers,' Janice said. 'See if they've heard anything from her.'

As Janice moved off in the direction of the dressing room, McNab called the station and made his request. He'd already considered driving to her flat himself, but this was quicker. Plus she might well walk in the door within the next few minutes. Although he had a gut feeling that wasn't going to happen.

Karen Bell had asked to be arrested because she was afraid. He'd persuaded her to appear tonight and had vouched for her safety, so eager was he to draw the missing Jason, or whoever was after him, here to the Red Dragon.

He'd suggested she message Jason, both on the mobile number he'd given her and also via her TikTok account, so that he knew she was okay and still dancing, and to hint that she had information for him regarding the death of his brother.

At this point in his thoughts, Janice reappeared, looking as worried as he felt.

'They're not happy. She's never late, just like he said. They've tried calling her, hoping that seeing a name she knew would encourage her to pick up. She didn't.'

'Did they know anything about her relationship with Jason?'

'If they did, they weren't going to admit it.'

'What about where she might go to hide?' he tried.

'Nothing on that either. According to the other girls, she

doesn't talk about her private life at all. Just arrives, dances and leaves again.'

The call from the patrol car arrived just as the manager took to the stage to tell the audience that Moondance wouldn't be appearing tonight. The punters weren't happy about that and voiced it by demanding their entry fees back.

McNab went outside to take the call.

'Flat was in darkness, Sergeant. A neighbour said she saw Ms Bell get into a car with a man around ten o'clock.'

'Did you get a description of the man?'

'He was tall and wearing a black puffa jacket and hat.'

'Hair colour?' McNab tried, praying it would be blond.

It wasn't the answer he'd hoped for.

'Unsure, but she thinks dark rather than fair, sir.'

54

Rhona's sleep had been filled with dreams of water. Initially she'd been floating on her back, looking up at a cloudless sky. Then she'd heard the sound of a child's voice, but try as she might, she couldn't turn to look for the child, her repeated efforts only propelling her below the surface, until she'd finally forced herself awake before she drowned.

Rising before dawn, she showered, dressed and made some toast and coffee, taking it through to the sitting room, where she lit the gas fire and opened her laptop.

She didn't need Magnus to interpret the nightmare for her. Her dream state had merely replayed her daytime worries. Like Marnie, she was imagining the child's presence, willing this ephemeral Tizzy to tell the whole story of her disappearance in the dream, if not in reality.

Jen's comment about the importance of the minutiae in an investigation had also been a trigger. The need to pursue the smallest detail to discover the truth of what had happened had made her question what, if anything, she might have missed in the farmhouse case.

The waiting required for the results from her various DNA

searches seemed interminable at times such as these. Patience on her part being in very short supply.

Despite her fervent hopes, her email was empty of anything that might have improved her mood. Plus a mobile check found nothing from Joan in either text or voicemail. Although, she reasoned, the woman had barely had time to check for Marnie this morning again.

She now turned her mind to what she would do if Joan reported back that Marnie hadn't reappeared. Her first thought was that McNab would have to be told. And what would he do? Marnie would have to be missing for longer than a day for the authorities to be interested. But perhaps her vulnerability would shorten that time?

Two thoughts on what might have happened to Marnie were competing for attention. Neither of them good.

Marnie, her mind further troubled by what she'd read in the paper, had decided to join her dead daughter by walking into the waves. A scenario that seemed more probable by the minute.

Alternatively, whatever she'd run from ten years before had simply caught up with her, and Marnie no longer felt safe in Kilcreggan.

Her mobile rang as she was getting ready to leave for work. Glancing at the screen, she saw that it was Joan. Taking a deep breath, she answered.

'I went by the cottage on my way to work this morning, Dr MacLeod, and there's still no sign that she's been back there,' Joan told her worriedly.

'Her outdoor clothes,' Rhona said. 'Are they still there? Her boots, coat, hat?'

'I checked and they're gone,' Joan told her. 'So she didn't just run out into the cold.'

'Any sign of a struggle?' Rhona posed the question that she should have asked the day before.

There was a moment's silence before Joan answered. 'None that I can see. No blood either.' She hesitated. 'No one around here would harm her, Dr MacLeod.'

'And nobody from outside has been asking about her?' Rhona checked.

'Not in my café, no,' Joan said firmly. 'Even if they had, I wouldn't have told them anything.'

'Could you check with the ferry?' Rhona suggested. 'See if she might have left that way?'

'I'll do that and let you know, Dr MacLeod. If no one saw her get the ferry, then I'm going to tell the police that she's missing.'

'Yes. Please do that. And call me if you find out anything,' Rhona requested.

Agreeing to that, Joan rang off.

Arriving at work, Rhona found Chrissy also had news. Although nothing about it was good either. It appeared that the young woman who'd been harbouring the missing actor had now disappeared herself, having failed to turn up at her place of work, the Red Dragon, the previous evening.

'I spoke to Janice earlier,' Chrissy said. 'She told me there was a near riot when Moondance didn't appear to do her pole-dance routine. After which McNab discovered she and a man had been seen leaving her flat together earlier that night.'

Chrissy handed her a mug of coffee and her usual morning roll.

'It gets worse. They're worried the guy she was seen getting into a car with might be the one who took Robert

Forbes from outside the Red Dragon, thinking it was the famous Jason.'

And Chrissy wasn't finished yet. 'Also, Ally says he saw someone like that outside a Linthouse pub the night of the murder. He has a snake tattoo on his right knuckle. Locals told McNab his name is Daryl Boyd. Probable cousin to *the* Jack Boyd the police are currently looking for. All of which you'll probably hear about at today's meeting.'

Rhona fitted some of these pieces into the puzzle that was slowly taking shape in her brain.

Chrissy, observing her reaction to all of this, said cautiously, 'We're getting closer?'

Rhona nodded. 'But we need the feedback on the low-level DNA lifted from the fingerprints.'

'We got one good lead from the familial search on the DNA retrieved from the skin flakes,' Chrissy said. 'If whoever helped him is also a relative . . . ?'

Chrissy's words echoed what Rhona was already thinking.

Of course, identifying the probable killers of Robert Forbes wasn't the same as catching them. She was aware that both McNab and Bill were operating on the principle that the hit team would remain in Glasgow until they finished the job they'd been given to do. And it now looked as though Karen Bell might be part of that plan.

Rhona decided it was the moment to break her own story, so she explained about Joan's call earlier.

'I think Marnie's done a runner,' Chrissy said in her forthright way. 'Maybe it was the story in the paper about the tortured guy with the sewn eyelids and mouth. That was bound to bring back what her so-called partner did to her. Then she reads about Ally going missing. It's like her own personal nightmare.'

Rhona thought back to her time with Marnie at the cottage. Her sense that Marnie felt her dead daughter was close to her there. Just as Magnus did with his father when back in their family home in Orkney.

As far as she and Magnus were aware, this behaviour had only begun when Marnie had returned to the home she'd happily shared with Tizzy from birth until she was four years old. Would she still feel that Tizzy was with her if she left the cottage and Kilcreggan? And if she felt Tizzy go from her, what would Marnie do then?

'McNab needs to know if Marnie's disappeared,' Chrissy said.

'I plan to speak to him,' Rhona told her. 'Joan said she would check if Marnie was seen catching the ferry. If not, then she would officially report her as missing.'

'God,' Chrissy said. 'Some folk in this life never catch a break, do they?'

Rhona didn't have the words or the will to argue with that.

55

Her decision had come from a combination of things. The first had been Tizzy's words regarding her promise that she would face her fear and tell the truth in the end.

The second had been reading the papers Joan had brought round to help light the fire. She'd avoided newspapers all the time she'd been in prison. Initially because she hadn't wanted to read what was said about her during the trial. Afterwards, she couldn't bear to read about bad things happening, because it reminded her of what she'd endured herself.

Despite everything, she'd felt safe inside what the women called the concrete mother. She was warm and never hungry or beaten. Or raped. Plus he couldn't remind her that he owned her and would do what he liked with her when she finally got out.

But there had been nothing worse he could do to her, she thought, than what he'd already done.

'Now's your chance, Mum,' Tizzy had said. 'Now's the time to fix things.'

Tizzy came with her on the walk to the harbour and was still there when she boarded the *Island Princess*. She was excited, just as she'd been when they'd used to travel over to swim in the Gourock pool.

Her chatting and laughter lasted half the journey, then began to grow faint as the outline of Kilcreggan faded from view. At that moment Marnie's legs began to crumple, just as they had done on her arrival, until she felt a small hand slip into hers and knew that she hadn't been abandoned.

Not yet anyway.

Once in Gourock, she headed straight for the train, where the warmth of the carriage enveloped her like the comforting feel of Tizzy's hand in her pocket. Choosing a window seat on the river side, she watched the Clyde flow past, knowing that the longer she kept its waters in sight, the better she would feel. The last part of the journey would be the most difficult, because she'd be heading towards the past and not avoiding it. It would engulf her, perhaps even consume her.

She wouldn't be the first woman to go back to what she'd previously fought to escape. The prison had been full of battered women who, once released, had simply returned to their abuser.

Better the devil you know, they'd used to say.

Switching from Central Station to the underground at St Enoch, she focused on the map in the carriage, counting off the stops until the one where she should get off. Yet constantly reminding herself that, should her courage desert her, she could always go round the circle once again.

Then they were at Govan and she found she could rise and her legs would carry her off the train and out into the freezing air in the place she'd vowed never to set foot in again.

Ten years had seen a change in Govan, that was clear to

see. Though the weather hadn't changed much, she decided, as she made her way along Govan Road until she could enter Elder Park and walk westwards towards Linthouse.

The park was as she remembered it, the boating pond and the clubhouse daubed with slogans of past and present gangs. None of her memories of this place were good, she told Tizzy under her breath. None of them.

Approaching the metal railing, she saw the burnt tree trunks and imagined the local kids using them to climb into the farmhouse grounds. They all did that, including herself, even before she was eventually released from the care system.

This was where the street stuff had been distributed, bought and sold. This was where you got high and hooked and fucked, initially for free, then for money, which you now needed to buy more.

This is where it had happened to her. It was where she'd first met him.

She thought about the boy who'd been taken. Him and his pals had been hanging out here. They were young, according to the papers, but not too young to write a slogan on a wall or climb into the old farmhouse.

According to the paper, the boy and his mates had found the body that snowy night, the night she'd seen Tizzy walking past the Lilias Centre. The night she'd believed – no, hoped – that somehow Tizzy would be waiting for her when she got out.

And she had been. Although she'd had to go home to Kilcreggan to find her.

She allowed herself to think again about the victim's eyes and mouth being stitched shut. How he'd been naked and hurt and how he'd been pushed from that upstairs window.

She'd known as soon as she'd read that paper who had likely done it. Alone or with one of the others.

That's why she'd come here. To finish what she'd started when she'd sent Dr MacLeod the doll.

She set off then, her head down against a flurry of sleet, her right hand cradling Tizzy's. They would head to a homeless shelter for tonight and, if she was still certain about this tomorrow, she would go see DS McNab and tell him what she knew.

56

He knew her as soon as he saw her. Dark-haired and slightly built, she was almost drowned in the padded jacket she wore.

Seated in reception, she'd looked up as he'd entered; then, their eyes meeting in recognition, she'd stood and he saw the hand that had risen to her face was trembling, even as a small smile met her lips.

Had he not been at the police station, he realized, he might well have embraced her, so glad was he to find her there and alive.

'Marnie,' he said. 'It's good to see you again. You had us worried for a bit when Joan told Dr MacLeod that you were missing from the cottage.'

She looked a little surprised by this, as though it was strange for anyone to be looking out for her.

'I'm sorry,' she said. 'I should have told Joan I was coming to Glasgow.' She hesitated for a moment. 'I wanted to see you,' she added.

'And here I am,' McNab said with a smile. 'We could head for the canteen and have a coffee or tea. I remember you prefer tea. And maybe something to eat?' He was feeling his way, remembering as he did how fragile she'd always seemed. Like a bird with a broken wing.

Her brief nod of acceptance had him say, 'Let's go to the cafeteria, then.'

He led her to the quiet table in the corner he'd recently shared with Rhona, and wondered if she'd learned yet that Marnie had taken the ferry, as she'd hoped.

'So a mug of tea and maybe a mince pie?' he tried. 'They're very good.'

When she nodded, he went to the counter, his mind turning over why Marnie Aitken should have come to Govan police station from Kilcreggan, now of all times.

As far as he was aware, Rhona had had nothing back as yet from the check on Tizzy's father's DNA. And if Marnie had wanted the results of that, approaching Rhona, as she had with the doll, would have seemed the most obvious choice.

Then there was the mobile. Why leave it behind when she could have just called to ask whatever she wanted to know?

As he approached with the tray, he noted that she was mouthing silent words to herself – or perhaps to Tizzy, her dead daughter, as Rhona had described.

He didn't comment on this, just laid out her tea and his own coffee, plus the mince pies.

He gave her a few minutes to eat and drink, while he did the same. All the time thinking about the recording Rhona had sent him and what Marnie had told her about the cruelty of her former partner.

Noting with pleasure that the hot tea and sugared pie had brought some colour into her pale cheeks, he eventually said, 'So why did you come to see me?'

'Tizzy told me to,' she said simply.

McNab wasn't often at a loss for words, but in this instance he definitely was. He found himself desperately wanting to repeat, 'Tizzy told you?' in a questioning fashion, but was aware how wrong that would be.

Instead he settled for, 'Why did Tizzy want you to?'

'You heard the recording I made?' she said. 'And what he did to me?'

Despair swept over McNab at her question, accompanied by a stab of guilt. He'd given up too easily six years ago. He should have fought harder for the real story of what had happened in Kilcreggan. If he had, Marnie would never have seen the inside of a prison. Never left that cottage. And might perhaps by now have come to terms with the loss of her child.

She was looking at him as though she should feel sorry for him and not the other way round.

'It wasn't your fault,' she said. 'It was mine. If I'd told you the truth then, maybe none of this would have happened.'

Professional training was warning McNab that whatever she wanted to divulge now should be done in the proper manner. Probably with the boss there too. But before he could halt her and suggest this, she continued in a determined fashion.

'I read the papers,' she said. 'Joan brought them for the fire. Before that, I didn't know about the murder in the park. I didn't know about his eyes and mouth being sewn shut. I didn't know about the torture. I didn't know about the boys finding the body and taking a picture. I didn't know that one of the boys had gone missing.' Her hand rose to her face again.

'Ally Feeney, but he's all right,' McNab told her. 'They let him go.'

Marnie looked surprised. 'He let him go?' Her voice rose in disbelief. '*He* would never have let him go. He would have killed him.'

'Who would have killed him?' McNab said.

'That's what I came here to tell you,' she said firmly.

She'd accepted his suggestion that they go to an interview room, where she would meet his boss, Detective Inspector Wilson, and repeat what she'd just told him.

Her only response was that she feared to stay away from home too long in case Tizzy would abandon her.

'And I want us to have this last Christmas together.'

McNab had accepted this statement without comment, although he was mightily troubled by it.

Once he'd settled her with Janice, he'd gone to the boss and explained what had happened. DI Wilson had immediately agreed to come and speak to Marnie himself.

It was a strange scene. One he'd never thought he would see. The boss and Janice sitting across the table from Marnie Aitken. Himself to one side. He'd suggested he watch from next door, considering that she'd already told him her story and three might be too many.

Marnie had disagreed and asked him to stay. Janice she also seemed comfortable with.

Once the recording was started, the boss thanked her for coming in.

'It's quite a distance from Kilcreggan,' he offered.

'And I can't stay away long,' Marnie said. 'For Tizzy's sake.'

'I understand your daughter encouraged you to come,' DI Wilson said without a hint of anything other than interest.

She nodded. 'We didn't know about the murder in Elder Park until Joan from the café brought us a pile of newspapers. I think I know who killed that man and sewed his eyes and mouth shut. His name's Jack Boyd and it was him who kept me locked up.'

She continued. 'The Boyd family were big in Govan and Linthouse. When I left the care system at sixteen, that's where I ended up. In the park buying drugs from him at the farmhouse. I thought he was my boyfriend, until I couldn't pay any more. That's when I ended up in a flat working for him.'

She stopped and took a deep breath. 'When I knew I was pregnant, I made up my mind to get away and I managed it. Me and Tizzy were okay. Then I took her to the Gourock pool and someone took a photograph of us there, because she was such a great wee swimmer. It got in the papers. And there was also a photo of her as a Highland dancer. He must have seen it or someone showed him.

'Anyway, he came looking for us at the pool and was told we lived in Kilcreggan. So he came there to find us.' She paused there briefly, before she added, 'He owned me, you see. So he thought he owned Tizzy too.'

She fell silent and McNab prayed she wouldn't stop there, like she'd done with Rhona.

Seeming to steel herself, she continued.

'We went to the games. Tizzy was to compete with the youngest dancers. I took her to the tent to wait, then I saw him. I had to keep him away from Tizzy, so we left and headed back to Kilcreggan but keeping off the road. I took her to the cave at Portkil Bay, to be safe from the bad man, and left her there.

'He drugged me to try to make me tell him where she

was. I don't know if I did or not. I remember thinking, is she still there in the cave? When I came to I ran there, out of my mind that he'd found her. That I'd told him and couldn't remember.

'She wasn't there and neither was he. I knew right away that she'd drowned. I knew it. I think she ran into the water because she thought swimming away from him would save her. You see, I'd told her once that being able to swim might one day save her life.'

57

'Thank you for coming in and telling us all of this,' the boss said.

McNab had served his superior officer long enough to know the impact Marnie's story had had on him. Had had on all three of them.

'Would you be willing to look at a few photographs with DS McNab to confirm the identity of the man you call Jack Boyd?' the boss asked.

She nodded. 'But I must catch the last ferry. I promised Tizzy I would.'

'DS McNab will make sure you do.' DI Wilson rose. 'I'm afraid I have a meeting to go to, but I want to thank you again for your help. And for Tizzy's support in getting you to come here.'

He motioned to McNab that he wanted a brief word outside the room.

'I'm sorry, sir, about the child thing,' McNab began. 'I wasn't sure how to handle it, but Rhona and Professor Pirie had recommended that we go along with Marnie on that, because it's not uncommon for the bereaved to communicate with their departed.'

'I can vouch for that myself,' DI Wilson said. 'I know Margaret's dead, but that doesn't stop me talking to her. Nor does it stop her giving me advice, which I always listen to, just as I did when she was alive.'

McNab nodded, relieved.

'That was a harrowing tale she told, which I suspect we should have uncovered long before now. I'm sorry, Sergeant, that you weren't listened to. If she's right about what happened to the child and that Jack Boyd was involved in her death, then we got that very wrong. But that's for the future. See if she knows this Daryl character that Ally Feeney identified as the dark-haired man. I have an online meeting now with my counterparts in Chicago.'

'Okay?' McNab checked as he re-entered the room. 'We can get some tea and coffee if you'd like. Even some more mince pies?' he offered.

Janice said, 'I'll sort that out while you two take a look at the photos.'

McNab logged onto the system. 'While we wait for the images to come up, there's another name I'd like to run past you, if that's okay?'

When Marnie nodded, he continued. 'Did you ever meet a guy called Lewis McLean during your time with Boyd?'

There was a moment of stunned silence before she responded.

'You think Lewis is involved in what happened?' She shook her head. 'I don't believe that.'

'So you did meet him?' McNab tried.

'He was part of the gang that sold drugs to the student crowd. We got together a couple of times.' She stopped there as though remembering. 'He was kind. He wanted to get away from Glasgow. From Scotland. He had plans to go to America to be an actor. That's what he told me.'

'Well, he did exactly that,' McNab said. 'Became quite famous. On TikTok anyway.'

Her face broke into a smile. 'He did?' she said.

McNab passed her his mobile. 'Meet Jason Endeavour – or Lewis McLean as you knew him.'

She stared at the picture, open-mouthed. 'He did it,' she said. 'We'd both been in care. We both had shitty lives. We both had dreams. I'm glad his came true.'

Her pleasure was so palpable that McNab hesitated before continuing the story.

'The man who was murdered in Elder Park was Lewis McLean's younger brother, Robert Forbes. They were split up when his mother died and only reconnected recently through social media. They look – looked very alike and we believe Robert was mistaken for Lewis.'

'They wanted to kill Lewis, why? Jack has a long memory but . . .'

McNab decided to tell her what they knew about the movie. She listened carefully, before saying, 'Lewis hated Jack. He wanted to help me escape.' She shook her head as though back in that terrible place again. 'Does Jack know he got the wrong brother?'

'He does now,' McNab said.

'Then he won't give up. Just as he wouldn't give up on me. He didn't kill me when he found me in Kilcreggan. He did something much worse.'

With those final words, the woman who had talked so succinctly in the interview, who'd unburdened her soul to them in that room, seemed to evaporate and he was looking again at the tortured soul he'd interviewed six years before.

McNab realized they'd expected too much from her and castigated himself for it. But, he reasoned, she'd wanted Jack Boyd caught. She'd wanted them to know the danger he posed. She'd wanted them to know the truth.

He watched as she slipped her hand in her pocket as though to take hold of her daughter's.

At this moment, the door opened and Janice arrived with a tray. He caught her eye and indicated with a look that all was not well. Janice put on a smile and said, 'Look what I found in the canteen. Christmas tablet. Maybe not as good as Joan's but Tizzy might like a piece while we look at the photos.'

Afterwards, his partner would say that she'd never decry the power of a sugar rush again.

As though humouring them, Marnie slipped a piece of tablet into her pocket. The simple acknowledgement of how she felt seemed to steady her and, taking a sip of tea, she pronounced herself ready to look at the photographs.

The ease with which she identified both Jack and Daryl Boyd confirmed what McNab already believed. Marnie Aitken was a key witness in this case.

The question now was whether she could in any way identify the location of either of the two men. Even as he considered this, she seemed to be reading his mind on the matter.

'I came here to tell you that I believe Jack had something to do with the killing in the park. I can also show you the place he kept me.' She halted there as though something else had occurred. 'Is Lewis still in danger?'

McNab glanced at Janice. How much more should they tell her?

'Lewis knows who killed his brother and we're concerned he may intend to take revenge for that,' Janice explained.

McNab came in then. 'We think that Jack Boyd, assuming he is the killer, hasn't given up on getting his target, which is Lewis. As for Daryl, he's in the mix too.'

'Then what more can we do to help?' Marnie said.

58

Rhona was uncharacteristically late, although there was a good reason for it.

'The meeting's already begun, Dr MacLeod,' the desk sergeant told her on entry. 'A lot has been happening here today.' He raised an eyebrow.

'I could say the same, which is why I'm late,' Rhona replied.

As she slipped in at the back of the assembled group, she could sense the excitement. *So something big has happened*, she thought, *which could be either good or bad in the present circumstances.*

A quick scout round the heads indicated that neither McNab nor Janice were present, which was odd. DI Wilson was currently on the dais talking to their counterparts in Chicago.

From what she could gather, entering mid-conversation, the DNA she and Chrissy had retrieved from the skin flakes on the tape and thread used on Robert Forbes had found a match in the Chicago records.

'However, the name we have for him isn't Jack Boyd,' Detective Johnson was saying, 'it's Tony Capanni, who was involved in an altercation here in Chicago five years ago. And who we believe may be involved in organized crime.'

When the photograph of Tony Capanni appeared on screen, a ripple went through those present. It was the usual standard mugshot of a dark-haired guy, with a neat black beard and brown eyes who might, Rhona registered, well fit the description they had of Daryl Boyd.

'And is this Tony Capanni currently in the US?' DI Wilson asked.

'He hasn't returned here according to passport control. However, should we identify him on entry, he will of course be detained here.'

McNab won't be happy about that, Rhona thought, Chrissy having reported McNab's opinion on cross-Atlantic cooperation via Janice, and his intense annoyance at the Yanks muscling in on their territory.

DI Wilson came in again. 'We have a witness, recently come forward, whose story strengthens our belief that Jack Boyd is one of the two men involved in the murder of Robert Forbes. However, we believe, as mentioned earlier, that their mark was in fact Lewis McLean, known as Jason Endeavour. Can you confirm if Jason Endeavour has returned to the US?'

'He has not. Although we would have no reason to detain him if he did. His record is clear.'

'Let's hope we can keep it that way,' DI Wilson said.

The exchange at an end, Rhona made her way to the front.

'Apologies,' she said, 'for being late, but I have a good reason.'

'Want to come into my office and we can exchange stories?' DI Wilson suggested, opening the door for her. 'So how much did you catch of the meeting?' he asked, once they'd got seated.

'That their Tony Capanni is not our Jack Boyd, who is likely still on these shores,' Rhona told him. 'And something intriguing about a new witness?' she added.

Bill leaned back in his old and favourite chair. 'We had a visit this morning from Marnie Aitken. Turned up at the front desk looking for DS McNab.'

'My God,' Rhona said. 'I heard from Joan she'd been spotted boarding the ferry, but I had no idea where she'd gone.' She paused, trying to assimilate this surprising move on Marnie's part.

'Can I ask why she came to see McNab?'

'You can listen to the interview she gave after her initial conversation with him,' Bill said. 'Suffice to say her abuser was none other than Jack Boyd. It was he who sewed her mouth shut and locked her in a dark cupboard. It was him she ran away from.'

Bill then told her a story of a photograph taken of Marnie and Tizzy at the Gourock pool having ended up in the newspapers, which had brought Jack Boyd to Kilcreggan looking for them on the day of the Highland games.

'She believes Tizzy ran into the water to try to escape him, and that's how she drowned.'

The image this painted was all too clear to Rhona. Marnie hiding the child in the cave at Portkil Bay to be safe. Then her abuser finding her, resulting in the child trying to escape by swimming away.

'The soil from the cottage came from a cave in Portkil Bay. It's quite unique archaeologically.' Rhona paused there, thinking. 'Is Marnie here because she read the stuff in the papers about the murder in Elder Park?'

'She recognized Jack Boyd's handiwork. Something she knew only too well,' Bill said. 'It appears Tizzy persuaded her to come here and tell McNab that.'

'And you believed her despite the fact she takes advice from a dead daughter?' Rhona said.

'I think I believed her because of that,' Bill said. 'Margaret died some time ago and I still listen to her advice.'

Rhona smiled, knowing how true that was. Partnerships 'made in heaven', as her adoptive dad used to say, 'don't end with death'.

'Marnie told us something else,' Bill went on. 'McNab asked her if she knew Lewis McLean. Turns out he dealt drugs to the student body for Boyd, and hated him. She and Lewis were friends.'

Rhona smiled. 'They were, I think, more than friends.'

Bill was trying to work out what she meant. When he couldn't, she explained.

'The result came back on Tizzy's DNA. Lewis McLean – or Jason Endeavour – is Tizzy's father, not Jack Boyd.'

Bill looked dumbfounded. 'D'you think Marnie knows that?'

'I suspect she hoped he might be,' Rhona said. 'Perhaps Tizzy didn't live long enough to show the likeness, except maybe in the hair colour. That glorious shade of strawberry blonde.' She thought back to the lock of hair hidden inside the Highland doll. How big a thing it must have been for Marnie to part with it, even for a short while.

'Has Marnie gone home now?' Rhona asked, wondering if she might tell Marnie the truth in person.

'She's gone out with DS McNab and Clark. She's showing them where Boyd kept her in Govan, and anywhere else he might choose to hang out when back in Glasgow.'

'While he searches for Lewis McLean?' Rhona said.

'As Marnie said, Jack Boyd has a long memory and a thirst for revenge on those who thwart him.'

'Then Marnie took a chance coming back to his patch,' Rhona said.

'She's well aware of that,' Bill told her, 'but she – no, *they* were determined to do everything they could to have him caught.'

Rhona tried to put her niggling fear about Marnie's immediate welfare to the back of her mind and mentioned the other reason she was here.

'Whoever left the skin flakes on the thread used to shut the victim's eyes and on the tape round his wrists is a relation of Jack Boyd's,' Rhona said. 'We know that Jack has a record, so his DNA is stored in our database. He knows that too. Whoever did the sewing and taping knew they weren't on the database, here anyway. But they forgot about the US.'

'You think that photograph the Chicago team showed us of their Tony Capanni was in fact Daryl Boyd?' Bill said.

'You'll have to confirm that with one of your super recognizers, but whoever it is, their DNA was on our victim,' Rhona said.

'If Jack Boyd was that careful, even if we catch him, how do we prove he was involved in the killing?'

Now was the time for Rhona to tell him what Chrissy's dedication and determination had achieved.

'When we swabbed the body in situ, we collected multiple blood samples. Only one of which did not belong to the victim. Nor did it match the DNA from any of the skin flake samples,' Rhona told him. 'This particular sample was collected from the right-hand knuckle of the victim. It appears he managed to get a punch in and drew blood from one of his attackers.'

She paused, giving Bill time to absorb this, before continuing.

'Chrissy, in charge of lifting samples of the blood splattering on the floor of the room in the farmhouse where he'd been tortured, found a match with that deposit on the knuckle. Both belong to a person already on our database.'

'Jack Boyd,' Bill finished for her.

59

Their run round Govan had taken longer than McNab expected. And in truth they were nowhere near locating Jack Boyd's current location.

All the trip had appeared to do was lower Marnie's mood. The enthusiasm with which she'd set out had dissipated and McNab had the strong sense that Tizzy's presence in her mind had diminished.

They'd located the tenement property she'd shared with Boyd, and Janice had checked with all the current residents. None of whom had any knowledge of the man or the fact that he'd effectively run a brothel in their building a decade ago.

Govan had definitely changed in the interim and hopefully, McNab thought, for the better.

Glancing in the rear-view mirror, he noted Marnie's pale demeanour and realized she'd likely had nothing to eat apart from a couple of mince pies since she'd set off from Kilcreggan. So he decided to take a run past Leo's in the hope that he might persuade her into having a fish supper. When he motioned eating to Janice, she immediately cottoned on and gave him the thumbs-up.

As they drew up alongside the chippie, Marnie seemed to come to, and suddenly said, 'Is Leo still around?'

'Still frying,' McNab told her. 'This is where the boy Ally, who went missing, came with his mates. Leo really liked him.'

'I used to come here too with my mates before . . .' She tailed off.

'You okay to go in?' McNab asked. 'Or shall I just fetch you something?'

Marnie thought about this for a moment. 'No. I'll go in with you, if that's all right?'

Janice gave him her order of a haggis supper and said she'd wait in the car.

Inside, there was only one customer in front of them and once Leo had served him and sent him on his way, he turned to McNab.

'I'm glad you came in, Detective Sergeant, because I was going to call you.' Leo gave Marnie a quick glance as though he should maybe not talk in front of her.

'This is Marnie,' McNab said. 'She's helping us look for Jack Boyd.'

Leo gave Marnie a long look. 'Have you been here before?'

'Ten years ago,' she said. 'And I was with Jack Boyd.'

Leo's face darkened. 'You were only a wee lassie back then.' When Marnie didn't respond, he added, 'Well, I'm glad to see you're not with him any more.'

He now focused on McNab. 'We take online orders. I've had a couple I wanted you to have a look at.'

He put the snib on the front door and, turning the sign to say 'Back soon', led McNab through to the back office, where a laptop sat open.

'Take a look at the two orders I've highlighted,' he said. 'The first one was picked up in person. By Dreep's big brother.'

'Darren McGowan?' McNab checked.

'Exactly,' Leo nodded.

'And the other order?' McNab asked.

'A delivery. Three suppers to this address.' He pointed to the screen.

McNab's heart upped a beat. 'And who delivered the order?'

'The young lad you met helping me out last night. Same guy came to the door, he says.' Leo was studying McNab's reaction. 'You think this helps?'

'It does,' McNab confirmed, already considering what exactly they should do with it.

'Can you wait here while Leo does our order?' he told Marnie as they emerged from the back room. 'I need to chat to DS Clark.'

'What's up?' Janice said as he slid in beside her.

'We have an address where Darren McGowan's holed up with two others,' he said. 'They've been ordering food online from Leo.'

As Janice absorbed this, he added, 'Not far from here. Opposite the Old Govan Arms pub.'

'Assuming you want to take a look, what do we do with Marnie?' She glanced towards the shop window, where Marnie sat at a table looking out at them.

McNab had already considered this. 'We could leave her with Leo while we suss out the address. Or we can drive her back to the station before we take a look.'

Janice contemplated the two options and offered a third. 'If we're going round there, we have no idea what will happen. We should call the station and have someone pick her up, just in case.'

McNab considered this and knew it wouldn't work. Marnie had agreed to come here with him. To hand her over to a stranger, even a policeman, might spook her altogether.

Checking the time, he realized the strategy meeting might still be in progress or perhaps just over. So he rang Rhona's number, hoping she was still about.

She answered immediately. 'How's it going with Marnie? Bill told me about her turning up at the station.'

McNab gave her a brief explanation of what they'd learned from Leo and what they were planning. 'I was going to call for a patrol car to pick Marnie up,' he began.

'She wouldn't like that,' Rhona said. 'I'll come for her. I want to speak to her about today anyway.'

'Good thinking,' Janice said when he rang off. 'D'you want to explain what's happening to Marnie or shall I?'

'My job,' McNab told her. Heading back inside, he found Leo boxing up their food. Paying him, he told Leo under his breath what they had planned for Marnie and was answered with a smile and a nod.

In contrast, Marnie's face was pinched with fear, although she was trying to muster herself.

'I'd like you to stay here with Leo and eat your fish supper,' he explained. 'Dr McLeod is on her way to pick you up.'

She took this in. 'You think you know where Jack is?' she asked quietly.

'Leo gave me an address that myself and DS Clark need to check out,' McNab told her.

'You'll be fine here, lass,' Leo said cheerfully. 'And I'll make you a mug of tea to go with your food.'

Marnie nodded. 'Okay, but Tizzy wants you to be careful.'

'Tell Tizzy I promise I will.'

Lifting the two boxes of hot food, he headed back to the vehicle. While he drove, Janice radioed in where they were headed and asked for back-up in case of trouble.

'I take it the plan is to pretend a delivery from Leo's?' she said. 'See who answers?'

McNab indicated with a nod that she was right.

'Then I'll be the one to do that,' she said firmly. 'If they say it's not theirs, I'll apologize for my mistake and say it must be for next door.'

McNab, seeing her determination, gave her the okay.

Drawing up outside the Old Govan Arms pub, he pointed across the road. 'That's the door. The previous order came from 1F2, the first-floor flat.'

'Any name on the door?' Janice checked.

McNab shook his head.

'Then 1F2 it is,' Janice said, exiting the vehicle, Leo's boxes in hand.

'No going into the flat,' McNab warned. 'Just straight back here again.'

Janice gave him a look that spoke volumes before she headed across the road.

McNab watched her press the entry buzzer. The first time brought no response, so she tried a different button. A moment later the door was set free and Janice stepped inside.

McNab immediately exited the vehicle and, springing across the road, caught the heavy door as it moved to close itself behind his partner. Slipping inside, he waited as, unaware of his presence, she continued up the stairs. It wasn't that he didn't trust her to do what she said she would. It was more that he didn't trust whoever might open the door of 1F2.

At this point she must have reached the said flat, because he heard her rap at the door.

When there was seemingly no response, she tried again, this time calling out, 'Delivery from Leo's.'

McNab listened as she knocked again.

Why would no one answer, he thought. According to Leo, they'd ordered before, so there should be no surprises when the recent order arrived.

He heard Janice rap one more time, then call out, 'Anyone in there?'

Hearing the change of tone in his partner's voice, McNab decided it was time to appear and raced up the stairs.

'What's up?' he said as he saw Janice's expression.

'Something's wrong in there. I can hear groaning.'

McNab put his shoulder to the door. Once. Twice. But the catch wasn't about to budge. This time he braced himself against the banister and used his foot.

The determined kick sprang the Yale lock and the door swung open.

Now the groans could be clearly heard.

The horrible thought of his partner walking in on another naked tortured guy in a chair made him head in first.

Two bodies on the floor. One male. One female.

Karen was curled in a corner, motionless. The groans weren't coming from her, but from the male who lay nearby, his gut a bloodied mess, the knife still in there.

Janice was already on the phone, even as she felt for a pulse in Karen's neck.

'She's unconscious but alive,' she told him.

McNab knelt by the man he believed to be Darren McGowan and, looking into the face, immediately thought about his skinny wee brother, Dreep.

60

Dark now, the street lamps formed a halo of light in the freezing fog, the intermittent snow showers crisping the pavements like frosting on a cake.

Rhona hadn't required directions to Leo's because she and Chrissy had taken Ally's advice that night and gone there for a fish supper. Added to that, they'd swabbed and tested his numerous boxes that had littered the upstairs room of the farmhouse.

It seemed by this latest call from McNab that she wasn't finished with Leo's yet.

Passing the dark outline of the old farmhouse, surrounded by the skeletons of the encompassing trees, she understood why Ally Feeney had been drawn back there.

Places where a life had been taken, especially in violent circumstances, held such a power. If the perpetrator of that violence was caught and brought to justice, that might help in some instances, but often a building had to be bulldozed before the spell was broken.

When McNab had called, she'd been listening to Marnie's interview with Bill. In fact, she'd already decided to wait around until McNab returned, hoping to speak to Marnie in person regarding the results of the DNA test. In truth, she had no idea how Marnie might react to the news. *If she'd already suspected Jack wasn't Tizzy's father, it won't come as so much of a surprise to her as it did to me*, Rhona thought.

Drawing up outside the chip shop, she could see Marnie through the window seated at a table, nursing a mug of tea.

The appetizing smells on entering reminded Rhona that she hadn't eaten as yet.

Leo, serving a line of three folk, gave her a nod to show he'd noted her arrival, then carried on as normal.

She looks exhausted, Rhona thought as she took a seat opposite Marnie.

'How are you?' she asked.

'Okay,' Marnie told her. 'DS McNab's gone to check out an address for Jack Boyd.'

'I know,' Rhona said. 'Don't worry, McNab knows what he's doing.' She paused. 'I'm to take you back to the station. I understand you wanted to return to Kilcreggan tonight?'

Marnie considered this. 'I did, and DS McNab said he would take me to the ferry, but if he . . .' She tailed off.

'I could drive you to the ferry?' Rhona offered.

Marnie paused for a moment, then said, 'I think I'd rather stay in Glasgow until I know what's happened.'

'And what does Tizzy think about that?' Rhona said quietly.

'She says she won't leave me. Even though I'm away from home,' Marnie told her.

'Good,' Rhona said. 'I wanted to speak to you about the lock of hair you sent me.'

'You gave me that back when you came to the cottage,' Marnie reminded her.

'I did,' Rhona said. 'And since then I've learned something.'

A shadow crossed Marnie's face. 'Can we go to the car, please?'

Rhona rose. 'Of course. How about we head for my place? You can meet Tom, my cat, and we can have a chat there.'

The drive home was silent, although Rhona had the feeling that Marnie was talking with Tizzy. What about, she didn't know.

Marnie's silence lasted until she entered the flat and met Tom, who, delighted to see not just one person but two arrive home, went to town on his affectionate feline routine.

That alone was enough to put Marnie and no doubt Tizzy at ease.

Settling Marnie in the sitting room, Rhona put on the kettle and checked for something to eat. It'd looked like Marnie had only picked at the fish supper, perhaps too worried by the situation she'd found herself in, so Rhona decided to offer her something now.

'What about a bacon roll?' she suggested. 'I'm not much of a cook, but I can do that for you.'

'If you're having one, that would be good,' Marnie told her.

After they'd eaten and drunk mugs of tea and coffee, Rhona said, 'I have a spare room if you'd rather wait until morning to head home?'

Noting the mix of pleasure and concern her offer produced, she added, 'It's no bother to me and by then we'll know what happened with McNab.'

'If you're sure?' Marnie said. After a moment's silence, she added, 'You can tell me now about the DNA.'

'Okay, but I suspect you might be aware of what I'm

going to say because of the forensic discussion in the Lilias Centre,' Rhona said. 'And that's why you sent me the doll with the lock of hair inside.' She waited until Marnie gave a small nod. 'As I explained back then, a child gets fifty per cent DNA from their mother and fifty per cent from their father. I believe you want to know who Tizzy's father was?'

Marnie's face was pale but resolute when she indicated that that was true.

'Well, it definitely wasn't Jack Boyd, whose DNA is stored with his criminal record on the national database,' Rhona said firmly.

A wave of relief mixed with conviction crossed Marnie's face. 'I *knew* she couldn't be Jack's. I *knew* it. Not with her nature. Her joy at life.' She halted there, her expression becoming one of acceptance. 'I was working as a prostitute. Her father could be any one of those men.'

'Except he wasn't,' Rhona told her. 'We had to check the victim in the farmhouse murder against a missing actor, one Jason Endeavour, who you knew as Lewis McLean.'

Marnie had lifted her head again and was gazing at Rhona questioningly.

'I can tell you now, without any shadow of doubt, that Lewis McLean is Tizzy's biological father.'

Marnie's surprise and joy at this news was short-lived as she appeared to consider what that might mean should either Jack Boyd or Lewis McLean find this out, because she immediately said, 'I don't want Lewis told. Ever. For him to know that Jack killed his brother, then his daughter . . .' She halted there, her horror obvious. 'And if Jack found out that Tizzy was Lewis's child, it would make him even more determined to kill him.'

Rhona had already addressed both these thoughts herself.

'Who knows about this?' Marnie said.

'Just DI Wilson, myself and my assistant, Chrissy,' Rhona told her. 'It's not part of the official investigation into Robert Forbes's death, so neither man needs to know.'

This seemed to ease Marnie's worries a little, because she relaxed back in the sofa and was swiftly joined by Tom, who put his head on her shoulder.

'Tom always knows who needs his company,' Rhona told her. 'Cat intuition.'

Marnie sat in silence for a while, her hand stroking Tom's head, the sound of his purring apparently making her smile. Rhona wondered if the smile was indeed for Tom or was more about her happiness at the news of Tizzy's real father.

Lewis, it seemed, had been her friend and ally at the worst time of her life. And he'd given her Tizzy, a child that she'd loved more than life itself. Despite everything that had happened since, it was a precious moment for Marnie to savour.

Eventually she said, 'Tizzy wanted a cat. I don't know why I didn't get her one.'

'I didn't choose to get Tom,' Rhona recalled. 'I came home one day and found him here. A friend got him for me.' She didn't mention it was Sean's idea. 'I wasn't happy about it back then, but I am now,' she said honestly.

'Maybe I'll get one when I go back to Kilcreggan. Give it to Tizzy as a Christmas present,' Marnie said, checking for Rhona's reaction to this.

'That sounds like a good idea to me,' Rhona told her.

When Marnie went through to bed, Rhona settled down with her laptop and mobile alongside, in case McNab should call.

Earlier, listening to Marnie's interview with Bill, she

couldn't help but reflect on some of the parallels with her own teenage years. She had become pregnant around the same age as Marnie. Her boyfriend at the time, a fellow student at Glasgow University, hadn't been cruel like Jack Boyd, but he had been controlling.

When she'd told him about the pregnancy, he'd basically ordered her to have an abortion. He said that a child wasn't in his life plan. A plan that would eventually lead him to practise law and become an MP.

When she'd refused to countenance an abortion, he'd informed her that he wanted nothing more to do with her or their son. Troubled and alone, she'd decided to give Liam up for adoption, never telling her parents about their grandchild. Something she would always regret.

McNab called at eleven, immediately apologizing that he might have woken her.

'I'm still up,' she assured him. 'I was expecting you to call. Marnie's here with me.'

McNab sounded surprised. 'I thought she wanted to get back to Kilcreggan?'

'She decided to wait and find out how you'd got on,' Rhona explained. 'I brought her here because I needed to tell her the results of the DNA search on Tizzy's father.'

McNab went silent at that, then said, 'I assume it was Jack Boyd?'

'It wasn't. Tizzy's father was Lewis McLean, aka Jason Endeavour.'

McNab's expletives were colourful and extensive.

'My God. When did you discover that?' he finally said.

'Just before the meeting, which I was late for. DI Wilson knows, as does Chrissy and now you. Marnie doesn't want Lewis to find out. They were friends back then, both wanting out of Jack Boyd's clutches. Lewis made it away. She didn't. She doesn't want to give Lewis a bigger reason to go after Jack than he already has,' she told him.

When McNab remained silent following this, Rhona felt a niggle of worry developing. 'Are you going to tell me what happened tonight?' she said.

'I'm outside,' he said. 'Can I come up?'

61

He hadn't wanted to arrive at her door without warning. So he'd parked up near her flat, then phoned her, knowing she was probably expecting a call.

Hearing the news about Lewis McLean being Tizzy's father had flummoxed him. That was something that hadn't entered his head, even when Marnie had confessed to knowing Lewis back when she was with Boyd.

Having it confirmed now put a whole new slant on things.

On the drive over, he'd decided to phone only if her sitting-room light was on. Despite his pleasure at finding it was, he'd waited a further ten minutes before he'd made the call, worried as he was about what he had to tell her.

That die now cast, he exited the car and, crossing the road to Rhona's building, was surprised to find the door already released. Reaching the top landing, he discovered she'd also left her own door ajar and briefly considered remonstrating with her about this, before reminding himself that Dr MacLeod didn't like being told what to do. Even when it was in her best interests.

He found her, as expected, in the sitting room, her laptop and mobile nearby.

'Don't you ever stop working?' he said.

'I could ask you the same thing.' She returned his smile.

He didn't know how to soften what he had to tell her, so he just blurted it out.

'We visited an address in Govan, given us by Leo from the fish shop. It appeared Darren McGowan had previously ordered a meal for three people from that location.' He paused there, conscious of the frightened look on her face.

'We found Darren inside, in a bad way from a knife wound, and Karen Bell unconscious. We transferred both to hospital. From the little Darren was able to tell us, we believe that Daryl and Jack Boyd have taken Lewis.'

Rhona glanced swiftly at the door, worried, he realized, that her visitor might have heard what he'd just told her.

'Have you any idea where they might have taken him?' Rhona managed.

'None,' McNab admitted. 'And we don't know exactly when it happened. When back-up arrived, they set to work questioning the neighbours, hoping for a sighting of whatever vehicle they'd arrived in, while DS Clark and I followed the ambulances to the Queen Elizabeth Hospital.'

Rhona was silent, although he knew her mind was racing with the news and its consequences.

'They may have already killed him,' she said quietly.

'On the other hand, they could intend to carry out their original plan and torture him first,' McNab said.

It was a horrible thought, but if true it would at least give them some time to find him.

Rhona had assumed a different expression, a more studied and calculating one.

'I think you're right,' she said. 'The torture they inflicted on Robert Forbes while believing him to be Lewis McLean was sustained and thorough. They also took him to a place that held meaning for them, when they could have just killed and dumped him.'

She began pacing between the window and the door.

'Marnie told me the farmhouse was where it all began. That's where the Boyds dealt drugs to teenagers and recruited young females like her into prostitution. That's where Lewis and she met and where he began to work for them.'

McNab came back in. 'So that's why they took him there when he wrote about them in the movie script.'

'Retribution,' Rhona said. 'Killing him quickly won't work for them. Plus, when they got the wrong man, that made them look stupid on both sides of the Atlantic. To the Chicago gang that sent them back here to do the job. Plus the remainder of the Jamesie gang still operating here in Glasgow.'

McNab realized she was talking sense.

'So we have to know where else they might take him,' she added, 'and as quickly as possible. Remember, we believe Robert Forbes survived the torture. What he couldn't survive was the fall from the window.'

Rhona stopped there as though listening, then put a finger to her lips, indicating that Marnie might be outside. At this point the cat jumped from the back of the sofa and headed for the door, mewing.

Following it, Rhona opened the door. 'Marnie,' she said quietly. 'This involves you too. Come and sit down.'

Marnie looks like the frightened young woman I first met back in Kilcreggan six years ago, McNab thought.

'How much did you hear?' Rhona asked.

'I heard DS McNab arrive, but I thought maybe you

would want to talk to him alone.' Marnie glanced from one face to the other. 'Then it sounded bad, so I came and stood at the door. I heard Lewis's name mentioned. Is he hurt?'

McNab looked to Rhona, who mouthed the words 'the truth' to him.

So he repeated what he'd just told Rhona, softening it a little in the repetition.

'So Jack has Lewis,' Marnie said in distress.

'We have officers out looking for him,' McNab told her. 'But we need help to think where Jack and Daryl might take him. The farmhouse was chosen the first time—'

Marnie interrupted him. 'Because that's where Lewis was initiated into the gang.'

'I believe so,' McNab said, hope rising now that she understood their thinking on this.

Rhona came back in then, speaking directly to Marnie. 'They didn't kill Robert right away, and we believe they won't kill Lewis immediately either.'

'Jack will torture him. Just like he did to me.'

'So if we knew where to look,' Rhona said, 'we might have time to save Lewis.'

'Is there anywhere you can think of that would be symbolic enough for Jack to take Lewis there?' McNab said.

'You think this all happened because of the film Lewis was making?' she asked.

'We believe so,' McNab said. 'And so do the police in Chicago.'

'So we need to look through the script,' Marnie said.

McNab had only skim-read the script when he was choosing a scene to illustrate to his fellow officers his thoughts on what was happening. So he now felt at a loss.

Rhona had taken a seat beside Marnie and he realized she was already accessing the script on her laptop.

'While Marnie takes a look through the script,' she said, 'I suggest you contact the other half of the scriptwriting team, whatever his name is. Tell him what's happened and see if he can come up with any fictional location that might be applicable.'

'Steven John Jarvis,' McNab told her. 'And he's in LA. Eight hours earlier than us.'

Taking himself into the kitchen, McNab made the call. Late night here, it would be mid-afternoon in LA, so no reason for SJ not to answer, especially when he saw the name of the caller on the screen. On the other hand, maybe that would be a reason for him not to answer.

'Hello, Steven John Jarvis here?' a voice finally said.

'DS McNab from Police Scotland.'

'Has Jason been found?' SJ immediately asked.

'We found where he was hiding, but unfortunately his pursuer got there first,' McNab told him. 'His life is now in serious danger, and we need your help in trying to locate where he's been taken.'

A pregnant silence followed as SJ digested the bad news. 'How can I do that from LA?' he eventually said.

McNab explained about the significance of the script in how this might play out, then added, 'If we're right, then there may be a window of opportunity before they kill him.'

He could almost smell the panic rising on the other end of the phone.

'I don't know what was true in the script and what Jason made up,' SJ said.

McNab had a dozen other questions that he knew

instinctively SJ would have no answer for. He was wasting his time here.

'Okay. I want you to go through the script again right now and send me all the Glasgow locations featured, especially if they involve violence.'

'I'll do that, Detective, right away, and get back to you.' SJ's relief at being let off the hook was obvious in his voice.

As the line went dead, McNab emitted a string of curses. SJ, he realized, may well have been leaned on to keep his mouth shut, just as the major players in the *Snake House* had swiftly departed Scotland.

Serious organized crime was international, after all.

Deciding he needed a caffeine fix to help him think more clearly, he checked out the machine and found some still warm in the jug. Pouring a mugful, he drank it down and poured a refill.

At that moment Rhona appeared.

'There's a scene in the script at a nightclub called the Red Eye.' She placed the laptop on the kitchen table and motioned him to take a look. 'Marnie says it reads like a scene she's experienced herself. There's an upstairs room where young women are paraded naked on a stage and the men bid for them.' The anger in Rhona's voice resonated with his own.

'The Red Eye. Was that the name of the club she was taken to?' McNab said.

'No. The one she was taken to was called the Red Dragon.'

62

Climbing into his car, he decided to check in with Janice before heading for the Red Dragon. 'You home yet?' he asked.

'Just got here. They sent an officer to replace me at the hospital. Before you ask, Darren's in surgery and Karen is still unconscious from a blow to her head.'

'Well, get some sleep. We've done what we can for tonight.'

'Wait. What happened to Marnie?' Janice said.

'Rhona took her back to her flat. There were things she had to be told.'

'Such as?' Janice said.

'That Lewis McLean was Tizzy's father.' No matter how often he said this, even to himself, it surprised him. 'I'll explain more about it tomorrow.'

'My God,' Janice said. 'That changes a lot of things.'

'It does,' he agreed.

'I take it we've had no luck finding out where they took Lewis, dead or alive?' Janice said.

'No solid info,' he told her. 'I'm going to check in with headquarters regularly, though.'

'And get some sleep,' she ordered.

'Sure thing, partner,' McNab said and rang off, assuring himself that he hadn't actually lied. He just hadn't told the whole story of tonight in all its glorious technicolour.

Driving through the city streets, he found them largely deserted although, come closing time, the numerous clubs would disgorge their festive customers to liven the area round George Square.

Noting the fairly spectacular Christmas decorations, McNab confirmed to himself that he wasn't into Christmas, having spent too many Christmases alone or working.

Maybe this one will be different, he thought. *Especially if I end up at Chrissy's place.*

Entering the Merchant City, he found the movie set disbanded. Even the trailer he'd visited recently had gone, which suggested Ragnar had been pulled out too, and was probably even now on his way back to enjoy Christmas in the States.

This time round, the proximity of the Red Dragon to the abandoned movie's location wasn't lost on him. If indeed it did include a scene at a place called the Red Eye, it would have been easy enough to make use of the club's frontage. If not also the inside.

Had Jason planned to use the real club in his movie? If so, had that literally been the final nail in the movie's coffin? And maybe in his own?

Driving past the open door and red welcoming light, he noted that there was no bouncer on duty. Or else he'd moved inside to avoid the freezing air.

McNab chose a spot a little way away to park his car. Not wishing to make his visit official by using the main entrance, he now set about checking for any fire doors to the premises where he might enter and take a look around on the quiet.

According to Marnie, the room upstairs had been used for more than just pole dancing. Were Moondance or the other girls currently working here aware of its existence and usage? Or had that practice ended in the intervening decade, during which Marnie had given birth to Tizzy, then been jailed for six years for something she'd not been responsible for?

At that moment, Marnie's haunted expression when she'd learned of Lewis McLean's capture returned to remind him of why he was creeping round the back of this building, looking for an entry point.

He was finally rewarded when he spotted a metal fire escape that climbed to the third floor, with apparent access on each intervening level. All three of which were in darkness.

After another quick look to check there was no one around, he hoisted himself up and began his climb.

The air being still and cold, and the late-night traffic infrequent, he found himself wishing for the raucous laughter of revellers to dwarf the clang of his feet on the metal steps. Reaching the first floor, he stopped and, pressing himself against the wall, tried to see inside. Eventually, with the aid of a not-too-distant street lamp, he made out the shape of the room and its shadowy contents.

There was a central dais, with what looked like a single pole in its centre. Might this be a room for private dances? He could only assume so. One thing was certain, though. It was in almost total darkness – until, that is, a light was suddenly switched on in the neighbouring stairwell accompanied by the sound of approaching voices.

Moving out of view, he waited. If the men – for they were definitely male voices – were intent on coming into the room at this level, further lights would be switched on, which might expose his presence.

Imagining his shadow might be visible where he currently stood, he decided to climb a few steps higher. Immediately having done this, he realized the men weren't coming into the room with the dance pole after all, but were heading up to the next floor.

This time he waited halfway up the steps to see whether the lights on level two would be switched on. Within minutes they were.

First he heard the click, quickly followed by the crackling of a fluorescent bulb going into action, then the window just two steps above him was flooded with white light. At the same time, he heard a loud groan, as though the bright light was unwelcome and had caused a possible occupant of the room shock or pain.

McNab, his mind racing on what that might mean, forced himself to remain below the window and listen.

This time he could clearly make out the two main voices, both guttural and definitely male. As for the other person in the room, they had gone completely quiet, as though listening as fervently to what the voices were saying as he was.

By now, he'd decided that the third voice belonged to a prisoner of sorts. Or at least someone, by the sound they'd emitted, who was likely gagged. Desperate now to discover the identity of all three men, he eased his head up a little so that he might see better.

The image of what looked like a hospital trolley below the expanse of fluorescent light gave the impression of being an operating room.

From his angle of sight he could see the bare legs and feet, a view of one shoulder and the top of a man's head. There was blood there too, but it didn't prevent his view of the hair, whose colour resembled his own.

In a moment, he was the one in there, bound, gagged and blindfold, hearing his tormentors discuss what they might yet do to him.

Feeling nausea rise in his throat, he ducked down and, concentrating on breathing, forced that memory back into the recesses of his mind where it belonged.

The man in there was not him. He was out here on the fire escape. He could climb down at least one level and call this in. Have officers here swiftly who would free the man he believed to be Lewis McLean and arrest his tormentors.

A strange screeching sound forced him back to the window.

The men had raised one end of the bed so that their naked victim was now in a sitting position, legs stretched out. The bed, being on wheels, had swivelled a little and sat at an angle to the window, offering McNab a partial view of his face.

Swollen as it was, he could still make out the cross-stitched eyes and mouth, the lacerations to the chest and the one bloodied hand on the left side.

Revulsion swept through him and he felt himself gag again.

Turning outwards, he bent his head between his knees, willing himself not to retch. Knowing the sound of it couldn't fail to be heard.

The moment passed and he made his decision.

As quietly as possible, he felt for his mobile and extracted it. At that very instant he heard a shout from the alley below. The bouncer, missing from the front door, had spotted him and was shouting about his presence on the fire escape.

As he fumbled with his mobile, it slipped from his hands and fell, clanging against the metalwork on its way down, no doubt alerting those inside the room to his presence.

Aware that the bouncer would be with him in seconds, McNab decided to head upwards rather than down.

He only got halfway up the steps before a hand caught his ankle and dragged him back down.

'What the fuck are you doing up here?' a voice demanded as McNab scrambled to his feet.

His hope that he was about to face the same bouncer as before was quickly quashed when he saw the guy's face.

'Police,' he said, reaching into his pocket for his ID and handing it over, aware that he was well out of line here and could quite rightly be escorted off the premises.

The bouncer didn't bother taking a look at it. 'You still have no right to be up here.'

'Then I'd like to go back down,' McNab said.

The bouncer was eyeing him the way you might view a prize salmon caught on your hook, wondering whether to smash its head on the nearest stone or throw it back in the river.

'Your boss and I have met before,' McNab tried. 'I suggest you take me to him. Then I'll explain.'

'He's not on the premises and we're about to close. I suggest you come back tomorrow and use the front door this time,' was the reply.

'There's a man hurt in that room.' McNab pointed to the window below, which was now in darkness.

The bouncer laughed. 'Really, Detective Sergeant?' he

said. 'Are you sure you haven't had a little too much to drink? And while on duty too.' He tutted.

As he spoke, he'd been quietly propelling McNab downwards. Now, with their feet on the platform outside the said room, his captor made his move.

The blow that met the back of McNab's head had the power of a boxer behind it. A fraction of a second later, his legs gave way and darkness overtook him.

63

She'd waited until she heard Rhona go through to the kitchen and shut the door before she'd risen, still dressed, from the bed.

When Rhona had suggested she try to get some sleep, she'd immediately agreed. Mainly because Tizzy had urged her to.

Once in the bedroom, she'd listened to her own thoughts, which were in tandem with her daughter's. If they'd taken Lewis to the Red Dragon, that's where she had to go.

Also, she had sent DS McNab there with her story of the auction. What she hadn't told him was what the men in that upstairs room were actually bidding for. And it wasn't just sex. They would own the girl they bid for. To do with what they wanted. Just as Jack Boyd had done with her.

Jack had been the one to run those auctions using the girls who, like her, he regarded as his property.

Whatever he now did to Lewis, she suspected, would be even crueller than what he'd done to his brother. Jack did not like to be thwarted. She of all people knew that.

Quietly closing the bedroom door behind her, she prayed that Tom wouldn't arrive to herald her presence in the hall before she could escape. It was at that moment she heard the kitchen window being raised and Tom being encouraged to go out onto the roof.

Using this as cover, she opened the front door and slipped out.

Taking the steep steps nearby, she made for the top of Sauchiehall Street where she could be sure of picking up a taxi. The bars and clubs were still open and busy, so she didn't have to compete with revellers heading home.

The taxi driver sounded a bit perplexed by her choice of the Red Dragon as a destination.

'You do know that's more of a male hang-out?' he checked.

'My sister dances there,' she told him. 'I'm going to meet her.'

He shrugged his shoulders at that and said no more.

Being dropped off a street away, as requested, she paid him from the remainder of her meagre funds, then watched as he drove away, her courage leaving with him.

She'd spent ten years trying to escape Jack's clutches and was now doing what so many of her fellow inmates had done. Walk back towards the horror.

This isn't the same, Tizzy told her. *You're going to help my daddy.*

She knew Tizzy's words were conjured up by her own mind. She'd known this from the moment she'd seen her daughter's imagined figure trudge past the Lilias Centre. She also believed that everything Tizzy had told her had brought her to this point and for a reason.

The snow had come on again, falling in big wet flakes that melted on her face. Raising the hood on her jacket, Marnie approached the Red Dragon.

As she watched from across the street, a couple of men exited the red-lit entrance and three more were allowed inside by the bouncer. She'd already decided that she wouldn't try to use the front entrance, knowing it would attract attention.

There was, she remembered, another way in from the right-side lane, because she'd been marched through it a decade ago. If it was still there, she would try to enter that way.

It was at that moment she heard a clanging sound like something hitting off metal, at which the bouncer departed his post and made for the left-hand lane. Marnie, still on the opposite side of the road, followed him.

When she reached her vantage point, she saw that he was halfway up the fire exit staircase towards a figure who was trying to get away by heading for the roof.

She instinctively knew who was being chased. She also anticipated the outcome of this before it happened. McNab was initially giving the bouncer the police officer story, which she doubted he would buy. Then McNab was on his way back down, the bouncer behind him.

Marnie had an image of what might happen next. A good shove would send McNab hurling down two storeys. But that didn't happen. The blow to the head buckled him, but he was stopped from falling forward. Instead, he was pushed through the open fire-exit door on the second floor, the bouncer quickly following.

Marnie stood there shaking as though she had been the one struck on the head.

What are we going to do now? Tizzy asked in a subdued voice.

At that point Marnie had no thought except to run as

fast and as far away as she could. But she'd got McNab into this mess, so she couldn't just abandon him. Her next thought was that the bouncer would not have struck a police officer unless he had something to hide, and that something was inside the Red Dragon.

64

After McNab departed, Rhona had persuaded Marnie to go back to bed. At least to rest, if not to sleep. She seemed to have gone willingly, which Rhona was grateful for. At times like these, she found it easier to be alone with her own thoughts, rather than worrying about what was going on in the heads of others.

Moving into the kitchen, she opened the window a little to let Tom out on his midnight prowl. He took advantage of it immediately, while she stood looking out on her favourite view of the neighbouring convent garden and its statue of the Virgin Mary cocooned in warm golden light.

With no religious conviction on her part, she'd frequently wondered why the statue's presence provided her with solace, exactly when she needed it.

Perhaps it was the certainty of its presence in an uncertain world. Or as a symbol of hope. Or because of its beauty.

For it is beautiful, she thought. *But that's not enough tonight.*

She'd brought through her laptop, intending to peruse the *Snake House* script herself. Better that than try to sleep with her head full of all that had happened over the last twenty-four hours.

McNab had indicated that he planned to visit the Red Dragon. He'd also mentioned checking in with Janice. It wasn't until that moment she realized she didn't know in which order he planned to do that.

Surely McNab wouldn't have gone to the Red Dragon on his own?

At this point, something made her rise and go to check on Marnie. Listening at the door and hearing nothing, not even the sound of sleep, made her turn the handle, open the door and take a look inside.

The mound of a body with its back to her fooled her for less than a minute. Pulling back the duvet proved her right. The bag Marnie had brought with her from Kilcreggan was there, but she was not.

Now she understood why Marnie had immediately agreed to go through to bed when McNab left.

And I was so relieved that she did so that I never questioned it, Rhona thought.

It took only moments while she pulled on her coat and boots to decide where Marnie had gone. She was no stranger to Glasgow or the Red Dragon. Her travel bag she'd left behind, but there was no purse in it. So assuming she had some money, she could have picked up a taxi easily enough at this time of night.

A taxi that would take her to the Red Dragon.

Heading for her own car, once inside she called McNab's number, then listened to it ring out unanswered. Setting the phone on speaker, she tried Janice's number only to hear it go to voicemail.

She tried to tell herself that this was good. They were partners, so likely were together. Maybe at the Red Dragon. Then another thought occurred. Why, when seeing her name on the screen, did neither one assume it must be urgent and answer her call?

The snow had come on again. Big white flakes that, thankfully, were wet enough not to lie, although they blanketed her windscreen with such regularity that she had to have her wipers on at full speed.

The late hour meant there was little traffic on the roads, which made each wait at a stop light like a red rag to a bull. Rhona wished that she, like McNab, could set a blue light flashing on the roof of her vehicle and simply cruise on through.

As she finally approached George Square, her mobile rang with Janice's name onscreen.

'Janice. Thanks for getting back to me. Is McNab there? I've been trying to get through to him.'

There was a moment's silence, followed by a sleepy reply.

'He's at home, like me, as far as I'm aware. And probably asleep, like I was, which would be the reason he's not answering.'

'So you two didn't go to the Red Dragon?' Rhona said.

A puzzled moment followed before Janice responded. 'Sorry, why would we go to the Red Dragon?'

Rhona delivered a potted history of the night's revelations regarding *Snake House* and Marnie's story about the Red Eye club in the script possibly being the actual Red Dragon club.

'Christ,' Janice said, all sleep now gone from her voice. 'I know nothing about this. McNab did call me, just as I got home, and told me to go to my bed. I told him to do the same.' She halted there in exasperation.

Sounding as though she was now on the move, Janice asked Rhona where she was.

'I'm on my way to the club, hoping to catch up with Marnie.'

'Marnie's gone there too?' Janice said.

'I think so,' Rhona told her.

'Right, I'll head there and call for back-up on the way. Wait for me there and definitely don't go inside. Under any circumstances. D'you promise me, Rhona?'

'Okay,' Rhona said quietly, although instinct told her that her promise might not be kept, depending on the circumstances.

Aware that once Janice raised the alarm, the whole area would be cordoned off, Rhona sought to get as close to the club as possible, parking in a nearby back lane, despite the sign that told her not to.

The plan she'd formulated en route was to enter the Red Dragon by the front door. She might be regarded as an odd type of customer but if challenged she would come up with some story about looking for a friend or even a partner.

If Marnie was in fact there, she would tell her that the police were on their way and to come back to the car with her and let the officers do their job.

Reaching the entrance, she found it shut, the red light no longer shining out. Her anxiety rising, she brought up McNab's number again and set it to ring.

Maybe Janice was right and McNab had gone home to bed, after discovering his trip here to be a waste of time. He was a sound sleeper, added to which he may well have put on the 'Do Not Disturb' mode on his mobile, which she often did herself.

When the call went to voicemail, she left a slightly panicked message for him to call her back, then tried to decide whether she should return to her car.

But what about Marnie? Where had she gone, and without taking her bag? *And why hide her departure from me?*

She contemplated calling Janice back to explain that the club was shut for the night and there was no sign of McNab in the vicinity.

But you haven't checked that yet, she thought. If he did come here, and was still around, his car would be too.

Retracing her steps, she glanced up each alley she passed, seeing no sign of McNab's vehicle. Maybe he didn't bring his car as close as this, she reasoned. Perhaps he parked further back to avoid the vehicle being recognized as the cop car from before.

She'd almost given up searching when she finally spotted it. And for a brief moment she even imagined she could see McNab's figure seated inside.

But that was just a hope and the true scenario was already playing out in her head,

McNab had come here and likely entered the Red Dragon, which was now shut for the night.

Which begged the question, was McNab still inside?

65

McNab wasn't out of it any more, although he was doing his best to play that role.

Their entry – his and the bouncer's – to the torture chamber had definitely come as a surprise to both the torturers and likely also their victim.

Having been dumped unceremoniously on the floor at their feet, McNab strove to maintain his unconscious status, at least until he might overcome the pain in his head enough to work out what to do next.

Seemingly accepting for the moment his comatose state, the two men began to discuss his presence and what it might mean.

'He's definitely a cop,' the bouncer assured them.

'Are there any more of them?' the demand came.

'No. He's a loner.'

When the toe of a shoe prodded him hard in the ribs, McNab swallowed his cry of pain.

'So we finish the job and get out of here,' a voice said, 'before anyone comes looking for him.'

McNab roused himself, realizing that playing dead wasn't going to stop them from killing their captive.

'I'd already called for back-up before he reached me,' he managed, his words sounding both weak and unconvincing.

'Bullshit,' the bouncer said. 'He dropped the mobile in fright when he saw me coming. It's lying in the alley somewhere.'

'Then go and fucking get it,' the order came.

Watching the two men exchange looks as the bouncer departed, McNab decided they hadn't been totally convinced by his story, so he decided to elaborate.

'I made the call whatever he says,' he offered them with an attempt at a satisfied smile.

He could practically taste their indecision before the older one, whom he took to be Jack Boyd, pulled the younger one aside. 'We finish the job and go.'

'The fucking cop's seen us,' the younger one said, glancing back at McNab with a look that revealed his thoughts clear enough.

McNab had been edging his way along the floor towards the trolley in the vain hope of taking them by surprise by propelling it into them. Lewis, his face stitched together like a ragdoll, was still breathing, even if he couldn't use his mouth. McNab knew he couldn't see him either, but maybe Lewis could at least hear his whispered warning of what he was about to do.

As he began to make his move, the door suddenly flew open and the bouncer reappeared, agitated and dragging a figure behind him.

Any small morsel of hope died in McNab when he realized who it was. And he wasn't the only one to be in shock at the latest addition to their gathering.

Daryl Boyd hadn't a clue who the female was. Jack, on the other hand, did, although it took him a moment or two.

Shaking herself free of the bouncer's grip, Marnie stood her ground and fixed her stare on her previous tormentor.

'Where the fuck did *you* appear from?' Jack managed, with what sounded like a laugh.

The bouncer came in then. 'She was one level down and she had his mobile. She says she's called the police with it.'

As Jack considered this, Marnie caught sight of the battered figure on the trolley, her eyes losing their defiance to be replaced by horror. Noting her reaction, Jack appeared to be mentally calculating how he might play this out in the cruellest and most vindictive way possible.

Until, that is, he picked up the distant cry of a police siren.

At this time of night, in central Glasgow, that wasn't an unusual sound and there was no guarantee it had anything to do with them. On the other hand . . .

'I told him I called the police,' Marnie threw at Jack's furious face. 'They're on their way.'

Marnie's voice was one of conviction, but McNab didn't entirely buy it. She may have tried to make the call, but he wasn't sure she'd succeeded.

The siren was growing louder and more insistent. It would soon either pass them and fade into the distance, or else screech to a halt nearby.

'Fuck, Jack?' Daryl said as the bouncer exited pronto.

McNab prepared himself for whatever decision Jack Boyd was about to make. Would he deal with Marnie first or focus on finishing off his mark, Lewis McLean?

Jack Boyd had been given a job and that was to kill the actor Jason Endeavour. And he wasn't going to fail on the second attempt.

Marnie, realizing this, tried to push the trolley away, but

her small slight frame had no chance against her former tormentor.

McNab saw the flash of a knife as Marnie grabbed at Boyd's raised arm, biting into the bare flesh even as the siren's wail grew ever more intense.

Now McNab made his move. Throwing his weight at the trolley, he sent it flying to hit the far wall and topple, but not before Jack had plunged his blade into some part of the strapped body that lay on it.

Then Jack too was gone.

McNab, head swimming, struggled to his feet. The trolley was on its side against the far wall with a frantic Marnie trying to stem the flow of blood that was steadily pooling beneath it.

66

Marnie went with Lewis in the ambulance, McNab having told the paramedic that she was the injured man's closest relative. She glanced out at him as the door was shut, mouthing a thank you.

'I'll see you at the hospital,' he promised.

He was next, despite doing his best to argue with Janice that he was okay.

'We'll let the doctor decide that. Concussion, as you are aware, can be pretty serious.' The manner in which she said this made him think she would like to land a blow on his head herself.

'We can't let the Boyds leave the country,' he said.

'Go get checked out and let me do my job. Dr MacLeod will follow in her car to make sure you get there without incident.'

What she meant, of course, was he couldn't tell the ambulance to stop and let him out.

McNab decided to accept a win on Janice's part, since she deserved it and he definitely didn't. He felt for his mobile, which Marnie had retrieved from the alley. The screen was badly cracked but it was still operational and she had used it to call Janice, who'd apparently been on her way already, after being alerted to his trip via Rhona.

As McNab climbed into the back of the ambulance, still insisting it was unnecessary, he gave silent thanks to the women currently in his life.

Rhona stuck with him all the way through Accident and Emergency, and his examination, which resulted – against all argument on his part – in a recommendation that he remain in hospital overnight. Deciding that this meant he might get a chance to speak to Marnie and keep track of Lewis, he'd eventually agreed.

There was another reason, of course. Two in fact. Namely Darren McGowan and Karen Bell, who were also in this hospital. According to Janice, Darren was out of surgery, and Karen had regained consciousness.

Darren's part in all of this he had yet to learn. He suspected that was probably also true of Karen. At least neither of them could disappear without talking to him, when that was permitted.

Rhona had reappeared with his requested coffee from the machine and taken a place alongside his bed.

'You can go home now,' he told her. 'I didn't escape and have no plans to do so during the night.'

She gave a small nod. 'I plan to stay anyway. I need to be here for Marnie.'

He felt bad at that. 'I'm here for Marnie. You could go home and get some sleep.'

'I could, but I won't. Not while they still have Lewis in surgery.'

McNab's mind went back to those final moments. He found himself relating the scene as though in flashback.

'Marnie was trying desperately to stem the blood. I told

her not to take the knife out. For fear that Lewis would die if she did.'

He met Rhona's eye, knowing her thoughts matched his own. She remembered, just as he did, that they'd once been in a similar situation together, where she'd been the one to tell him not to remove a knife from a killer, but he'd done it anyway.

That action by him against her express wishes had put a wedge between them on both a professional and personal level. It was a wound that had taken time and effort, particularly on his part, to repair.

Silence followed until she reached over and touched his hand.

'They think he'll be okay,' she said. 'Thanks to you, and Marnie's actions.' She gave him an attempt at a smile. 'That doesn't mean it's all okay. When you left my place I understood you had called Janice.'

'I did call . . .' he began, then stopped himself. 'You're right. I thought Marnie might be, I don't know, in that other world of hers. Remember, I'd already visited the Red Dragon. Nothing had been said about it being used in the movie, so what she suggested didn't quite fit. Plus, if we'd gone through the correct channels, we'd have had to apply for a search warrant. So I thought I'd just do a recce on my own by climbing up a fire exit and looking in a window.' He stopped there, aware that he might be laying it on a bit too thick.

'Lewis McLean has a lot to thank you for,' Rhona said.

'No. It's Marnie he should be thanking.' He halted there for a moment. 'D'you think she'll tell him about Tizzy?'

'Maybe,' Rhona said. 'I suppose it depends on what happens when he realizes that Marnie's the reason he's still alive.'

67

He'd kept his word and waited to be officially discharged by the resident doctor the following morning. After which he did his own rounds, beginning with Karen, who gave him what sounded like a truthful account of what had happened in their Govan hideaway.

'Darren took me to Lewis. The Boyds found out where we were and came for him. The younger one knocked me out. I only found out what had happened to Darren and Lewis when I came to, here in the hospital,' she said. 'Is Lewis going to be all right? I know Darren is.'

'Lewis is going to be all right,' McNab said.

McNab's biggest interest now was how Darren came to be involved. That was the bit she'd seemed less easy about explaining.

'I didn't know him,' she'd said. 'Lewis just told me he was a friend from his past, who didn't like the Boyds.'

McNab also made a swift visit to Darren, who, according to his police minder, was still heavily sedated and unlikely to be discharged any time soon.

'So not able to give a statement as yet, Detective Sergeant.

You took a bit of a beating yourself, sir,' he added with a concerned look.

McNab, having not looked in the mirror as yet, just nodded and left it at that.

Regardless of what he might look like, it could never be as bad as Lewis McLean, he thought, when he pushed open the door to his room.

Marnie immediately rose from where she'd been sitting alongside the bed, and the look she gave McNab confirmed the officer's earlier remark.

McNab waved her concern away. 'I'm fine. Discharged and going back to work. How's Lewis doing?'

'He'll be okay,' she said. 'Thanks to you.'

McNab shook his head. 'No, your coming to the Red Dragon saved us both.'

Silence fell between them like an unwelcome guest, before Marnie lifted her coat from the back of the chair.

'Now that you're here, I can go,' she said.

McNab was puzzled by this. 'Don't you want to stay until he wakes up?'

She shook her head. 'I don't need to, now I know he's okay.'

'But don't you want to tell him about Tizzy?' he said.

'Tizzy's dead. What would be the point? And Jack Boyd's still out there.'

It was the first time he'd heard her say this out loud and it made him sad. He'd thought referring to her dead daughter had been weird, regardless of what the boss had said about it, but now he found himself disabusing that fact. 'It was Tizzy who made you come to Glasgow, wasn't it? Then to the Red Dragon.'

Marnie seemed to take pity on him and with a small smile said, 'She did.'

'Which means Tizzy saved him and me,' McNab said. 'He should be told that, don't you think?'

As they exchanged determined looks on the matter, a sleepy voice from the bed said, 'Who's Tizzy?'

'The person who saved your life, along with Marnie here,' McNab said. 'I'll leave you two to get acquainted again.'

Having said his piece, McNab chose that moment to leave. As he closed the door quietly behind him, he was pleased to hear Lewis say Marnie's name in recognition.

Exiting the hospital, he flagged down a taxi and asked to be taken to Govan police station.

'Jesus, mate. What happened to your face?' the driver said in a shocked voice.

'You should see the other guy,' McNab retorted, realizing this would be his life for the next couple of weeks and he'd better get used to it. As they passed George Square, where the festive fair had yet to open for the day, he wondered if he might change his story to one about falling off the big wheel, for variety if nothing else.

From the time he was dropped off at the station to reaching his desk, he'd been subjected to even better suggestions as to how his injuries had come about.

Taking his seat alongside Janice, he gave her a grin that made her laugh out loud. 'Don't make that face again or we'll get no work done at all today,' she informed him.

Accepting that sympathy definitely wasn't on the menu, he asked where they were with locating the Boyd brothers.

'No sightings as yet but we're on it, Detective Sergeant,' Janice told him. 'They're not booked on any flight leaving Scotland today. Or northern England,' she said.

'Ireland?' he said. 'Dublin's the place to go if you're heading for America.'

Janice gave him a look that would have floored lesser men.

'Why don't you look on the system and read what's happening instead of making me repeat it?' she suggested.

He accepted her criticism with another gargoyle smile. 'If I were one of the Boyd brothers, I'd go to ground and let the police spend all their precious time trying to discover our flight plan.'

Janice decided to change the subject. 'How's Marnie and Lewis?'

When McNab gave her a potted version of what had just happened at the hospital, she said, 'You got that bit right, then.'

McNab accepted the compliment with good grace. At this point the boss shouted him to come through.

'Good luck,' Janice offered as he rose to comply.

McNab knew he would need all the luck on offer, regardless of the positive outcome.

'Sir?' he said on entry, trying to gauge the mood from his superior's expression and failing.

'Lewis McLean?' DI Wilson said in a clipped tone.

'Looks terrible, but doing okay. Marnie is with him, sir. He remembers her from before.'

The boss's expression softened. 'Good. And the other two?'

'Darren McGowan is still heavily sedated. Karen Bell gave me an account of what happened, which I'm about to write up, sir.' McNab shifted a little under the boss's stare.

'I believe the positive outcome in what was your mess is entirely down to Marnie Aitken, Detective Sergeant?'

'It is, sir. I'm about to write that up too.'

'I look forward to reading it, Sergeant. Go and see if you can find out where the Boyds went after you messed things up.'

Smarting a little from the boss's interpretation of how and why Daryl and Jack Boyd had managed to escape, McNab took himself back to his desk, where Janice was waiting with a sympathetic look.

'He blamed you for their getaway?' she suggested. When he nodded, she said, 'The boss has a point. If you and I had gone together, with back-up in tow . . .'

'Without a search warrant? And on the advice of a woman whose dead child from six years ago tells her what to do?' His anger and frustration had finally won. 'Or maybe waited for that search warrant and eventually discovered Lewis McLean tortured to death in that upstairs room?' He stopped there when he saw the look on Janice's face.

Shaking his head at his own stupidity, he rose, telling her he was going for a coffee and asking if she wanted one. When she indicated not, her face still smarting from the onslaught, he departed.

Ignoring the coffee machine, he headed for the canteen instead, where he bought a filled roll and a sugared doughnut in lieu of the hospital breakfast he'd missed, and took himself into a quiet corner to nurse his wrath, which was directed at himself.

This would end badly if they didn't lift the Boyd brothers. Free, Jack would be set on revenge. Which meant both Marnie and Lewis would remain in danger until he was caught. Marnie would be in even more trouble than before, because Jack Boyd now knew that she'd been aiding the police in their search for him.

These thoughts just contributed to the head pain he was already suffering. Also, in a bizarre fashion, the bullet scar on his back seemed to have come out in sympathy.

Or, he thought, *I'm just feeling sorry for myself.*
At that point in the proceedings, his mobile rang.
Looking at the cracked screen, he noted it came from an unnamed number. He answered it anyway.
The wee voice that spoke was immediately recognizable as Dreep McGowan.
'Hey, mister. It's me, Dreep,' he began. 'We need to speak to you, mister. Me, Kev and Ally.'
'What's this about, Dreep?' McNab asked.
'Gonnae come and meet us, at the entrance to the cycle tunnel. Can you come right now?' he said in a frightened voice. 'It's about that bloke Daryl.'
'Okay, Dreep,' McNab said. 'I'll come now. Just stay there.'
McNab rose, taking his half-eaten roll, but abandoning the doughnut.
He went by Janice and told her what had happened. 'D'you want to come with me this time?' he said pointedly.
She stood up. 'Of course.'
They exited the police station and, as they climbed in the vehicle, she asked, 'D'you think they're in danger of some sort?'
McNab didn't think so and told her. 'It's more likely they've found out something they want to tell me to my face.'
Parking on Govan Road, McNab led the way down to the cycle entrance to find the three boys standing with their bikes just past the open gate. Delighted to see them unharmed at least, he demanded to know why he'd been summoned.
'Ally wouldn't phone you,' Dreep told him. 'So I did, because I started all of this,' he added.
'Get on with it, then,' McNab ordered.

Dreep pointed at Ally. 'He thinks he saw him, standing at a window.'

'He saw who standing at a window?' McNab checked.

'The guy with the snake knuckles,' Dreep said dramatically. 'Daryl Boyd.'

McNab turned to Ally. 'Is this true?'

Ally hesitated. 'It was only for a minute but I – I think so.'

'Okay,' McNab said. 'We know you're a super recognizer, because Ollie said so. Which means you're correct at least ninety per cent of the time. That's right, isn't it?'

Ally, looking a bit calmer at his words, nodded.

'So when was this?' McNab tried.

'This morning. Just before Dreep called you,' Ally told him, his voice trembling.

'Where exactly did you see Daryl?' McNab said.

'It was on Hutton Drive, halfway along, second floor up, at the big window, near the tree.' He said this as though he'd been practising.

So Mags might have been right when she'd said if Daryl had been drinking in the Vital Spark then he couldn't be far away.

He glanced at Janice, who said, 'Maybe they did decide to go to ground here while the heat was on. Go take a look,' she added. 'I'll call it in and follow you.'

'Okay, you two guys go straight home and take Ally's bike with you,' McNab told Kev and Dreep. 'As for you,' he said to Ally, 'you and me will go on a recce.'

They walked along Govan Road, cutting in by Clachan Drive and the Vital Spark.

'What if I'm wrong?' Ally said in a small voice.

'I asked you to phone me if there was anything, however small. You did that,' McNab reassured him. 'Or Dreep did,' he smiled. 'Okay, we walk along and chat together like father and son.' As soon as he said that, McNab realized how stupid it was, because neither of them knew how such a relationship worked, since he had no son and Ally had no father.

When they reached the tree, McNab glanced across the street at the first-floor bay window of the house opposite. 'That's the place?' he said.

'Aye, it is,' Ally told him with a nod.

'Then I want you to walk on and go straight home. Understood?' he ordered.

Ally gave another nod and headed off. Once he'd disappeared from view, McNab crossed the street to the building Ally had indicated and, tucking himself out of sight, kept the said window in his view. What he dearly wanted now was a glimpse of Daryl or Jack Boyd, just to be sure, before he went in, all guns blazing.

At this point, his mobile buzzed.

'Car is in position at the end of the road. I'm walking down to meet you now. Back-up is on its way,' Janice told him.

'We're gonnae look a right couple of arses if Ally got this wrong,' he muttered.

'The boy's a super recognizer, Ollie said so.'

'Maybe Ollie was just trying to encourage him. He's a big softy, remember?'

'A bit like yourself,' Janice said. 'See you shortly.'

When she arrived, she was carrying a bag that turned out to hold an enforcer. After McNab nodded his pleasure at this, she pressed the buzzer for the first-floor flat three times in succession, which resulted in an answer by a male voice expressing his extreme displeasure in colourful terms.

Janice looked to McNab for confirmation that he recognized the voice. When he nodded and mouthed 'Daryl', she said in a pleading tone, 'Sorry about that. Could you open the door, please? My key's not working.'

A moment later, the buzzer sounded the door's release. Glancing along the road, McNab saw a police car turn in, followed by a second, both with sirens blaring.

Heading up the stairs, they took up their position at the door of the flat, the enforcer at the ready.

'Police,' McNab shouted. 'Open the door or we'll break it down.'

Just as in any community, the word had got out that the police were in Linthouse. How they knew it was for the Boyd brothers, McNab had no idea.

By the time they brought them out, handcuffed, he suspected the entire clientele of the Vital Spark had amassed at the end of the street, with Mags and Archie among them.

He was sorry, then, that he'd sent the three boys home, because they should have been there to see it happen. Ally in particular.

Deciding to make good on this, he called Mags when he'd safely installed the prisoners in the police van and told her how Ally, together with Kev and Dreep, had made the arrest possible.

She was mightily pleased by that, she told him, and would make sure to show their appreciation on Christmas Day.

68

His motorbike was back. Parked in front of the police station, as though it had never been away. Despite his amazement, tempered with annoyance, McNab found himself smiling, which might have been the result of spotting the large red ribbon bow attached to the front. Plus the 'Merry Christmas' sign propped up on the passenger seat.

Taking himself inside, he met the astonished gaze of the desk sergeant, who just happened to be the same one on duty when the bike had been stolen in the first place.

'Is this all your doing?' McNab demanded.

The sergeant shook his head. 'Had I been the one to take your Harley, it would now be gracing the premises of a new and worthy owner. Plus my bank account would be the better for it.'

'Did you perhaps see who delivered it, Sergeant?' McNab tried.

'I did not, Detective. However, I did find this envelope on the counter with your name on it, although I never saw who put it there.' He handed over a pink envelope. 'It also smells nice.'

McNab did not immediately pick up the said envelope. Neither did he sniff its perfume.

'Someone's taken a len of you, Detective Sergeant. That would be my estimation of the proceedings.'

'Well,' McNab said. 'I'm glad it's back.' He lifted the envelope and, making a big show of not opening it, strode off.

His bike theft had been a running joke since it had happened. Plus he was pretty sure a great many folk in the building had spotted it back and tarted up outside the front entrance, and were eager to know who had left it there.

He, on the other hand, preferred to discover this in private.

Once inside a cubicle in the Gents, away from any interested onlookers, McNab examined the envelope in more detail. Lifting it to his nose, he sniffed it, hoping, at closer quarters, to recognize its scent. Stumped at that, he had to admit to the fact that if any of the women in his life wore perfume, he'd never really registered it.

Except maybe the imagined scent of Ellie in his flat, after she'd left him.

Tearing open the envelope, he found a card with a sketch of a skull like the tattoo on his back that had been inked by Ellie. The breadth of his smile grew even wider when he saw the date, the time and the location of the party this was obviously an invite to.

Below was her name: **Ellie xx**

It looked like he would be celebrating Christmas after all.

69

Rhona had been woken by the winter's low sunlight streaming into the room.

Rising, she went to the window to look at the park and university hill. The snow had almost disappeared, apart from a few patches dotting the grass and an occasional hard mound indicating there had once been a snowman built there.

In truth, the fact that it was Christmas morning didn't register at first. Not until she chose to listen to BBC Sounds on her mobile and heard excited voices declaring it to be so.

Last night, after she'd spoken with a delighted and relieved Magnus about Marnie and Lewis, she'd gone to bed, thinking sleep unlikely. As it was, she now realized that she'd slept for well over twelve hours.

Something she felt very much the better for.

Heading to the kitchen, she put on the coffee machine and stuck two slices of medium-stale bread in the toaster, and hearing Tom's plaintiff meows, restocked his food bowl.

The idea of a long lazy day stretching out in front of her, doing nothing apart from what she chose, seemed at that moment to be a vision of heaven after the world of the last few weeks.

Except you've been invited for Christmas dinner at Chrissy's place.

'Three o'clock exactly,' she heard Chrissy's voice repeat in her head.

That gave her a little over three hours to shower, read a book or watch something on TV.

It didn't seem quite long enough. Still, she had said that she would go, and besides, there was next to nothing in the fridge. Plus anything that was there she, as a scientist, could not recommend eating.

Heading for the shower, she stood under it for longer than normal, since she wasn't in a hurry. Only emerging when her mobile rang insistently, then repeatedly, when she didn't hurry to answer it.

The caller didn't come as a surprise.

'Just checking that you're up and getting ready?' Chrissy said firmly.

'I am,' Rhona could honestly tell her.

'Good, because we have a mountain of food and drink to get through.'

'How's wee Michael?' Rhona said.

'Jesus is born and in his cradle. So he's happy about that. And opening presents has been entertaining.' A squeal from somewhere had Chrissy saying her goodbyes. 'See you soon, Dr MacLeod.'

As she laid down her mobile, it rang again. She was pleased to see McNab's name on the screen.

'Merry Christmas, Dr MacLeod.'

'Merry Christmas, Detective Sergeant McNab. Are you heading to Chrissy's for Christmas lunch?'

'I am not,' he said, sounding very happy about that.

'And why not exactly?' Rhona demanded. 'Chrissy's arranged it especially for us sad singles.'

'Of which I am not one,' McNab told her. 'Despite my gargoyle looks.'

A pause, before Rhona said, 'It was Ellie who took the bike?'

'It was. She returned it yesterday, all spruced up as though by a Harley specialist, which she is. Along with an invite to a Christmas party today.'

Rhona laughed, delighted for him.

'And what of your Irishman?' McNab said.

'He's in Dublin,' she told him, hoping she didn't sound as saddened by that as she suddenly felt.

There was a moment's silence before McNab said, 'You haven't listened to his voicemail, have you?'

'How d'you know about that? Did Chrissy tell you?'

'No. Sean did. That night we ate together in your kitchen. He suspected you hadn't listened to it.'

Rhona was momentarily nonplussed at the thought of this conversation between Sean and McNab.

'The Irishman's good for you, Dr MacLeod. Just like Ellie's good for me. We're not the easiest people to partner. Can't think of anything but work most of the time. Some would say we're impossible to live with. To love even.' He halted there for a moment. 'Anyway, I plan to try harder this time round. Give my namesake wee Michael a Christmas hug for me. He already has his present.'

When he rang off, Rhona stared at her mobile for a while, thinking about what McNab had just said. They were alike, she thought. In particular their obsession with work.

She realized she couldn't even remember exactly why

she'd fallen out with Sean. It had definitely been her falling out with him, because the truth was Sean didn't fall out with anyone. That was what had drawn her to him in the first place. His easy-going nature. His view on life in general.

Curling up on the couch, she chose that moment to listen to Sean's voicemail, registering how good it was to hear his Irish voice on this Christmas morning.

The message was simple and straight from the heart.

I hear life through music, Rhona . . . I'm sorry I don't always hear you.

When she rang him, he answered almost immediately, wishing her a Merry Christmas.

'How was last night's gig?' she said.

'Excellent,' he told her. 'Despite the fact that most of my extended family were at it,' he added with a laugh.

When a silence fell between them, he said, 'You heard my message?'

'I did,' she said.

'There's an early flight to Dublin tomorrow morning. Come over and I'll repeat it in person.'

70

It was weird to be asked to a Christmas party in a pub.

At first his mum had said no to the invitation. But when Mags came round herself and explained why the locals wanted to do it, his mum had seemingly changed her mind.

Initially, she'd told him to leave the room and let the adults talk in private. He had, of course, listened at the door, but their voices had been low and he'd had difficulty working out what was being said.

He had, however, heard the words 'Christmas party' and 'the Vital Spark', plus his name, Kev's and, more than once, Dreep's, although they'd used his proper name, Brian.

They left the house at midday, because his mum said there would be food at the party. Gran was there, of course, having arrived on Christmas Eve. They collected Dreep, with his mum, and Kev and his parents on the way.

It had been weird at first, with no one talking. Even Kev and Dreep had been quiet, despite the three of them walking ahead together.

Eventually Dreep broke the silence by saying, 'We're heroes. That's what my mum says. If we hadn't called DS

McNab and told him where Daryl Boyd was hiding, him and his brother would still be out there.'

'It was Ally who recognized him,' Kev reminded him in his usual straightforward fashion.

'If I'd actually met Daryl Boyd in person, I could have got it right,' Dreep suggested.

'You started it all,' Ally reminded Dreep jokingly. 'When you dropped Darren's phone next to a dead body.'

Remembering the horrors of that night made them all drop into silence again.

'How is Darren?' Ally eventually said.

'A bit better. Not out of hospital yet,' Dreep said.

Ally wanted to ask what would happen to Darren when he was discharged, but didn't like to. They'd heard that Darren had been helping the missing actor, who was speaking up for him. It seemed they'd known one another back in the days when the actor was still living in Glasgow. Plus Darren's gang didn't want the Boyd brothers murdering folk on their patch.

He thought about Darren and how he'd known that the murdered man was naked, and supposed Darren must have been hanging about the farmhouse that night, because he thought something was going on there.

Ally decided he was glad that Darren had done something good for someone, but he still hoped Darren would stay away permanently from Dreep and his mum because Dreep's house was a better place with Darren out of it.

When they arrived at the Vital Spark, there were decorations and Christmas lights round the door, which stood open. They could hear voices coming from inside, plus Christmas music playing.

Ally heard Kev's dad say he would lead the way, which seemed to please his mum.

Silence fell as they all trooped in, in an embarrassed fashion. Then there was cheering and clapping as Archie and Mags came out from behind the bar to welcome them.

71

It was Joan who brought them the cat. It was a rescue that Tizzy promptly named Daisy.

Daisy had arrived on Christmas Eve, together with more food and a man to turn her power back on.

'I sorted that out, when you were away in Glasgow,' Joan said. 'I'm glad you're home safe and sound.'

Marnie had been touched by her kind thoughts, but even more by Daisy, who'd immediately investigated her new home. Including the cat dish filled with food that Joan had put down for her.

'Now, remember, you're welcome to come round to the café tomorrow for Christmas Day. We always have open house for folk that are on their own and could do with some company,' she said. 'And they're not all old folk either. You can stay ten minutes for a snack or share the turkey. There's always plenty to go round.'

When she'd left, Tizzy had suggested she should take up Joan's invitation. 'Talk to people other than me,' she'd said. 'I'll be okay here with Daisy.'

Marnie wasn't convinced, but didn't argue, of course. Tizzy liked to boss her around and, in truth, she liked it that way.

Christmas morning came and Tizzy had woken her as usual at an unearthly hour so that they could open the presents. It was so early than even Daisy couldn't be coaxed from her bed beside the stove, regardless of what enticing morsel Tizzy tried to offer her.

The early start meant that she could catch the fire, which was still smouldering, and feed it more wood.

She was sleeping in her bedroom again. Tizzy in hers. Both of them keeping their doors open, like they used to, to let the warmth flow through the cottage.

After they'd admired what was in their embroidered stockings, Marnie made a breakfast of pancakes and honey. After which Tizzy decided it was time to go to the beach and look for blue stones, like always.

Aware of how important this was for both of them, Marnie organized their coats, hats and boots, and together they went outside, leaving Daisy in the kitchen by the stove.

'She'll eventually want to go out,' Marnie told Tizzy. 'Joan says she's an outdoor cat, really. She's just getting used to us and her new home first.'

And so their days together continued as before, but with the addition of the new member of their family, who soon joined them on their walks along the shore.

Shortly after the turn of the year, on a gloriously bright morning, while on their way back from their daily walk on the beach, they noticed a car coming down the track to park outside the gate.

'Who's that?' Tizzy said, hurrying a little to see who was about to get out of the car.

For a brief moment, fear entered Marnie's heart again, but Tizzy's laughter soon melted it away.

She never had to worry about him again – DS McNab had promised her and she believed him.

Perhaps it was Tizzy who knew him first, Marnie could never be sure. It took her a little longer. When he eased himself out of the vehicle and turned to face her, she saw that she was right.

He'd been lucky that the knife wound hadn't damaged anything internally, but he was obviously still feeling its effects. The damage done to his face was more obvious, but it too would heal. Marks from the stitching would fade. She knew that for sure, because it had with her.

He said Marnie's name, and Tizzy, who was holding her hand, gave it a little squeeze.

'We have a lot to talk about,' he said. 'Especially about Tizzy, my daughter.'

Marnie heard Tizzy's laughter at that and smiled.

Looking into her eyes, Lewis said, 'Is Tizzy with you?'

'Always,' Marnie told him.

Acknowledgements

With thanks to:

Forensic scientist Dr Jennifer Miller. Inspiring and supportive, she is my main go-to for all things Rhona. In the case of *Whispers of the Dead*, what happens when we swallow a bullet comes to mind. Plus how to deal with a naked dead body that is anchored to a chair.

Dr James H. K. Grieve, emeritus professor of forensic pathology at Aberdeen University, who is more than generous in answering all my queries about modes of death.

Professor Lorna Dawson, of the James Hutton Institute, for her advice on the soils of the Rosneath Peninsula and for inspiring the creation of forensic soil scientist Dr Jen Mackie.

And, finally, a big thanks to my wonderful commissioning editor Alex Saunders and all the team at Pan Macmillan for their help and support. Thank goodness they appear to have kept a bible of this long-running series and can remind me of things I have forgotten.

Introducing Rhona MacLeod . . .

Lin Anderson's series of crime novels featuring forensic scientist Rhona MacLeod are set in and around Scotland. From the beautiful remoteness of the Orkney islands to the dark underbelly of urban Glasgow, the locations she chooses to write about play as much of a role in her novels as the characters that she populates them with.

Go back to where it all began with the thrilling first novel in the Rhona MacLeod series.
Read on for an extract now . . .

I

THE BOY DIDN'T expect to die.

When the guy put the tasselled cord round his neck, grinning at him, he thought it was just part of the usual game. The guy was excited, a dribble of saliva slithering down his chin and falling onto the boy's bare shoulder. He nodded his agreement. He was past feeling sick at their antics. He lay back down, turning his head sideways to the greyish pillow that smelt of other games, closed his eyes and shifted his thoughts to something else. There was a goal he liked to play out in his head.

On the right, the Frenchman, arrogant, the ball licking his feet, thrusting forward. The opposition starts to group and there's a scuffle. Bastards. But no worry 'cos the Frenchman's through and running, the ball anchored to him, like a child to its mother. The crowd breathes in. Time stretches like an elastic band. Then the ball's away, curving through the air.

Wham! It's in the net.

The boy can usually go home now. Not this time. This time, before the ball reaches the net, his head is pulled back, then up. The intense pressure bulges his eyes, bursting a myriad of tiny blood vessels to pattern the white. His body spasms as the cord bites deeper, slicing through skin, cutting the blood supply to his brain. At the moment of death his penis erupts, scattering silver strands of semen over the multicoloured cover.

2

SEAN WAS ALREADY asleep beside her. Rhona liked that about him. His baby sleep. His face lying smooth and untroubled against the pillow, his lips opened just enough to let the breath escape in soft noiseless puffs. No one, she thinks, should look that good after a bottle of red wine and three malt whiskies.

Rhona has given up watching Sean drink. It is too irritating, knowing the next morning he won't have a hangover. Instead he'll throw back the duvet (letting a draught enter the warm tent that had enclosed their bodies), slip out of bed and head for the kitchen. From the bed she will watch (a little guiltily), as he moves about; a glimpse of thigh, an arm reaching up, his penis swinging soft and vulnerable. He'll whistle while he makes the coffee and forever in her mind Rhona will match the bitter sweet smell of fresh coffee with the high clear notes of an Irish tune.

They have been together for seven months. The first night Rhona brought Sean home they never reached the bedroom. He held her against the front door, just looking at her. Then he began to unwrap her, piece by piece, peeling her like ripe fruit, his lips not meeting hers but close, so close that her mouth stretched up of its own accord, and her body with it. Then, with a flick of his tongue, he entered her life.

When the phone rang, Sean barely moved. Rhona knew once it rang four times the ansaphone would cut in. The caller would listen to Sean's amiable Irish voice and change their view of answering machines, thinking they might be human after all. Rhona lifted the receiver on the third ring. It would be an emergency or they wouldn't phone so late. When she suggested to the voice on the other end that she would need a taxi, the Sergeant told her that a police car was already on its way. Rhona grabbed last night's clothes from the end of the bed.

Constable William McGonigle had never been at a murder scene before. He had stretched the yellow tape across the tenement entrance like the Sergeant told him and chased away two drunks who thought that police activity constituted a better bit of entertainment than staggering home to hump the wife. Constable McGonigle didn't agree.

'Go home,' he told them. 'There's nothing to see here.'

He was peering up the stairwell, wondering how much longer he would have to stand there freezing his balls off when he heard the sound of high heels clipping the tarmac. A woman leaned over the tape and stared into the dimly lit stair.

'Sorry, Miss. You can't come in here.'

'Where's Detective Inspector Wilson?'

Constable McGonigle was surprised.

'Upstairs, Miss.'

'Good,' she said.

Her fair hair shone white in the darkness and Constable McGonigle could smell her perfume. She lifted a silken leg and straddled his yellow tape.

'I'd better go on up then,' she said.

The click of Rhona's heels echoed round the grimy stairwell, but if she was disturbing any of the residents, they didn't show it by opening their doors. No one here wanted to be seen. If there was a fire they might come out, she thought, in the unlikely event they weren't completely comatose.

A door on the second landing stood ajar. She could hear DI Wilson's voice inside. If Bill was here at least she wouldn't have to explain who she was. She could just get on with the job, go home and crawl back into bed.

The narrow hall was a fetid mix of damp and heat. The sound of her heels died in a dark mottled carpet, curled at the edge like some withered vegetable. She paused. Three doors, all half open. On her right a kitchen, on her left a bathroom. She caught a glimpse of a white suit and heard the whirr of a camera. The Scene of Crime Officers were already at work.

The end door opened fully and Detective Inspector Bill Wilson looked out.

'Bill.'

'Dr MacLeod.'

He nodded. 'It's in here.'

He allowed himself a tight smile. The two other men in the room turned and stared out at her. Dr MacLeod was not what either of them had expected.

Rhona looked down at her black dress and high-heeled sandals. 'I came out in a bit of a hurry.'

'McSween will get you some kit.'

Bill nodded to one of the men, who went out and came back minutes later with a plastic bag.

Rhona pulled out the scene suit and mask, put her coat into the bag and handed it to the officer. She took one shoe off at a time and, hitching up her skirt, slipped her feet into the suit. Only then did she step inside.

Rhona took in the small room at a glance. The hideous nicotine-stained curtains stretched tightly across the window. A wooden chair with a pair of jeans and a tee-shirt thrown over it. Two glasses on a formica table. A pair of trainers on the floor beside the bed. A divan, three-quarters width, no headboard but covered with heavy silken brocade in an expensive burst of swirling colours.

The boy's naked body lay face down across it, his head turned stiffly towards her, eyes bulging, tongue protruding slightly between blue lips. The dark silk cord knotted round the neck looked like a bow tie the wrong way round. The body showed signs of hypostasis, and the combination of dark purple patches and pale translucence reminded Rhona of marble. Below the hips blood soaked into the bedclothes.

'I turned the gas fire off when I arrived,' Bill said. 'The smell nearly finished off our young Constable, so I put him on duty outside for some fresh air.'

'Did anyone take the room temperature?'

'McSween has it.'

Rhona took a deep breath before she put on the mask. The smell of a crime scene was important. It might mean she would look for traces of a substance she would otherwise have missed. Here the nauseating odour of violent death mixed with stale sex and sweat masked something else, something fainter. She got it. An expensive men's cologne.

'McSween and Johnstone have covered the rest of the room. The photographer is working on the kitchen and bathroom.'

'What about a pathologist?'

'Dr Sissons came and certified death. Then suggested I get a decent forensic to take samples and bag the body because he needed to get back to his dinner party.'

'Important guests?'

'He did mention a "Sir" somewhere in the list.'

Rhona smiled. Dr Sissons preferred analysing death in the comfort of his mortuary. Taking samples of bodily fluids in the middle of the night he regarded as her territory.

'That's some bedcover!'

'We think it might be a curtain, but we'll get a better look once we take the body away.'

'Did the doctor turn him over?'

'Just enough to tell if he's been moved. He said the left side of the face, the upper chest and hips had been compressed since death occurred. He's lying where he was killed.'

Rhona opened her case and took out her gloves. She knelt down beside the bed.

'There's a lot of blood under the body.'

Bill nodded grimly. 'You'd better take a look underneath.'

Rhona lifted the right arm and rolled the body a little. The genitals had been gnawed, the penis severed by a jagged gash that ran from the left hand tip to halfway up the right side. One testicle was mashed and hanging by a thin strip of skin.

'This must have been done after he died or the blood would be all over the place.'

'That's what Sissons said.'

Rhona let the body roll back down. The boy's head nestled back into the dirty pillow.

'Any sign of a weapon?'

Bill shook his head. 'Maybe it wasn't a weapon.'

'A biter? Did Dr Sissons check for other bite marks?'

'He muttered something about bruising on the nipples and the shoulder.'

'I'll take some swabs.'

'How long do you think he's been dead?' Bill said.

Rhona pressed one of the deepening purple patches, and watched it slowly blanch under her finger. 'Maybe six, seven hours. Depends on the temperature of the room.'

Bill risked a satisfied smile.

'Matches the Doc.'

Rhona raised her eyebrows a little. She and Dr Sissons didn't usually agree. He had a habit of disagreeing with her on points like the exact time of death.

It was almost a matter of principle. Rhona had done three years' medicine before she switched to forensic science. She liked to practise now and again.

'How did you find him?'

'An anonymous phone call.'

'The murderer?'

'A young male voice. Very frightened. Maybe another rent boy came here to meet a client?'

'Alive, this one would have been pretty,' Rhona said.

Bill nodded. 'Not the usual type for this area,' he said. 'A bit more class, but rented all the same. I'll leave you to it? Just shout if you need anything.'

She was nearly an hour taking samples of everything that might prove useful later on. After she'd finished with the surrounds, she concentrated on the body, under the fingernails, the hair, the mouth. Dr Sissons would take the anal and penile swabs.

The skin felt cold through her gloves, but with the blond hair flopped over the empty eyes, he might have been any teenager fast asleep. Rhona lifted the hair and studied the face, trying to imagine what the boy would have looked like in life. There were none of the tell-tale signs of poor diet and drug abuse. This one had been healthy. So how did he end up here?

'Finished?' Bill's timing was immaculate. 'Mortuary boys are here.' He looked at her face. 'Go home and have a hot toddy,' he said.

A hot toddy was Bill's answer to almost any ailment.

Rhona got up from the bed and unwrapped her hands. 'Any idea who he is?' she said.

'Not yet. But I don't think he was Scottish.' He pointed to the hall. Behind the door hung a leather jacket and a football scarf. 'Manchester United,' he said in mock disgust.

'There are people up here who support Man U,' Rhona suggested cheekily, knowing Bill was a Celtic man.

'Yes, but they wouldn't flaunt it. Not in Glasgow anyway.'

Rhona laughed.

'All right then?'

'Yes.' She began to pack her samples in the case.

'The Sergeant will run you home.'

He walked with her to the front door.

'How's that Irishman of yours these days? Still playing at the club?'

'Yes, he is.'

'Must get down and hear him again soon. Good jazz player. You'll ring me as soon as you've got anything?'

'Of course.'

Sean was still asleep when Rhona got back. With the heavy curtains drawn the room was dark, although outside dawn was already touching the university rooftops. She had stopped at the lab on her way home and checked the swabs for saliva. It was there all right.

She left a note on the bench for Chrissy in case she got there first, giving her a brief history of the night's events, then she headed home for a few hours' sleep.

Rhona pulled her dress over her head, kicked off her shoes and slid under the duvet. She wrapped her chilled body round Sean's. He grunted and moved his arm over to take her hand.

'Okay?' he mumbled.

'Okay,' she said, but he was already back asleep.

Rhona closed her eyes and tried to relax into his warmth. She had been at many murder scenes, some more horrible than the one tonight. Death didn't scare her, not when it was reduced to tests and samples. But tonight was different. There was something about that particular boy. Something she hadn't been able to put her finger on. Not until the Sergeant had put it into words for her, coming back in the car.

The boy who had been abused and strangled in that hideous little room looked so like her, he could have been her brother.